"This is a gorgeous, brutal dream of a book. It
about time and magic and love, and every sentence pulses with danger and beauty. It will
haunt me for a long time. I implore you all to lose yourself in its strange enchantments."
SARAH BROOKS, bestselling author of *The Cautious Traveller's Guide to the Wastelands*

"Extraordinary. Helen Marshall channels the best of Angela Carter then takes it up
a notch or three. A gloriously bewitching new tale from one of our best fabulists."
ANGELA "A. G." SLATTER, award-winning author of *The Briar Book of the Dead*

"*The Lady, the Tiger and the Girl Who Loved Death* blew my mind, and
forever changed how I looked at writing. Haunting and soaring, transcendent,
and masterfully executed – Helen Marshall's talent is unparalleled."
TASHAN MEHTA, author of *Mad Sisters of Esi*

"Lyrical, beautiful and brilliant, *The Lady, the Tiger and the Girl Who Loved Death*
is a magic puzzle box that surprises and delights with every revelation."
KAARON WARREN, author of *The Underhistory*

"Chillingly beautiful, with wonder and dread in every word. Fans of *Pan's Labyrinth*,
The Night Circus and *The Cautious Traveller's Guide to the Wastelands* should be first in
line for the big-top spectacle of Marshall's lyrical storytelling and wild imagination."
CHRIS AND JEN SUGDEN, authors of *High Vaultage*

"It is a rare story which manages to be thoughtful and colourful at once. Angela
Carter did that, and now Helen Marshall does it in her own way. A book
which you can't stop reading, and then you can't stop thinking about."
FRANCESCO DIMITRI, author of *The Dark Side of the Sky*

"Helen Marshall's writing is, as ever, mesmerising. She has a vivid, keen-eyed
vision of the past and its possibilities, of hope and hatred, of cold realities
and dark dreams colliding. This is a sensuous, spellbinding read."
ALIYA WHITELEY

"Gilded in bone-dust, with the breath of a predator, Marshall's *The Lady, the*
Tiger and the Girl Who Loved Death is a pageant of the masks myths and politics
alike wear as they pace their cages, and the bloody chains that bind them."
KATHLEEN JENNINGS, author of *Honeyeater*

Also by Helen Marshall

THE MIGRATION

THE GOLD LEAF EXECUTIONS

GIFTS FOR THE ONE WHO COMES AFTER

HAIR SIDE, FLESH SIDE

SKELETON LEAVES

THE SEX LIVES OF MONSTERS

THE LADY, THE TIGER AND THE GIRL WHO LOVED DEATH

HELEN MARSHALL

TITAN BOOKS

The Lady, the Tiger and the Girl Who Loved Death
Print edition ISBN: 9781803369518
E-book edition ISBN: 9781835413609

Published by Titan Books
A division of Titan Publishing Group Ltd
144 Southwark Street, London SE1 0UP
www.titanbooks.com

First edition: June 2025
10 9 8 7 6 5 4 3 2 1

This is a work of fiction. All of the characters, organizations, and events
portrayed in this novel are either products of the author's imagination
or are used fictitiously. Any resemblance to actual persons, living or
dead (except for satirical purposes), is entirely coincidental.

A CIP catalogue record for this title is available from the British Library.

EU RP (for authorities only)
eucomply OÜ, Pärnu mnt. 139b-14, 11317 Tallinn, Estonia
hello@eucompliancepartner.com, +3375690241

Typset in Fournier MT Std & Esmerelda Pro.

Printed and bound by CPI Group (UK) Ltd, Croydon, CR0 4YY.

To Vince Haig and Malcolm Devlin.
The Twins.

IN THE BEGINNING

1

"There is light. At least that's how the story goes, isn't it, my love?"

AND IN THE BEGINNING

2

The girl follows the road past the hidden sunflowers. It was her husband who showed them to her, a field of dry earth that would blossom like cloth-of-gold in the height of summer. Dead now, he must be, though she hasn't seen his body. Her name is Sara Sidorova; she is eighteen years old and a widow already.

Days pass as she searches the wildwood for his remains. She marks the hours as the sun rises in glory, then sets in a blue gloom. Birch and alder line the dusty track that brought her this way. Skeleton trunks. Alder is good for sleeping, she knows. Feliks taught her that. Before they were married, they'd lie beneath an alder as high as a steeple, listening to waxwings and bluethroats. Now she cares only for the shriek of the mourning birds, her guides in this terrible business.

She knows these woods well, all this beautiful, terrible sliver land. Mountains in the west, the impassable spine between this little world and the next. The lakes, the coastland, wild and dark, the plains, then the forest, the killing zone, and beyond it the border. Nothing here is easy. In Strana, her people say: *We are small but we will make you bleed. We are the bone that will choke you if you try to swallow us.* Her people say: *We are invaded but it will cost you to take us.*

Strana. Country.

If this thrice-tenth nation had another name once they have forgotten it as they have forgotten so many things.

She stumbles on, her clothes shredding to rags, her feet bloody, her painted nails gone wretched as talons. On the fifth day she discovers a body in the woods—not her husband. This one is too old, over forty. Tawny hair, thinning near the crown. Big shoulders, a big man. The hole in his woolen gymnasterka seems smaller than a thimble. She could dig out the bullet if she wished, but he is only so much meat now.

Still, needs must.

Sara Sidorova takes the dead man's knife, misshapen from over-sharpening. His boots, which are too large. A week ago Captain Olender asked her to dance. Once she loved dancing. She knows she will never dance in these stolen boots, even as she hacks strips from the dead man's uniform and stuffs the rags in her toes.

"'Juniper, juniper, juniper, my juniper,'" she sings as she goes about her work. "'Under the green pine, lay me down to sleep.'"

Then in the distance—the livid shadows of others approaching: a legion of soldiers. The dead man's friends? His murderers? They all wear the same jackets, speak the same language, so how could she know? Sara Sidorova vanishes beyond the treeline.

Her grandmother told her a story about the devils in these woods who turn men into smoke. Remembering it, she fits herself between birches bleak as old houses—invisible. She doesn't know these soldiers but she hates them anyway. She never knew hate before, but now it's an animal inside her.

Storm clouds gather, drench the earth, and then retreat. Afterward, Sara Sidorova trails the legion with nothing but the knife in her hands. She could slit their throats while they slept in the mud if they weren't so watchful—but they *are* watchful. And for all the days she has spent learning to hold herself straight, learning never to bend, still she is too weak.

At night, she howls her grief. The soldiers huddle round their campfires, blowing warmth into their hands, pretending it's the damp that has prickled their skin.

"Listen, do you hear that?" says one. Local accent. He is sixteen, maybe. Younger than her and certainly younger than the others. A stripling with a mop of pale blond hair and a delicate, pointed chin.

"It's nothing. The wind."

"*Listen*, I said! There's a tiger in these woods. A man-eater. I heard it tore through a camp not far from here. Gorged itself on the captain and ate everything but his heart."

The boy is canny but all they see is a coward. Perhaps they'll kill him on their own.

"Something is out there," he says again.

The old reflex: "What kind of man are you then? Are you afraid?"

Soothsayer, *prorok*, elf-child. Sara Sidorova doesn't expect anyone will listen to him.

This time she is wrong. Their commander doubles the guard and no one sleeps that night. In the morning they muck out pits and whittle birch spears to lay inside. One among them knows how to hunt a tiger.

The girl's stolen knife isn't sharp enough, her body isn't light enough. She still leaves too many tracks. She abandons them for a time to hunt for cloudberries and the tender shoots of cornflowers. She chances the mushrooms with their delicate fringed veils and wonders whether she might poison herself. If it would matter. What is she living for anyway?

The baby kicks. Her name will be Else, if it's a girl. If it's a boy she will have to strangle him.

She hushes her hate. Back to the road.

It's close to dawn when she makes her second mistake.

All around her, the wildwood is alive, first with warblers and rose-finches, then the rest of the noisy lot. Sara Sidorova moves through the undergrowth, letting the birdsong hide her business. But she isn't as silent as she thinks. Suddenly, a bullet slams into her shoulder. The crack like thunder comes too late in warning.

She falls in a slow spiral. No pain, not yet.

Was this how it happened, husband? she wonders. *Is this how they killed you?*

Then there's wet loam beneath her, sweet smelling. She wants to stay, sleep in her pain now death has come. She puts her thumb to the wound. Her blood is coming out in spurts, and, with it, her fury and helplessness.

The soldier boy's face hovers over her: pointed chin, fey-blue eyes. "I thought you were one of them!"

Sara Sidorova doesn't believe him. After all, she's wearing the same jacket he is.

"You're just a girl," he says though she is older than he is. At eighteen strands of bone-white gleam in the tawny thicket of her hair.

"I'm sorry," he mutters, staring at the knife.

"Go away!"

"If I do, you'll die. Gangrene or blood sickness. I've seen it before. Why are you so dirty? Why are you so thin?"

Scarlet smears across his cheek as he tries to wrestle her up. Her belly is cramping, a deep, bleary pain that tightens and loosens. The child mustn't come yet. Too soon.

"Leave me alone!" she hisses, for above all, she doesn't want him to see the bulge beneath the jacket.

"I'll take you with me."

Now she is fumbling with the blade. She can't work her right arm properly but all she needs is a bit of cunning.

"Who *are* you?" he cries as she stabs out wildly.

She doesn't tell him she is the circus master's daughter.

She doesn't tell him how loved she was in these parts once. The tiger's wife.

Instead she whispers: "My name is Baba Yaga and I'll eat you if you stay. I'll chop up your flesh and grind up your bones. I'll put a candle in your skull and hang it from my belt as a lantern." The knife point scrapes his thigh bone and he staggers away in fright. So young. She almost smiles. Dragging his poor limbs like that, leaving a trail of gore. She'll find him later if she must.

For now, soft needles beneath her and the world going dark. Noises in the forest, the silken swish of something out there moving. Two golden eyes, like two bad moons. The pale curve of teeth.

"Hush now, my love. I'm with you," says the Tiger.

"It's you then, is it?" asks Sara Sidorova. She feels as if her spirit has already left her body. "Old man, Grandfather Death. The devil in the wood."

"It was you who loosed me."

"I told you to take them and you did. Thank you." Somewhere else, her breath whistles between her lips in little gasps but she is smiling now.

"The boy was right. This wound will kill you."

But she isn't afraid. "I stuck him. Follow his blood and you'll find a meal big enough to sate your hunger."

"Is that what you want?"

"I want an ending," she says.

"Good. Come away with me then," the beast whispers in her ear.

Sara Sidorova watches as a magnificent, curved claw drags itself through the air, which parts like the stripling's flesh. Then there is a road—a second road, shimmering black, winding, impossible. That second road becomes a staircase, a great twined chain thrown down to the earth. Inside her the baby moves like a song. Or is it a white bird? Smoke?

Sara Sidorova doesn't remember standing.

She doesn't remember setting her feet upon the path, but there, it's done.

She is walking, then rising upward. She sees the black arc of the heavens, stretched like a widow's veil above her, the forest beneath now, then all of Strana. She imagines the trembling of small creatures.

"Welcome, princess," says the Tiger.

DAYBREAK

3

Sara Sidorova climbs until her legs ache.

She climbs until her soles bleed and her lungs constrict like drying leather. The soldier's boots aren't made for such dainty feet as hers. For an hour she rests on the stairs. What is the world now? A tiny thing, dwarfed by chaos and the killing cold.

There are stars here, but she doesn't recognize them. Too close, too many. Then comes the dawn like warm light spilled under a doorway— breathtaking. The blue hand of evening lifts away and an orange sheen burnishes the earth's surface. It resolves itself into a form she can understand. A burning figure in the heavens. A man.

For one wild moment, she thinks she knows him. Feliks had a way of moving... *Husband*, she thinks. But no, it's a foolish thought. Whatever she spies traveling through the gloom—a god, an angel, some immortal thing passing on through the black—it isn't her husband. Feliks is gone now.

Perhaps there are impossible things in the world but when a man is dead, he stays dead.

✦ ✦ ✦

Sara Sidorova climbs and the world falls away. The pain slips from her limbs. She comes to a gate with great spindles of ivory and bone and eleven chattering skulls. They whisper in a secret language she does not understand. She would stay to learn it but something pulls her onward, a silver thread anchored in her soul, winding tighter and tighter.

"Enter, my love."

The Tiger's voice fills her up.

Sara Sidorova has always had a rebel spirit, hating orders of any kind but the thread tugs her onward and—oh, mercy!—what an elegant place she has arrived at. She is accustomed to cramped hostels, the cuss of the wind against her traveling tent. But now a crenelated dome stretches above her. White marble, glossy and nacreous. It reminds her of a skullcap, the mollusk shells she'd rescue from the river.

Then she closes her eyes, opens them, and she is in a cave.

Limestone drips like melted wax, layering itself into fantastic shapes. The damp air steadies her, redolent with the rich smell of smoke. A blazing peat bonfire makes the walls dance with movement.

So. It's all an illusion. She smiles.

The cave is empty, but for two women in animal-skin cloaks, crouched beside the flame. Despite the quivering glow, no light seems to touch their faces. Sara Sidorova knows they are queens, though she could not say how, exactly. Only that she remembers the stories her grandmother told her. *Sweet Sara, little Sara, I know a place the birds go in the winter and our souls go after death.*

There is a second gate set into the farthest wall of the cave but it's nothing like that first one she passed through. This one is iron—and that means something, doesn't it? Everything in this place means something. Isn't that how stories work?

She tilts her head and blinks the palace back into existence.

Can she even call it a palace? It's more like a mausoleum. A hundred passageways honeycomb outward. There are no tables here, no carpets, no soft furnishings of any kind, except for two iron chairs sat upon by two regal women with gossamer veils obscuring their features. Before them is the fire, but the fire is also...

Oh. Oh yes. There he is.

The Tiger is impossibly huge. His head is the size of a wagon and when she tries to follow the lash of his tail she finds no end to it, only the flame and the darkness, braided together, long enough to cinch itself around the world.

Fear freezes the breath in her lungs but she won't let the beast scent it on her. She is *still* the circus master's daughter. Even here she is the circus master's daughter.

"I knew you once," says Sara Sidorova. "You were flesh and blood and I held you in my arms, didn't I? Such a small thing you were. Not anymore, it seems. You've come into your strength."

"Devil, you called me. Have you no kinder words for an old friend?"

She lifts her chin. "Tell me: who are you? Who are you really?"

The Tiger huffs and the stink of ash is on his breath. "I am Amba. That great beast of legend who some say will devour the constellations when the storm blows in at last from Paradise."

He is playing with her. She knows his moods, his affections, and his petty jealousies. She *did* raise him—or one like him, his shadow self. She remembers the scent of milk laced with brandy. How the cub used to suck it from the nib of the bottle she held.

"And these others?" she asks.

His tail twitches in amusement. "They are my sisters."

"Of course," murmurs the circus master's daughter.

"Come now," says the elder woman in a voice old and creaking. She moves slowly, raising a withered hand to her brow where sits a diadem with a single fist-sized fire opal at its center. "We can speak for ourselves. I know the circumstances are strange, but you are long awaited, Bright-Heart—and very much welcome. My name is Zorya Vechernyaya."

Gently the old woman pulls aside the glittering widow's veil, revealing a face weathered by the ages: crepe-like skin, hair the color of mercury, a pair of dark, burnished eyes.

"You know me then?" asks Sara Sidorova. Should she be surprised? Truly?

"We do," the marquessa replies. "We are watchers. We know everyone our brother befriends."

"Watchers?"

Zorya Vechernyaya lifts her hand. Beyond the iron gate, the light really is extraordinary. It summons the spirit of color into all it touches. The dense forests of the earth below, the sleeping fields, and the wide ocean beyond, the deepest blue the circus master's daughter has ever seen. She would stare and stare, drown herself in that blue...

But then a story comes to Sara Sidorova, about two sisters bound to keep order and the beast who rests his head beneath their fingers. A story of destruction, the end of the world. A story of fire.

"I know all of this," she says slowly. "It's like a dream I once had, isn't it?"

Suddenly she feels that moment—the moment that comes in every performance when the light shifts, the music swirls, and the story *changes*. The words are there, waiting for her to speak them.

"It is your duty to close the gate of heaven," she says to Zorya Vechernyaya. Called the Evening Star in all the old stories. "And her," she turns to the old woman's sister, Zorya Utrennyaya, who has remained as still as a statue, "she will open it again, won't she?"

"Perhaps," says the Evening Star drily, "in a little while. When the time is right."

Sara Sidorova contemplates the three of them. The two queens—the elder and the younger—and the fire-beast between. An iron chain is all that holds him back from devouring the world.

It's such a little thing to do so much work, isn't it?

Ah, but the Tiger, it seems, knows her thoughts. "To be chained thus is no great burden, my love." His lips curve in mimicry of a smile.

"The one I knew was too proud. The one I knew hated any kind of confinement."

"I'm not the one you knew, Sara Sidorova."

"Of course you aren't," she says though she recognizes the scent of him: carnival musk and sweat and buttery sebum. "What is this place then? Where am I?"

"There are many names for it. Lookomorie, the Thrice-Tenth Kingdom. Sometimes it is called the Palace of Stories," says the Evening Star. "Now come. I see you are cold and weary, half-starved, lovelorn. Please. Will you make yourself comfortable?"

Still her sister does not speak.

"I'm your guest?" asks Sara Sidorova. She knows there are rules for guests, special considerations. In a story, everything has a rule that binds it.

"You are *my* guest," says the Tiger possessively. "None have rights upon you but me." His tail lashes the air, a hook of flame in the darkness.

✳ ✳ ✳

As it turns out, Sara Sidorova *is* cold and weary.

Her muscles ache but the practiced grace of her childhood returns to her as she settles herself against the warming flanks of the Tiger. There is no other place for her and he, at least, is not a stranger. Not fully.

Amba, the great beast of legend.

The sound he makes now is more like a barn cat given cream: contented. All at once he is no bigger than he should be, no bigger than her own tiger cub was when her father gave him over. She feels the bronze gaze of the elder sister upon her as she gathers him up in her arms and lays his gorgeous, striped head upon her lap. She expects it might burn to touch but it doesn't.

They are still watching her. Waiting for something else.

What is it? What has she missed?

Sara Sidorova lets her eyes linger, soaking up their beauty.

She is used to being around beautiful women—Lil and Lis, the circus acrobats—but these ones... Their beauty is of an entirely different order, isn't it? Their outer garments are of silk and fine brocade, indigo and violet, with sleeves folded back to reveal white lace cuffs, jeweled with garnets. Up her gaze travels to the dazzling headdresses formed of seed pearls and fountains of lace. Now she remembers sitting with her mother, listening to the radio for news from Hraná City, the progress of the war. Back then Sara Sidorova had lusted after such finery. A red corset with real whalebones, a comb adorned with ostrich feathers.

She touches the dead man's gymnasterka, finds the buttons, then moves upward, searching for the bullet hole with her fingers. They come away sticky with her own blood. For a moment, she had forgotten she was dying.

"It seems I have no need for stories anymore. Watchers, you called yourself. Then you will have watched. You will know the world is nothing to me now."

"We understand you have suffered," says the Evening Star.

"Don't demean me! Suffering I can bear. Thirst, hunger, pain, all of that speaks only to the body, but this is more. This is..."

"Desolation."

"Yes," Sara Sidorova answers slowly. "It's only the living who suffer. And I've passed beyond that, haven't I? If I'm here."

There are cycles, aren't there? Repetitions.

"The great beast of legend, the eater of worlds. I know you, don't I?"

Her fingers land upon the soft fur of his ruff, gently exploring. Then she discovers the thing she was searching for. The collar that circles his neck is cold to her touch. Iron, like the gate. It's always iron in such stories of binding. But who thrust the spike into the stone? Who could snare the Devourer? Her fingers creep further and she finds the catch. How simple it would be. Another little move and everything could be undone.

"So. This is why you brought me here," she says to the Tiger. "To set you free upon the world. That's the way, isn't it so? In all the old stories the princess must choose..."

Now the beast's muscles quiver with a killing spirit. That's all the answer she needs. Even at the edge of the universe, it seems, there's no escaping the past. Is it really a choice for one who has suffered as she has? For one who has lost what she has lost? She undid a collar very like this and there was blood after. She was glad of it.

"Take everything then. Take the world. Take the boy with his rifle, take his captain too, the soldiers, the trappers, the stalkers and huntsmen."

Her thumb slides toward the catch.

"Wait, girl, don't be so stupid!" cries the Evening Star. Her knuckles are bloodless and white as pearl.

"Ah, but she has chosen! It's done now, and easily too." The Devourer fixes Sara Sidorova with his yellow glare, urging her on. "Go on then, unchain me. You're finished with the bone orchard. What could possibly remain for you down there?"

His eagerness is hot and heavy, a scent as strong as sex.

But then a thought comes to her. The burning man traveling through the darkness. And another memory fluttering: "Bitter, bitter, bitter!" the men shouted at her wedding dinner. They drank samogon afterward and she kissed Feliks, to chase the bitterness of the world away for all of them—

"The matter isn't settled, brother," says Zorya Vechernyaya more quietly now. "Not yet, not so easily."

—and she knows this is a performance: the wonder and the strangeness, so shocking to her senses. It is all an attempt to astonish her.

"I've been forced," she says. "Forced and forced, stripped of choice. But I won't be your plaything in this, whatever it is. No more games now. Tell me everything."

"Everything," says the Evening Star with a note like irony. "That I cannot do. The world is too vast, my dear. But I can show you *something*."

"Sister..." A warning note from the beast. Or perhaps something else—an echo of longing?

The moment is over too quickly for Sara to parse because now the light is blinding: first silver and then the color beyond silver, the color silver strives after. The sky is rent. Then Sara Sidorova is falling, falling through the night...

THE EVENING STAR

4

There is a light blinding the girl in the cage.

Perhaps you'd call her face common: a smooth forehead, pale skin, sharp cheekbones above flat cheeks. Long limbs, a slight dimpling at each elbow. She wears a corset of crimson silk. Girlish hips, a pretense of breasts. The girl is barely sixteen but already she is a beauty in the making.

Her name is Sara Irenda Lubchen.

"What do I care about this one?" demands Sara Sidorova. "You promised me an answer and I'm tired of games."

"Be patient," says the Evening Star. "There is a proper order to stories. Let me tell it my way."

The cage is on a platform, lit by a spotlight, bordered by red velvet curtains. Beyond—in the darkness—is a sea of bodies, the girl's audience. She senses them from the sounds they make, the rustling and nervous breaths.

Now she begins to move as if in a dream. She knows what she must do, what she has promised to do. Out there is the man she has promised to kill. She is frightened, poor girl, but she masters her fear quickly.

"I love you," she whispers, to herself, to us. "I love you all." And despite everything, despite the cage, despite the corset, and despite the package of death hidden inside, she does love them. But her love is a feral, violent thing. She tells herself what she has set out to do, she can still do in love…

"She hasn't learned how to lie," says Sara Sidorova.

"That will come in time."

"Tell me, who is she? I think I know her…"

Carefully the girl steps toward the bars of the cage, her head cocked. It's instinctive, an animal gesture. Her nostrils twitch. There's a predator inside this cage with her, behind the secret panel. She knows he is there. She's afraid of him, in her own way, but not as frightened as she should be.

"It's him, isn't it? Your brother. Why? What does he want with her? Stop pretending now!"

"Oh, but the self is changeable, Sara Sidorova. Your father taught you the rules of magic and that's the very first, isn't it? A thing is what it is only as long as belief holds it in place. And belief can make a thing larger than it is, like a light throwing out a long shadow."

"Go on then. Show me what this girl can do."

The lights go out. A hush falls over the crowd.

Sara Sidorova draws in a breath.

"Do you wish to linger?" asks the Evening Star gently. "Of course you do. You think you're a renouncer, recanting life, cursing whatever your eyes fall upon—but I know differently."

"Enough! Let the beast take her if he's so hungry. What's one more, then? That girl is nothing to me."

"Has no one taught you patience? Never mind. I drank from the milk of the heavens and I have seen a thousand earthly kingdoms rise and fall. My years are infinite. I set the clock as I please. And I can turn it—like so..."

5

And so we have light.

The light of a new day, a new life.

Here is a babe—newborn and blinking. She has the same delicate skin, the same copper eyes. See that lovely brow? She knows no more of the miraculous than any other child. Yet all children are born miraculously. They emerge from a place of darkness and fall into—in the best cases—love.

"Would you tell me there's love in the world then? Liar."

"There was for you, Sara. Once you were in love and eager to greet the new day."

"Once I was young and my head was full of nonsense."

"What is this one's filled with? A babe's greedy anger and hurt. Someone must teach her to love, don't you think? But here she is, arriving into a world of chaos. It's good to watch from the beginning."

"What's that awful noise?" demands Sara Sidorova.

"Sirens. There's been an explosion. Three blocks from the hospital..."

The child feels the vibrations and lets out a cry. Cold air, bright lights, sweet air. Her mother holds her to her breast. "You wanted to be born, little mouse," she whispers, "and so here you are."

Her papa asks, "What shall we call her?"

"Sara," says her mother. It means 'princess'.

"Irenda," he replies, which means 'peace'.

Thus, they name her according to tradition. For her mother's mother.

"This is your granddaughter, Sara. Blood of your blood. If you choose to live."

"If I live." And Sara Sidorova's hands move protectively to her belly as she looks at the child's mother.

Else, her own daughter.

It is too much, too fast. She feels lightheaded.

"I think she sees us, don't you?" says the other. "Hush now, sweet thing, you have your name. No matter the noise, no matter the dark, no harm will come to you this day, I swear."

"And tomorrow? Don't lie to her. Don't let it begin with lies. Tell her what's coming."

"Tell her yourself, Sara," says the Evening Star. "For now we'll turn the clock again and leave the poor child to grow. When she is ready she will attend upon us."

And so the light flashes and the world whirls away.

MORNING

6

"Look, Sara. The light really is quite wonderful..." says the old woman with a chuckle.

Zorya Utrennyaya, the Morning Star, her still silent younger sister, is moving. The glow of the rising sun limns the outline of her robes. Sara still cannot see that one's face, but she breathes in the tangy air and tries to remember what she was thinking of. There should be a dawn song, shouldn't there? Waxwings and bluethroats and... What else? What *else*?

But the thought has vanished. Her body feels like molten silver beginning to cool. No pain now. Beyond the gate the earth is washed in hues of lavender and coral, sunflower.

Crimson.

Heart's blood.

There, now. Yes.

She remembers the seep of her blood through the jacket. How it felt for her heart to beat: the steady thudding, like the younger Estes' drum summoning the circus performers to the ring. *Thrum di dum, thrum di dum*—but where is that rhythm now?

"I'm dead, aren't I?" she asks. "That vision—it doesn't mean anything. The boy shot me. I felt the bullet go in."

"Dying, maybe. Yes. Almost certainly," answers the Evening Star. "Oh, child, is that what you want? Of all the wishes in the world that one is easiest. If you ask me, I'll unstop the hole in your shoulder and let your blood flow again. The birds will come for your body—"

Wings black as a seam of coal. Oh, she knows about the birds, doesn't she?

"—Or the wolves, wild pigs. Anything with sharp teeth and a growing hunger."

"That girl was my granddaughter. Irenda, they called her." She tries to feel the kick of her daughter but there is nothing. "So it seems I live."

"Maybe," growls the Tiger from his position of repose, feigning disinterest. She has seen this tactic at work before in her own cub. "Maybe you live. Maybe you die. Pffft, does it really matter?"

"This is a place of stories, Sara," says the Evening Star. Her copper eyes shine with reflected light. "Every story has a choice."

"So maybe I live."

"Yes."

"Then show me the girl. My granddaughter. That's what you want, isn't it? Let her speak for herself."

Now the old marquessa is smiling and Sara Sidorova knows she has stumbled into a trap. But how could she not? How could she know where the snare lies, the pits with their spears? All of this so far beyond what even she might understand of the world...

"Look again, Sara."

Then the Evening Star reaches out and clasps her chin, directing her stare with fingers immeasurably cold. Their gazes meet with the force of an electric shock. That face, almost plain beneath the layers of finery, but impossible to ignore.

The same face as her granddaughter: common but somehow beautiful. Except this one is older, far older. And her smile is like Sara's smile but... not. Less forced, yet it gives little away. The Evening Star tilts her head—Sara Sidorova has practiced the very same gesture a hundred times, a thousand—and it's like staring into a looking glass.

Curiosity. Wonder.

"Oh, Sara," says the Evening Star. "Grandmother. You were so different when I knew you in life. Omen of ill luck, I called you. Teller of tales, outcast, thief... Well, I never meant it cruelly!" Sara hears a young girl's laugh in that age-scarred throat. "In the lands of the living we're seldom our best selves."

"That child you showed me—it was you. My granddaughter? How can it be?" demands Sara Sidorova.

Still the smile.

"So I am. So I will be. A story can change as well as the self, can't it? It was you who taught me that. It grows as the teller grows, alters as the world alters it, sheds its skin like a snake—we are very like a snake, aren't we? You and I? A snake the devours its own tail... oh yes. I think so—"

Sara Sidorova blinks. She expects the other to vanish, for the world to *change* again, but still the old woman stands before her.

"—stories are like that," continues her granddaughter. "Sometimes they are a knife that cuts the master's hand. Sometimes they live and in living breathe new life into others. Sometimes they kill and sometimes they die. Would you know my story then, Sara?" Coyness, at the last, and something else: hunger.

"Yes," whispers Sara Sidorova.

"Good," comes the reply. "Then listen, my sweet."

THE GRANDDAUGHTER

7

"Shall we begin the old way then?" asks the Evening Star.

Once there was a girl. The girl was on a train headed to the capital, to Hraná City—best of all cities in the best of all possible worlds...

"I see green, nothing but green for miles," says Sara Sidorova. "Where are we?"

"In the east now, crossing through the wildwood. But perhaps you've never been this way. You always kept to the coast, didn't you? The harbors and the ports, the blue places. It's different inland: all evergreens, oaks, and black gum, a thicket of savage weald our people still haven't managed to tame. The land fights us. It always has and always will, so they say—but just wait a little and the shape will change. Soon the land will grow flat and tameable, chalky fields of monocrops, then rivers again and the summerhouses of the wealthy, then the industrial estates, the munitions factories..."

The girl in the carriage was an orphan. The girls in these stories always are, aren't they?

She clutched a letter in her hand and her heart was filled with death. The letter said very little she could understand, nothing of grief and even less of love.

The girl, of course was me.

I was a good girl but my parents had died anyway. I was a smart girl, a pretty girl. All the papers said so. They remarked on how somber I had looked at the assembly for mourning, how very beautiful in my black scarf and silk dress, kneeling before old General Cvetko's ikon.

In stories these things matter, don't they? Being good and wise and pretty. Being an orphan, even. In stories these can position a girl in a certain way: for marriage, if one is lucky—or happiness after certain violent trials. It is the good girl who tames the witch. Lady Pale-Throat, the loyal daughter, willing to serve if she must to get what she wants. She might be possessed of special talents. She might speak the language of birds or have a cloak that can turn her feral, claws and teeth and a taste for man's blood…

Well. What are those but stories?

"Tell me. How did she die? How will my daughter die?" says Sara Sidorova, her hands curling around her belly.

"A bomb blast in Assembly Square. Separatists, they said, and agitators. Seditionists, treasonists, collaborators, demagogues. It was widely reported at the time. So widely, some said, that a story emerged months later claiming certain news outlets had reported the explosion before it had technically occurred."

"Did she… suffer?"

"I can't answer that, I'm afraid. Not all travel the same road when their spirit slips away."

Mama and her dying…

In those early days after the blast I used to try to imagine it. How she must have seen a brilliant shingle of light and all the world receding. I like to believe she felt nothing though in truth my mother had never been afraid of pain. Pain, she often told me, lives only in the body. The mind forgets pain, which is why mothers have second children.

And Mama desperately wanted another child. Not because she didn't love me—no, she was a rare woman of love, my mother. She was much remarked upon in Stary, the little town where I grew up. It was not a place where there were many such as her: full of laughter, love for my father, love for me. Her house had wild dill in the yard and chamomile blossoms whose puffed-up lemony hearts she would dry in the cellar. She adored all the small, fragile things of the world and every kind of singing delighted her:

> *That love shining in your eyes.*
> *There's the missing moon.*
> *No harm done I know…*

Sometimes I wonder if she would have liked another daughter better than me. Even back then I was a difficult child, stubborn as a crab, my papa used to say, and secretive as all the children of Stary were.

Well, what else was to be expected? I had grown up in the shadow of a war I never understood. At school I was taught to love death. I wrote endless compositions about how I'd like to die in the name of… By the age of twelve I'd earned a reputation. My teachers took an interest and often I read my compositions at assemblies.

I was a good girl, you see? So very well-informed.

* * *

In Stary, for a time, my grief made me special.

I was the daughter of heroes. All the dead were heroes. I was told this daily by Miss Boban, my caretaker. She stayed in the house with me after. Her lessons included regular grieving exercises. Jumping jacks and journal writing. I wrote every morning in our parlor, rubbing my big toes together when I couldn't think what to say next. Grief-addled, she called me. She insisted I give her the journal for safekeeping before I slept.

"How proud you must be," she would tell me, brushing my hair, thinking the shock had left me feeble. Sometimes she'd whisper that she loved me and she wasn't the only one to do so. Eyes followed me when I ventured outside, a chorus of whispers. It seemed I'd become a rare object of fascination. Certain apparatchiks took to remarking on the paleness of my cheeks. These weren't lewd comments, you understand, not then—but comments of particular note, nonetheless.

Their attentions were observed, of course. Stary was a place of observation. Every glance was documented and disclosed to the proper authorities. Before long it was deemed an intervention might be necessary. Though we were many miles from Hraná City, it didn't take long for word to arrive. It would be better, everyone agreed, if I should find a home elsewhere. For my own sake.

So. My journey.

On the train now I was no one. Unloved, dispossessed. Poor too despite the promise of a state subsidy when I arrived where they had told me to go. I slept seldom and when I did it was fitful and anxious. Often I woke in tears. Sometimes a woman—often a mother—would take my hand and try to comfort me but I was afraid of strangers and didn't easily give myself over to their kindnesses.

In my hand I clutched a letter. The letter was handwritten on cheap paper and every so often I would press it against my knees to smooth the creases.

> *When you come to me, leave no trace of*
> *my daughter. No hair, no blood!*
> *Burn the clothes you cannot carry.*
> *Burn her books. Burn her bedsheets.*
> *Burn this letter.*
> *There is the body and there is the body.*
> *Bring only ashes.*

This letter was from you.

I was a good girl and so I had tried to do as you demanded. Beside me was a suitcase filled with my mother's refuse: old cotton dresses, her bedsheets, her most loved books. All of them had been shredded or torn—her *samizdat*, the few forbidden Rosettis and Ravenskayas she had hoarded—all cut to pieces by my own secret hand. I'd had no idea how to burn them without Miss Boban seeing.

"Let it be enough," I'd said to myself as I ripped through the delicate pages, "let it be enough."

I had loved my mother fiercely but now she was dead. I'd been forced from my home: wild dill and singing and yellow blossoms like little victory wreathes. I must forget the dead, they told me, it would be better that way, easier for me. Strana was a country that looked forward, only forward, ever forward. Here love grows tired, history vanishes, and nothing needs to linger past its day.

"I see something on the horizon," says Sara Sidorova, "what is it? It seems like a fortress of light... a thousand winking eyes in the darkness... I never saw such structures in my life. Is this the capital then?"

"Oh, we are coming to it, Grandmother. To Hraná City, the best of all cities. To Baba Yaga in her palisade of bones."

8

Morning arrived with a steamy blast from the engine that frightened the rooks from their perches. A cloud of dizzying blue-black wings met us as the train pulled into the station. Bad luck, if you were the sort to fear such things.

Not me, of course.

I'd left Stary but my grief had followed like a kind of glamour. That was clear right away from the face of the civil servant who had been called upon to usher me into my new life.

"I trust your journey was well?" he asked politely but his eyes lingered, searching, scrutinizing, attempting to suss out whatever it was that made me shine so.

Orphan, orphan, orphan I wanted to shriek, but the travel had cast a spell of silence on me. I nodded imperiously. He was a functionary—and that was enough for both of us. He took his place behind the wheel of a black armored sedan and slid shut the privacy partition. I suppose he was used to driving around a different class of passenger—the Deeps, perhaps. The Department for the People's Protection. Even in Stary I'd heard stories about them. How they were human lie detectors, how they didn't need to sleep.

In any case it didn't matter. I had nothing to say and was happy for him to drive in silence.

The outskirts of Hraná City were sprawling and the sprawl was both ugly and bleakly impressive. A shivering afternoon light slid between ashlar facades twenty stories tall. From time to time a bridge would cross us and in its blue shadow handkerchiefed women hawked mushrooms the size of lamb hearts.

The engine bled gasoline and the driver took his time. There were no sights to point out. Victory Square lay further west as did the fabled Fountain of the Princes, the Winter Palace with its thousand rooms and courtyards, its sea-green copper spires, the Capitol Buildings, the seat of the senate, of General Cvetko himself—but those weren't for me. I was the daughter of heroes but we were no longer in Stary. Already my mother's time was passing, *she* was passing, out of the realm of living and into…

Somewhere else.

As we drove along the magistrale, I set about making my own plan to join her. A rope would be best to end my life. Braided from my bedsheets, perhaps, if nothing better could be found. Poison would be hard to come by and painful if maladministered. Drowning would be difficult and fire more terrible than poison. Falling would be acceptable though the building must be high enough to guarantee certainty. At least there were enough of those around.

Thinking this way made me calmer so I dozed as the car carried me into my new life. My almost certain death. The light was weak and yielding. The asphalt whispered its secret song as it sped into the distance.

✦ ✦ ✦

Then:

"Who's this one? Speak up, girl, at my age I don't hear so well. What are you? A lump? A parcel? What's your name? What are you doing on my doorstep?"

"Well now, Granddaughter. I suppose you'll say that old crone is me," demands Sara Sidorova.

"What can I tell you, Baba? The years are seldom kind." A trace of a smile on her lips.

"But how old is that one down there? A hundred? A hundred and two? Her face looks like a pickled onion! I swear to you, my own mother was beautiful, even in old age she was beautiful! But her... her..."

"Oh, I confess my first impressions weren't good either."

You clutched the doorframe as if I'd woken you from a deep sleep. Rheumy eyes, a shapeless black frock and a briny aroma that followed you out into the hallway. One long severe braid hung like a noose from your scalp. But still you held yourself like a boyar-wife—mad perhaps, but your back was straight, your gaze fierce.

"The girl's name is..." my driver started but you yanked up my hand and held it an inch from your face as if you might read my fortune quicker than he could tell it.

"Sara Irenda Lubchen. Yes, yes, of course, I'm not a soft skull. Consider her safely delivered. Tell whoever you need to she's with family." With that you hauled me inside and slammed the door.

The smell was worse here. It hung like a sweat in the air. Thick preserving jars balanced on unsteady shelves: eggs and walnuts, beets swimming in magenta vinegar, cucumbers, cabbage, and tiny sour green apples. But I didn't have time to take it in.

"Did you do as I asked? Did you burn my daughter's things?" You were stamping your feet on a shapeless saffron-colored rug.

"Come now. Irenda—" you tasted my name in your mouth "—you must answer me quickly."

I shook my head.

"Foolish girl."

You snatched up my suitcase and set about unlocking it. Out came a strip of bed linen as long as my arm. A few scraps of poetry fluttered to the ground.

"This was my Else's, wasn't it? It tastes of her. Like lemons and apple blossom," you said as the ribbon traveled from your fingers to your cracked coral lips. "You should have consigned these to the fire, girl. You should have let her find her rest. Did no one teach you anything of value in that stinking place she raised you?"

I kept my silence.

"Answer when I ask you a question. I won't live with a mute."

"In Stary, I had excellent scores," I told you stiffly, "in geometry and history. I know how the seven princes died and the name of every man who fought at Cheyory Bridge."

"Trivia, trivia, trivia, just as I expected," you shot back with a scowl. "What a bad start you are off to, Granddaughter. But I'll do what I can. I'll have to, won't I?"

✷ ✷ ✷

Your apartment was five stories up, made of red brick balanced on rusted steel struts. Its spatial features were peculiar, the partitioned remnants of a communal style of living long since abandoned: narrow hallways and jigsaw rooms. The balcony held a glassed-in bathroom along with strings of dried red peppers.

"This is yours now," you told me as you pushed me toward a cramped room behind the kitchen. Inside it was a mattress. The rest of the furniture was modular: a standing mirror that doubled as an ironing board, a stack of four boxes I was told could be anything I wanted: a stool, a sofa, a bed, a table for the old sewing machine that took up half the closet. Immediately I hated it.

"It's make-believe," you snapped. "Just make-believe the furniture."

"Yes, Baba," I whispered. Imagine dull lead softening. Impossible? Well, your face did. Not much, but I swore I saw it. You thought I knew nothing but Stary had made me a careful observer.

"Well, girl, do you want tea? Do you need to pass water?"

I shook my head.

"You must be hungry at least, with all the miles you've traveled. Eat when you have the chance or starve later."

"No," I intoned. A hunger strike would do as well as anything else. I wanted to deny my body.

But then my stomach rumbled gassily and you were pulling me into the kitchen before I could refuse you again, saying, "Good, good. Only shadows don't eat."

Well, so what if I was hungry? It had been three days on the train and I dearly missed my mother's cooking. But in your kitchen were only more preserving jars stuffed with mummified cranberries, horseradish, and thick-skinned tomatoes. Did you live on these? It seemed intolerable. I'd have to kill myself soon and spare myself a horrid breakfast.

While you set about collecting specimens to fatten me up, I was left in an airless living room where a masonry heater piped warmth through a maze of black pipes. The bottom third of each of the walls had been painted moss-green, the work abandoned evidently. Above the divide, dusty cupboards hid an assortment of worn crockery and knick-knacks.

In Stary, snooping on one's neighbors was a time-honored tradition. When I opened one drawer, I found a blown-glass bulb that launched a snow-swirl of confetti as I shook it. Next was a fading picture of a girl. She stood barefoot in the flooding gutter, her knees splayed, gripping a pair of dancing shoes while a soldier with a black umbrella stood some paces behind. Seventeen or eighteen, rail-thin with a wild elation in her eyes. She had my mother's delicate, heart-shaped mouth. I pried the picture from its frame to search for some hint of when it had been taken. 'Mirko, after the war' was all I could find written there.

"I married that one," you said from behind me.

Who knew you could move like a panther when you wanted? I spun around to find you holding a board with buttered rye bread toward me. "Your deda was kind in his own way. You won't remember him, I expect. You grew up too far away. Put the picture back, child. The light will spoil it."

It was you then. Not my mother at all.

"But that can't be right," says Sara Sidorova. "My husband was Feliks."

"It hasn't come yet, Sara. The girl in the picture is still ahead of you."

"Why did you send me that letter?" I demanded. In truth, I suppose what I really meant was, what's to become of me now? I had no one in the world but you and by that point it was becoming clear to me you were a grotesque, a witch woman, a fossil gone grotty in the head. I had seen war widows like you in Stary. The state madhouse was full of them.

"You look like my daughter," you murmured as you sank into the wing-backed chair near the stove, balancing the board on your knee. "Else was so skinny when she was your age, like a little boy."

Oh, but just hearing Mama's name was a release. "Will you tell me about her? Will I sleep in her room?" I would have knelt at your feet had there been room enough.

"You want stories, go find a storyteller."

"Please!"

You pressed your lips together and said nothing.

"Tell me about her childhood, Baba. How was she born? What kind of girl was she?" I could see the questions were an affront but I couldn't stop asking them.

Suddenly rage pooled in my stomach, the back of my throat. Then I was thrusting the old photograph toward the stove.

"Tell me," I hissed, "or I'll burn this picture! I swear I will!"

Who were you supposed to be to me anyway? My grandmother? Mama had never spoken of you, neither her nor my father. All I had was your name and even that they'd never bothered to use. You had been happily abandoned and now you inched round the room like a whelk and I wanted badly to hurt you further.

Ah, but I was wrong about you—and not for the last time.

In a flash you were out of the chair. The bread flew, the board clattered, and the metal grate hissed like a cat as you flipped it open to show me the glowing orange flame. I swear your fingers must have been blistering from the heat but you didn't even flinch.

"Oh, child, you think I'm so easily cowed? There's a beast at the heart of the universe," you spat, "and he'll gorge himself on your wanting, if you let him. Some call him the fire in the night, the great devourer but not me, oh, not ever me. I tamed him, Granddaughter..."

The heat jellied the air and I took a step back. You smiled then, and that crooked smile of yours was worse than the heat because I could see you weren't lying.

My hand dropped slackly to my side and the picture floated to the floor.

But then your face changed, your smile twisted and a terrible coughing racked your body. On and on it went, bending you over like a question mark. When the fit passed, whatever it was I had seen in your eyes was gone. You slumped into your chair, boneless, just another old woman, just another husk who had held on long past her purpose.

This was why they had told me to forget. Some things lived too long. I swore I wouldn't make that same mistake.

Carefully you plucked the picture from the floor. "Your mother thought the world was a place for singing. Now she's dead. Let me mourn her. Tomorrow, we'll talk, Granddaughter. Tomorrow we'll set things right…" Then your eyelids drooped, slid shut and your body went slack as a windless sail.

You were asleep.

Was I sure?

You could have been pretending… but no. It was as if your age had crept up on you. Your skin was translucent as onion paper, the veins a crosshatch of velvety blues and purples. Maybe you thought you'd tamed the beast but it was clear as still water that Death had sunk his teeth into you.

But the anger was inside me, a red flush creeping up my neck. I took the iron poker and imagined bludgeoning you to death. I dreamed of driving you into the oven myself as all the brave girls did when they met a witch in the forest.

A beast at the heart of the universe, was there? Let him feed, I thought, let him take it all. What need had a girl like me to resist him? There was nothing for me here. No love, no kindness, only the great millstone of pain I'd carried around since the day my mother had left me.

✳ ✳ ✳

So.

I tied the bedsheet carefully under my chin, then tested the running knot.

In Stary, I'd learnt a basic knowledge of ropes but these specialist skills were beyond me. Never mind. Hopefully my neck would snap when I jumped. But if not… well, dead was dead, even if it was messier than you wanted. Pain lived in the body.

Outside the evening light was pink as a scar. Five stories up—I was almost certain it would be enough. Through the bedroom window I could see two bridges and a green-topped spire jutting out from the concrete morass of Hraná City in the distance. I almost abandoned my plan. Wouldn't it be good to see the Winter Palace? The thousand pale blue columns, the gardens like a paradise on earth? Mama had spoken of it often, had said she had visited it as a child once…

Then I shifted the pane and a warm wind gusted in. The whisper of traffic muffled by distance, louder now. There was no use waiting. Grabbing hold of the frame, I prepared to dash myself against the street below.

But then the scent of lemon and apple blossoms teased my nostrils and it was as if Mama was standing before me. Her face was reflected in the wavy glass and she was whispering the words of one of her forbidden poems:

I shall not see the shadows,
I shall not feel the rain…

A ghost, I thought. I didn't doubt it was her. There were stories about spirits and angels and all sorts of demons, weren't there? Stories about the kind of women who could see them, speak to them…

I sank down onto the dilapidated mattress. My fingers worked at the knot but I couldn't untangle it. I was tired now, and teary. The day had brought too much. But still there was tomorrow, wasn't there? Always tomorrow. *I can do it then*, I told myself. It was a promise. My secret strength. Whatever further pain the world brought me I could end it if I wished.

"I'm so sorry, Mama," I whispered.

Death hovered at my shoulder, winking. I cradled the rope like a doll until eventually sleep took me.

9

In the old stories there were warnings about women like you, Baba. A witch knows the secrets of the dead, she can speak to animals, she can bleed memories from a child's head and drink them like chamomile tea...

"Irenda! Irenda, girl! What shall we eat today?" you were bellowing as if I were three flights of stairs away rather than the next room over. Your strength had returned. "Why my cupboard's as bare as a bone. You'll have to go to the market. These knees of mine are dreadful."

A gray-green morning light sluiced over my bed, illuminating the linen, now miraculously straightened. Had you changed it while I slept? It seemed impossible I wouldn't have woken. But then I'd always slept deeply and there had been a time in Miss Boban's care when I had drowsed for days, mindless and inert. Perhaps I'd only dreamed the ghost and the knot.

Tomorrow, you had promised me. Well, it was tomorrow now, wasn't it? Perhaps there was another way to make my mother's spirit linger. If you were a witch, there might be secrets I could tease from you. If I were brave enough, if I were smart enough...

If I did as you said...

The old Stary line.

I crept out of the bedroom to find you dancing around the kitchen, searching through cupboards, then under the sink. When you spotted me, you thrust a handful of kopeks onto the table. "From now on if you don't eat, I don't eat."

"This won't be enough," I grumbled. I'd seen the shop prices as I'd been driven through the streets, close to double what they had been in Stary. But then I took hold of myself, grew canny, and tried again more delicately: "Besides, you said tomorrow… *today*…"

"Yesterday you're like a shadow, now you say this won't be enough? How much does a shadow need anyway?"

"What about the subsidy?" I tried.

"I'll be long dead by the time it arrives. Delays, delays, delays…" You scuttled toward the front door, threw it wide, and checked the hallway. "Out you go, girl. I've things to do that don't need little eyes watching. And don't let that old trout next door see you."

Obey and be safe, follow, follow, follow, never lead. If a boy breaks your arm then say nothing, grit your teeth, and be silent. Secrets are good, the secret life is the life best lived, but also keep no secrets, be as you appear, conform your inner self to your outer self. Forget the word private.

I had my secrets and I could keep them as well as you could.

✦ ✦ ✦

Summer was arriving early in Hraná City. The sun was a five-pointed star in a vaporous sky. Drowsy wasps threw themselves against the windowpanes, dropped senseless to the pavement where I had to step carefully to avoiding treading on them. Even the dead ones still had their sting.

I found a scattering of shops along the magistrale—a butchery with three chickens strung up, a key cutter, a bottle shop, a café with prices that made my eyes water. It was filled mostly by glamour girls squeezed into mini dresses, with thick velvety eyelashes and tenant-less expressions. I looked at the dirty kopeks you had given me and knew the situation wasn't good.

An hour's fruitless search turned up nothing until I abandoned the boulevard and discovered a maze of back alleys where brightly colored awnings dipped in the breeze. One shop had a huge vertical rotisserie with lovely smelling meats. My stomach grizzled at the scent. I couldn't help myself.

The man at the counter was old but lively. "What's your name, sweet girl?" he asked in a slow drawl. A foreigner then, or his parents had been.

"No one," I answered. Stary had made me suspicious.

"No one? Oh, child, everyone's got to be someone. Call me Fedkin if you like."

I browsed for a moment, mouthing the prices in the vague hope they might transform when I spoke them. Even here they were too high for what I had—but I remembered the glance the functionary had given me. Fedkin had the same look of wonder when his gaze passed over me: as if the touch of death had made me shine.

"Here, Mistress No One," he told me, giving me a fan of flat breads and a paste the color of old paper. He waved aside my attempts to pay him. "Keep your money and buy yourself a pretty dress."

I was still wearing my black mourning clothes. I hadn't brought anything else with me. "Thank you."

Outside I found a stoop and devoured what he'd given me. The bread was oven-hot and dusted with salt. The paste turned out to be ground sunflower seeds, but smoky and full of spice.

When I'd finished it off, going so far as to lick my fingers clean, I properly began to take in my surroundings. No glamour girls here.

Mostly it was grandmothers and aunties searching out their dinners, squeezing fruit and magicking it into their baskets when they were satisfied. A few old-timers skulked in the mouths of narrow alleyways—soldiers, I realized with a start. They weren't in uniform but they'd clearly returned from the war. I watched them with interest, remembering the many parades I'd been to in Stary, the little thrill that shot through me when I heard the rifles firing in salute.

Could these really be those same brave boys who had blown me kisses before they headed to the front? Some seemed to have taken to begging, with various ploys to attract the attention of those on the street. There was an uncle missing his left foot, the joint sealed up as smoothly as an elbow. He had a military supply sack with him and he shook it noisily, trying to get a bit of attention. Clank, clank, clank went whatever it held inside but the women didn't care, bustling past with grim, tight-pressed lips.

I felt sorry for him: his hangdog expression, his too-long fingers and ungainly way of moving. Perhaps he'd been a coward. Perhaps they'd generously stripped him of rank rather than shooting him in the back for desertion.

He reached into the bag and pulled out a length of chain, then another, and another until it coiled at his feet, gleaming slickly in the morning light.

There was no patter, no polish. Slowly he bound his wrists, one after another. Then he began twisting and writhing, making furious grunting sounds. He moved like a python. Somehow he squeezed the military supply sack over his head and then maneuvered his hands to yank a cord that seemed to pull it tight against his windpipe.

There was something unnerving about the strange figure as he stood there, his body shaking, some kind of keening, choking noise coming from beneath the canvas.

"No," I whispered to myself, then: "Please." Something terrible was happening inside the sack. I imagined his pale, purpling face, his tongue thick as a worm as he fought for breath, struggled again something. The bright shingle of light receding...

"Enough of that," shouted one of the grandmothers, waving a loaf of bread. She yanked the sack from his head. "You're only shaming yourself!"

"Spare a kopek to fill a hero's belly, gran?" the uncle said with a death's-head grin. Bound tight as a sausage, he still managed to hobble toward her. She staggered back in surprise and a moment later he had wriggled free of the chains.

"I've children of my own to worry for," she snapped.

"Then mind that Cvetko doesn't call for them." With regal dignity, he balanced like a stork on his one good leg and collected his discarded shackles.

I wondered if there had been a parade for him once. If that old grandmother had yanked at her braids or cast rose petals in the air for the dead. Maybe, maybe not. Hraná City was a very different place than Stary.

I left him the first of my kopeks and brought home nothing but potatoes that evening.

"Well," you said dubiously when I returned, "I suppose it's better than starving."

That night I boiled them carefully as Mama had shown me, then pounded them flat and stirred in the remains of the rye loaf you'd been hoarding.

"It would be good with dill," I told you. "You could grow it there by the window."

"Find me some seeds and I will," you answered.

An hour later, you sniffed the dumplings I pulled from the oven, tasted one, and smiled.

10

The next day I brought you a dill cutting I'd filched from a nearby garden and we set it to root in a teacup filled with water.

It was the first time I'd stolen and it gave me a shameful, hot-cheeked shock of alarm to do it. Time passed and you and I began to eat better after that, which was a relief. As much as I wanted to deny it, my body had its own needs. It was sprouting quickly, same as the dill.

I suppose I was feeling a growing responsibility for myself and for you as well. Aye, you were difficult, secretive, and ornery too. I think it was the fits that seemed to take you from time to time, leaving you weak and churlish, the breath wheezing in and out like a broken bellows.

Tomorrow, you had promised me but whenever I pressed the issue you were quick with an evasion. "Not today, child," you'd tell me, "but soon. Now go outside. I've things of my own that need doing."

What you did in the hours I took to the streets I couldn't imagine. The little apartment seemed unchanged, dingy as a forgotten cupboard. You hadn't touched my mother's things since the day I arrived. But sometimes you dropped hints of her. How she'd hated eating eggs as a child because she had such sympathy for the hens. How she'd got the scar on her cheek from playing with twisted metal in the camp where she'd grown up. These were like breadcrumbs you set in my path. Perhaps you enjoyed the company of her ghost as much as I did, the sometimes scent of lemon and apple blossoms, a cool breeze that seemed to cut through the rising afternoon heat.

If you did, it was her company and no one else's. You hated your neighbors, it seemed, and took great delight in scandalizing them. You'd blare the radio at five thirty in the morning then claim deafness when complaints emerged.

"Why torment them, Baba?" I asked. "You can't even hear yourself think when it's on."

"They're dull as posts and twice as thick. Did you know we used to share this apartment? Your deda and I, your mama—and them too, that old trout and her brood of troutlings."

"But you're so hard on them!"

"It's different after you've lived so close to people. You learn what they're capable of. And I know, don't I? Oh, yes, I know."

Another secret, another mystery. Very well, I thought, tomorrow I'll try again. Tomorrow and tomorrow and…

Perhaps it would have been all right if it stayed like that. My trust was delicate but it was growing hour by hour. Sometimes when I think back on those days, I wonder if you knew what was coming. You must have, if only because I know better myself how time loops and gathers like a thread in a loom. If you're hearing my story, Sara, then of course you will take it with you. Of course it will change you in turn…

But we mustn't rush it, Baba. Those were happy days—or happy enough.

⁕ ⁕ ⁕

The weeks crept by as I counted down the days until my mother's spirit would leave the land of the living. Forty days, it had been, then twenty, then three. Still you wouldn't speak of her, wouldn't tell me if we would keep her close, bind her to us, or let her fly…

My blood was beginning to itch. High summer was a time for fighting and the border skirmishes were always fiercest when the mountain passes were cleared of snow. More state funerals appeared on the television. I'd recently taken to watching Cvetko as he addressed the crowds. He was a handsome man, I thought, though he must have been nearly as old as you were. His pale eyes sparkled like opals.

"What are you doing?" you barked when you caught me copying his words in my exercise books.

I slammed my book closed and clamped it between my knees. "Nothing, Baba!"

"That man's a hoodnik. King Fiendish himself! I swear to you, Irenda, no good word ever passed between his lips. It's only them—" you thumbed toward the wall "—who listen to the likes of him."

"But, Baba—"

"But nothing! You stay away from him and his jackals. What would the Deeps do with you, eh? Put you to work as a *devushka*, I'm sure. Young girls are always good for raising a soldier's spirits."

With that, you yanked out the plug from its socket and dialed up the radio broadcast instead. But the message was the same everywhere: the war was reaching a critical stage. Our imminent victory had sparked a last-ditch effort along the border. There was a need to be extra-vigilant. We should expect dancing in the street, spontaneous parades—or else spies and foreign agents. It was every citizen's duty to keep tabs on any strangers.

"It's good news for Strana," I tried to tell you but an evil spirit had swept in with your rage.

"Child—" a new pronouncement "—what you know about the world could fit in a thimble. It's bad luck to listen to the Devil."

I could see you were in a superstitious mood and your company would be bad for the rest of the day.

✳ ✳ ✳

In disgust, I searched the streets for Fedkin whom I hoped might offer me some breakfast. But arriving at his shop I saw the words 'Closed' scrawled in paint across the door. Nothing was visible through the newspapered window.

I felt uneasy. Perhaps it was just that it had been days since I'd had a sign of my mother's presence. But I couldn't concentrate. My stomach rumbled like a diesel engine. What now? Sometimes the café threw out old pastries but I'd learned to be careful scrounging there. Vagrancy was a crime and I'd been chased off more than once when the glamour girls and their hoodnik boyfriends were around.

Even under the yellow-striped awning, the concrete burned the backs of my thighs. I'd scout the café and if that was no good I'd just have to go hungry. I wrenched myself from the stoop but someone caught my attention. A soldier.

He was far younger than most I saw on the streets, no more than a handful of years older than me, with movie-star good looks: wavy gold hair and bright blue eyes. Honestly I don't know what made me rank him among the uncles as he wasn't in uniform and he didn't have a war wound on him.

Of course, there had been a time I'd been curious about sex. Some of my girlfriends had been mad for it in Stary, always going on about what they'd done—or been asked to do—for their boyfriends. Most of it sounded disgusting. Later it seemed the part of myself interested in such things had withered and I'd little cause to miss it. In fact it had saved me a great deal of bother. In my final days in Stary there had been offers... It was considered good luck to sleep with a widow in her time of grieving. Some said there was a certain public spiritedness to it. And if I wasn't a widow exactly, if I were an orphan with better than passable looks, well, what of it? It was all to the good, wasn't it?

No one had touched me though.

Have you ever seen robins wrestling over a worm? Sometimes the rush of the flock spares the morsel, as they say. Or perhaps Miss Boban had been a better guardian than I'd thought. Either way I hadn't taken note of their sidelong glances, the passionate confessions of respect for my parents, sweaty brows, sweaty palms, the inadvertent touches for which they'd apologize instantly and insincerely.

So now it took some time to know what I was feeling: a kind of wildness and wonder shooting to my lips, the soles of my feet.

The fellow had a face like any other face, maybe more symmetrical, aye, but there was a nose, there were eyes, a mouth. Nothing special. But still I couldn't help looking—he just seemed so different!

And he was a watcher like me. I could see him studying the other former soldiers as they went about their panhandling. When they shucked off their chains and bowed to their little audiences a small crease appeared in his bottom lip. Suddenly I wanted to kiss it away.

What? Kiss it away? Who *was* the person thinking these thoughts?

But so it went. He noticed me noticing him and my skin flushed scarlet. Blood in my cheeks, muscles weak as noodles—what a fool in love I was. It was just as you said: everything I knew could fit in a thimble.

I crept closer. Not too close though. Still there was a street between us, and that was good, that was inoffensive to moral standards. But then I crossed the street, feigning an interest in the architecture. Oh, what strong lintels these were! Good construction! Yes! I was three doorways away, two. I sat on the same stoop, both of us watching, him casting a glance my way, me not daring to speak.

"No good," he said. I blushed so hard I must've looked like a radish. "See how no one listens? See how no one bothers looking at them?"

He was staring at the uncle with his chain, performing to a crowd that never bothered to applaud. I said nothing. For hours—days? weeks? what was time anyway?—we watched the people drift by like breeze-blown pamphlets.

"Why do they ignore him, do you think?" he asked as another uncle shucked off his chains. The gloomy-eyed escapist reminded me of a whipped dog.

"It doesn't mean anything. They don't know him. Why should they care?"

"Why do *you* care?" he had to know.

My answer was halting. "I want him to be free."

"Why?" Whip-fast, like being quizzed. "He put himself in chains, didn't he?"

"I don't know why!"

"Not good enough. You know but you're not telling."

I gritted my teeth and said nothing, feeling provincial and stupid.

Abruptly he stood. "What's your name then?"

His good looks had thawed my suspicion. Isn't that how it always is?

"Irenda." I took a deep, steadying breath. "Sara Irenda Lubchen."

"Come back here tomorrow, Miss Lubchen. Promise you will?"

He touched his fingers to my lips and a painful jitter rushed

66

through me. No one had ever touched me like that, making me want to be touched even more.

"And wear your hair loose," he said consideringly. "Do you have a white dress?"

"No," I breathed.

His eyes were nearly violet, lovely and electric. "I'll make do. I'm good at that. You'll see."

It's good news, I'd told you, Baba, and that's just what I thought as I skipped into the three o'clock sunshine. But I didn't know back then how trouble has a way of wearing a boyish grin.

11

That night it seemed a wild animal had slipped on my skin and was tearing around the apartment. Absurdly I found myself singing my mother's song while I combed my hair:

> *That love shining in your eyes*
> *There's the missing moon,*
> *No harm done I know...*

No longer horrified with my appearance, I went through every piece of clothing I'd brought. It wasn't much.

You stuck your head into my bedroom. "What's all the fuss?"

"My clothes are too small. These buttons are pinching me."

"So take the buttons off." There was a slight droop to your left eyelid, a sign you'd been sleeping.

"It won't do," I moaned. "Don't you have something I could try on?"

"What do you want, then?"

"A white dress."

"A *white dress*?" Your eyebrows beetled upward in surprise. "Who are you, Lady Pale-Throat preparing for the Sun-King's wedding? Have you found yourself a husband then? Won't you invite your old baba to the ceremony? I'll need a new dress myself, something that shows off my calves, I think. Mirko always said I had the *loveliest* calves he'd ever seen..."

"Any dress will do," I snarled. "Did my mother leave one?"

Your face went stony. "I burned them all. Didn't I tell you to do the same?"

"There must be something!"

"There must, must there? Well, I'm sorry to disappoint, little mouse, but you wanted to be born and this is how it is. Better ask the spiders to spin you some lace." You turned on your heels and disappeared.

Outside the sky was settling into velvety evening as I slumped on my mattress in despair. All over the city little lights were shining like glimworms. Mama and I used to watch them in the garden when the long summer twilights would shift and deepen, apricot to raspberry to mulberry to licorice-black.

"Mama, will you help me?" I whispered.

This was the way of certain stories, wasn't it? A prayer of desperation. I waited for an answer, for her face to appear in the wavery pane of glass.

But nothing happened and nothing I had was right. What was worse, it seemed my only living kin was a wrinkly old trout who'd be no help at all.

✳ ✳ ✳

In the end I pulled the buttons from my mourning clothes, tore open the seams, and restitched them with your old sewing machine. It took all night.

"I see you've found what you needed," you told me at breakfast, huddled over the stove, brewing coffee in a long-handled pot. "It's amazing what can be done when you've a will for it."

"Don't expect me until late," I shouted as I threw open the front door.

"Anger at last?" The pot bubbled and you rescued it from the flame. "You'll have to try harder to impress me. I once beat a girl with a metal rod just to let her know I'd a temper worth minding."

I turned with what dignity I could muster. "Maybe I won't come home at all. What would you care?"

"If houses were as easy to come by as new dresses, I'm sure I'd never see you again."

If there was a warning in your voice, I didn't want to hear it.

* * *

I found my movie star by the usual spot. When he saw me coming, he slapped a hand to his forehead and made me spin around like a ballerina.

"Very simple, very pretty," he said.

Boom! went my heart.

"You sure you've never done this before?"

I shook my head.

"Well. You're a natural dazzler."

His breath went shallow as if some ghostly thing came over him. His hands hovered near my shoulders, almost touching, not touching. He seemed stupid as the heat-blind wasps until he snapped his fingers and wagged off the jinx.

"Help me into this," he said.

He had brought with him an old gymnasterka, the kind my grandfather had worn in the photograph. Olive-green, with wide shoulders and flaring sleeves cuffed smartly round the wrists. It looked as if he had fit it especially with hundreds of leather straps.

"Like this?" I helped him slide the jacket over his thickly muscled arms.

"Not even my sister could do it better."

My fingers were small and the cinches difficult. I had to yank them a hundred times to get them tight enough. Pretty soon the closeness of our bodies was becoming difficult to ignore. He was hot as a grille though his face was pale and sweatless. He had to shut his eyes as he told me what to do.

Once I was finished he tried the straps. "You'll have to pull it tighter or else they'll think I'm bluffing." I tugged hard where I'd left it slack and he tested it again. "What a clever thing you are!"

I reached forward to touch his cheek.

"Not that, Miss Lubchen. Please."

Boom! went my heart again—but now the strain of his gaze was forcing me to back away. By then the crowd had thickened around us. He hadn't even spoken yet but still a little girl stared with eyes wide as cuckoo eggs. "Has it started?" she whispered to her mother.

There would be dancing in the street, the radio had promised. I had no idea what had drawn these people in the first place.

My movie star didn't stand, he couldn't, not with the contraption I had fixed to him. "Friends, my friends," he called out. His voice sailed through the streets, rebounded off shut windows, which miraculously lifted a crack. Doors opened and eyes glinted in the thick interior darkness.

They were listening. People were listening to him.

A peculiar feeling bubbled up inside of me, part hotness, part rage and withering grief. I remembered standing before the crowd at my parents' funeral. How the officials had marched me on stage with a gaggle of other sad-eyed children, Miss Boban clutching my hand like I might fly off in the wind.

It had been a wet day, the shoots drinking up the morning showers while twenty-two caskets gleamed with a soapy sheen.

Ours are a people who live for parades and speeches and any kind of public revelry. The rapport of a cannon, the bright skirl of a banner kicking up in the breeze. Anything that makes us think our lives are a little better than they are.

So.

Now a spark of light was moving from body to laughing body, from hand to clapping hand. Where had these people come from? They had crept from their houses and corners. They'd altered their daily routines and abandoned their principles. And there at the heart of it was my movie star, restless as a charger.

He flexed his spine, drew air deep into his lungs. His voice was pure as a priest's. "Who among you has been bound in shackles? Who among you has been in the grip of some heavy chain you couldn't throw off?"

He shifted as he spoke. Small movements, almost shrugging in apology.

"I've been to places you cannot imagine and seen things you wouldn't believe. I was at the front. No, I won't say where! You know why, you know the necessity for secrets. So many of us died there but I swear I was lucky. I lived, didn't I? Would you hear my story?"

"Yes," they breathed.

"Are there any faint-hearted among you? Any cowards or caitiffs?"

"No! Not here!" Even the child screwed her voice with courage.

"Of course not, my friends. Isn't it said the people of Strana have steel in their spines?"

They roared their approval. He waited. They breathed in and prepared to listen. With a mournful sigh, he swept on with his story. "When the enemy took me, they put me in a cell and I swear I thought my life was over. What soldier wouldn't? What soldier doesn't believe in his heart that his life is no longer his own from the moment he puts on the uniform of Strana? But I was wrong, my friends. For it was in the prison of our enemies—the place every soldier fears more than the grave—that I met the stranger.

"He was an old man, his limbs scarred by the things he had suffered at the hands of the other side—taken by our enemies, just as I'd been. He had spent many years already in the hellhole and one look at his body showed me what I was in for."

"Oh mercy," gasped a voice. "Angels, protect us!"

My movie star looked toward the speaker, tipped his head, and acknowledged it calmly. "They tortured us. I'll spare you the details except to say, aye, it was bad. But the stranger never made a sound. They'd ask him questions and they could've been asking a stone for all he gave a damn."

His words floated into the open ears of the crowds. Tears glistened in their eyes and it was as if I could see their spirits blowing out of their mouths, lifting above the waving hands like a sparkling, silver cloud.

"When I spoke to the stranger, at first he would only whisper of home. He wasn't from our country, but neither was he from theirs. He was a traveler, he said, a wayfarer. A mirabilist, he called himself. He'd say nothing of his ability to resist our captors but he was as curious about me as I was of him and little by little we grew friendly. Three years we spent together and I never saw his face, only heard him breathing, heard the stories he whispered about his life. The silence as he denied our enemies what they wanted.

"Who among you could stand it, my friends? Who among you could remain silent as he did, to protect the ones you love?"

The crowd moaned as one and my movie star fixed his gaze on their faces. This was the moment they might break, I thought. Feet shuffled but he held them.

"The mirabilist was growing weak from hunger. By then he'd spent years in that prison, aye, centuries for all I knew. And at last he confessed to me it was clear he wouldn't live much longer. 'How do you do it?' I asked him. 'Won't you tell me?' And he did."

A pause now, as they hung on his words, craning in to listen.

"It was a spell he had learned from his mother. There was a door inside his mind, a door to Paradise. He could open it and walk through whenever he pleased. If he did this, he came to a beautiful place where he couldn't feel a thing.

"When our enemies came to him, he'd fly away to that place. 'Why do you return?' I asked. And do you know what he said? 'I return because I love the world.'"

The soldier was rocking back and forth wildly by this point but the straps still held him, the leather cinches I had tightened around myself. He looked like a worm, a snake thing, barely a man at all.

"There were two spells he taught me. The first, he told me, would take away pain. The second, he told me, would allow me to escape any confinement."

The crowd was listening with a rapt and wondrous attention. *I* was listening. The scent of lemon and apple blossoms swirled up in a storm of sweetness. I could feel my mother hovering close then as it is known the spirits of the dead may do when emotions run high. When passion or joy or a welter of deep sadness can draw them from the darkness.

Then my movie star called to me and my hands shook. "Sister," he said, "I can see you bear a weight of grief. Would you set it down a little while? Shall I take it from you?"

I didn't need to be told what to do. His words had set a hook in my soul. I didn't want the burden of Mama's ghost anymore, her hand on my cheek, her spirit voice whispering to me. I wanted to forget. To sever myself from longing, from wanting, from wondering what if it had been different and did she feel pain and what would she think of me now.

I leant my face close and he whispered a word in my ear. The sound vanished from my mind the moment he said it.

Then it was like a cool wind blustered through the streets. The heaviness of my limbs lifted and the dark shadow of my loss passed away from me.

"It's gone!" I couldn't have said if it was wonder or horror that sent my voice rising. "You've taken my grief away!"

He smiled up at me, and then beyond, to the others in the crowd. They were waiting for this. A walloping cheer traveled away from him, then slung back, doubling in volume. The movie star waited with a lifted chin. When it was over, I think he smiled.

I *think* but I don't know for certain.

With the noise came a violent movement all around me. The crowd stumbled forward. Eagerly they touched him, whispering love songs in astonishment as their fingers grazed his skull, tousled the blond waves of his hair. He received them with his eyes closed like a saint.

Then he burst out from among them, shouting "See! I'm a free man now! And you could be too! Free men and women!"

An old codger—it might have been Fedkin, even—exploded into tears and clutched his forehead. "It's gone," he said, "all my soreness is gone!"

I yearned to touch my mirabilist again. He had promised to take

75

away my pain and he had. But even now my pain was returning, the leaden grief. Wanting, wanting, wanting.

"Mama," I whispered but there was no answering murmur. In the midst of the clamor a deep stillness seemed to surround me. Try as I might I couldn't recover the clear conception of the divine my instructors had instilled in me: a bright and beautiful space where my mother and father would drift for eternity, their substance rarefied—almost like song. I dreamed I was going deaf. I couldn't remember Mama's voice. I dreamed the world was falling into darkness. There was nothing left of my mother but the pure pain of her loss. I wanted to give it back to him. I wanted to cast the grief from my body.

Then the wail of sirens shook the crowd from their frenzy and sent them fleeing in all directions. "Go!" someone urged me. "Run, girl. Don't let them find you here!" But my sense of self-preservation had vanished with the ghost of my mother. Where could I go? What place was there for me in the world?

And so when the black sedans arrived, they found me with tears on my cheeks, waiting stunned and docile as a slaughter lamb.

12

I felt myself lifted like a child, carried, deposited into a sedan very much like the one that had brought me to Hraná City: tinted windows, gleaming slickly like a coffin.

There were two Deeps—black-suited men from the Department for the People's Protection—one knuckling the steering wheel while the other stared ahead with a face sharp as barbed wire. Neither spoke. The car door opened and the shorter of the two pushed his snout toward me so that I had to press myself away from him. His eyes were comically narrow. In his left hand was a canvas sack which he roughly pulled over my head. A cord was tugged tight, cinching the bag beneath my chin. I clawed at the canvas but his meaty hand swatted my own away.

"Breathe," he told me and I did: fast and desperate. The canvas exploded into my mouth with the taste of stale, seditious sweat. My pulse was drumming in my wrists.

Soon after the engine started.

"Where are you taking me?"

Neither bothered to answer me.

＊ ＊ ＊

Sometime later there was an argument between them. The words were difficult to make out. The sedan pulled to a halt and I heard the door opening, felt someone reaching across my body to unbuckle me. He steered my shoulder and then his hideous orders were in my ears.

"Come with me and behave."

At the time I didn't know where he was taking me. Through the streets first—I could tell from the clatter of my boots on cobblestones and the bustle of traffic around us. Then through a door, its heavy hinges groaning. After were hallways, many hallways, where our footsteps echoed off stone walls. The air grew damper, mustier. Tight passages where my shoulders scraped both walls as they made me turn sideways, and then cold metal ladders, their rungs slick beneath my palms. Again his hand dwarfed mine and curled my fingers around the struts. "Climb down," he whispered and so I did.

We moved carefully, he and I, but sometimes I stepped badly and he would hoist me under the arm. I snatched around for support, clutched at air, even grazed him once but his chest was solid as brickwork.

Down, we went, down and down and down.

The smell of sweet-rot and damp crept into my nostrils. I imagined we were traveling through an underlair, a whole inverted city, one with roots rather than spires and steeples. My fingernails skidded against the corridor wall, then sank into old paint, peeling a strip off like the skin of an apple.

Then my foot struck some sort of wooden platform and my steps made a hollow clack. His handling was gentler now and it made me relax a little. I was sweating badly though the canvas mopped it up. He guided me to a chair, made me sit, pulled my wrists behind me and snared them together.

"Wait," came his voice from somewhere beside me. Then the footsteps receded.

I had thought the journey was bad but what came next was worse.

An hour I spent twisting on the chair while the metal bit into my skin, bruising, then drawing blood. I stamped my foot and listened for the echo: bright and tinny. The pain drifted beside me like a river.

I fell into a dreamless sleep, then shot myself awake with the sense of a sudden drop.

"Miss Sara Irenda Lubchen, I believe," came a whisper from right beside my ear. Not the jackal's. This one was bereft as a desert. Suddenly the hood was yanked away, my head jerked up. I tried to focus but glittery white lights exploded in my vision. "You may answer if you like—if you feel ready to begin."

"Yes," I said slowly. The old Stary instinct was taking hold. Listen and be safe. Keep no secrets. The face was still in shadows despite the glaring light, a wraith-form. I couldn't make it human. Beyond it was nothing but shapes in the darkness.

"You may call me Uncle."

"Yes, Uncle." I was mad to obey.

"Good. Let us begin then."

He asked me many questions and each of them I answered as best I could, at first considering my responses and then, as the pace quickened, blurting out whatever it was that jumped into my head. How long had I lived in Hraná City? With whom did I live? Was I well cared for? Did I love the General and was it true my parents were dead? Had I ever read the books my mother kept? Did I know there were certain materials which were forbidden? Which poems of hers had I liked best? Why those and not others?

Sometimes he stopped and appeared to check my words against

a register. But how could he know what was truth? He was pulling out my dreams and passions, the little things I whispered only to myself. I gave them up to him eagerly, remembering what it was like to stand before the other children in the school auditorium, reciting my compositions. How the green grins of my teachers made me sway with pleasure.

But he was beyond pleasing. After an indeterminate length of time, difficult for me to parse with only the lights and the heavy sphere of darkness beyond, I was permitted to rest. Thirst clawed at my throat. When he understood this, he brought me a cup of water and held it to my lips. The water dribbled over my chin, which he wiped with a clean white cloth.

"Don't worry, child," he told me. "You're doing very well."

That swooning sense of accomplishment again.

I still couldn't make out his face, even as he administered to me with a brisk touch. The light swung close and glib starbursts of blue sparked in my vision. A spasm tunneled through my shoulders but there was no way for me to release them or alter their arrangement.

Then his fingers were kneading into soft muscles, sending shoots of agony up and down my arms. I groaned but he didn't stop and after a minute the pain receded. I found I could move my neck more freely again.

"Were there others?" I asked him as he settled back into his previous position. I was thinking of my mirabilist, if they had taken him as well.

"Yes."

"Did you bring them here?"

"Oh yes, they're watching us. Watching you. What you have said has been a great help."

I didn't know if he was toying with me. I tried to listen for the sound of breathing but there was only the creak of the floorboards as he settled.

"Is there anything you would like to say to your fellows?" he asked me.

I hung with indecision. *Teach me the word*, I thought suddenly, *teach me how to open a door in my mind*.

"Shall we continue?" he murmured after a long length of silence.

What was the quality of my sentiment now? Did I feel anger or pride in Strana? If I could have uttered one word of warning to my mother while she was alive, what would it have been? Why her and not my father? Was it not said that the father was the head of the household? Didn't I owe my father my passionate defense?

On and on it went until a knot had scratched a bloody thumbprint into my wrist. Then it seemed the questioning was over and Uncle went away again. Another face swam into view. The lights dulled and gave me a clearer image. This man seemed very old. The hair on his wrists was as thick and wiry as a greyhound's. His ears were stuffed with hair too but otherwise he was completely bald. His eyes were a poisonous opal blue.

"Do you know who I am, child?" he asked me.

I did and I didn't.

There were rumors the General was desperately paranoid, that he employed body doubles. Sometimes he would disappear from public view for months on end and when he returned there would be subtle changes: a misaligned nose, a mouth that creased differently than it had before. The voice of the man on the radio had been silky but this one let the consonants click together.

What to say to this man, if he was who I thought he was?

"All other states pressed against Strana but we weren't despondent." I was an echo throwing back the speech I had heard on the radio. "We didn't lose heart. Didn't we throw back the interventionists? The back-stabbers? The saboteurs and falsifiers? We recovered lost territories and we buried many friends. But what is a country that has no bones?"

The General laughed softly and a little thrill ran through me.

"I'm rarely available for these interviews," he told me, "but sometimes I find it pleasing to speak with my citizens. To understand them better, you see. A man is only so good as his information, wouldn't you say? And while one must trust to one's own stewards and second selves in matters of life or death I've found that from time to time it is useful to involve myself more deeply in the detail work."

I could feel the sharpness of his gaze, the lamp light of other imagined eyes on me. The Deeps would be watching.

"And that one"—he jerked his thumb toward the shadows—"knows I have an especial interest in certain preoccupations that touch upon yourself and your comrade. The spectacle of the two of you, so he called it." He paused in his delivery and studied my face. "I understand your parents are dead, Miss Lubchen. They were heroes, were they not?"

I said nothing.

"I called them heroes and so they were."

A prompt—but still I couldn't speak. A great shudder went up my spine.

"Do you know what death is?" the General asked without blinking. "I have spent my life making a study of it." I shook my head and he smiled a slow, careful smile. "Some say it is only the other side of life."

Then he reached toward me. For a moment I thought he might caress me—but no, his fingers darted past, then returned, revealing a silver coin with his own imprinted face winking in the light. He made the kopek dance over his knuckles like a cartwheeler.

"Such a little thing it is, with you one moment, then gone the next."

The coin vanished.

Or so he clearly wanted me to think. I could see the crook in his thumb as he palmed it. I kept silent and waited.

"Here," he said at last, "have this."

The coin appeared between his fingers. He tucked it gently into my shoe. Then from the shadows emerged one of the Deeps who put a mouth to his ear.

"It seems I'm needed elsewhere," the General said. "Have no fear, Miss Lubchen. Your country thanks you for your cooperation." I expected him to turn then but he lingered close, still regarding me with a python's rapt attention. Then he did touch me. He placed his palms on either side of my face and leaned forward to kiss the crown of my skull. "This will be good for you," he let slip into my ear. "They'll remember how friendly we were."

I heard a sound, the clearing of a throat, the slow release of another breath. It was only then I knew for certain it was really him. He had placed his mark upon me.

13

After, the interview was over.

Someone with a black, mirrored gaze escorted me up through those same winding passages, past the damp walls and rusted ladders, until we emerged into the night air. They led me to a car—some heavy sedan that smelled of leather and cigarettes—and we drove in silence through the sleeping city. When we reached my grandmother's apartment building, they told me to climb. Of course I climbed, one shaky foot in front of the other, each step on the creaking stairs threatening to buckle my exhausted knees.

You were awake when I entered. The instant I appeared in the doorway you took stock of my clothing, my bruises, the weightless panic behind my eyes. "What have those jackals done to you?"

When I couldn't answer you acted swiftly. "Here, tea," you said, setting dried knots of chamomile to loosen in the pot. While the water boiled, you forced me to drink a thimbleful of samogon which you'd brewed yourself from beetroot sugar. Fat bubbles quivered to the surface as you swirled the bottle.

I slumped in the chair and drifted off, the little chimney blazing with warmth. I dreamed questions and more questions. I dreamed that Uncle was listening to me even now, taking notes, weighing me up. I told him what I saw: a killing coldness, stars too close to name. A staircase. My spirit hovered above me. I was ready to fly away to wherever my mother had vanished.

Hours later, I cracked my eyes open. A greenish light was settling through the windows and a cold mug of tea sat before me. The apartment was redolent with sizzling onions. Seeing me awake, you brought tinned meat spread on toast sprinkled with dill. It made me smile a little. Always there was dill with you now. Dill on potatoes, dill pickles, a loaf formed of goose-meat and dill, dill mayonnaise, dill sweets.

You poured me broth stewed from old lamb bones, saying, "This is how my own mother made it." I didn't feel hungry but the warmth was welcome. "You have a touch of her look here, there, the eyes. And my papa's stubborn jaw."

And so we were at it again, trying to make sense of what we meant to one another. I needed a way to understand what had happened. The trick Cvetko had performed for me. My mirabilist too. Was he imprisoned as I had been? Had he watched me deliver myself up without a protest?

I told you my story and your face didn't change as you listened.

"You were careless out there. And for what? All for a stupid man!"

"You don't know what he was like." How weak my answer sounded. Was this the substance of the world then? Strange happenings? A kind of marvelous, terrible chaos? What was the point of it?

"You think I got to my age by being stupid? I tried to teach your mother but she was stubborn in her own way, aye, she thought all the bad had been done in the world already. Done to me, I reckon. She thought a man who laughed would be enough. And you—you thought a man with a bit of shine would heal your pain. Is that right?"

"He was *more* than that, Baba."

"And less too!"

"So teach me!"

Her expression hooked with interest. "Teach you what, girl?"

"I want to know…" I couldn't finish. There were fairy tales Mama used to tell me before bed. Everyone in Stary knew them though no one would say where they came from. How easily you slid into those stories: a woman with hair like silver and a cloak of secrets. Omen of ill luck, outcast.

"A storybook villain, is that who I am?" demands Sara Sidorova.

The other is silent for a moment. "I didn't know who you were. I knew only that I would have died for a touch of love right then. Tomorrow and tomorrow, you'd promised. I'd waited but the answers hadn't come. You hadn't given them to me, always hiding behind rules I didn't understand, knowing things I wasn't supposed to ask of anyone."

You grimaced. "What has no hands, no feet, but passes by? My papa taught me that riddle. He organized the circus caravan but that summer they went on without me. They left me alone. And… something happened. Something awful. Do you understand?"

"I remember that. I remember them going…" murmurs Sara Sidorova. And it is there in her mind: a glinting, painful recollection.

I told you I didn't understand anything.

"Good," you said. "A girl shouldn't think about such things. And you're just a child. You're so young—aye, was I ever so young myself?" You stood shakily and went to the cupboard. "Help me with this."

My shoulders were aching but I forced myself to kneel beside you. Inside was an ancient wooden chest with three broken brass lever locks.

I asked what it was but you weren't ready to answer. Instead you lifted the lid carefully. Inside were shredded newspapers, yellowed and curling, the dates unreadable. I plunged in my hands, expecting what I don't know. But beneath the papers were objects: a dried sunflower, leather dancing shoes, a hunk of spindly copper, a span of black lace turned scabrous in the gloom, a mildewy whip.

I took them out carefully and set them nearby, but still your eyes urged me onward. My fingers touched cool and satiny cloth. Hidden in the chest was a corset of red silk shot through with purple. Thousands of mirrors had been strung in a loop beneath the bust. A bloom of taffeta and, tucked away beneath it, an elaborate headdress attached to a silver-toothed comb.

I ran my fingers gently at first, then more greedily, over ostrich feathers as long as my arm. Soft and luxurious. As I shook them a cloud of dust burst into the air. The fabric flashed in the uneasy light and glittering beads clinked together. I couldn't help it, already I was in love with the thing.

"I loved it too once," you said to me, "when it was my turn to wear it." Then your skin seemed to harden as if someone had poured gold over you. You took on the aspect of a lizard or a dragon, some shining and terrible creature. "I told you there is a beast at the center of the universe. One day, he told me, he'll burn up the sun, the moon and the stars—but I'll teach you a spell to tame him a little while. But you must listen carefully and do everything I ask of you."

The hairs on my arms pricked up but all I wanted then was to strip down to my parachute bra and try the thing on.

But still you were speaking in a voice I didn't recognize, older, distant as the stars. "Child, you must tell me what you want."

"What I want?" I knew how fairy tales were supposed to work. Children abandoned in the woods, witches with lanterns made from human skulls, Lady Pale-Throat striking her bargain. "I want riches," I said, thinking of my hunger.

"Of course."

"And a husband," I said, thinking of my mirabilist.

"What else?"

But I was cautious and didn't say the last thing. Instead I let it grow in my mind. Suddenly the scent of my mother was around me, apple blossoms and chamomile and all the sweet, fragile things of the world. They faded so quickly. Everything beautiful vanished. The riches of the world, seized or shattered or hidden away. In dirt holes scrabbled out by desperate children. Stuffed into cellars, beneath floorboards, in chinks in the walls. My mother was already dead. The thing I wanted most could not be returned to me, not even by you.

"Tell me." Your eyes were bright.

"I want to tame death."

"Oh, girl. Is that not what everyone wants?" asks Sara Sidorova.

"Perhaps, Baba. But you did not deny me."

You took my hand gently in yours. "Once I was the circus master's daughter. I can teach you what I learned. But you must give something up in return." And for the first time since I had arrived you let yourself acknowledge the thing I had brought with me into your house. "It is time we let your mother go."

✦ ✦ ✦

You were gentle as you opened the suitcase, as you took up a handful of the papers I had shredded so carefully in my mother's house. I watched in silence then mounting horror as you pulled wide the grille of the stove and stuffed them in.

"Baba, no! What are you doing?" I tried to snatch a curling page from the fire. Were you really cutting her loose as easily as all that? My finger blistered where the tender skin met searing metal but I had to rescue the little snatch of poetry.

> *Now we are half lost in silence*
> *and the dream that was shaped between us.*
> *Night is falling too quickly for pauses.*

Jekaterina Rovenskaya, my mother's favorite. A burning red eye appeared in the page's center. Soon it was nothing at all.

"We cannot keep her here."

"Why not?" Wasn't this what I had asked for? Wasn't it my wish?

"Because the dead aren't ours to command, child. They are neither our servants nor our handmaids. We keep them by us at our peril. It's better to let them go."

"Go?" I demanded. "Go where?"

You closed your eyes. "All people are born with a song inside them. When they die the song flies from their mouths and travels to Paradise."

I told her that was just a story, it wasn't real.

"Of course it's just a story. But is it a good one or a bad one?" I didn't know how to answer. The fight was going out of me. "We both loved her, Irenda. Everything has a cost. Would you really bind her here?"

"But the beast…"

"Ah, that is another thing entirely. Let her go, Irenda. You can take her pain away. Let her go."

What was I to do? There were tears on my cheeks but she was gone already, wasn't she? I had done that. I had asked for it. So what did it even matter now?

I took a handful of torn pages. They still smelled of her: of apple blossoms and chamomile, as if she had pressed the flowers between them, trying to keep them as long as she could. But all we love we are destined to lose. That is the way of the world, isn't it?

"Or you were wrong," says Sara Sidorova. "Girl, you were a fool to agree to the bargain. And for what? For silk as red as blood? Has it done you well? Are you content in your palace in the sky?"

"If the price was too high it was because you set it yourself. And if I was a fool, well, you must answer that yourself."

Together we burned my mother's things.

When we were finished you took the ashes and corked them in a bottle with some samogon.

"Will we drink that?" I asked.

A look of horror on your face before you burst out laughing. "Of course not! Leave them happy where they lie. When the dead leave us, it is said they can make a path for those brave enough to follow."

I let the fire fill my vision until when I looked away I could still see blue bursts of color flickering through my tears. "What now?" I asked eventually.

With unexpected tenderness you touched my hair. But still your voice was distant, as if it wasn't me you were speaking to, but some other granddaughter, better loved, better cared for.

"Now," you told that other girl, "you and I have work to do. Tomorrow I shall make good on my promise. Tomorrow you shall tame Death."

14

Then it seemed I awoke. My eyes drifted open as the sun rose: pale shades of rose and amethyst giving way to a bright, searing blue. A wave of light broke over Hraná City. The green domes of the Capitol Buildings glistened like dewdrops.

I yawned, stretched, and looked over the previous night's growth. Hips, breasts, hair curling to my shoulder. How long had I been asleep? A day? A year? I knew then I was passing into the realm of superstition and fantasy.

Your voice from the next room, the notes broken, held too long.

> *Juniper, juniper, juniper, my juniper,*
> *Under the green pine, lay me down to sleep.*
> *Oh you dear pine, oh you green pine,*
> *Don't you rustle so loud over me.*
> *Beautiful maid, dear maid,*
> *Won't you please fall in love.*

"You're up then," you said when you saw me emerge. You seemed to have found your own strength in the night. Your back was straighter and you had brushed your hair until it gleamed like polished silver. Almost you seemed beautiful: like the girl in the photograph, wild and unafraid. "Today we have work to do, child. Are you ready?"

I told you I was but of course it was a lie.

* * *

It seemed that Death lived at the State Circus.

There it stood. Sixteen marble columns supported a balcony with bronze figures: dancers, jugglers, strongmen, and clowns all whirling about in tableau. A pair of peacocks blustered and shrieked to one another in the courtyard beneath a poster with bold slashes of red, yellow and black. **SEE FOR YOURSELF THE TIGER LOVER!** it read. **NO MAN CAN PLEASE HER. COULD YOU?**

"What is this?" The hairs on Sara Sidorova's neck begin to prick.

"Wait," says the other, touching her hand. "Wait and watch with me."

Standing before the circus I was overcome with a sense of recognition though from where I couldn't have said. It seemed I knew this place, had always known it, though of course that was impossible. I had never left Stary in my life.

Inside, a winding marble staircase led up to the gallery. Bold geometrical shapes gave the impression the space was suspended in the driving shaft of some great machine. Looking downward, I saw the mural of a dancing chimpanzee, wise beyond his years. All about him, tiny lights flared with an old-world glamour. Everything here glittered and danced—it was extravagant and wasteful and glorious. I drunk it in.

You led me toward the lower stalls and together we entered the hall. It was a vast semi-circle draped in red velvet, with sweeping murals of elephants and snow leopards picked out in tesserae. The stage protruded like a great discus, the vestige of an older kind of performance: the touring caravans with their menageries, long since gone out of fashion.

"Do you like it, child?" you asked me.

"Yes," I breathed.

We took our seats near the orchestral pit where the velvet coverings were threadbare. Paint flaked from the cherubs and grapevines, the pillars canted dangerously, but it didn't matter. The point was improvidence, the point was a sheer lack of restraint.

Yet among the rustling crowd none seemed to see the glory of that place but me. Their eyes were flinty. They stuffed programs in their pockets, smoked, and flicked cigarette butts at their neighbors.

The lights dimmed and the musicians struck up a jaunty tune. It wasn't enough to win over the crowds and even I could pick out the sad violinist whose instrument pitched awry—but I felt a thrill, just the same. My skin began to hum.

"Watch as it begins," you whispered. "A magician must choose his moment perfectly. Will he ravish them or entice them in? We'll see, we'll see. Look, he comes—*now!*"

A circlet of light appeared and a man strode into it. What was I expecting? My mirabilist returned to me? This one was different, taller, perhaps, but his presence was far less compelling. His suit was of fine slate-gray silk but the cut was bad. He was pigeon-chested, baby-faced. "I am the great Erastus Fortunato!" he declaimed in an off-key tenor. "You may think you understand the laws of physics, but I'll show you those laws by which we have been bound since the beginning of time are mutable. You see, I hold power over life and death…"

He held up his right hand and showed the palm. It was empty...
and then, of course, it wasn't. Now he held a spoon in his hand. His
left hand floated nearby, the fingers outstretched. As he concentrated
the spoon began to bend. But he wasn't a master and the crowd could
tell. Whatever the man pretended, he couldn't offer them true magic.
They might see a man make a broken egg whole, but in the world they
knew when a thing was broken it was gone forever. Their applause
was limp as the spoon.

Was this what I had given up my mother's spirit for?

Another egg appeared in the magician's hand, and another. He
juggled the three eggs without effort. Then a fourth egg appeared in
the air, levitating, now growing larger and larger. Suddenly it burst
apart. A flock of white doves flashed toward the upper balcony. I
imagined her soul going out of her, traveling with them, and oh how
I wanted to fly away.

But then... but then...

* * *

There is a moment that comes in every performance when the light
shifts and the story you think you are watching becomes another. So
it was that night. The air itself seemed to thicken. Even the audience
could sense the change. They stopped their filibustering and perked
up. There was something here, something *more* than what he'd shown
us so far. Even you felt it. Your face was still and rapturous.

Now the stagehands were bringing out a cage. It was big as a
trapper's hut.

"Let me tell you a story." The magician strode out to the rostrum.
"In the beginning, there was an ancient tribe that wandered the
northern reaches of our country where the thunderclap shines white

and unsparing. Among them lived a hunter renowned for his prowess. He wanted a beautiful woman."

In Stary it was said that God wore a gray suit to work every morning. In Stary it was said that to deceive was to divide. But as she stepped into the cage, hips swinging like a pendulum, I understood at last: This was what you had brought me for.

The Devil was a woman, a *chingara*, a glamour girl. What depth, what hideous brilliance she had. *Deliver me from every evil*, I thought, *Mama, I want to be like that one!*

I was so caught in the sweep of her movements I almost missed how your fingers had gone white-knuckled on the armrest, how your breath had caught and held at the sight of her.

"But the hunter would leave her often and the princess became lonely. He spent many months in the forest, killing and killing so that a trail of bones followed behind him wherever he went. And his strength was so great and so terrible that it was up to Amba—" that word awoke a shuddering breath from you "—the great god of the forest, to tame him. But the tiger had his own appetites. When the hunter returned from his wayfaring his lover greeted him with open arms. Softly, slowly, she ushered him into the bedroom…"

His movements were fast as he lowered the curtain but I wanted them slow. More time to gaze on her thighs, the curve of her calf muscles, her ankle, the points of her stilettos. I had never understood the ravishment of a disappearance until then.

"But the woman had become greater than her lover. For she'd been remade… And now she was hungry!"

The cage floated into the air. There was a flash of gold and the stage lights flickered. Some wild presence hurtled into the room as the curtain drew back.

"He's here. The beast. He's here at last..." whispers Sara Sidorova.

"Oh yes, Baba," says the other hungrily. "It is him. It is always him, isn't it?"

The tiger was magnificent. His body moved like fire, sleek and sinuous, eyes golden as polished stones, the pupils dark as oil drops. I didn't know him—but you did, it seemed. You had been waiting, and something in his movements seemed to echo in my own blood, like a language I should understand but couldn't quite grasp. Each time he turned his head, the light caught his stripes like shadowed script, and I felt the same patterns burning deep in my bones.

"A big animal makes you think of death. That's what my father told me," you whispered. "Be ready. What comes will come. Only know that I'm sorry for this and all that comes after."

I didn't understand, not then, how wild and full of power you were, not even as a hideous grin curled across your features.

Your nails dug deep enough to draw blood but by then all my pain had dropped away. Numbness, then a warmth spreading outward from my gut. Delight, cutting as a sword. Blood chuntered in my ears. What was happening? The beast in the cage seemed to loom above me, his grin gorgeous and deadly, flame-orange and black. With each passing moment, I felt you growing tenser beside me, your spine straightening vertebra by vertebra like a serpent about to strike.

"Behold," said Erastus Fortunato, "Grandfather Death. Is this not his very face?"

Then as if in utter anguish, you stood, back straight, chin lifted and began to howl.

What can I say, Baba? Your howl was magnificent. Long and keening and full of a glorious dolor. My own grief rose up in my throat but I couldn't speak. You did it for me: a howl of loss for what has been taken, rage and fear and fury. I could see on the faces of the others it was the same for them. A release, a way to pierce the universe with their longing and their pain.

"Yes!" they cried as one. "Oh, yes!"

Now they listened. Now they wept. The flinty-eyed crowd who had sneered at Fortunato's tricks sat transfixed, their faces slack with wonder. You had done what his magic could not—made them believe.

"Please," cries Sara Sidorova. "I can't bear it. I know that pain—why must I hear it made so naked for them? What need have I to see one more widow pulling out her hair and weeping for their pleasure?"

"This isn't your story, Baba. It's mine. So listen."

You drew in a breath and the silence thickened as they waited for you to speak.

"Who here has seen the face of death?" Your voice was deep and sonorous, your face full of cunning. "Oh, I know you, don't I? Once I was called the tiger's wife. That one is mine! I have tamed him. I am the one who tamed Death and placed him in a cage."

In that moment, you were transformed. Gone was the sharp-tongued old hag with her cryptic warnings and hidden truths. Here stood someone else entirely—someone declaring her power openly at last.

Your howl had turned the audience blank and willing. You could have told them you were the General in disguise and they would have genuflected.

Everyone was quiet except for the tiger. His starburst face tilted toward you and he balked in agitation. Then with a noise like a bomb blast the cage crashed down to the boards. Panic on the stage as the house lights went up. The assistant appeared beside us, begging you to stop. "You mustn't, you mustn't. Please, this is dangerous. You need to be quiet now. Will you come with us, Grandmother?"

Gracefully you rose up, a countess with red triumph in your eyes.

* * *

But you didn't take me with you.

Whatever you said to the woman and her magician—whatever truth or lies were spoken—you didn't share them with me. I saw your eyes as they led you away: a sharp look softened by tenderness. You had set something terrible in motion, I knew then. Even if I had asked for it, even if I had told you what it was I wanted...

But I didn't know, did I, what would come of it? How could I?

It was only later I would turn our compact over in my mind, wondering when it was the threshold was crossed. Had I ever really had another choice? Or had time trapped me, your story, my story, braided together, the dark and the light?

We are never truly ready for what comes for us. That's the way of things, isn't it, Baba?

* * *

What had happened? Was it a plot of some kind? Badges were flashed, guns slipped from their holsters, and suddenly there were Deeps spreading out among us.

Your spell was failing. In its place whispered the spirit of unease. I waited and watched the restless crowd moving in their seats. The tiger thrashed backward and forward in the cage, his spectral gaze raking over the watchers. Each time his claws scraped against metal, another tremor ran through the audience. They could smell his wildness now, his hunger. The crowd were spooked by the presence of the beast, murmuring first to one another until at last it was too much for them.

"Let us out!" came a high reedy voice. There was a mad hurly burly as the panic broke over them. The Deeps let the doors swing open. They wore evil half-smiles on their faces. Breathing in the pulse of alarum, savoring it. With each gasp of fear, with each cry of panic, they seemed to grow larger, darker, as if feeding on the terror they had cultivated. This was how their power grew—not through force, but through the slow poison of dread.

Yet all my unease had vanished. I recognized the cage and the beast it held and I knew what I must do. It was clear as a story I had been marked for this. Marked by you. I had told you I wanted to tame Death and you had delivered to me the means.

The crowd's screams seemed to come from very far away now. Each step I took toward the cage felt like walking through a dream I'd had a thousand times before. My eyes never left the tiger, my body cool as stone, limbs weightless, my future laid out perfectly before me.

The force of his gaze was terrifying. His eyes held centuries of secrets—your secrets, Baba—and I knew this was your final gift to me, this moment of perfect terror and perfect clarity. I wanted to crawl into the black tunnel of that one's throat. Aye, here was the true freedom from grief.

"Is that how you came to this place?" asks Sara Sidorova. "Did the beast take you up, just as he took me?"

"No," says the Evening Star softly. "It didn't happen like that for me. Not then. As much as I may have wanted it."

You had sent my mother's spirit away. Now I felt a sharp tug in my soul, an urge to follow after. I felt myself in the midst of an impossible moment, my flesh turned to light, then shadow, then rarefied song.

The bars of the cage seemed to waver, and I understood at last what you had known all along—that the strongest prison was only a suggestion, that flesh was merely a costume we wore.

There is the body and there is the body.

You had taught me that, and for what, except this final surrender? How easy it seemed now to slip out of my skin, to pass through even the sturdiest of iron bars, to let oblivion claim me so I might join my mother at last...

MIDDAY

15

Now Sara Sidorova seems to be moving with her granddaughter. She feels the breath of that other burning in her lungs. Blood pounding, the heat of the lights, and the wild, dark beast before her. They are joined, one inside the other, stitched together by blood and memory both. She *knows* this. She knows this just as she knows the beast—the godhood. Together she and her granddaughter reach out...

✳ ✳ ✳

Like a comet, a joyous flame streaking through the Palace of Stories, the Tiger leaps to meet her. "Come, my love. Let us make an end of it together!" he roars.

Then he is upon her, the crushing weight of muscle and bone. And this too she remembers—the trick she herself used to perform when she traveled with her father's circus. In the old days she would meet him as he stood on his hind legs, the two of them eye to shining eye. For a moment the Devourer hangs in the air. His great hooked claws rend the darkness between them but she will not let herself flinch away. After all, it is only a performance. The chain still binds him.

Then Zorya Vechernyaya herself is rising up, an aureole of silvery light spinning around her. "Enough, brother. Leave her be. She isn't yours."

"Was it not I who brought her here? The girl is *my* guest," snarls the Tiger. Behind him the sun glows like a torch and the world glows with it: a tapestry of gold-touched greens, purples and molten blue.

"Then treat her as she deserves."

At this Sara Sidorova catches something new between them, closer to affection or perhaps even deeper than that. Still, she clenches her jaw. "Outcast, ill omen, bad luck, and bad tidings. You were right. I cursed you, didn't I? Somehow I cursed you to this."

"No," says the Evening Star. "Not a curse. Or not only a curse."

"Tell me."

"Lady Pale-Throat, the people called me. It is true, Sara. They came to love me, just as I desired."

"Who profits from getting what they desire?" the circus master's daughter replies bitterly.

There is more to the story, Sara knows, but now the Tiger is pacing, his great shoulders rolling as he charts the boundary of his prison. He speaks: "Maybe you lied, maybe you told her truly. What does it matter? This world is a heartbreaker so let me end it. Your granddaughter will suffer as you suffered. Isn't that right, sister? Tell her truly now—"

"Yes," says the Evening Star because it seems somehow she must.

"—so let it go, Sara. Let *me* go. I can send you and all that would come after into the dark. There will be no pain. They will never feel the wind on their skin, their mother's touch, the darkness, the rain. No sickness shall take them, no wound shall harm them, no love will kindle their spirit."

For a moment this is all Sara Sidorova desires. Her wanting moves across her features like a cloud. The Tiger can see it, the sisters, too. But she told them she would not be forced.

"*Is* that what you want?" Silence now as Zorya Vechernyaya places her hand on the girl's forehead. "It's your choice, Sara."

"Is there no better world than this? No better choice?" she asks.

At this the great beast settles his golden glare upon her. "How many worlds do you see out there? In those thrice-nine lands and thrice-nine kingdoms and thrice-ten countries, how many live without pain?" His voice is deep and hypnotic. "Ask my sisters how it was in the beginning. The All-Dark, a squalling goulash of sea and sky—and then came the world egg, which housed Father Serpent. And the egg cracked open. From it issued forth light and from the glare of the light came shadow."

Suddenly Sara Sidorova can see it: a darkness crossing over the universe. One by one the stars wink out, the bright sun gutters and dies, drowning in the black. A great thundering... Nothingness. The earth recedes and in its wake is a cold as still and awful as forgetting.

"Tell me then what happens to my granddaughter!"

"You said she meant nothing to you."

Shivering, she searches the palace for succor but it is empty. Ice creeps up the gymnasterka, freezing her blood into tiny crimson rosettes. She is alone here. The Morning Star and Evening Star have shuttered their light. The only warmth is that of the Tiger himself. His fur bristles and moves like an inferno. Sara Sidorova knows he would welcome her touch, that it would be enough.

"You don't want to know, my love," he says. "Look into the darkness instead. Isn't it beautiful? Painless, joyless, cold forever. Nothing but—"

"Hunger," whispers Sara Sidorova. She can sense it.

"There is always hunger." And his devilish grin is large enough to swallow the world. "You think there's hope for her, don't you? There is *none*—I swear this to you. Her road is the path of thorns and every step she takes will draw blood."

But now it is Sara who is beginning to laugh, first softly, then with a wild whoop of abandon. Because his grin is a lie. She knows it is a lie. "But I am your guest. So show me," she shouts, "show me, show me, show me!" until the walls resound with her mad chanting.

"Enough!" cries the beast. "Oh, Dear-Heart, if you ask me, I'll show you

107

what lies ahead. I'll show you what this world does to those who choose the path you've set your granddaughter on." His eyes flash with violence. He is not the one she knew, not some tame beast she could conquer with a touch. He is older, bloodier, strong enough to survive the darkness and the cold...

"Tell her what happens next," says the Tiger to the Evening Star. "Let her see for herself the harm she has done you."

THE BEAST GIRL

16

Around and around the universe turns like a great spindle, yarning out story after story. That's the art of the mirabilist, I've learned: kenning the warp and weft of the world's affairs, pulling a thread here, a thread there, weaving ill fortune and good, dyeing each strand in heart's blood.

But some threads are more stubborn than others. They tangle and run crosswise. My tiger—ah, that was already how I thought of him—he was one such errant strand. I've heard it said there are elements in this world that last forever. Always they come back to us, sometimes as we remember them, sometimes altered in appearance. Ghosts and figments, phantasms, dream-stuff.

"Grandfather Death," I whispered as I reached toward him. I swear his eyes went liquid and shining as molten gold. I knew it instantly—he was what you had promised me, Baba.

"What I promised you? What I cursed you to suffer, if that one speaks truly."

"Decide for yourself, Sara," says the Evening Star gently. "Let no one else tell you what it is this story might mean."

The iron bars were between us. Whatever I desired, I hadn't found a way to shed my skin or pass through cold metal. I was only human: a girl, nothing more than that. Still, the warmth of his breath washed over me. The purr in his throat was an engine throttling. In that moment, it was enough.

I don't know how long I stayed crouched before the cage, the two of us staring at each other while around me the crowd emptied from the theatre. I longed to trace the dark calligraphy that covered his spine, to sink my fingers into the dandelion-ruff of his neck. I didn't know where they'd taken you, Grandmother, and if I'm honest I didn't care. I could feel my world changing again, just like...

I shall not see the shadows,
I shall not feel the rain.

Rough hands yanked on my shoulder and swung me about. "What are you doing, girlie? Get away now!" came a voice close beside me. Its owner was a man nearing sixty. He stood barely to my shoulder, his spine twisting his stance into a perpetual, painful slouch. "Come now—fast as you can." Despite his bent back, he moved swiftly, letting fly with a leather bullwhip.

"He wouldn't hurt me," I hissed.

"A beast like that'll make ribbons of you, give him half a chance," rejoined the old fellow as the whip cracked and cracked again until my tiger retreated to the back of the cage.

"He *wouldn't*," I insisted but the old man's eyes held me, squinting with intelligence: a surprisingly handsome oyster-gray.

"Maybe not. He's past his prime and we cut up his meat for him these days. But how would a little thing like you know that?" It wasn't what I'd meant but the matter seemed settled in his mind. "Call me Leon," he said. "If His Nibs takes a bite of you, it'll be my hide that gets a tanning. So, enough chat. The mistress will see you now."

He led me through a black-painted door and down a lengthy corridor, moving so quickly I had to sprint to keep up with him. A moment later I was panting and out of breath as he flung open another door.

Red hips, red breasts, red lips.

"Miss Sara Irenda Lubchen," came a woman's voice from inside and each syllable of my name was perfectly weighted. "You're to stay with us now, do you understand?"

It was the *chingara* from the show. She didn't turn, not right away. She was standing in her dressing room in front of an ornate triptych mirror that revealed each and every crimson angle. The blunt angle of her hair fell straight as a guillotine across her neck.

My breath went out in a gust. "For how long?"

"Leon will find a room for you. Work hard and we'll get on. Everyone earns their keep in Mistress Sostary's show." Her voice was deep, different from the simpering pitch of the café glamour girls. *She* was different. Hadn't I seen the magician raising her from the dead? Hadn't I seen her in the cage with my tiger? Didn't she wear the same blood-red corset that you had once? What had you promised them for this? Had it been your plan all along? *First, child, you must tell me what you want,* you'd said to me—and what had I asked for? Riches, a husband, the chance to tame Death.

"Don't worry your head about your grandmother, sweetling. She wouldn't be the first to get rid of an unruly child in these dark times. It's hard enough keeping one belly fed, let alone two. But there are worse places you could find yourself than this. There's no misfortune without a blessing in it, as my own mother used to say."

The tilt of her head showed me she knew I was regarding her. Ruby-colored sequins glittered beneath her collarbone. Her thighs were a flash of snow-pure white above the black silk stockings.

Touch me, her body seemed to whisper, *and do not ever dare to touch me. If you touch me I'll curse your line and poison your blood forever. But if you don't I swear you'll die of a heartbreak no other can cure.*

A flush crept across my cheeks but her beauty only seemed burnished by the heat of my gaze, my thoughts. Red lips brushing mine, caressing the soft skin beneath my jaw… Then she turned and her eyes lit on me alone, inviting but also repellent. A gorgeous, glittering spider.

"My grandmother promised this would happen. She promised today I would meet Death. But I thought she meant…" I couldn't finish.

"Death is everywhere. She needn't have brought you to my doorstep if that's what you were after."

"Will you use me in the show then? Will you teach me?"

She laughed in derision. "You think you're beautiful, do you?" The scent of lemon and apple blossoms flooded over me, incongruous, like perfume in an abattoir. She didn't seem to notice. "You may be younger than me," she was saying, "but then age isn't everything. Look at that cheapnik dress you're wearing and those stockings. Are you a child? Those are children's clothes. Maybe you were something where you came from but—Kitten, my love—*this* is Hraná City. Now keep quiet and do as I say."

In truth that was exactly what I'd been thinking: that I was beautiful, that she had chosen me. Her laughter told me how wrong I was.

"Obey and be quiet," I repeated slowly.

I'd met others like Mistress Sostary before who didn't care if they hurt me. They wanted only that I should know my place. But hadn't you too refused me once, Grandmother? I'd found a way to turn you. I'd do it again if I had to, I'd use what you'd begun to teach me…

"Maybe you're smarter than you look," said Mistress Sostary as I lowered my gaze. She tapped her fingernails, a sign between her and Leon. "If so you might find a place for yourself here. If not, well, His Nibs is always hungry."

The circus master's hand nudged me out into the hallway where he spoke softly, carefully. "I know Mistress may seem flinty but if you work hard she'll take good care of you."

He loves her, I thought. I couldn't blame him. For all her scorn I was halfway in love myself.

17

So. You had left me here, it seemed. I felt like a leaf blown heedlessly from branch to bluff, always in motion, skimming the ground but never settling for longer than a moment. I had nothing of my own, not a letter of scrawled instructions, not a scrap beyond what I was wearing—a cheapnik dress, Mistress Sostary called it—and whatever it held in its pockets. A trace of ash, the coin the General had given me.

Nor did it seem my accommodations were to be much improved. Leon showed me to a derelict office with a thin mattress on a trolley bed that stunk faintly of stale perfume. In one corner stood a makeshift railing hung with old garments.

"These belonged to Aleena Alexeeva. She was our fancy girl but she's gone now, so there's little harm if you take what you need," Leon told me when he saw me eyeing them.

"Where did she go?"

"Left us for Madam Nikolayevna, didn't she? Scheming little shrew. She was in close with the master." He spat as if it were a curse. The viscous lump hit the floor and for a moment he had the decency to look apologetic.

I summoned up the name of the magician I'd seen on the stage. "Erastus Fortunato?"

"Not him," said Leon. "The old one, Arkady Pavlovich. But when he was done for, the little shrew must have got spooked and

run off. Took the secrets of our best swindles with her too, I reckon."
He rubbed his lips against the sleeve of his shirt. "For her sake I
hope it bought some favor. Everyone knows Madam Nikolayevna's
girls make their kopeks on their backs." He blinked, then said more
kindly—half proudly: "But it isn't like that here. This is a show of
quality."

I was barely listening. Two corsets had caught my attention, one
red, one green. Both trailed stray threads but to my eyes they seemed
alive with the glitter of paste gems and goldstitch. I touched the
smooth-spun silk and felt a warm glow inside of me.

"Try the crimson, if you must. Red is a color the punters never
forget."

I remembered how Mistress Sostary had looked in the light. If I
stood just so—just like her—they would see a slice of white thigh,
the sickle shape of my shoulder blade. "And the green?"

"Green's the color of life. Mistress always said a lie in green is
easily exposed. So Arkady Pavlovich found out. But best to use these
old togs for now." Leon pointed to a pair of faded-black muslin
trousers and a worker's shirt. "No fancy work for you."

"When—"

"When the Mistress trusts you, hear? It was Master Fortunato who
agreed to take you. The likes of him have their own reasons, I reckon.
That one promises and promises and leaves others to pay the bill so I
can't say Mistress was happy about it." He looked suddenly ashamed
his tongue had wandered away from him. "Change right quick, will
you? Best we find something to keep you busy, else the others will be
at your throat. They're a jealous, squint-eyed lot and they don't take
kindly to strangers. Not if they think you're on wages."

Minutes later I joined him outside the room, dressed in the

ill-fitting clothes he had suggested for me. I suppose I should have been more grateful. Fate had struck again like a thunderclap.

Orphan, I thought as I stared at my reflection in the old man's gray eyes. *Double orphan*. I saw myself as he must: a scrounger. What had you told them about me? Too many mouths to feed at home? In Stary I would've been cared for but here... I could see things were different in Hraná City.

"Come along," he muttered, shuffling off through a series of back hallways where the peeling paint had given way to brick. What had the theatre been before it was a theatre? A cathedral, a temple, a grotto, a bunker? Then came the smell of greenery as we entered what must have once been a boyar's courtyard. There were dozens of derelict flower beds, now overrun with the creeping bell flowers of virgin's bower.

The scent of animal was thick here and soon I saw why. In the northwest corner stood a wire perimeter fence three meters high. It circled half the breadth of the courtyard. My tiger slunk out from his den, his tail scribbling signatures behind him as he went. His chuff was a rhythmic, guttural exhalation—but not unfriendly.

"Hello yourself, Grandfather." Leon went toward a feed stall outside the cage. "I reckon His Nibs has taken a shine to you, girlio. That's good. He's often ornery with new folk."

He picked up a pale ash wood cane and handed it to me. It was lighter than I expected. My tiger watched as I tapped it against the wire, ears pricked up. He chuffed again.

"That's him being inquisitive. If the noise were deeper, he'd be warning you off. Listen for that. And keep an eye out: ears back means he's in a temper. All right?"

"Aye."

Leon took the cane back, pointing out the particulars as he instructed me. "You've got to be careful. Clean every bit of sawdust from your hands before you haul in the meat for him. The stuff will clot his innards if you aren't tidy."

The sun was casting long shadows below the crenelated edge of the courtyard. I wanted to hear more but I was exhausted.

"Tomorrow's early enough," Leon said when he saw me sagging. "Be back here at six and we'll begin. Meantime, you can find grub in the mess hall, just follow your nose. Some will be venturing out to the Strelka in the evening—that's the canteen across the road—but I reckon keep yourself to yourself for now. Stay out of everyone's way."

I was practically swaying on my feet.

"What else?" he mused. "See Renata and her girl if there's any seamstering you need. Fingers and Ears they call those two, so mind what you say when they're close. The rest'll be sorted in time."

* * *

I wandered the hallways searching for my room, playing Blind Alley, Dumb Alley, Deaf Alley as I had in Stary as a child. The door when I found it was unlocked but inside all was as I had left it—which wasn't much. Just my old dress draped over the chair and the General's coin burning a hole in my pocket. I'd never lived in shared quarters before and had only the rumors of the boarding school girls to go by. Mostly they weren't good. I pushed a stack of old crates against the door then slumped on the trolley bed.

For the first time since I had come to Hraná City I found myself missing home. I remembered how the blue-gray hills used to multiply in the distance. There was a river that ran through Stary and an old wives' tale said if you drank from it you were destined to return. I used to play there when I was younger. Had I truly wanted any of this?

"Mama?" I whispered—but there was nothing, just the whiff of my predecessor who had fled this show of quality.

I tried to sleep but it was too easy to remember that first night I had spent in your apartment, Grandmother, and the ghost of my mother on the glass. I had sworn to myself to make an end of it, yet somehow my choices had brought me here. I had lost my mother and found…what?

Sleep must have come because a moment later I woke with a start. A sound was coming from underneath my barricaded door. Sad, slow singing in the hallway.

"Not that old dirge," came a slurred voice. "Something faster, man. You were in the army, weren't you?" My heartbeat leapt at the rattle of my bedroom door. It creaked open an inch before the hornbeam knocked into the crates. Then a wedge of amber light appeared a handspan from my bed. "I hear you've put the new girl in Aleena Alexeeva's old room. Leon, you've seen her, haven't you? Did I do well? You know what the poets say: *I wish that the world were enfolded in love! The world in love needs not the frontier lines…*" A belch then. "That was Martynow, I think. I may have gotten it wrong."

"Take your look when the sun's out, man," I heard the old circus master say fiercely. It must have been him who was singing so sadly.

"Oh, you should be kinder to me. What is it the reviews say? *The pleasure of Erastus Fortunato's performance is that pleasure that comes from being deceived, and knowing you are being deceived in an artful way…* Never forget, I have the power over life and death." Another belch then and another shove at the door.

"Of course," said Leon sounding much less drunk. "Aye, that's what Master Arkady said too. But then the Deeps came, didn't they? They hauled him out to some back alley and slit him open from smile to sternum. I heard they butchered their way through his ankles like a hatchet-man through gristle. Stuffed his severed feet beside that peacock silk pocket square of his."

Silence after that, then the sound of heavy breathing.

Leon again: "What color's that silk pocket square of yours? Green, I reckon?"

At last spoke the magician. "Unkind, my friend. Unkind and undeserved."

But the light vanished as the door snicked shut again. Soon enough I could hear their footsteps leading away.

18

That night I had a dream. My mother was washing her hair in a basin scented with vinegar. I used to dream of Mama doing this often, I don't know why. She would call me close to her and wrap the towel around both of us. "Tell me, little mouse," she'd ask, "what have you learned today?" I'd report back the nonsense trivia I had gathered from school.

But today her hair formed a veil and I couldn't see her face. "Mama, where are you?"

"I know a place where the birds go in winter," she said to me lightly. There was a glittering staircase behind her. When she turned her head and the fringe fell away, it was Mistress Sostary's kohl-blackened eyes that stared back at me, shimmery with gold dust. "Obey and be silent," she hissed in my mother's voice.

Obey and be silent. Follow, follow, follow. These things I could do well enough. Hadn't I been one of Stary's prized pupils?

I met Leon early, just as he'd promised. This time I scratched tally marks in the rotting paint as I navigated the back halls of the theatre so I could find my way. Still the sun had painted the sky the color of roseships by the time I arrived. Leon stamped his feet for warmth in the chilly spring air. Somewhere in the depths of the animal pen I could hear the gentle *whuffs* of my tiger snoring.

"Coffee?" He poured me a cup from a thermos and revealed a butterbrot topped with marmalade, which I devoured greedily. I was grateful for his intervention last night but still wary. Momentary kindnesses were a far cry from loyalty. He was Mistress Sostary's man, that was all I knew about him. That, and Amba seemed to be his responsibility.

"Most of the lads steer clear of old Amba," Leon told me as he set my cup aside. "They treat him badly and then wonder why he's quick to turn when they're lax. A bad situation. But I reckon you've a better temperament. What do you say, girlio? It isn't fancy work."

Obey and be silent. "Yes. Of course."

"Righto," he said.

And that was all it took for me to become his beast girl.

* * *

How many days had I sought instructions from you, Grandmother? A sense my life had direction and purpose? I listened carefully and set myself to doing exactly as he said, the first time, without reservation or hindrance. I helped arrange Amba in his pen while we hauled in the meat. Six days of feed Leon told me and one day of fasting. Like a holy saint.

It was hard work but I enjoyed it. I was outdoors most of the day and Leon was firm but fair. If I wasn't sharp enough he'd cuss me out as quickly as any boy. I had to keep my wits about me in the pen. Perhaps my tiger was more generous than rough with me but that didn't mean he was tame. Leon said I must be alert to his movements and keep him in my sights at all times. Sometimes I sensed Amba was amused by the attention. Who was this pretty young thing come to tend him? Her skin was so soft! But other times I felt him watching me slantwise, feigning disinterest but plotting carnage. Then the hairs on the back of my neck would stand on end.

The day stretched on and as the sun dropped below the courtyard walls, Leon touched me gently on the shoulder. "You've done well. You're keen and that's not nothing in a place like this. Come along with me."

The mess hall was long and narrow, with high ceilings and a trencher table that ran down the center like a whale spine. I was starving by this point, and the sour-sweet smell of solyanka bubbling away was enough to drive me half-mad.

In the training yard we had been left undisturbed but here I could see the full company of troupers assembled before me. Leon pointed out a handful for me with sly nods and a faint, fierce grin. "Aye, there's Otto the carpenter, best you leave him be. He wakes early and his nights are full of temper. And that's Estes with him." The former was as old as Leon, with an explosion of darkened capillaries spreading from his nose. The latter was barely older than me but huge as a howitzer.

"It smells of beast," Otto moaned when we went searching for a place at his table. "Can't you hose the girl off at least before you bring her to dinner?"

The other one—Estes—stayed quiet but the rest of the crowd looked up with undisguised interest. One among them a ballerina-skinny girl, with velvety eyelashes and painted red lips. "Are you sure she's housebroken, Leon?" she sneered.

My cheeks grew hot-pan red and I tried to hide them, tried to make myself small. She was right. The smell of my tiger still clung to me.

"What's that? Cat got your tongue?" With that she smacked the pewter bowl Leon had set in front of me aside. The greasy soup splattered down the table. "Clean it up, Lady Pale-Throat," the girl demanded.

Suddenly, a hot, fresh feeling: it was like the shadow of Amba was moving beneath my skin, hackles rising as his did when I made a misstep and vexed him. Rage boiled inside me and I lunged toward her. As she startled away from me, sputtering, my nails raked her pretty cheek.

"You cheapnik bitch," she squealed as she touched the ragged tracks I had left behind.

"Leave off, Teresa," called Leon, intervening at last. "You wanted to see if my girl has claws. Fair enough—but it's no one's fault but your own that you've been scratched."

The others were staring at me, po-faced. The giant coughed, then looked away. Teresa turned from face to face, sussing out where their loyalties lay. She took note when their glances sheared off and she smiled at me deliberately. "Good," she said, wiping the blood away. "I'm tired of these whey-faced little *sukas*, anyway." A performer's voice. "Is she one of us then, Leon?"

Now it was the circus master's turn to cast a look at me in appraisal. A heartbeat passed, and then another. "Never know 'til the show," he said eventually.

What seemed like faint praise to me was enough for the others. Teresa slid me her own bowl, saying, "I couldn't eat this filth anyway. Enjoy." Her tone was amused, fatalistic. The giant Estes pushed over, careful not to crowd me.

After that I let the talk of the company wash over me. Mostly it was gossip and mostly I was ignored, which suited me well enough. But when the meal was over Estes leaned over. Tobacco-colored with chestnut hair, his shoulders protruded like wings beneath his round face. "Let me show you something," he whispered, producing a tiny grain of rice and a looking glass the size of a coin. Both he handed me with a furtive expression.

I took the glass and inspected the grain, seeing nothing at first, and then the contours of a whole landscape: a river and a bridge, the outline of mountains in the distance.

"My father gave it to me," the giant said. "He was a strong man in the old days and he *said* he got it himself from a sorcerer." When Estes took it back he clutched it like it was the most precious thing he'd ever held.

"Keep it safe then," I told him.

"Oh, aye," he said with a grin that made him seem younger than his years. "I only show it to my friends. What's your name then?"

I thought about this for a moment. I didn't feel like the girl from Stary any longer.

"Lady Pale-Throat," I replied. He looked hurt for a moment but the smile I gave him brought him around.

"Aye, m'Lady," he said at last with a little half bow. "Welcome to the circus."

19

The days passed quickly after that as I fell into the routines of my new life. Early to rise, early to bed. At first I kept my door barred as best I could but no one ever disturbed me. Still, Estes borrowed what he needed from old Otto's workshop to help me put in a bolt so I could secure it myself.

A week later, the giant appeared in the training yard near the end of my shift, drunk on samogon and weeping. By then Leon had begun to trust me to put away the day's equipment on my own so I was alone. It wasn't much but it still felt like something of an honor.

"Why are you crying?" I asked Estes when he stumbled into my sight. I was oiling the whip to keep it supple while Amba watched from the shade with an amused look.

"I've lost it!" cried Estes.

"Lost what?"

"My talisman! The one I showed you." It seemed he had been playing Fool with one of the delivery boys, a known card shark. "I loved it too dearly," Estes moaned between gulps of air. "Teresa said not to. Love is a trap, she told me." He must have weighed three times as much as I did but he came to me and laid his head in my lap. He wouldn't calm until I stroked his hair and sang him one of my mother's lullabies.

He was quiet for a time afterward and I found myself enjoying the feel of his hair between my fingers, the softness of his breath.

It felt good to be touching another person who wanted only a little gentleness.

After a while he stood, went to the training stall and tugged at a wooden panel hidden by a dirty canvas covering. He emerged from the darkness with an emerald-green bottle. It had a fat body and a long, slender neck.

"This is the good stuff," he told me shyly. "They say Tsarina Sofia Anastasia commissioned it, especially, to be drunk at her funeral. Of course it wasn't ready in time. But then only angels and executioners know the hour a spirit will be called away." He pulled out the cork with his teeth, and then poured out a finger's worth for each of us. "It was Arkady's. Leon hid it. He won't notice if we have a taste."

We talked, he and I, in low voices made mellow by the brandy. The sky darkened from plum-wine to black. In Stary I had known all the constellations but here they seemed misshapen and ill-formed: missing limbs, wounded warriors. "The Thresher, The Trammel…"

I pointed out those I knew and Estes told me of his own life in the provinces before he had come to Hraná City. How his older brother had been larger than he was but it had never done him good. Deep down he despised how he was always knocking into things. Then the local hoodniks had gotten to him and his size made him a target. When some sort of drug deal went sideways, they'd thought it was a double-cross. Estes had found his brother's body a couple of blocks from the house. "Now I cry at strange times," he told me. "I know I shouldn't but I can't help it."

"I cry too, sometimes," I told him. When he had settled, he shared out the samogon with me. It burnt as it went down, just as it had when we had drunk—you and I—to my parents' death.

Then it was weeks—a whole month—that had come and gone. I was Leon's beast girl now, or Lady Pale-Throat when the company were deep in their cups. "Watch old Baba Yaga doesn't slit you open," they joked at the mess hall, meaning Mistress Sostary, of course. "She's been waiting for a child just your size." Then with liquor-sweet breath, they'd kiss me on both cheeks before hauling their heavy bodies over to the Strelka where they often finished the night.

Not that I saw much of Mistress Sostary. My work kept me backstage or underground mostly, ferrying Amba through the tunnels that ran beneath the stage so he could make his appearance on cue.

By then summer was peaking and the air sweltered. The upholstery made a smooching sound whenever anyone moved in their seats. It was like playing to an orgy when the show lagged, which it did now, more and more. Despite Master Fortunato's aristocratic mien, he lacked charisma, more like a schoolteacher than a magician, slightly peevish, half-afraid of his pupils. Still, I liked to watch him when my duties let me.

Master Fortunato often began with a twist on the famous bullet trick, which Leon himself had devised. "It plays well with the cadets on leave but poorly for the uncles who've come home," the circus master confessed. For that the mistress needed a black powder cartridge smuggled on the inside of her corset. Dangerous. It had a fiddly tackle that had to be prepped just so. I had seen him doing it out in the yard while I tended to Amba's food and watering. He was the only one who handled the powder, the only one she seemed to trust enough to make a fuse she would set alongside her own flesh.

"Does it ever go badly?" I asked him.

"Aye, once I knew another girl who tried the trick, Agnessa Zaytseva whom they sometimes called the Swallow of the Night. Well, she'd had an old lover who meant her ill and he paid her apprentice to fit the squib badly." With a grimace he told me of the hole it had punched in her chest: a fist of muscle and bone strewn about the stage and her gasping once, twice, lungs shredded, heart pulverized.

While Master Fortunato was barely passable at this trick, he was better with the coins. Some of the hands joked it was his coin-play that first attracted the Deeps' attention. "Men like that," Estes told me one evening as we watched from the wings, "often have that gallows humor."

"Men like whom?" I asked.

"Victor," he said in a superstitious hush. "Have you never caught sight of him? You can see him at the back there. They say he's the General's second self."

Following Estes' gaze, I caught sight of a figure near the door: a bullish man with hair shaved so close the layers of skin visibly sediment around his neck. He wore the nondescript black suit I had come to recognize as the uniform of the Department for the People's Protection.

"I heard Master Fortunato was an accountant when they came for him. An amateur magus, a baby magician at best."

"Who told you that?"

"Otto, I think." He shrugged.

This was how it was at the theatre, all whispers, half rumors, and endless chains of speculation. Estes was no better when it came to his love of prate and scandal. Still, it didn't mean he was wrong. I could imagine Master Fortunato well enough as a comptroller, cashier, or some other bookkeeping type. He was good with his hands—subtle, well-practiced—but otherwise the spotlight left him red-faced and sweating through his jacket. When Mistress Sostary appeared her walk was sensuous as silk, cool as water. The crowd was hers—but only for the moment. She'd slant her eyes toward the magician, hold her shoulders so their gazes leapt toward him.

"There was a trick she used to do—her first signature." His gaze drifted away. "It was called the Goddess of Love. The old master—Arkady—they say he invented it. 'You think you know what love is?' he'd croon to the crowds." His voice lowered then, a raw attempt at hoodnik patter. "'You do? Let me tell you about love, friends. See I've always been a traveling man, a roamer—wasn't a girl could tie me down. But one day this geezer sidles up, whispering about a place out east called the Temple of the Sun where dwelled the most beautiful woman in the world…'"

"And that was her."

"For a time," he said. "For a time, it was her. The old master set her on the stage. 'Not for the like of you or me,' he'd whisper to the crowds, 'But let one among you come before me, a child—yes, you, little man!—and I'll show you what I saw.'"

"Her signature," I said. "How did it work?"

His eyes sparkled. "They needed a boy. Ten years old was best, old enough to be trusted, old enough to mount the stairs without a chaperone. Arkady would bring him onto the stage where she would be waiting.

"'See how lovely she is?' he'd purr, hanging his hand upon the poor lad's shoulder. "'See how she sparkles in the air, little man? The temple-keepers told me if she chooses she can grant a blessing… nah, not for me. She's never once touched a poor slicker like me. But you, my son! I believe love can still thrive in one such as you.' And he'd whisper in the boy's ear as he swept him up so she could touch his forehead."

I saw it in my mind: Mistress Sostary hovering in the air, bathed in the spotlights, shimmering like a diadem. And the boy... the boy... It would have to be wires, invisible at a distance. They would hold her aloft so she appeared to be floating.

"That close, and he must have seen the trick of it."

"Of course the boy could see. But when the old master put his hands around the nipper, he'd start to squeeze and squeeze, smiling 'til he felt the lad's ribs nearly pop between his fingers. Then he'd whisper, 'If you ever tell anyone about this, I'll slit your throat. I'll know and I'll gut you, kiddo.'"

The laughter barked out of me.

"Still, she isn't leading the show, is she?" Estes confided. "That's because Mistress Sostary is feral. She likes things her own way. But Master Fortunato's as much a mark himself as a magician. Whisper something in his ear and he'll spout it off like gospel the next day. I've seen the mistress doing it. I reckon the Deep is doing the same damn thing."

I thought of what I had heard Leon saying that first night in the hallway. About Arkady Pavlovich, the one the Deeps had left dead in the street, same as Estes' brother. A chill ran through me despite the humid musk of the summertime crowd beneath us. "But what's his game?"

"Who knows the games those sorts are running? Money, maybe? They say the old boy, Arkady, owed a ransom in debt to all the wrong people. After him, Mistress Sostary had to cut our pay twice just to keep the show afloat. But now the pay's back and the seats are filling faster than ever. Strange, that." When he saw my blank expression, he leaned in close. "Maybe you'd have to be a long-timer to tell but look at them. Look at the crowd. What do you see?"

It was dark as doldrums in the auditorium but there they were: the men with their migratory hands, and dolled-up wives. Mouths inhaling with gusto, lips smacking, clothes rustling—but their eyes were flat and loveless.

"Freeloaders, pigeons, and half-price moochers," whispered Estes. "Someone's brought them in. But why so many? And why for *him*?" When the giant turned back to me, I caught the smirk of the scandalizer on his lips. "Even Arkady couldn't muster a crowd like this and he was *something*."

"It's not money."

Estes had never been among the Deeps but I had. And I remembered the questions they had asked me, their especial interest in certain preoccupations…

"Maybe not," Estes agreed. "I reckon we're no better than pigeons ourselves to those lot."

While we talked, the magician drew his rifle for the bullet trick. Even from a distance, I could see the muzzle shaking. But the crowd was indifferent to drama and clumsiness alike.

"The laws of nature that bind other mortals are nothing to me. Let me show you how little a thing like death is…" Master Fortunato whispered, insensibly soft. Then he pulled the trigger and the squib exploded, sending a shower of crimson as Mistress Sostary swooned on cue before him.

20

When the finale was over, it was my job to tame the tiger and keep him cool-headed for his exit. The others were afraid of Amba, just as Leon had said, but we seemed to have come to an arrangement, he and I. With me he went as a gentle as a yearling. "Amba," I'd coo and his whiskers would sketch out a love letter in reply.

This made the others nervous. An animal like that shouldn't be meek, I heard them saying. But what did they know of it? Perhaps it was good they feared me. The company were wild in their own way: misfits and old-time seditionists, malcontents, and cripples. Freaks, castoffs, lepers—and me now, the beast girl. Lady Pale-Throat.

This lot knew something about mutiny and now I was becoming one of them. Whereas once the theatre had seemed a maze of hallways, by now I had taken to learning its secrets. The third and fourth floors were reserved for the dressing rooms and the manager's office. But the basement was riddled with corridors that led to bare concrete rooms, more than one bearing the iconography of a dancing bear scratched into the door. Was I imagining their gamy odor, far less delicate than that of my tiger, still clinging to dank air?

As the beast girl I was clearly beneath notice, but this could be a boon. It seemed I could make myself invisible when I chose. I learned how Otto would visit Renata the seamstress every night, how even though Teresa might doll herself up to play the glamour girl, she had a quiet, steely reserve. No one touched her unless she desired it.

I learned that Leon loved the mistress. I could see it in the way he watched her, the same look as my father in those moments, a green shoot of tenderness that surprised me. Hraná City didn't seem a garden of love. But when they prepared for the show it was like clockwork. Leon and she moved effortlessly alongside each other, two cogs driving the whole company into motion. If there were night-time assignations between them, I found no evidence of them. Perhaps she would touch his shoulder from time to time—she never showed gentleness to anyone else—but that was all. For Leon it seemed enough. I minded my tiger, he minded the mistress. And the more I watched, the more I could see her true supporters were few enough and the Deeps seemed to be everywhere.

And so I wondered about what Estes had said: about the Deeps and whatever arrangement she had come to with them.

It was only as I watched her take her own bow (always shorter than Master Fortunato's, but more elegant as well, more likely to capture the applause) that I began to understand. Mistress Sostary didn't like the crowds, not *these* ones, not even if it meant the receipts had doubled since the start of my tenure. Sometimes I'd follow her gaze and watch it snag on the black-suited man Estes had showed me. Victor. And I'd see that one grinning a shark's heartless grin as he gave her a tiny salute.

As the beast girl, I knew that look in her eyes. She had the stiff-spined stillness of prey.

✦ ✦ ✦

On Thursdays when we took our weekly layoff, Estes would head with the others to the Strelka but I never went with them. It was then I would practice in the tiny, cracked mirror Aleena Alexeeva had left

135

behind, testing the mistress's gestures, trying to match her litheness and poise.

"Why? What was she to you then?" asks Sara Sidorova.

"Who else was there for me to love? My mother was dead, you had vanished. I was young and my love had to go somewhere, I suppose."

At first I wore only my working togs, which I washed in a sink and strung up to dry in the courtyard. As I grew bolder I would put on the red corset. It hung loose for I couldn't manage the laces myself but I adored the way it glimmered as I turned my body this way and that.

I must move like water, I told myself. I would repeat the mistress's lines over and over, trying to remember her cues, her precise position on the stage.

During the day I made it my business to know her comings and goings. Truly, I don't know why: only that she had secrets and Stary had taught me the value of knowing your neighbor's heart better than you knew your own.

And so I came to see how it was between her and the magician. I hadn't forgotten how he had come to my door that first night, the pong of his breath stealing into the room. *I wish that the world were enfolded in love! The world in love needs not the frontier lines...* He hadn't spared me a second glance after that but Mistress Sostary was more than an ornament. He'd taken to dragging her to the hall after hours with concocted stories of faulty machinery, some urgent issue with the wiring. But what he wanted was advice—or worse yet, it seemed, to show her his ideas.

"Leon's not here, is he? There's no bloody fire," I heard her telling Master Fortunato after another emergency visit to the main stage. I had hidden myself behind the curtains as I often did so I could listen to them.

"No." He looked shamefaced at least and his syllables had lost some of their lisping plumminess.

"What d'you want then, Erastus?"

"I can do this better," the magician started promising, "I want to. I *need* to."

"Of course you can." Her smile was tight.

"I mean it!"

He knew he was a fraud, it seemed. He couldn't read the crowds and even if he could they were hardly ever candid. They'd been bullied or bribed to be there but the Deeps couldn't make them do more than clap like crows when a trick was over. So who were they performing for? For us? For each other?

"All right—" she was feigning niceness now "—show me then."

Out came his notebook, and she almost batted it from his hands. But he held steady and she rifled the pages. "What is this? Egorov or Oblonsky? Poetry?" She pushed it away. "Don't you understand? None of this matters if you can't seduce your audience."

"I *know*," he whined. "I see how they are with you."

"So?"

"I want you to teach me."

"You want—what?"

He gritted his teeth. "Teach me, Vesna. Please."

"Let Victor teach you." Her tone was dangerous. "He knows this business."

"We aren't—*friends* but… Couldn't you just—?"

"Ye angels and all things holy, enough now. Yes, you're terrible," she snapped.

"So you'll help me?"

I was certain she would refuse him. If I had learned anything it was that while she tolerated the magician there was little in the way of respect that bound them together. But as her gaze raked over him, her face took on a sudden stillness. She seemed to teeter on the edge of a decision.

But what could she do? Where was his strength? He wasn't all bad, I thought. It was just that he was waiting for them to love him, without coaxing, without effort.

Her mind was working through these same thoughts. It was as if my mimicry of her had made the secret portions of her more visible. I knew what she would say even as her lips parted. "A seduction starts here——" she jabbed the pit of his stomach "——not here. Hold your breath. Feel it as a warm ball of energy completely under your control. Now hurl the words out."

"Gentlemen and ladies!"

"Not good enough. You're putting on airs. Do it again. Relax your shoulders more."

He thrust out his pigeon chest. "Gentlemen—and *ladies*!"

"Stop acting like you need permission." It was better, I thought, but still more than halfway bad.

"It doesn't come so easily to me, Vesna."

"Quit whining, man! Why should it come easily? This is *life* and *death*. But you're a magician. You're supposed decide when and where."

He tried. Give him credit he tried—but he wasn't anything like my mirabilist. The words didn't make sense for him.

"He's in the wrong story," I whispered.

Or I thought I did.

Suddenly Mistress Sostary was yanking away the curtain that had kept me from their view.

"What are you doing here, you little snoop? Doesn't Leon keep you busy enough?" Her eyes slid from me to Master Fortunato. This was a woman with many enemies, I realized. She trusted no one. Except Leon, perhaps, and even then I suspected she never gave herself over fully.

"Let her speak," the magician pleaded. "What's the harm, Vesna?"

"Fine," she snapped. "Take advice from the beast girl, if you want. We can ask the cleaners next, or maybe the cooks. Ask the cockroaches, they've been in this damn place long enough to have picked up a thing or two."

Master Fortunato ignored this and motioned for me to continue. "When they look at him," I began, trying to arrange my own thoughts into something sensible, "they see weakness. A man pretending. But why's he pretending? What's he got to pretend for?"

"What would you have me do?"

I chewed on my thumbnail, then stopped when I realized what I was doing. "The story doesn't have a proper ending." I struck a pose—*her* pose. I'd spent weeks honing the slope of my shoulders, the tilt of my chin so it matched hers.

"He's a hunter," I said, "and he's found a beast in place of his lover. Is he the sort of man who'd suffer a beast like that to live?"

As I spoke my accent lifted her vowels and hard consonants. I moved like a shadow girl: the Lady Pale-Throat. It wasn't the way my mistress moved, but then I was younger, wasn't I? I could still play the innocent.

"Oh Amba, lord of the forest. I can see you bear the burden of death." I let the Lady speak. "Shall I take it from you?"

Both their eyes were following me now, wide as a jackdaw's.

"Let the beast be released from the cage." I could see it clearly in my mind: Amba stalking through the aisles, the slither of his spine as the light slid over it, his eyes glowing like hellfire in the darkness.

I moved as my tiger would move. His hunger burned inside me like a live coal.

"Shall I set you free?" I stalked toward Mistress Sostary. My tiger could have passed through her like a shadow, cutting her to ribbons. And she *knew* that. I could smell the fear-scent on her—like I was her own death approaching.

"And then what?" asked the magician greedily.

What next? What *next*? I imagined the hunter on the stage. He would raise his rifle, wouldn't he? My elbows glided up in mimicry, pointing toward Mistress Sostary. I knew what it was to want to kill. The violence inside me was building and building and building…

"Enough," she snarled, slapping me hard across the cheek. "We don't keep you on for this. Settle yourself down or I'll have Leon tan your bloody hide. I don't want to see your face again, you hear?"

The shadow slipped away from me with the shock of her assault. I touched the place she had struck me and felt an island of heat. I wasn't frightened exactly, but more complex than that: a kind of victory. She had struck me because I had made her.

"As you like, Mistress," I whispered, just a girl again, just a bit of gristle, spindle-shanked and hungry. I sloped back into the darkness that had hidden me.

"You could be kinder," I heard Master Fortunato saying after a moment. His voice was soft but the stage could make a shout of a whisper.

"And what do you think our patron will do with her?" my mistress replied furiously. "Maybe you've forgotten how much kindness dwells in his heart but I haven't. Let her feed the tiger and she'll learn not to get bitten."

The magician thumbed his muzzle. "Maybe she will," he said thoughtfully. "Aye, maybe."

21

"She loves me, she loves me not. She loves me, she loves me not."

That was Estes plucking the delicate white petals from a chamomile blossom, mooning after Teresa.

"She doesn't love you," I told him with a sidelong smirk. "Nor will anyone else, I reckon, while you're carrying on like that." Now he was rolling his eyes at me while he plucked another flower. "Hey! Mind you leave some, Estes." I had planted the seeds myself two months ago in a cracked ceramic pot and they had only just begun to bloom.

It was late in the afternoon, that time after the feed where Amba could be made to do little but take his leisure digesting the meat. Though my tiger was always sweet enough with me, even I had learned not to test him when he was bothered. These were my rare moments of freedom: no training to do, my tasks all completed. Estes often visited me then and often enough his complaint was love.

"Show her to me, will you?" Estes asked, tossing the newly denuded flower aside. "Please, just for a moment?"

"Who?"

"You know who! Teresa…"

It had been nearly a week since Mistress Sostary had banished me from the theatre and if I were honest I was feeling as lovesick in my own way as Estes.

"I don't know what you mean," I insisted—but of course I did. Whatever it was I had felt on the stage that day had stayed with me:

sometimes a shadow, sometimes a shining in my soul. When I closed my eyes I could feel it—*her*—waiting for me. The Lady Pale-Throat. And she was whoever she needed to be, a mistress or a glamour girl, a servant or a queen.

It unnerved me how easily it happened when I practiced in front of my little mirror, as if in those moments Irenda the orphan was just a tale I had told myself of who I was. As easily as that, it could vanish. As easily as that, I could become someone else.

"Please…" Estes was begging me. "Just for a moment. I only want to imagine it. How she might be. With me."

I had never tried Teresa before. I closed my eyes and let my mind drift over what I knew of her. She was older than she looked, that much I had come to understand. Though she flounced like the other fancy girls she had a steeliness they lacked, a knife blade in the darkness. She had accepted me because I'd fought—and she hadn't cared that I'd hurt her. So. She was someone who wasn't afraid of pain. She neither coddled her body nor worshipped it. It was just a thing she had, another resource she could exploit.

I plucked the straw from my clothes and tried to see myself as she would. Perfect fingernails, but they could be a weapon too, couldn't they? Only the men never saw that, never knew what she might be capable of…

It was harder in the harsh sunlight that slanted into the courtyard. There was nothing to hide behind but the mask.

"Well, now," I said—but it was Teresa's voice, her sly, detached cadence. I let my body take on her cant and flow. Her heavy-lidded stare, her barely parted lips. "I hear someone has been pining for me. Is that you then, sir?" A beat later. "What can I do to ease your heartache?"

Estes watched, wide-eyed, as I advanced toward him, slinging my steps with Teresa's saunter. His throat pulsed with the rhythm of his heart. "Tell me I'm handsome," he whispered.

"You're a giant, aren't you, Estes?" I murmured as a flush crept into my own cheeks. The heat of his gaze was awakening something new in me. Even now Teresa would be toying with him. She would have decided what she wanted and how she would take it. But he wouldn't know that. "Would you like to show me how big you are? Is that what you want?"

"No!" he protested, voice strangulated and raw. "I mean—that's not…"

But still I came toward him. It was as if I could feel Teresa moving with me, her haughtiness melting into the heat of her own true desire. She teased, yes, but that didn't mean it was only a tease. I passed deeper into her. I had been wrong before: her body was more than just coinage. She wanted them to know she was a woman. She wanted to see herself as a woman in their eyes. It hadn't always been that way for her but… "I don't care if the others watch," I told him, leaning closer, until my mouth was a hair's breadth from the soft, inner lobe of his ear. "Make love without love, that's what I always say. This will be good for you. They'll remember how friendly we were."

"Stop it!" Estes gasped. His heavy fingers locked around my wrist. He had wanted the fantasy of her but I had given the truth: her desire and her scorn all at once.

"It's only an act, Estes," I tried to reassure him—but I knew it had been more than that. Whether it was Teresa's heat or not, I had felt it rising inside of me. I had made her body my own.

Ashamed now I turned, seeking to hide what I was remembering: the pulse in his throat, beating just for her. I had only felt such a thing once before, when I had stood with my mirabilist on the streets of Hraná City. He had looked at me like that too. But then he had…

"Irenda!"

Leon's strident voice broke through my reverie.

He rushed through the entrance to the courtyard, his face pinked, in thrall to some high emotion of his own. "What in the ever-loving name are you doing here?" he cursed as he caught sight of Estes. Then his gaze darted between us as he took in my friend's own obvious embarrassment and came to his own conclusions. "Enough now," he hissed through clenched teeth. "Out, you hear?"

"What is it?" I asked as Estes scarpered, untucked shirttails flying behind him like pennants. The disturbance had roused Amba from the darkness. He sniffed along the perimeter of the fence.

"It's the bastard Deep, is what it is." Leon ran a hand through his sparse gray hair. "Victor. The General's second self. He wants to parlay with the mistress."

"Here? In the yard?"

"He picks his own places. Said he wanted to see the beast for himself…" Now he was snapping out orders like a commandant. "Go with Estes, girlio, I want you gone from here. Find a corner and keep yourself well-secreted. That one has an evil eye and it's bad enough he's calling on her like this."

Amba let out an inquisitive bark and the hackles on his spine formed a sharp ridge.

With one hand Leon shoved me toward the door and with the other he was already making a sign to the tiger. From the hallway I could hear him muttering in the quiet, calming voice of his: "Easy, Grandfather, easy now. Play nice for this one, will you?"

Obey and be silent. That was what Leon had asked of me. And he had treated me well, hadn't he? Didn't he deserve my obedience?

Perhaps.

Yet something in his command had rankled. Perhaps it was just Teresa's lingering recalcitrance, clinging to me like her musk. Currant leaves, lingonberry, wild-growing things. She wasn't afraid of anything, no matter what she feigned.

Perhaps it was more: my own desire, which she had well and truly awoken. What was my obedience buying from this lot? My silence? I wanted to understand the engine that drove Mistress Sostary's fear. Who was Leon to say what I should or should not do? They would give me nothing—*nothing*—unless I seized it for myself.

And so for the second time I found myself a space in the shadows to watch. The courtyard, I knew, was overlooked from two vantage points. One was the mistress's own office, which none of us were ever allowed to enter, but the other was an abandoned prop room where much of the debris of the show had been stored over the years. It was there I took myself. Through the weathered pane of glass I could see the training yard clearly.

Soon enough I had the man himself in my sights. I recognized the hulk of his shoulders beneath the suit, like Estes, except whereas my friend had a certain ungainliness, the Deep stood squarely. He had a thick, purple neck and a bald patch the color of an onion. He had chosen a place close to Amba's pen where he could survey the courtyard.

"They say I should make a movie," I heard him proclaim.

"I know that voice..." says Sara Sidorova.

"Every bastard one of us knows that voice," whispers the other.

146

"That voice is Death in the night. That voice is bad news coming your way. You hear that voice and there's only one thing to do: run and never look back."

"A guts-and-gore type. Reckon you know what I mean, Vesna. But for that hoodnik shit you know there'd need be blood."

"Hello, Victor," said Mistress Sostary, striding into view. It was the same walk I knew from the stage, cool as water, designed and deliberate.

"Hello yourself, you old damn-bitch." He grinned and though his eyes followed as she passed, they were frigid. "You think I should do it? Give me your professional opinion."

"My mother always said however you feed the wolf, he still looks to the woods for more. So, tell me. What else could a man like you still want from life?" She was smiling as well. I had heard her using this coaxing voice with Master Fortunato.

"Fuck off and die, is that what you mean?"

Mistress Sostary had made it as far as the training tools when he spoke. Now she stopped in her tracks, her face bleached bone-white at his words. But he laughed then, a sharp ha-*ha*. "Well, this wolf is still hungry. But I reckon you know where the best meat is. I never went in for movies, anyway. No weight to them, no *presence*." Victor pushed himself away from the wall, coming up close to her. "Your tiger's getting a bit old, a bit thick around the haunches. Ever consider cutting his grub? You need to manage your costs better."

"A hungry tiger can be dangerous. Even if he's past his prime," I heard her say to him. It was brave, that. I could tell she was afraid. He moved again and she flinched. But he was only stepping past

147

her to pick up the leather bullwhip. Its handle was dwarfed in his double-sized fist as he released the coil.

She raised her hand to stop him and right away I saw she had made a mistake. Suddenly the popper cracked an arm's length from her face. She held herself very still.

Now it was my tiger I was watching. Strangers made Amba anxious as it was—but this one with the whip? Fretfully he had begun to pace, his body moving back and forth in a sinuous figure-of-eight.

"Try touching me again and I'll break your left hand. The right hand—you need it. So no marks, nothing that might spoil the entertainment. But you wear gloves, don't you?"

My heart was beginning to race. If she screamed now would Leon come? Would anyone?

"You're a fine-looking woman, Mistress Sostary, or you were back in the day. You could even be in my movie. Maybe you'd like that?" He was enjoying the performance, expanding, taking up space—like it was his stage now and it felt good for him to own it. "You'd have to audition, of course. Plenty of fine-looking women around. But folk esteem you. They think you're some sort of faery queen. I know Arkady thought that way—so what about this new one? Master Fortunato." He cracked his knuckles viciously. "What kind of regard does he hold you in?"

To her credit, she held her place when he moved toward her. Now it was like they were dancing. He might hurt her but she would not give an inch unless he took it. "That one isn't used to the crowds yet. You saw him, he can't keep up the show. Our agreement isn't possible with him. Get me someone better. Someone with experience…"

Victor examined the whip carefully before he offered it to her. Still the deadpan stare. His left hand covered hers as she took it. "Needs must, Mistress Sostary. Waste not, want not."

Amba was watching as closely as I was. His ears were pressed flat against his skull, a low growl building in his throat. But still the Deep ignored him.

"I'll get the money but it'll take more time," said my mistress.

"More time." The Deep pretended to turn the words over in his mind. "Time's not the substance of our conversation today."

This was it then. I knew the shape of a finale. He was dangling her along to prepare her for what was coming. *Run*, a part of me wanted to yell. *Get away from him*.

"What if I said we—that is, myself and those I represent—are willing to offer a new arrangement?" he asked. I tried to will my body to stop sweating. There was a bulge beneath his right breast pocket and I knew what it was. The Deeps didn't like guns but they wanted you to know they had them.

"What sort of arrangement?" She kept her tone neutral.

"Certain members of the Party have asserted their interest in this production. I'm only the facilitator, understand, but I have backers. My own patrons and grubstakers. I'm relaying what it's been asked of me to relay, nothing else." Victor leaned forward. "Their interest in this operation is more than purely financial. Stratagems are being devised."

"Agitprop?"

"If you like." He paused. "I say there may be a queen's place in what will follow and you're the regalest damn-bitch I ever saw. If—" he held up a finger "—you can be friendly."

"What do you want me to do?"

"A show is all," he said, "but it must be pitch perfect. Victory Day is approaching and the man himself has called for a spectacle."

She breathed in slowly. "Cvetko?"

"None other. He's a long-time enthusiast of your craft."

"We're unworthy of his attention. Surely there are others who would be better blessed with this opportunity? Madam Nikolayevna perhaps?"

"*The pleasure of Erastus Fortunato's performance is that pleasure that comes from being deceived...*" He grinned again. "The General reads the reviews, it seems. They've piqued his curiosity." Another pause. "See I'm your protector, Vesna. Your supporter, sponsor, and best ever-loving friend in the world. This is a good opportunity for us."

She nodded slowly, but he was still holding her hand, touching his finger to her pulse. They said the Deeps were human lie detectors. Behind him my tiger was responding to her fear-scent, lashing the air with his tail. Here it was then. My own body burned with adrenaline.

Suddenly Amba went off like a landmine.

A flurry of muscle and teeth, he hurled himself at the fence like I'd never seen in my life. The fixture shuddered, the fence bulged, the metal rasped as his weight sheared it from the rivets.

"Down!" cried my mistress. "Amba, no! Get back!" She tried to let the lash fly but the Deep had caught hold of it.

"Not yet," he was saying, his own voice alive with some new emotion as he stared at my tiger. The fence was old, I knew. I'd seen the rust eating away at the tension bands. But then everything here was in such disarray: re-used and repurposed, mended only when no other choice remained. It wouldn't hold.

"Please," Mistress Sostary whispered. "Victor, let me—"

"Not yet."

They were dancing still as Victor's knuckles whitened.

"Come at me!" he called with a wild laugh to my tiger. His skin was a livid red. "You think you could take me? You'll choke on me first, you old bastard!"

There were other curses then but I didn't stay to hear them. In Stary I could run a mile without panting but my body had grown soft without the rigors of school calisthenics. My blood moved too slowly in my brain. I was gasping for air as I hurtled down the stairs.

Then I was in the courtyard. The sun was bleeding crimson and the last sprays of orange lit up old Amba like a demon. The fence was coming away along the top of the post, rivets *sproinging* into the dust. I saw Victor and Mistress Sostary, locked together. His other hand was grappling with her wrist. He had turned her to make her face the tiger, holding her close against him.

Amba was going mad inside the cage, body slung low to the ground, jaws wide open revealing incisors three inches long. His lips crinkled with rage as he launched himself forward, his barrel chest slammed into the weakening metal. Then he seemed to hang in the air as stud by stud the fence sheared downward.

I threw myself in front of Mistress Sostary and the Deep.

"Hold now!" I screamed to the tiger, running through all the training signals to calm him I knew. But this was more than simply pacifying an unsettled beast. Victor was goading him and he knew it. If there was one thing my tiger couldn't abide, it was a challenge.

No time to think.

At school I had been taught to love death, and, in your home, Grandmother, I had longed for it. As I passed Mistress Sostary my nostrils filled with the scent of lemon and apple blossoms.

> *I shall not see the shadows,*
> *I shall not feel the rain...*

I must be that girl again, I thought. I must be the girl who welcomes Death.

One step, a second, and a third. Now I was close enough to touch him, let him take me if he wanted it so. His roar vibrated my bones. My own ribcage shook and shook. Slick-palmed, I raised my hand and brought it close. My fingers were barely an inch away from his slavering muzzle.

"You're mine," I whispered to the tiger. "I claim you as mine."

The metal curled beneath him like a petal until his great paws touched the cobblestones. Nothing stood between us. Freedom was his if he wanted it now. Lambent eyes, flecked with their own inner light: little golden pyramids. Then my vision went strange. I swore I could see something—another tiger, eyes glowing like an inferno, his fur midnight black but the switches somehow deeper, a darkness beyond what any mortal knew.

"It was him, wasn't it?" asks Sara Sidorova. "It was the Devourer."

"It is always him," answers the other. "One way or another, it is always him."

But then the tension slunk out of his tail and he burrowed his maw against my hip. *Chuff-chuff.* The flick of a delicate pink tongue, a rumble of satisfaction.

"Go on now," I told him, voice firm as my mother's. Meekly he turned and his tail flicked a final question mark. I watched him disappear into his den, my muscles aching with rigid, relic terror.

Behind me the Deep was muttering, voice low and rhythmic, like a lullaby. "Shouldn't have done that, Grandfather. Shouldn't have given up so easy." I recognized the inflection with a start. *Don't worry, child,* he'd whispered. *You're doing very well. What you have said has been a great help.* That voice wheedling from the shadows while a single light glared down.

He breathed in, let the air gush out his nostrils, then turned to Mistress Sostary. "Organize yourself. This isn't a reprieve, understand. We're being generous with you. We have *chosen* to be generous." No response. Her body was still seized with tremors. Then his gaze touched me, soft as a gypsy moth. "Use this one," he said. "We like her very much, indeed."

His eyes glinted and his smile was all teeth. When he turned his neck was cool and sweatless as if Death hadn't been an inch away from taking us all right then and there.

22

Breakfast was a tense, talkative affair as a nervous wire of energy threaded the company. They knew—or they knew *something* in any case. Though the sunlight was barely creeping through the windows, Teresa had brought out a jar of Otto's homebrewed samogon, which she poured out liberally for any who would take it. Which was most of them, to be fair. "What shall we drink to?" She stood like one of those ancient plainsmen warriors with her cup aloft, a dangerous glint in her eye.

"To the rope that holds," grumbled Leon from the benches, "and to keeping the wolf from the door." He looked as if he had spent the night at the Strelka.

Estes was much the same. He'd barely managed more than a few grunts since I'd taken my place beside him and whenever I tried to engage him, he only clutched his forehead like it might unlatch. Too many rounds last night. He would have had news and they would have been eager to twist it from him. Gossip made one a king for a day in the company.

"To money in our pockets," cried Otto with a touch more enthusiasm. He had been mutinous during the weeks of half-pay, I'd learned.

Teresa drained her glass and was quick with the bottle for the next round. "A good toast. Shall we use it again?"

"Toasting twice is bad luck, girlio, or didn't your dairymaid mother ever teach you that?" answered Leon, though he hadn't touched his own. "Besides, we should be drinking to the General and his health. May the tables break with the abundance he provides, eh?"

"To Victory Day, then!" She was up on the trencher table now, performing a slow, graceful spin. A whoop went out from the onlookers. She knew her audience and she knew how to smile.

Estes slammed a glass down in front of me, spilling half the liquid, but like Leon I was slow to lap up what remained. They hadn't seen Mistress Sostary last night. *To what purpose?* she had asked. It wasn't the kind of question that Otto and his like bothered with. Either your pockets were full or they weren't, who needed to know more than that?

Then Leon was at my elbow, sliding the glass away from me. He did it quietly so the others wouldn't notice, Estes most of all whom, I suspected, wouldn't have seen if the old circus master had suddenly sprouted feathers. "Keep a sober head now. Let these others prattle on. I reckon you'll need it for what the mistress has planned."

"What's that, Leon?" I asked as another huzzah lit up the mess hall. Teresa had taken to an elaborate dance of stomping and roosting in rhythm while her adorers applauded wildly.

Leon gave them one last baleful glance. "Come along and find out."

His brow was furrowed as we left the circus, untangling some angry thought. I followed him across the central courtyard and down a narrow, tree-lined street called Stradaniye. A good neighborhood. The buildings here were four stories of rough granite cladding, carved columns, and delicate miniature balconies.

Mistress Sostary was waiting by the door to one, dressed in black velvet. Her figure was accentuated by puffed sleeves and an exquisite silver belt. I regretted I'd worn my working clothes and barely scrubbed my face this morning. Her perfect crimson lips and plucked eyebrows were immaculate.

"Master Fortunato is expecting us," she reported tersely. "Say nothing, understand? You aren't here for your wit." A curt nod sent Leon back the way we had come.

We entered beneath an elaborate frieze: curling vines and laurel leaves spilling out in profusion. Mistress Sostary's stilettos clicked against the marble tiles. She knocked lightly and another door opened to reveal the magician. His silk shirt and tailored, powder-gray trousers were rumpled. "It's trouble, isn't it? I saw Victor leaving yesterday. He had that look—" His breath was boozy.

"What look?" snapped Mistress Sostary.

"The look of a man who's happy."

"He *is* happy. Be pleased he's happy."

Master Fortunato nodded twice, jerkily, then let us into his apartment. It was well appointed with plush carpets, fine china, and all manner of books: old books with cracked leather spines, new books with fine dust jackets, banned books, pamphlets. It reminded me of Mama and her little *samizdat* library.

"What's the girl doing here?"

Mistress Sostary's gaze silenced me. "We need her." She took a seat at the table and pushed aside a plate of half-eaten butterbrot crowned with onions. She gestured for me to join her, which I did. I still had no idea why she had requested me.

"What did Victor say? Last night at the Strelka there was all sorts of talk. But half of what that lot says is nonsense and the other half... if the Deeps heard it, well—"

"He is commissioning a performance," she broke in smoothly.

His blue eyes widened further. "A performance?"

"A very special performance, Master Fortunato. With many high-placed partisan personages. There's no room for your heavy-handedness."

He fidgeted with an olive in a fine porcelain bowl. "I told you I want to do better."

"This is your chance."

"But why this? Why now?"

She hesitated, deciding how much to dole out. "The General is a connoisseur. They say his father sat at Valentin's deathbed, that he wanted to see if the old clown would laugh as he died. Now he wants to see you, Master Fortunato."

The magician looked like he might chunter at this news. "If he catches me out, then I'll—I'll vanish, won't I?"

"Oh, you know what will happen." The severe black velvet rustled as she re-arranged herself. "You'll disappear, Master Fortunato, you'll be decamped. Someone will come for you and someone will put a sack over your head. Someone will lodge a bullet in your brain and they won't find a drop of blood after on that same someone's hands."

"Then—" His panic was riper than his breath.

"Remember *I* didn't do this to you." She looked pointedly around the apartment. "You're feeding from Victor's nosebag and you're wearing his wealth. What did you bloody well think would happen?"

"They came for me once and it was exactly as you said. They put a sack over my head. They told me to…" The whites of his eyes gleamed. He grabbed for her wrists but she was faster snatching them away. "I never *wanted* this damnable show."

"You're not an innocent. Someone marked you for a reason."

What had Leon said? *That one promises and promises and leaves others to pay the bill*. He gave off a little moan.

"Whatever it was, we don't have a choice. Besides—" she was slyer now "—you've been practicing, haven't you? That's what I wanted to discuss today. Perhaps it's time for a new finale." Her eyes flicked meaningfully to me.

"You really think so?" He recovered fast with the praise.

"Of course." Softly, softly now she reeled him in. "You're our luminary, aren't you? I've been weighing up your strengths and thinking on your plans. Your control over the human eye is extraordinary—*but* we've been wasting you. The show needs something fresh. Not just tricks, something that will touch them deeply."

"Of course I've always said so. But what would be…" he gulped "…fitting for one such as the General?"

"A proper ending." Her smile was full of teeth. "The hunting of the tiger, just as Miss Lubchen here told us. Imagine if you will: darkness sweeps over the theatre and the beast has been set loose. Is he here? Is he there? They'll see the gleam of his eyes, feel the passage of his body among them, and then you with your rifle on the stage…"

"Let old Amba loose? But, Vesna! What we need is something with mirrors. Or a trick prop, some sort of double. Maybe Leon could…"

"Of course I had the very same thought, Master Fortunato. No one has done this before, no one would even *dare*—certainly not Madam Nikolayevna. But that's the heart of the matter. The General has seen mirrors and doubles and trick props, of course he has. He'd spot those swindles in an instant."

"And so…"

"And so we must do the thing he *can't* imagine. We must do it *because* it seems impossible."

I could see her words had hooked into him.

"But how would we do it then? Who could we trust with the tiger?"

"Kitten," she said softly, her gaze swinging to me at last, "I've seen how Amba is with you. You could do this, couldn't you? Keep him calm enough? Under control?"

Master Fortunato blinked at me: the unprepossessing scrap of gristle, the orphan. But I thought of the way Amba had gentled in the yard. "Of course, Mistress. If *you* ask it of me." I raised my chin.

"Then all that remains is your role, Master Fortunato. Can *you* hold the show?"

"I aim and..." Already his face was changing from terror to vanity.

"Why, it's your own wife you've shot through the heart. We'll use the bullet trick. Let me die in the General's arms." Her face had a curious expression. *A glittering spider*, I thought for the second time. "Let him be close enough to see the damage you've done. Only a master spectacle can bear such scrutiny."

"Tragedy plays best," he murmured. "The death of a beautiful woman."

"But it won't be a tragedy, will it?"

"You're right, of course. The woman must live." He snapped his fingers in excitement. "I'll bring her back. I'll breathe life into her with a word..."

That was all it took to stoke the flames, a voice that smothered his good sense. Promises, promises.

"This is what you were born for," she whispered in his ear.

"Think of it—Erastus Fortunato, the people's prophet, advisor, and archimage to the very highest echelons of power, why to General Cvetko himself."

"I can see it," he breathed.

I could see it too. That was the power of what she was doing, weaving her web around him, trapping him with honey and praise. The only question was, could I *really* do what she'd asked of me?

"Yes," whispered a voice in my own mind, sweet and seductive. "Who else but you? What else were you made for but this?"

That voice belonged to the Lady.

23

There must be no mirrors, she'd said, for the General would be looking for them. That much he knew of the methods of magicians. New swindles were rare in the world, Leon had told me once. It was all embroidery and alteration: a switch here, a variation there. But this would be different. The swindle was in what *I* could do—what they believed would be impossible.

Estes thought it was mad, of course. I'd been sworn to secrecy but I trusted him as I did no one else in the company. But if I expected words of comfort, I was mistaken for he seemed more frightened by the enormity of the task than I was.

"Ye angels and little fish, Irenda!" he said as he set about checking over where Otto had mended the fence. He didn't like how I let the tiger snooze at my feet, how I coddled his dreaming head on my lap. "His Nibs may be old, but he's far from tame. You don't know, you never saw what poor Gavrie looked like after Amba startled. No one even know what caused it. The lights? Some simple shock from the crowd? Or maybe it was nothing more than his own bad temper. But even after the surgeon saw him, Gavrie lost half the fingers of his right hand. Now he's good for little but tearing a ticket and even then he's as slow as you'd reckon."

"You worry too much," I called to him, sinking my hands into the soft ruff of Amba's fur. He blinked sleepily and yawned, his tongue a pink curl of ribbon. Harmless. "You're like a grandmother yourself, has anyone told you that?"

He didn't understand how it was between my tiger and me. I tried to show him how Amba went gentle as a titmouse when I spoke a word to him. There would be training involved, of course. I'd need to map his path through the hall precisely and guide him through it. But Mistress Sostary was quick to see we would be given the space and secrecy to master it.

For six days the company were released from duties. They drank at the Strelka and counted their blessings, and despite his protestations, Estes was quick to join them. I never did. I hardly left the yard except with Amba by my side. We ate together, he and I, whatever Leon brought us from the mess hall. We slept together too, stretched out in the shadows when the day grew too hot for movement. I wouldn't permit the cage to separate us. Our bond would have to be absolute, beyond trust or love or fear.

By the third day I couldn't tell our scents apart. I didn't wash lest I make myself strange in his eyes. With the theatre empty we were free to practice the route he would take, sliding gracefully between the aisles. A hundred times we walked the course, a thousand times— then a thousand times more when the lights were extinguished, then a thousand again with starbursts to blind him, the crack of black powder. But my tiger would not be dazzled. He roared when I bade him roar, he made himself as still and silent as a ghost, passing from place to place in the shadows.

He would be everywhere, that night. Death walking among them.

We didn't practice it with a genuine audience. Who would we trust? Not even the company. I'd seen how Estes had reacted. He'd promised silence but the more time he spent in the Strelka, the more he vented his misgivings to me. "Let it be another trick, Irenda," he begged me. "The mistress can't be serious. It *is* impossible. And foolish! What if he startles?"

"He won't," I told him firmly but I could see he didn't believe me. He thought some calamity was coming for us. Hraná City seemed to feel it as well, waking and sleeping, convulsing and stirring. It dreamed its own complicated dreams. There were more unreported bombs, a spate of arson and knifings. At night the city burned and smoke clotted the upper reaches. There were lights in the scarp beyond, in the hills. We all breathed ash and detritus and hummed along with the old war songs piped out over the radio, me most of all. The General was coming and I would be ready for him.

24

Then it was the evening before. The show was ready, or as ready as it could be. We were taking a chance and the whole company seemed to know it. Renata had spent the day adjusting costumes—new sequins, new seams—and even I had been given togs with fresh hems that hung where they were meant to, hiding my wrists and ankles. I wouldn't wear them though. I'd decided to keep all as it was during my rehearsals, minding what Estes had said, knowing it didn't take much to set my tiger in a foul mood.

"Come to the Strelka," pleaded Estes after I'd finished my work in the yard. Today was a day of fasting for my tiger and even this I dared not alter though he was ornery when his stomach was empty.

"Another time, my friend, when all this is finished."

All this. Back then it seemed so, that life truly had endings and beginnings. That a thing could really be over.

I'd never joined him before and I couldn't have said why except I didn't trust the place, not since the night Master Fortunato had pounded on my door, quoting lines about love.

"You'll like it, I promise." Estes' round face was shining with that look of sincerity he alone seemed to possess. "Well, you *might*, anyway!" He must've been the only fellow I'd met who couldn't dissemble. It was sweet. Still I turned away, thinking I should check my marks and rehearse again.

But even after he'd stropped off without me, shaking his head

164

at my stubbornness, I didn't return to the hall. My nerves jangled. I sipped water but it did no good, nor did the swallow from the half-finished bottle of samogon Estes had stashed nearby.

I'd never performed before, not truly. Yes, I had played my role in the show to this point, minding Amba, but nothing had relied upon me. Even with my mirabilist in the streets there had been no decisions for me to make. He'd marked me out and made use of me. I had been a prop to him, nothing more.

A wave of homesickness swept over me. But it wasn't Mama's home I longed for, with its tidy garden, its hidden library. No, Grandmother, it was yours. I longed for the smell of coffee in the morning, brewed thick and dark as tar. Your jibes and grumbles, your mischief with the neighbors.

"Did you come to me then?" Sara asks.

"No. Truly I can't say why. Only that you had asked me what I wanted and now I had gotten it. And I wanted it still—the show, the chance to be seen, badly, and there was a thought in me that if I went to you it would vanish."

"But..."

"Aye, there was something else too, even then. A gnawing discontent. A tremor of fear."

I shook my head. I needed fresh air—I was suffocating!—that was all.

A narrow staircase led me to the theatre's roof, which no one else ever seemed to use. The concrete was stained with pigeon droppings and the wind whipped violently against my cheeks, stinging them raw.

Still I circumnavigated the sharply angled dome, the triangular prows like a tangle of barbed wire. I slipped between the legs of a massive bronze-cast statue: a strong man holding up a teetering globe.

Beyond it I found a ledge and swung my knees over easily, despite the four-story drop below me. Heights had never worried me. The brutalist concrete block bit into the meat of my thighs but I let the pain bring me back to myself. Up here, the light was calm, an elegant ivory-blue tinged with gold. As a child I'd loved these long summer evenings when the sun seemed to waver but never truly set. Sometimes I'd run through the deep woods that circled Stary— hornbeam and ash, strips of silver-papered birch—chasing after the glimworms which I'd cap in a glass bottle to light my way home.

But there were no glimworms in Hraná City, only the gilt-glass windows of the Capitol Buildings, the streetlights illumining the wide magistrales with their lines of banners. Cvetko, Cvetko, Cvetko, his face, everywhere, his slogans, his Party, his promises. Like the city was dreaming a single dream and that dream was the General himself.

The kopek he'd given me danced over my knuckles, his face flashing again and again. I'd been practicing. I was better now than he had been and tomorrow would show how much better. A curious thought, that one. Only a treasonist would tack to that line. So, what *was* I now? What would Mama think of me?

> Now we are half lost in silence
> and the dream that was shaped between us.
> Night is falling too quickly for pauses.

Just so.

How many days had it been since I'd threatened to throw myself from the bedroom you'd given me, Grandmother? I remembered the clarity of the desire, how singular in purpose I had felt. Perhaps I should've done it: how good a daughter I would have shown myself, how devoted, how loyal.

I didn't feel the loyal daughter any longer. What real loyalty did I know now? I shivered uneasily, a dark thought growing in my mind.

The wide curtain of evening enriched the pale colors, draping the cityscape with mauve and heliotrope. The stars struggled to pierce the glow. I'd named them for Estes. The Thresher with his scythe, the clustering circlet which formed the Trammel. What had stopped me from going with him? It would have been good to have a friend tonight. Nothing lingers, nothing stays, not in Strana, perhaps nowhere in the world, not even over the border.

A premonition, though I didn't see it as such at the time. But now I wonder who else might have shared it. Leon? I never asked him, not that night, nor in all that came afterward. He was an old army man himself, a long-time survivor on the front lines. I had seen when he stripped off his shirt in the heat what it had done to him: how it had carved a hole in his body that never truly healed, no matter the time that passed. Would he have felt the same as I did? That there was something evil coming with the darkness?

And then it happened. It had been the same way in Stary the night after my mother died.

A shadow leeched the color from the sodium lamps that lit the magistrales. Lights out, silence around me, the darkness whispering over all Hraná City. I kept my gaze on the horizon, straining. Of course, there they were. Red sparks, a cigar-tip smolder that multiplied and flowed down the boulevards. Military jeeps. I knew what they were and what their business would be tonight.

"Keep away from the window, Irenda," Miss Boban had told

me. There had been terror in her voice. Grief-dumb as I was in those days, still I had known it. Hadn't that same terror lived in my parents? Mama with her *samizdat* poetry, Papa her willing accomplice, seeking out those forbidden pamphlets and chapbooks. Heroes, they had been called after—the angels of our nation. But they had been traitors.

Oh yes, I knew what would be happening tonight. What the Deeps would do. Bodies dragged unresisting through doorways, with hoods over their heads, their muscles limp and spiritless.

Cvetko's coin bit into the flesh of my Venus's mound. From here I could see the Strelka, shuttered in gloom, the Deeps hadn't reached it yet. I closed my eyes. Whatever happened next…

> *I shall not see the shadows,*
> *I shall not feel the rain…*

What could I do for them? What warning could I give? How would it change things if Otto had been named in a register somewhere, now stamped and officialized? Or Renata? Or even sweet, inculpable Estes?

In Stary we children had been taught to hunt out secrets the way pigs sought truffles in the forest. Later we learned to see without seeing, to feel without feeling. I turned away from the knowledge crowning inside of me. *Forget, forget, forget.* Nothing was happening, nothing need concern me.

"I've always liked this place. Good sight lines: you can see as far as the Capitol Buildings and no one would ever know you were up here," a voice announced behind me. I recognized the provincial drawl, laden with irony.

Startled, I turned. There was Teresa, clutching a cigarette, leaning against the thigh of the bronze giant. The wind tangled strands of her golden hair across his knee.

Below us came a shout from the street, followed by the scabrous laughter of men. Other things too. The discharge of a pistol—again and again. Then a silence of a different pitch and quality, a waiting silence.

"So, Lady Pale-Throat. Do you know what's happening out there? What those sounds are?"

A high, keening after, almost animal in its grief. Only a fool wouldn't know what it meant.

She slipped down beside me and the ruby eye of her cigarette glowed between us. She offered one to me, shrugged when I refused.

"The others have gone to the Strelka," I said.

"Of course they have."

"But you didn't. Not this time."

"I'm not a fool, am I? Nor are you, it seems." A long exhale, smoke clouding the limpid air. "You have to admit, the General's tastes are nothing if not theatrical. Someone planned this. And look— we've got the best seats in the house."

"Careful how you talk."

She grinned a vicious grin. "If anyone asks, tell them I'm loyal."

"Are you?"

I stared out at the gloom, thinking of Victor, imagining him comfortable in the formless hours before dawn. This was *his* time, the creeping time.

"Loyal enough. I used to be in the army, same as Leon—though that poor bastard had it far worse than me. He was at Cheyory Bridge with the General, did you know that? But then most of us were military at some point or other." She was holding her cigarette the way I'd seen certain officers doing it. A lifetime habit: brownish stains on her joints. "Life is short, m'Lady." That edge of irony. "They knew what they were doing, going out tonight. Sometimes a drink with friends is worth the risk."

"Did Estes know?"

Teresa shrugged again. "That one's a romantic. You don't see so many of them in Hraná City. Romantics expect too much of the world so a place like this will always disappoint them. But you're not from here, are you? It must be different out east: factories, aye, but none of the ghettos, none of the sprawl."

"I haven't seen stars like this in some time," I said. Without the streetlights, the cityscape was black. Above us spun newly revealed galaxies. The sky seemed as deep as an ocean, ready to swallow us.

"I was born in the south, near Iloropol—the Village of Kindling, it was sometimes called, for the deep forest that surrounded it. Do you know it?" Teresa asked.

I shook my head.

"I'm not really surprised. Mostly shepherd-folk living the same way they lived a hundred years ago. Hand to mouth, but honest enough, not like here."

"Why did you leave then?"

"That's a strange story." She flicked the butt of the cigarette over the side of the theatre, where the wind snatched it and sent it tumbling away. A heartbeat later, she had another clenched between her fingers. "It's an old border town. Lots of outposts. Even if you weren't a guard you knew to watch for strangers. From our side crossing over and from their side too. When I was a wee thing—twelve, maybe, or thirteen—I learned to plant landmines in the valley with my brother Tars. See, I knew all the best hiding spots. Alders were good.

They give the best shelter and the catkins are edible if you're hungry enough. So. We planted our mines near the biggest. *Boom*, we'd hear at night sometimes. Deserters were always waiting for nightfall. *Boom, boom!*"

She gave me a sidelong look. Testing me, I thought. I stared hard at her face. There were fine wrinkles at her lips, on her brow. I'd never noticed them before.

"Now Tars got all the credit. When he was sixteen he enlisted and because I didn't want to be apart from him, I went too. I was fourteen, maybe? At first the officers all laughed at me but by then there were other girls in the village whose brothers were joining the war effort. So a group of us went to the local militia office and they turned us away but we kept at it.

"Eventually they let us in and that was good. Our commander was an honorable man, not welcoming the lot of us exactly but tolerating our presence. He had us training as snipers because he thought that way we'd be kept out of the worst of the fighting." A pause then. "Can you guess how many men I killed?"

"Less than five." The cigarette was dancing between us. More lights on the street now, more noises from below. I focused on the sound of her voice.

"More."

"Less than ten."

"More."

The edge in her voice stopped me from guessing further.

"See, it doesn't matter how many I killed beyond the first one. Killing changes something inside of you. The first time I killed a man it was close to twilight. The sky was glistening with light and already there were stars—just like tonight. I remember that. I could barely

171

see them because the moon was so fat and I'd been planning to use its light to shoot over his head, just to give him a scare. I remember breathing in, breathing out, and pressing the trigger—just kissing it, really. But the bullet flew lower than I expected.

"No one found him until the morning, which seemed amazing to me. I kept waiting for the alarm to sound, but it never did. I was with one of the other girls—they always paired us up—and I was crying and she was telling me to hush because they hadn't found the body. She cradled my head in her hands and eventually she started kissing my mouth just to stop me from making noise."

Another sidelong glance, another cool drag from the cigarette. I was thinking of the mistress then, how her lips had tasted on mine. Not sweet, not that exactly—but somehow comforting.

"Then it was deep night," she continued after a beat. "The moon was gone and she made me count the stars with her and she told me all the names she'd learned for them. The Trammel, the Shield, the Hanged Man, and the Thresher, which I'd never heard of before. One star was brighter than the others and she told me that star was for the man I had killed and that I was a hero. Can you believe it? But then we were always telling each other how brave we thought we were."

Her hand brushed mine. I let it linger there, our little fingers touching at the knuckles. "So what happened after?"

"Well, I don't think my commander had really expected me to kill anyone either. I suppose he thought we'd play dolls out there or plait each other's hair. You know what men are like. But afterward he began to talk to me seriously about killing. He made me learn the markings so I could spot officers by their uniforms. He let me eat with the men and gamble with them. They often told stories into the night and most of them were exactly what you'd expect—about women—but I was allowed to listen because they didn't think of me as a woman anymore. I killed for them wholeheartedly. I knew they were in the right—that *we* were in the right—because I loved them."

The noises were growing distant now. The bright clusters of red were traveling down the magistrales, headed elsewhere. I asked her what happened to her brother.

"Ah well. He was taken as a prisoner. They let him go eventually but he never came home. He wrote a letter saying we wouldn't recognize him. He'd been very handsome. My mother guessed he must've been wounded but that's not what he meant, I think. So I came to the city to look for him."

"Did you ever find him?" I asked.

She inhaled softly and shook her head. "I found the company. The same as you did." The cigarette had burned down to her fingertips again. She pushed herself to her feet. "We'll need to be careful tomorrow. Someone is smoothing the way, I think. That's what tonight is. They'll all be in on it, whoever's left standing when it's over. They'll be happy, just you wait—more *relaxed*. Nine months from now I expect we'll see a glut of babies."

Then she was gone. A ghost, a specter who offered her warning and vanished.

The darkness seemed thicker, clotting the doorways below in shadows barely pierced by the ashy moonlight. I imagined the chamomile flowers shivering in the courtyard, my tiger pacing back and forth, his eyes burning sulfurous as they had when he'd almost got free.

25

The Deeps didn't come to the circus that night. Dawn set the sky to smoldering while outside the street washers began their work. Viscera, bone shards, bullet casings hosed into the gutters. All that remained would be the traces searched for by the desperate, the suicidal. Those left behind in the wake of violence—as I had been once.

Orphan, I thought upon waking. *How many other such girls would there be today?*

I hadn't thought sleep would come to me that night but it had. Easily I had followed the needs of my body which were simple: food, rest. When I woke the day seemed like any other. But I was thinking on the mistress and what she had said to me about the games Victor was playing, why he was doing what he was doing. And home. I thought on that too. The last memory of my mother. She had been drinking coffee at the table, her fingers twisted carelessly with my papa's. Neither were smiling but both were happy. Happy in their love for one another, their love for me.

Did other families have such happiness? Mistress Sostary could have been the same age as my mother, though she wore the years better. But for all her happiness I knew that Mama was lonely as well. She never spoke of her family, not of you, Baba, nor of the friends she had made. Perhaps she had none. Perhaps she couldn't allow herself to trust and so she had kept her world tiny and controllable: herself, Papa and me. What would she have asked for had you made a bargain with her?

Or perhaps you did. Perhaps she had her heart's desire. I would never know now.

Nine months from now I expect we'll see a glut of babies.

Mama seemed everywhere around me then, a ghost image of her face reflected in the little cracked mirror. Was it only that I was growing older, leaner, more like her? No, it was more than that. The parades in the streets, the smoke in the air. I remembered these things from my grief-stupor. Rain lying slickly on a line of coffins. Kneeling before the General's ikon in a black scarf and a simple mourning dress. Miss Boban whispering in my ear how proud I must be.

And I *had* been proud, hadn't I?

I left my room quietly, keeping to the back hallways as I always did. Black trousers, a black shirt, clothes to make one invisible—they still smelled of my tiger, just as I wanted it. I had worn black the day of the funeral as well.

First I tried Estes' door, rapping sharply. There was no reply, not even when I called to him. *Don't be such a baby!* I chided myself. *He often sleeps likes this. Later he'll complain someone must have lodged a pickaxe in his skull.*

I wanted to believe this was true. Wanted to believe it desperately. But the scent of lemon and apple blossoms was all around me, sweeter and fiercer than even the tiger's musk. I found myself at Mistress Sostary's dressing room door.

It was an old habit of mine now, this creeping from door to door. I suspected you would have hated it, Grandmother, but for me it was only another kind of protection. Mistress Sostary had lied to me. She had wanted me calm and biddable. If Victor was making his plans then she was making her own.

She would be preparing, I knew. The routines of the theatre were as familiar to me now as if I had fashioned them myself. Moisturizer, foundation, primer, color. She would be brushing her hair, then shaping it to hang just so—straight as a guillotine. She never let another help her. Estes said it was because there were tales of girls who had poisoned their mistresses with lead and arsenic in their powders, belladonna in their perfumes.

It was why when I pressed my ear against the door I was shocked to hear another voice with her. I had seen Leon earlier that week, carrying packages wrapped in oilcloth, speaking in whispers with the mistress. At the time I'd thought nothing of it—props for the bullet trick, surely. But now...

"I can lay in more gunpowder—three, maybe four squibs, each of them larger. It'll widen the blast radius. But must it really be this?" It was Leon.

And then my mistress: "This way I choose for myself. You understand, don't you?" There was something in her voice I recognized, perhaps because I myself had felt it as well. The weight of pain and the longing for it all to end.

Once upon a time there was a little girl who lived in a village in the forest. The girl dreamed of fire, every night she dreamed of fire...

Suddenly I saw her as I had that first day in the theatre: she was the beast that spat when cornered, that clawed and scratched, that gave its life to maim the bastard hunter. I understood now why she had chosen the bullet trick, why she moved through our rehearsals with such fierce determination. She wasn't practicing for a performance—she was preparing for her death.

"Leave me now. The General will be here soon and I must be ready for what comes next."

A moment later the door was opening but my blacks kept me invisible, just as they were designed. The old stagehand limped away, never knowing how close I was. My instinct guided me. Quietly, I slipped into the room behind him.

There stood my mistress by the mirror: red as a rose, red as the slaughterhouse.

"I know what you're doing," I said. Her breathing caught. I watched in the mirror, saw a flash of scarlet appear on her cheekbones, then vanish again. I came up behind her and touched the laces, feeling the curve of the bone bands. There she was and there was I, two bodies reflected back at me.

"What did you say, Kitten?" Her voice was perfectly controlled and wonderfully casual but I sensed a danger note in it. Every bone knew its breaking point.

"I know what you've placed upon your person." A package of death, I thought, a swindle within a swindle. It was why she had chosen the bullet trick.

"How?" Just that single word, nothing more.

But I was tired of her layers of deception. If what I believed was true then this would be the final one. "My grandmother is a witch."

"All grandmothers are witches." Her eyes were still very wide, studying me carefully in the glass. "Why are you here, Irenda? If you know what you say you know."

My hands were still touching the corset. I pulled gently at one of the knots, slipped my fingers into the lacing and loosened it. The corset gaped and fell away—with it the munitions that Leon had placed there.

"Is this a good death?"

Her skin was pale where I'd stripped away the cloth. She was shivering but she smiled into the mirror anyway. "Never know 'til the

177

show, Kitten." Then she turned and caught my wrists. For a moment I thought she meant me violence but when I looked in her eyes that wasn't what I saw.

She raised her hands—raised mine with them—and the corset fell around her ankles. Before me she was naked now, her skin smooth and velvety. There were blemishes, a prune-colored oval the size of my fingertip that sat below her right breast. Below it was the puckering of old scar tissue. A series of thin, white flourishes and raised circlets that stood out like stars. Cigarette burns? She saw me looking at it and said nothing, only offered herself up to my gaze. Slowly she released my wrists and brought my hands to her hips. I could feel the bones of them, sharp but finely made.

"What do you want, Irenda?" she breathed.

My body brimmed with a mongrel light. Desire, yes, that was part of it. Her eyes were large and liquid, she smelled of bergamot and rose, vanilla, iris. But buried within those heady scents were others: apple blossoms and lemon.

"Let me take away your pain," I whispered.

"Oh, no. Please, no, Irenda..."

"Hush now, Grandmother. Whatever happened, happened long ago. What does it matter now?"

"Is this what I did to you? Was this my gift to you?"

Now the other's eyes are flashing. "Some things are given, aye, but not all. Not this..."

As if in a dream, she released my wrists. Now, her fingers worked at the buttons that secured my black canvas shirt. When they were undone, she freed me of the trousers so I stood naked as she was. The cold air licked my skin and my hands fluttered upward like birds. She moved them away, tracing the jut of my rib with a perfect, red lacquered nail. The skin that covered it was taut and shivering, but unmarked.

"Say it again," she commanded.

I remembered what it was like to stand in the school assembly. How right it had seemed then, reading aloud my compositions. That swooning sense of accomplishment. "When I die…" I started but I couldn't finish. *What else had I been made for but this?*

You had promised me I would tame Death, Baba. How better than this? I thought of the tiger beyond my tiger, the way his teeth had gleamed in the darkness. At least now my death might mean something. Not what they had told me in Stary but something I could choose for myself.

"You thought you were making it your own," says Sara Sidorova.

"Aye, Grandmother. I was, don't you see?"

"You were a fool."

"Perhaps," says the other with a faraway look. "But less fool then, than I would prove to be…"

It was as simple as that. She understood what I was offering, understood I meant it. Perhaps lying for a living had given her a canniness about the honesty of others.

With a gesture, she bid me turn around. Her fingers grazed the laces. I thought of my mother brushing the tangles from her hair, the sound of her voice singing to me. But Mistress Sostary was silent.

With each yank of the cord, the corset gripped my ribs. It hurt. I think it was meant to: her warning to me.

"Lace it tighter," I told her.

She paused, then with a vicious wrench she crushed the air from my lungs.

"You need to season it." Her lips were close to my ear. "Wear it unlaced for an hour every day until your body learns what you want it to do. If I had time, I could teach you. But there isn't time."

She showed me the mechanism, the boning lined with cartridges. She showed me the trigger, made sure I understood what it was.

Afterward, she looked at what she had accomplished, a flower from every angle. "You're beautiful," she said. Still, she pinched my cheeks, pinking them further. "But can you hold the show? You will need to be perfect, flawless, if you are to get close enough…"

"I've been practicing," I told her.

Wryly then: "Of course you have. But there's something I want to tell you. About the cage. How it feels inside." She touched my hair and hesitated.

"It doesn't matter." I was growing impatient. My heart beat a military tattoo in my skull. I had chosen, hadn't I? It was enough. This time when my pain left me, it wouldn't return. I would make something of it.

"If you fail they'll hurt you."

I stared at the scars on her body, none on her face. None where another could see them. "Can you tell me nothing wiser than that?" I asked.

"Don't be afraid of what you are," she said. "They'll try to make you hate yourself, but you mustn't, not ever. You know the story of Lady Pale-Throat, don't you?"

"Which one?"

"Once upon a time there was a little girl who lived in a village in the forest. The girl dreamed of fire, every night she dreamed of fire…" Her voice was husky and she leaned in close, touched her lips to mine. A pulse of heat strung itself between my groin and my wrists. "Smile for them, Irenda. If you're lucky, no one will look deeper than your smile."

26

"She knows what will happen? What she must do?"

Leon's voice held a quiet fury my mistress refused to acknowledge. He stood at the door to the dressing room, looking me over: the corset and finery, my lips and cheeks touched with red. She had taken scissors to my hair, let the bronzy thatch fall upon the floor of the dressing room so that what remained hung in the same sleek, blunt cut she herself was accustomed to wearing.

"I know," I told him as firmly as I could. He didn't like it, that much was clear, but he still had a cadet's sensitivity to orders. His eyes were on hers, still asking the question, hoping, I think, for a different reply. Whatever it was that held the two of them together was being strained to the point of breaking.

She touched his shoulder, but he flinched.

I hoped he understood, or would come to. But perhaps he wouldn't and perhaps it didn't matter truly, so long as he was loyal. And what else was he but a loyalist? Here was a man who had been at the front. He would know about martyrs.

Before he could press me further, there was Renata coming at me with her pins and persuasions. "Mistress Sostary…" she started and then stared agog when she saw who it was wearing the costume. But whereas Leon had gone stubborn, there was a slyness that slipped into the seamstress's eyes. She dropped her head, bobbed in a premature curtsey, and waited for me to speak.

Mistress Sostary arched a delicate eyebrow and said nothing. I would have to tame them, I understood. It was to be my first test. I closed my eyes, then, and let the Lady come into me.

My back straightened and my shoulders went back. "There has been a change of plans. This is how it will be."

Both of them said nothing: *Obey and be silent.* They knew the old line as well as I did.

I was made ready, prepped and primed and sent to the wings to await my cue.

The punters tonight were more flushed than I expected, boorish and loud, jeering to one another. From my vantage I saw money changing hands, secrets whispered from ruddy lips to waiting ears. They smirked like best friends, but they were hatchet-men, all of them. Their loyalty was the law of the pack. Grovel when faced with strength but wait for your moment.

And General Eduard Cvetko—there was the man himself. A pulse of excitement rippled through me, building in the soles of my feet and shooting upward, into my palms: an old reflex that. Even then, knowing what I did, with the little packet of death hidden beside my ribs, the blood thundered in my ears. I remembered the portrait Miss Boban had kept of him, a poor likeness. He had been younger then, his rust-colored hair cropped close, eyes impassive but alert. Now, the flabby wrinkles and weathered pate were more obvious. He wore a beige kilim jacket with a soft turn-down collar, the austere cut of a uniform.

Would you believe when I saw him, I thought of you, Baba? He was a relic, a statue crumbling beneath his own weight. All it would take was a little push. Was this what you had prepared me for? Your revenge for whatever it was that had happened to you, and for my mother's death, a fuse lit, smoldering, burning its way toward the powder. And then what? Then I would be with Mama again.

The house lights settled with a swell of music—an old war song from the days of Cheyory Bridge. I hoped the General would appreciate that touch. It took longer than normal for the punters to settle into their seats. They weren't here for our performance, not truly. They were performers themselves. All this was an elaborate pantomime directed at one person only.

King Fiendish, you had called him. A thug, a hoodnik.

There had been hate in your voice. I hadn't understood it. But then, what had I understood of hate? It is a different thing to grief. I had known loss, of course, but I had thought my parents' death formless, shapeless, a thing without cause or reason.

Now I was beginning to wonder. They had been called heroes. But it is easy to give such a name to the dead. I had never said to anyone what I knew of my mother's library but in Stary there were eyes everywhere. And what child didn't tell stories? The tale of so-and-so who did such-and-such?

I looked out over the crowds and tried to feel my way to the truth of them. If they were jackals it was because they had been forced to be such. They clawed and bit and fought over the scraps, a bitter, laughing snarl resounding across the length of the country. But inly they were quiet, always quiet, even when they were frightened or happy. With that kind of quiet you could give a child bread or cut her throat. Oh yes, I could recognize an orphan when I saw one, hollow-eyed and white with pallor. Strana was a country of such orphans.

"I love you," I said to them, meaning it truly, "I love you all."

It is possible, I was learning, to love and hate at the same time.

27

"Listen now! There's a story I've heard of an ancient tribe that wandered the northern reaches of our country…"

That was how it was supposed to go. A cage set out at the center of the stage: wide enough that when the woman entered she could give the impression of spaciousness. It was a difficult trick to perform in the round, requiring perfect precision, an awareness you were watched on all sides, that every part of you must be part of the spectacle. How many times had I seen Mistress Sostary perform it? How many times had I dreamed of doing it myself?

"Among them lived a hunter renowned for his prowess. He wanted a beautiful woman."

I breathed in deeply. Now I was upon the stage. It was hot under the lights and my footsteps echoed more loudly than I had dreamed possible. I lifted my chin, fought for balance. I wasn't used to the corset stealing the breath from my lungs and making each movement a battle of its own. When I had practiced in my room it had been simpler, with only the mirror watching.

Master Fortunato's eyes widened when he caught sight of me, blue as larkspur, blue as surprise. I tried to give him that imperious smile my mistress often deployed but I was uneasy in her stilettos. They pinched my toes viciously, I tottered on the spikes. He saw this as well, good man, and offered me his arm with a gallantry that seemed unforced. Then it was all right, it was all right if I appeared uncertain.

This was my bridal chamber, wasn't it? I remembered what it had been like when my mirabilist had touched me.

Boom! went my heart.

And so would hers—the princess. She wouldn't know what was coming. Wasn't her magician a man of power? Not to mention desperately in love? All he had promised would have seemed within her reach then: riches and safety, the much-desired marriage bed. Unused to such attentions, what could she do but cave to his affections?

"The hunter would leave her often and the princess became lonely."

Now the cage lifted into the air and I had to move with it, swaying gracefully from side to side. My knees were weak and rubbery but it merely added a flourish to my almost-swooning. My lover had abandoned me. *Orphan*, I thought, *orphan*. I was alone. Who could I turn to? When I touched the bars of the cage, I recoiled in horror. Only now did I understand it was a not a palace but a cage he had placed me in.

But the Lady—ah, the Lady, she was clever. Not a good girl, not a pretty girl, but subtle. Her grandmother had been a witch and her grandmother before her. Who was she to be so easily cast aside? There were other powers in the forest: demons who turned men into smoke, wild beasts that could slip on the guise of a lover.

The magician had forgotten this, it seemed, forgotten that a princess abandoned could make her own way in the world.

Was he returning at last to me? Well, well. My spine straightened, my eyes filled with a dangerous fury. I'd smile and smile and smile while inside I lit up my vengeful heart like a coal. That was what the crowd wanted. The hoodniks and the lager louts, the ballroom thugs. For a moment—a heartbeat only—I sought out the eyes of the General. He was watching with some interest, leaning forward in the chair that had been freshly upholstered for him.

He would have seen many girls in his time, I thought. Orphans—yes, and widows too. Sycophants and loyalists. I remembered how Miss Boban used to kiss his portrait each evening, how I had kneeled before his ikon, how I had not spoken when I had seen the kopek tucked away in his palm.

Had it always been this way? A perfect universe, a universe perfected by one man. How could it possibly be resisted?

"How indeed?" murmurs Sara Sidorova, leaning in.

Well. There were ways, weren't there? No universe exists without the possibility of further perfecting. Thus the purges, arrests, expulsions, and ejections. Thus the cleaning up of the streets. Thus the establishment of borders. Thus the succession wars and internecine fighting.

There would always be treasonists. Malcontents, freaks, castoffs, lepers, traitors, witches. And if we were not there waiting, why, they would make us themselves, wouldn't they? We were the whetstone for their blade, the beast they stalked for their own sport in the wildwood, never fearing our claws and our talons and our teeth.

"When the hunter returned from his wayfaring his lover greeted him with open arms. Softly, slowly, she ushered him into the bedroom…"

I had to act quickly. As Master Fortunato drew across the cage a curtain of red velvet, my disguise dropped like snakeskin. We had only a moment. Then Amba was leaning his weight into his haunches, sheathed claws, tendons flaring, as the barrier dropped away. His throat roared to life. And, aye, in the hollow of the cage, with death riding close, the scent of it thick around me, I felt my senses flying out.

Now I was hovering over the stage, my spirit floating outside of my body, hanging in the air like a jeweled pendulum.

"What did you see?"

The jackals.

They were watching. They had liked seeing the girl in the cage. They had liked how she glittered like a glacier. She was younger than they expected, younger than they'd heard. Was this the famous Tiger Lover, then? Why, she was almost a child!

Some of them were thinking they might pay a visit backstage. Bold with booze and their own heady prospects, why shouldn't they take what they want? They saw the way she glanced at them. They saw her fear and they told themselves they would protect her. As long as she was loyal. As long as she was obedient. As long as she wanted nothing more from the world than they were willing to give her.

And they were making a new world, weren't they? It was *good* she was so young. The children she'd bear would have the brightest of futures.

The rook beside her didn't matter. He wasn't a true magician. It was all a bit of chicanery. Mirrors and sleight of hand, oh, it didn't even matter how he did it—because what power was there really? It was all words, words, and more words and words were nothing. The poets and prophets were gone now, they had made sure of that. This one was telling a story, that was all, and they'd heard the story before.

Was there a tiger coming? Of course, but they were tigers themselves. Last night had seen them hunting. They weren't afraid now.

Then the lights went out.

28

At first there was only a murmur of surprise. Surely this was part of the show? One more step in the dramatic unveiling?

Too long for the show, they told themselves after a minute had passed. There must have been a mistake. Had a fuse blown? There'd be trouble, if so. Trouble but not for them. They were safe. Another's mischance was as good as a fete in their minds. They traded knowing glances, touched their fingers to the round rims of their glasses.

The moment stretched.

A laugh pitched too high. The first brine of fear-sweat in the air.

They squinted and smacked their lips. They expected a flash but none came. It was still too murky for them to see properly. Sudden movement behind them. Had the doors to the circus hall closed? Their pulses were galloping now. Nervous murmurs whipped up the air. A voice on a radio whispered: "Can you see him? Where is the General?"

Then came a nerve-deadening roar rippling from the front. Could it be a bomb? Surely not! Surely tonight at least they were safe? Now they were stumbling in their chairs, unsure of themselves, unlaced from the drinking. A howl of rue as someone—somewhere—got trampled. The fear was in them, a kind of growing terror.

They couldn't see the magician. They couldn't see *anything*.

Lights out.

And then that fusillade sound swept over them again. Not a

bomb, but a growl so loud it resonated in the pits of their stomachs, vibrated along their spines, turned them gutless and afraid. Only then did they begin to understand. There were creatures that loved the darkness as much as they did.

The lights sputtered and flashed to life and the punters beheld the platform, the collapsed cage with its door hanging wide open, empty as a spent cartridge.

They saw and they understood: Grandfather Death was walking among them now.

Flashlights dazzled their eyes as armored bodies moved through the crowd. Good, the Deeps at least were prepared for this. That was their job, wasn't it? The cold snouts of semi-automatic weapons touched shoulders, crystal crunched underfoot and fizz soaked the runners. "Where is he? Do you see the General?"

The stage torches strobed as the magician came into view, picked out in a circlet of light. His voice rose up like a snare roll: "Some say there is a beast at the center of the universe. He comes from the darkness and to darkness he will return the world. They name him Amba, the lord of the forest. A beast of vengeance, of blood and flame and destruction."

Then the circus plunged again into a second darkness and it seemed as if the show had taken on a life of its own. That was when they noticed the smell, the ugly carnival fug. They saw the beast's body, a halo of orange and gold that glimmered like a firebrand.

"Found him," crackled the radio and there was the General in the aisle, the great man, eyes bursting with fear, his jowls quivering.

Glints and flashes. It was impossible to make out what was happening. They saw an animal head appearing like a starburst. Slashes of orange and gray radiated outward.

And then their eyes flew back to the magician. They could make out the rifle in his hand. It was a prop surely, but no one carried arms around Cvetko. This was known, damnit, so what was the magician up to?

"Oh Amba, you think these forests are yours. The mountains and foothills, the rivers and the plains. But you have grown old in your time upon this earth. They say you carry the burden of death—shall I take it from you? Shall I free the world of death at last?"

From the stage the magician raised his rifle and the Deeps were trigger-happy and alarmed. They tensed, swerved their own weapons, and wavered. It was the tiger that concerned them. The man was nobody, he couldn't hurt them, but a beast like that? Hunting? *Here?*

The lanterns were sending off tracers of glaring light—dark and then brilliant, then dark again. There was the tiger. He was picking up speed.

The General smiled stupidly. "Come," the old man whispered, welcoming annihilation.

Ten feet. Three feet. Then the tiger was upon the old man. A blinding coruscation as fireworks seemed to explode all around them.

And then there was the girl, somersaulting through the air, the crystals of her garment winking. And then—what were they seeing? A flash of crystal scales, a liquid movement that could have been fur or silk or fire. Something twisted through the air that was neither fully beast nor woman.

Suddenly the tiger was gone—transfigured into this astonishing creature. She landed with a flourish. She was close to him now, close enough to kiss him. Close enough to—

"Is this it then?" begs Sara Sidorova. "Is this the end?"

"No," whispers the other. "It was only the beginning."

Her eyes were gold and murderous.

Suddenly they wondered: Had the beast vanished at all? Was it a girl or a tiger? Look how she was *moving*, damnit! What were they seeing? The beast's shadow behind her, his killer claws coming forward.

The magician was raising his rifle, sighting toward the General. Their own fingers tensed. The muzzles went up but not soon enough. A sharp rapport broke the silence. Who had done it? The magician? No, now he had a squint of incomprehension as if something was wrong, something unexpected was happening.

And with that noise, the girl seemed to freeze.

At last she sensed their gaze upon them. Her eyes were wide, a look that might have been fearful. They would argue about this afterward, those who were in the hall that day, those who claimed to be afterward when it was seen as fashionable to have been in attendance. Definitely fear, they would argue over their cups of samogon, for who wouldn't be afraid, come face to face with General Cvetko himself?

But those who were closest would grow quiet during these arguments. Of course the girl must have been afraid, they would think to themselves, but still their guts would churn with unease. For it *hadn't* been fear they had seen in her eyes, those closest, those few living witnesses. Love, they would have said, had their companions pressed them. What they saw in her eyes was love—close enough to fear, in its way.

The moment lengthened. A breath, it seemed, could have swayed it.

But then the princess sank down before the death-struck General with all the fluid grace of a blade being sheathed. Her hands touched the floor, her head bowed low enough that none could see her face. "All honor to you this day," she said as the sound of applause rose up like a hornet swarm around her.

AFTERNOON

29

The noise is deafening, a roar that shakes Sara Sidorova's teeth, rattles her bones, obliterates thought. She cannot see, she cannot think. Is it the tiger? The cartridges her granddaughter had set upon herself? Or something else, far worse?

"Wait," she says, "wait please. I want to see–"

But it is as if the lights have all gone out at once and she is staring into pure darkness. It is the gate–or whatever lies beyond it: rage, emptiness, hunger. The howling All-Dark, which it seems is sound as much as freezing cold. Sara Sidorova has lived a life that has taught her about terror. But even the terror of the soldiers, their captain with his murderer's smile, is nothing next to the terror of the open gate and that noise–oh, mercy, that noise!

Whatever is out there is howling for *her*. Howling for her to have done, to end it all.

She presses her hands to her ears. Even with her eyes clenched, a red stain seeps across her vision, light glaring across the insides of her lids. She forces herself to breathe, to open herself to… whatever it is. To face it as she has faced so many calamities before.

And joys too, a voice whispers in her mind. *Once. Before…* A tiny voice, barely worth minding.

Then suddenly–

"It's over," whispers Sara Sidorova. But she knows it isn't, not truly: something flew away from her in the moment between breaths. She saw it go, a white sheen, a flutter of... She was thinking of the captain... but what did he do? She remembers his face, his scented hair and gentlemanly way of speaking. But who was it that he took from her?

"Aye," says the Tiger. "The Lady's performance is over. You've seen enough, haven't you? You know what she did--what she chose to do."

And it seems he too is here with her again, him and his sisters, unmoved by the fury and the killing cold.

Sara Sidorova is in the cave, the limestone walls slick with damp: shades of pale gray, ecru, toadstool green, and soap. Or they should have been. Now they gleam as if someone has washed them in gore. A red evening. Through the iron gate the sun seeps light like a wound in the darkness. So close, too close. One of the sisters should be rising, should be opening the gate for the burning man who looked like...

"Was it really as you said?" Her voice is livid as she turns furiously from the gate. "Granddaughter, I saw you *bow* to that one. Why? You had the means, you could have..."

"Indeed," says Zorya Vechernyaya softly. Her robe glitters, the bodice flaming into titian, her mantle the palest mauve as is the fall of the long gown to her ankles. For a moment, Sara Sidorova feels ashamed of the filth that crusts the dead man's gymnasterka. But what has she to be ashamed for? She is *proud* of what she did, the vengeance she took.

"King Fiendish, you called him. You knew. You knew what the General was. What he must have done to your mother, him or one of his loyalists, it doesn't matter."

She raises her chin. "Yes."

"Yet you let him live."

A slower answer this time, twisted out of her. "Yes."

Now the Tiger is grinning a deep and vicious grin. His tail flicks like a lash in the space between them, his eyes gold and murderous as her own granddaughter's had been before she decided to bend her knee.

"What was that noise?" Sara Sidorova demands of him. "I could scarcely stand it!"

"The All-Dark," he whispers in a low and seductive voice. "The end."

"The end of what?"

"The end of everything, just as you desire. Come now, my love. Have done with these stories. Haven't you had enough? What have you really learned from this?"

"That my granddaughter is the worst kind of traitor," spits out Sara Sidorova. "The kind who betrays those she loves. And for what? A sniff of power? Is that why you did it?"

Despite her granddaughter's stiffness, the mulish set of her mouth, each accusation is a poison dart that Sara knows has hit its target. The Tiger's smile deepens, his purr of satisfaction thrumming in her bones. It sounds like charcoal hissing and sputtering.

"Set me free," he orders. "And I shall make it right for you."

Now he is beside her, his muzzle between her fingers, the great spear-heads of his ears twitching as he moves. Now her hand is at his throat. Sara Sidorova can feel the coolness of the metal chain, awaiting just the smallest movement.

"Aye, why not, Grandmother?" says Zorya Vechernyaya bitterly. A high hectic spark of color reddens her cheeks. "Mistress Sostary would have scorned me for my choice as well. And you? Well, you did worse, didn't you? And why?"

Sara's head jerks up. She had been ready, just a moment before, her thumb poised on the latch. But the question has confused her. She remembers so much of that night. The captain beside her, how all he had craved was a performance. Such a little thing for her to give. And afterward, she had found bodies on the road. She had done that, been responsible, *wanted* it. But as she sifts through her memories she finds them patchwork and fragmentary. As if something is missing, something important.

"What's happening to me?" she asks.

"Pay no mind to her," wheedles the Tiger, rubbing his cheek against her, nudging her hand back to the collar.

"That is what death does," says Zorya Vechernyaya, gray-haired and ashen-faced beneath the shadow of her elegant aristocrat's headdress. "It takes what you are, the good and the bad. But always the good first. The best parts of you. It is why there are so many angry spirits."

But still she doesn't understand. Worse yet, she despises how the queen is looking at her. She doesn't want her granddaughter's pity.

Sara Sidorova sinks to the floor beside the Tiger. Her fingers graze the bare rock, cold to the touch. Smooth as bone. And she feels a sudden pain in her shoulder and when she touches the bullet wound her fingers come away red with blood. There is a roaring in her ears, an echo.

Now Sara Sidorova can feel soil beneath her fingers, not the smooth-curled wax of the limestone. She is among the trees of the wildwood: the birch and the alder, laid down as she used to lie with Feliks when the summer sent them seeking shelter. Overhead she can hear the call of the rooks who, it seems, saw the bullet strike her. Black wings, mourning birds. They know how to find a good meal.

Soon she will be dead. She never found him—the one she had been searching for. And now it is too late, he is vanishing even from her mind. The best part of her.

"You watch and you watch," murmurs Sara Sidorova, "while down there we're born, we suffer and we die."

"It is the way of things," growls the Tiger.

"What does it matter then? Either I die in the wildwood or I don't. I raise my daughter, watch her leave me. I live alone, far from her, so far they must send me a letter to tell me of her death. And then, what? I meet her daughter, my granddaughter, and I send her out into the world as once I went out into the world where she suffers and suffers and suffers and falls in turn..."

"Why did you do it then?" asks Zorya Vechernyaya quietly.

"I don't know. I'm not that woman. She lived a life I never had."

"Of course," murmurs the other.

"Just as you have."

And at last the Evening Star bows her head: "Yes. Judge me how you will, I lived my life. Perhaps I suffered, perhaps I fell..."

Sara Sidorova's hand pulls away from the collar. She stares at her fingers as if she has never seen them before: callused and dirty, blood in the creases. A ring on her right hand, touching a vein that runs straight to her heart. A trammel of its own kind. She had wanted to wear red to her wedding. Her mother had refused her, saying it was bad luck.

"Why did you betray my daughter? Why didn't you end it?" she asks her granddaughter.

"You heard her command, brother," says the Evening Star then. "She is our guest. And she is not yet satisfied."

"Have it your way," the beast snarls but there is no surrender in his voice. Nor does Sara Sidorova expect it, not of this one, not of the Devourer. "It matters little. Your time is coming, sister, and I can wait a little longer."

Though his eyes flash with impatience, still that predator smile never leaves his glorious face. Sara Sidorova looks up sharply but now the sun is in her eyes and all she can see is red, red, red.

LADY PALE-THROAT

30

Red hips, red waist, red breasts.

"Wait until Cvetko is close," Mistress Sostary had told me. "None of this means anything if the General lives." I wanted to believe my death could set her free.

In the darkness of the cage, I held the image in my mind: her leaving the theatre at last, boarding a train headed north, just as she'd said she might. In the distance, the concrete towers and six-lane overpasses would yield to silver-green hills, dusk spilling over the cracked platter of the plains, the indigo shadow of mountains on the horizon. Thinking this made it easier to do what we'd planned.

See, the cage didn't scare me, Baba. I was exactly where I wanted to be, in the darkness with my leman, my soul spirit. Even then I wanted to do it. Hadn't my whole life been moving toward this moment? Mama's funeral, your bargain with me, fulfilled at last.

The air felt sweet and porous. I touched the bars and they melted. No one saw, not even Master Fortunato. His eyes were rapt and remote. He too must have felt the possibilities of this performance—but not as I did.

Then Leon snuffed the lights and it was simple as an equation. Amba was beside me. I let the spirit of death enter and I leapt. It was joyful, really. The men in their seats were afraid, just as we had planned it. The General too—but of what? Weren't they hatchet-men themselves? The stink of blood was on them, Cvetko most of all. He was dying already. The rot had set in like trench-foot. I was bringing him a gift, really, and he knew it.

Which is why he smiled when he saw me. He wished to be devoured, just as I'd once wished to be devoured. We were the same, he and I.

And I *could* have done it. Loaded up with death, close enough to kiss him, I had the wherewithal, I could have burst apart right then, flayed him to the bone. I *had* wanted to, no hesitation. The scent of lemon and apple blossoms hovered around me, stronger than the fear-stink. Mama felt so close I swore she must be watching me.

"Why didn't you?" asks Sara Sidorova. "Why didn't you do it?"

"Because he smiled."

"Oh, Granddaughter. A man can smile and still have murder in his heart."

"Yes, but in that smile I saw something I can't explain: a chance, perhaps, an opportunity."

When I appeared before them, his apparatchiks stared at me in wonder. I'd opened them up to a way of seeing beyond the scrimmage of competing powers. Their bodies trembled then went still. They were frightened, yes, but they were ravished too.

Obey, obey, obey... but was that all there really was? Could there be nothing in all the world but that?

Their eyes sparked a torch in my soul. I was raw and untested, my skills were crude, there was little enough of art in what I'd done, but it didn't matter. They were *watching* me, waiting to see what I would do next. Everything hung on it—my choice: Would he live? Would I die? What wondrous strange world would I deliver to them?

In that moment of possibility I saw them come alive to themselves.

"So you knelt," says Sara Sidorova.

"A woman can smile herself and wrap up her vengeful heart like a coal."

"Was that it then? You were biding your time?

But now she turns away, her eyes softly lit, distant but unafraid. "No."

Everything that followed was born from my decision.

Afterwards—after I'd taken my final bow, after the cameras had sliced my image for the daily papers—the apparatchiks were eager for my attention. And the General himself, like a proud papa. He kissed my cheeks, his body close. I still could have done it if I wished but I *enjoyed* holding his life in my hands. I felt his power flowing into me.

"There's a touch of cruelty in you," says Sara Sidorova.

"Don't I know it, Baba."

"This will be good for you," he said. "They'll remember how friendly we were."

It seemed he'd forgotten our previous encounter. I smiled a smile I'd learned from Mistress Sostary: perfectly poised, revealing nothing. "I thank you for all you do, General Cvetko."

Then a danger note flashed in his eye, a warning or perhaps a welcome of its own. "Miss Lubchen. What a distance you've traveled in so little time."

Until then I'd kept my gaze slavish but now it leapt to meet his. "Not far enough," I told him.

His laughter was sharp. "Good." He laid a third kiss on my cheek. "For luck," he said. The smell of attar of roses trailed after, lingering as he left me.

✳ ✳ ✳

I was tired of the performance then, the jackals watching, the apparatchiks, the Deeps. They all wanted to know, how had I done it? Had there truly been a tiger? How had I mastered him? There are always questions after but when a man like the General is happy, one is never questioned too closely.

So I smiled for them and demurred. One tried to touch me—"Lady," I heard him calling, half dazed by my glamour—but he was too slow. Another slapped his hand away.

It was Victor. "Sweet child," he said, voice quiet as a gas leak. "What a rare treat you've offered tonight. Your mistress had no idea what she had in you, did she? Where is she now, I wonder?"

"Even I can't answer that."

"Call me Uncle," he said.

"Of course." I offered him a childish curtsey and he barked out a laugh. I could smell the adrenaline rotting in his veins.

"We'll palaver in time," he told me. "But for now you must be exhausted. Say nothing to the others. I'll handle them." Then he raised my chin and pressed his finger to my lips, a gesture of silence that stole my breath.

His hand was warm on the back of my neck as he guided me to Mistress Sostary's dressing room, a place I'd once thought as remote as Siberia—not for the likes of me. But now I saw it for what it was:

utilitarian, square, clean, and with few ornaments to distract. The wallpaper wore the shape of violets and orphan roses. A large vanity claimed the farthest wall, white with a gold tracery, a three-part mirror above it.

He took it in with a glance. A few items had vanished, but all else was left untouched. "It seems this is yours now. You've earned it tonight. Tend to yourself and I'll see you have space."

Then he was gone, leaving only my reflection for company. I stared at myself in the mirror. The corset was gorgeous, seedling pearls, the delicate plumes of the ostrich feathers, but my own face was a stranger's. Paler than I remembered, gaunt and adult. Reflected there, it seemed I saw my mother's shrewd eyes and say-nothing smile.

"Mama?" I whispered. Did she hate me for what I'd done?

But I was alone. The corset was just a corset, just a weight of cloth and boning which held me too tight, thick with my raw, unperfumed scent. I came into the awareness of my body with a start, unable to breathe. I tried to fill my lungs but the corset pinched them small as stonefruit.

And then—

"Vesna!" called Master Fortunato from the hallway, rapping furiously at the door. "Vesna, are you in there?"

My eyes clenched in panic. He hadn't known I'd be performing tonight, couldn't have guessed what I'd been sent out to do, what I'd chosen not to do. But he could still spoil everything if I wasn't quick enough.

"Please don't..." The words were stillborn, clutched close by the corset. He burst in like a shot.

"You!" His silk shirt was still laden with lather from the

performance. "It was you out there! I thought... You were wonderful. I mean, I fired but the squibs... they never... but you *improvised* so beautifully—" He was babbling to me, just as he had babbled to my mistress. It wasn't the beast girl he was seeing but someone else, someone miraculous.

Yes, I could use this. I pressed my finger to his lips, stealing the Deep's gesture for myself, then turned in a pirouette to expose the clenching laces. "Quickly! I can't manage myself. If you don't do it now then I'll die!"

He was dumb with indecision. "I never—with Vesna, she never asked me—" In the mirror, I saw his gaze darting side to side. What had Estes said? *Whisper something in his ear and he'll spout it off like gospel the next day.* All that was needed was the right voice.

"Please! *I'm* asking you now."

Obey, obey, obey.

Then he was behind me, trying to work his way through the complicated knotting. Ignorant, fumbling, fingers shaking. I panted with the need to get free. At last the corset slipped away and sweet air leapt inside of me.

But there were the blast charges with it and I knew I mustn't let him see them. He had never concerned himself with the details of the swindles but even he might recognize the cartridges for what they were. But how to keep them hidden? I wore no shift beneath, just my naked skin.

He was staring at me in the mirror: the length of my neck, the squeezed flesh below, newly released. My mirabilist had given me that same look and so had Estes. Only now did I understand what it was—ravishment, indeed.

"Don't be frightened, Irenda. No one will touch you here."

He was attempting gallantry but my body felt hot and slick after the performance, hungry as I'd never known it to be. My breasts were small but I thought—yes, they would do. I remembered him pounding at my door. *I wish that the world were enfolded in love!*

A burst of headiness came over me. In Stary the doors were never shut. But here—*here!*—anything could happen here and afterward whatever it was would be whatever I said.

I thought of how my heart had boomed when my mirabilist slid his glance my way. One had left me, now there was another.

The room still swam with my mistress's perfume: rosehips and bergamot, cypress and salt. Her dressing gown hung from a hook. I could have taken it but I didn't. I'd been meant to die that night. I'd prepared myself for it—for so long in fact that I'd forgotten what it was to live without the promise of death. I turned toward him and let my fists fall to my waist.

I'd never done this before—but suddenly I wanted to own my body, to feel it responsive and awake to possibility, mine to do with as I wished.

Tentatively, for the second time, I touched my finger to Erastus's lips. My own lips followed after. I loosened my hair so it flowed over my shoulder, reaching the curve of my nipples, which stuck out like little thimbles. I brushed one, then the other, surprised at the aching, electric surge.

    "Is this what I planned for you? Ye angels and all things holy."

    Hunger still, despite her age. "Maybe it was no one's plan but my own."

I drew back and used my eyes to command him, my body, everything except my words. He staggered to his knees, revealing the pale crown of his disordered hair. I smoothed it with a touch. This is how it would be between us, I decided.

"I am Lady Pale-Throat now. Do you understand?" It felt right. So the others had called me and so I would learn how to be. If I was to stay, I would need my own signature.

"Y-yes."

"I want you to say it now. Say who I am."

"Lady Pale-Throat."

I knelt so we were eye to eye, my body exposed but for the black silk stockings. Though the floor was cold, the air between us was warm and yielding.

"Good. Now tell me your name, master magician. Your true name."

He hesitated.

"There should be trust between us. This isn't an ordinary company. Today we set something loose in the world and if we don't trust each other we'll both be lost." It was true. Apprehension shimmered in the air. The hunger in Victor's eyes, the sting of triumph, pieces shifting into place.

"Albin," he murmured. "Albin Egoshin. Vesna never asked me."

"I'm *not* Vesna Sostary. It's better that she's gone, don't you think? Better that I'm here instead?"

I slid his shirt buttons through the slips that held them, expecting the dense thicket of hair all men had in Stary, but beneath the silk his chest was smooth.

Albin he was called. White as snow, white as eggshell.

Ah well, I thought. *There is the body and the body*.

31

The next morning I awoke beside my magician. Pale skin, pale sheets, pale light drifting in.

Everything was soft, the mattress stuffed with feathers, the sheets made of silk, and my body glossy and supple, ensconced in comfort. There was an ache between my legs. I hadn't known it would hurt. Only when Erastus—Albin—saw the blood did he realize I was a novice.

"It's an honor," he'd announced, red-faced, his body still moving and moving and moving, above, beneath, inside. Now he slept and his eyeballs twitched under the delicate, blue-veined lids. It reminded me of Amba and his dreams, how some nights I'd lain with him just to feel the warmth of another's breath on my shoulder.

"I love you," I whispered. It was an experiment. Did I mean it? There was a kind of tenderness, yes, but so much had changed so quickly. Was I the same girl I had been a day ago? I tried to imagine the rhythm of that other one, Lady Pale-Throat, what it must be like to wake in her body, how she would move, hold herself.

I had memories of Sara Irenda Lubchen, the old shadow of her grief, but where was she?

Quietly, I rose and slipped into Mistress Sostary's dressing gown—silk again, cream with a pattern of scarlet flowers—and cinched it closed. It was a beautiful thing yet she'd left it behind. She'd left all of this: the company, the corset, the waiting eyes, and ready hands. Baba Yaga in her palisade of bones. Now she was gone.

Oh Grandmother, was that why you said I must burn Mama's things? Not for fear her spirit might return, but rather that someone else might slip on the mantle of her life and claim it. I didn't look for her spirit now. I'd made my choice.

Had Sara Irenda Lubchen wanted death? Well then. I would give it to her.

✳ ✳ ✳

Quietly I left my magician to return to my old quarters. The sidewalks were empty along Stradaniye Street, but for those few hawkers forced by need to test their luck underneath the scarlet foliage of the snowcloud trees. Birds feasted on the purplish berries, which dropped to the pavement, smearing it with color. Many windows were shuttered. It would take time to forget what had happened, what would no doubt happen again.

I was in a fragile state of transition as I entered the circus. I moved with a light foot, unwilling to encounter another member of the company, Teresa with her scornful, half-lidded stare, even Estes himself whom I still longed to speak to. He at least would be proud of me, I thought, and eager for my gossip.

"Is the mistress really gone then?" he'd ask me in wonderment. "And you? You're to take her place now?"

But not yet. My triumph seemed too fraught, too friable. Had one of them seen me, I would have been reduced to the beast girl they had known, with her chipped fingernails, chapped lips, the musk of tiger in her hair. I needed to erase all relics of her before that happened.

My old quarters felt shabby and squalid next to the magician's apartment. A tiny storeroom with a thin mattress on a trolley bed and Estes' makeshift lock on the door.

For so much of my life now I'd been at the mercy of others, guided by regulations, diktats, customs, propriety, wont. But where had it got me? When I'd seen Cvetko I'd finally understood you might control the current of attention, subject to nothing but your own will. He'd been afraid of his death but he had smiled. *My kneeling didn't need to mean real obedience*, I told myself. Sara Irenda Lubchen had been loyal but Lady Pale-Throat was beyond such considerations. She might choose to serve for a little while but she was a princess. She held her own power.

I gathered my things. I would burn them.

✳ ✳ ✳

Last of course were the munitions to care for.

I'd distracted Erastus well enough but there was only one place I thought safe enough for the gift Mistress Sostary had given me. In the training yard Amba was waiting for me, his face orange as a daylily, pricked toward me at my entrance. There was a look hanging about his lips, self-satisfied I might have called it. I looked upon my tiger now I saw again that other, secret tiger. I saw the spirit of Death—and he was mine, tamed by my hand.

"Oh, child."

"Do you see me too?" I wondered.

But the shadow tiger said nothing.

I blinked, and there stood my prince once more. Now he was rising up on his hindquarters, placing his paws against my shoulders as if the two of us were dancing partners. His delicate whiskers quivered with anticipation. He nuzzled my shoulder until I took his head in my hands and scratched that special place beneath his chin.

"Sweet thing, I've not forgotten you," I said to him.

Suddenly I knew I didn't love Erastus, not the way I loved this one.

He dropped down again, rubbed his cheek against my belly. He wanted meat but it wasn't meat I'd brought for him. Instead I went to the panel Estes had showed me.

If I were honest with myself I didn't think this was the only such secret that had been hidden in the establishment. The circus was just the sort of place that attracted lowlifes and rebels, strongmen and acrobats, sword-swallowers, knife enthusiasts, trick shooters: all manner of masters of a certain type of violence. We might have been sitting on enough gunpowder to set Hraná City aflame for all I knew.

Had Leon and my mistress been working alone? Who else might have known about what they planned? It was a problem I would need to sort through another day. Today was for transformation.

After the munitions were hidden, I sank down next to my tiger. Instantly he curled around me, the great bulk of his body protective, possessive, those lungs of his moving the air in and out like a bellows. I was glad then for my two tigers, the dark and the light, glad for what it was I had done.

"Na na na, who fears death? Not the Lady Pale-Throat, not me, not me," I sang softly while Amba blinked his handsome yellow eyes in agreement.

32

I didn't search out Estes that day, nor the next, nor any day in the week that followed. Neither did he come visit me in the training yard. I thought nothing of this, of course, or rather I allowed myself to think nothing of it. It was an old habit of mine. Besides, there was much that needed my attention.

First of all, it seemed, was the magician himself. "Surely you won't eat in the mess hall! Stay with me," he begged, "here." My resistances were easily overcome. The feeling I had entered some liminal stage still lingered with me. I wasn't keen to encounter the company, not until I understood who I was, what I had become. In any case, there had been many deliveries since our performance: crates of wine, platters of other delicacies prepared by Hraná City's finest chefs. Each bore a handwritten note from Victor praising our performance. With these came a reprieve as well. The General had rewarded the crew with a fortnight of wages. There would be no performances. Our time was to be spent in the service of pleasure.

Having lived with only what was standard-issue I was willing to be indulged. The wine was red and rich, filled with the taste of the sun. It sparkled in my mouth. I enjoyed the other dainties as well: delicate pastries filled with apple jam, rosehip tea, caviar, and smoked fish the red-yellow of coral. With every bite I told myself, *I can live without this. It isn't necessary.*

I loved the oysters best. We ate them with a special knife with a short, sharp blade for stabbing. Erastus taught me to sip the liquor pooled in the crinkled shells. It made me think of the ocean, which I had never seen. That vast expanse of water made up of shades I learned from the cloth dyer: lead-silver, slate, and beryl. There had been a lake in Stary where Papa had taken me to swim. It was always very cold. I sank if I stopped pumping my arms. But I'd heard that the ocean was full of salt and the salt could buoy you up. It seemed amazing. But that was how I felt in the magician's apartment: weightless, protected.

So I drank rare wines, ate fine foods, and afterward, always, there was the feather bed with its silk sheets. Perhaps I didn't love Erastus but I still took comfort in the mastery of his affection. Our pleasuremaking was a thing of wonder for me. I was ill-prepared but a quick study.

I tried to remember what the older girls had said about sex. Much of it seemed oddly mechanical: touch him here for so long, then here, then here, with this amount of pressure. Working it out from first principles proved the best method. I judged the pitch of his breathing and adjusted my rhythm to match. It wasn't so different from how Mistress Sostary performed. Nothing she did was without a measured sense of the return on investment.

My magician took instruction well. I confess I may have been a ruthless taskmaster but the experience was so new I was unwilling to give over any opportunity to test my control.

Thus the days passed lazily, each one stretching out before me, blearing even my own memory of what it was I had done. The stories became easier to tell myself: that Mistress Sostary was safely vanished, that the bright star of the General's affection would continue to shine.

Even Victor himself seemed to have shaken off the worst of

his thuggish disposition. With our status elevated it seemed he had installed himself as our majordomo. He had a secret way of coming and going from the theatre. I would be about my business, on my way to see to Amba, and I would find myself alone in a hallway, no footsteps, no hubbub of voices. Then he would surface.

"Sara Irenda Lubchen," he would murmur in that rasping voice of his. In the beginning, he always said my full name as if to remind me how completely he understood my history, where I had come from.

"Uncle," I'd greet him. Then if I was feeling bold I would drop that little curtsy, a signal that we understood each other. If he wished to be Uncle so he would be. After all, wasn't every little niece obedient? Didn't she know who her betters were?

"This is yours now," he said the first time he came to me, pressing the key to Mistress Sostary's office into my hand. It was a cramped cubbyhole with a ramshackle desk and about a million cigar-cured caddies. They were crammed with ledgers and hiring contracts, bank statements, cancelled checks. Much of it was a mystery to me but he seemed to expect this and never took it upon himself to show me the inner workings, the obscure financial systems that governed our expenses and profits. Instead, I got used to keeping the samovar on the boil so I could pour his tea straight away. He'd told me he was civilized. "A drink in welcome is what civilized people expect when they discuss business." He drank his thick and black, quadruple strength as they do in prison.

The tea was stronger than I liked but it reminded me of home. Papa had drunk tea like this in the evenings, blowing out pipe smoke and philosophy in equal measure as Mama read her books of poetry. It was his professorial drawl I adopted now, cupping the blue-veined china in my hand and blowing a hurricane from the steam.

"You're learning quickly," he told me, plucking a sugar cube from the bowl. "Your mistress wasn't always so sweet-tempered in our collaborations. Have you enjoyed the provisions? Master Fortunato tells me how partial you are to oysters."

"They're very fine." A touch of red bloomed on my cheeks. I hadn't known those two were on equally friendly terms.

"Such things are appropriate to your new stature, Miss Lubchen. You'll come to expect them in time. When you're tired of the oysters, only say the word and we'll find another delicacy to tempt you."

"I'm certain that won't be necessary. I'm content, believe me."

"Content," he repeated, the word taking on a dangerous edge. "Be careful of contentment, my wonder-child. It can blunt ambition and such delights have a cost, understand? Now that the company has had time to… adjust, the General is eager to see the show resumed. Forge iron while it's hot, as they say, while the heat makes it willing to bend. And Mistress Sostary has left us lacking a leading lady."

His face didn't change as he said this. No indeed, I swore he didn't move at all, except for a raised eyebrow to tell me his teacup was empty and now he expected me to pour.

"Tell me," he continued after I'd finished. "Are you willing, Miss Lubchen? Will you do what your country requires?"

Follow, follow, follow…

I lowered my gaze. "Of course, Uncle."

"Good," said the Deep, covering my hand in his. A fat chunk of agate balanced below his knuckle, colored in hues of orange like raw tripe. "But I wonder, Niece, might you indulge in an old tradition?" He pressed the ring toward me and I knew he meant for me to kiss it. "No one does it anymore but when I saw you I reckoned, 'Here's one born of the old world. Here's one who might understand.'"

Without hesitating, I leaned forward and brushed my lips against it. A thick purple vein pulsed in his wrist and suddenly there was an answering pulse inside me, hot and liquid and stronger than anything I had felt with Erastus. The Deep had marked me once but now I was marking myself.

"What would you ask of me, Uncle?"

"Only that you're loyal. And you *are* loyal, aren't you, Miss Lubchen?"

"Yes."

He permitted himself a smile then and I allowed myself to match it. "I believe it's time our spectacle refined itself further. The people of Strana are waiting—it's time for you to dazzle them."

33

I had told the Deep I was loyal—and I was, just as I had promised. I knew what loyalty meant. You see, once I had known a girl named Alya and still sometimes I dreamt about her dark freckles, her shock of blue-black hair. I was only seven when she disappeared.

Her parents were the problem. We'd been warned in school against women like her mother who lacked mettle—what Miss Boban called a certain public-spiritedness. Alya's mother had a brother and something had happened to him. He'd been killed or taken or denounced or else he'd died in military service under dubious circumstances. Whatever it was had shaken something loose in her. She wept openly and often kept to the shadows on parade days though I never heard her speak an ill word against the General. But this sort of silence was normal. Indeed, Alya never spoke of her mother's affliction except to say she was sick but eventually she'd be well again and would I like a hot drink now or to play with her dolls?

Even then I knew what these questions were: mechanisms for shifting the conversation to safer ground. Only once did Alya ever speak honestly to me about it. We were upstairs in her bedroom. It was early winter. New snow blanketing the ground, frost etching flowers in the windowpane. I remember she'd taken to brushing my hair. She loved how easily the brush passed through it. There she was, tugging the brush along, saying nothing at all, until she suddenly leaned forward: "I'm afraid Mama will kill herself soon."

I was appalled to hear her speak so bluntly. Seconds later I was shushing her, hugging her to me but pressing my finger against her lips as well, telling her to think of other things.

The next day Alya and her family were gone. What was worse was that after it happened, no one would acknowledge the mystery. "Keep quiet," Mama told me whenever I mentioned her. "It never happened. She never lived here."

While I was used to Mama's cagey nature, in private my papa was often more open. He looked at everything slantwise, which was why Mama loved him so much. This made him bad at keeping secrets. But even he wouldn't budge. "I'll scream if you don't tell me where she is," I told him one night as he rubbed peppermint lotion into his back.

"Scream all you like, little mouse. How many times have I told you the walls are thick in Stary? No one will hear. She's gone away, don't you understand?"

"She wouldn't, she wouldn't," I wailed.

He slapped me hard across the cheek. "Her parents have taken her to the border."

I stared in shock, then with a cry I went to him and buried my face in the nook of his shoulder. Both of us were frightened by how quickly that violence appeared. First nothing, then *pchut*—it was there, and my cheek smelled of the balm he'd been using. Now he stroked my hair gently, murmuring a song he made up on the spot. "Na na na, little mouse. I won't hurt you, don't you fear your funny old papa. What a little man he is!" That was my father. Mama said when I was hidden inside her, he'd get on his knees and place his hands against her flesh to search for me. He didn't want us to be strangers when I arrived.

Soon after Alya's name was scrubbed from school attendance. So. I learned from my parents how to keep quiet, how to hold my joy within my own body, how to marshal my features into the same bland expressions as my girlfriends.

I learned what loyalty meant.

✢ ✢ ✢

Estes was gone.

As the theatre's operations were restored, the crew began to return, many of them with awful hangovers, their pockets empty but their mouths full with tall tales of the drinking they'd done. My friend wasn't among them.

Now there were new faces as well: cold-eyed men whom even Leon had trouble mustering. Not that we spoke of it. The few times I tried to seek him out I found him sullen as a stone. "Yes, Lady" and "No, Lady" and "So Victor has said"—never more, never less, exactly proper: unimpeachable, unassailable, unknowable.

Teresa was no better when I asked her where Estes had taken himself. Had he gone back home? When had she last seen him?

"Eh? Who?" she asked with a frown.

But she wore a new wariness in her expression. *Cheapnik bitch*, she had called me, *a whey-faced little* suka. Back then I'd been one of the company and now I was the Lady. She was measuring me up. There was a chance I would stumble and we both knew it. Perhaps she hoped I'd drop out of view myself in time. Hadn't she let them go to the Strelka that night? Let them go and watched from the roof?

If anyone asks, tell them I'm loyal.

Perhaps she had known even then what would happen. But Victor hadn't asked, not about her—and I'd kissed his ring. So now I did what I had learned to do. I smoothed my expression and blanched my voice and tried to forget I had ever had a friend named Estes at all.

34

There was more to being a leading lady, I would learn over the coming weeks, than a talent for mimicry. While I'd shown I had certain true-steering instincts I knew little enough about the intricacies of my craft: how to hit my marks, how to find the light, how to throw my voice to the rafters. It wasn't easy. My performance before the General had been a triumph, but not one I could reproduce reliably, night after night, as I would need to.

When the Deep came to understand how green I truly was, it left him in a fury.

"D'you know how you're holding yourself?" he demanded as he watched my rehearsal alone in the theatre. "What? Are you some vestal petticoat? Damn it all, I want you stately. I want balance and breeding. Time is short and I need a dazzler out there. What are you playing at? You're not some country milkmaid."

I tried using what I'd learned from Erastus, making my eyes wide with a touch of helplessness, my lips slightly parted. "I'm only doing what you told me, Uncle," I simpered.

A moment later he was out of his seat and up on the stage. He moved so fast I had barely a second to register what was happening before he grabbed my arm and pulled me so close I could feel the lariat strength of his muscles.

"Don't you try to play me," he hissed.

Then I was thinking of what Mistress Sostary had told me, about the girl who dreamed of fire. Every night she dreamed of fire…

But he only pushed harder against the bone with a laugh, a strange ha-*ha* sound that reminded me of a hyena or some other small but deadly scavenger.

"That's better, but it isn't enough. Who'd want to watch a scrap of provincial ass prancing about? You think that's what they want? I see you, Miss Lubchen. I see you now and I saw you then. Maybe all those little dainties have made you go soft. Where's that damn-bitch I saw bowing before the General? She's the one they want to see out there, a she-beast who knows how to kneel."

"Oh, I *want* you to see me, Uncle." I knew there was a high hectic spark of color in my cheeks. Then it was me laughing back, mimicking his ha-*ha*, showing him I knew well enough what I was and that he couldn't fool me into thinking otherwise.

"Like a pussycat ready to scratch my eyes out. Is that what you think they want? What *I* want? That's what Mistress Sostary tried with me…" With those words, his face went gray with the only thing I'd seen that seemed close to pleasure. "I've got a line of girls with their claws primed. *Other* girls, you know, dozens of girls more darling and dear than you. You're nothing to me. I see you and I say, Sara Irenda Lubchen, you are *nothing*."

He was trying to cow me but now the Lady was sweeping in and my body was cold and unfeeling as ice. Who was he to tell me what I was? I'd held Cvetko's life in my hands. I'd tamed Death that night, so how could he truly hurt me?

"Better," he whispered, breath rank. "Better, child…"

Then suddenly he was at it again, bending me over, trying to make me submit. His hands were hot except for the band of his agate ring, which was cool as iron. I kissed the ground while he held me like

I wasn't anything. Everything before had been a threat, the promise of pain or just the whiff of it but now my tendons were screaming. It was the first time I felt truly forced.

"Push me further and this arm will break." My voice faltered but that was just my body. It wasn't me.

"Let it break then."

"What good will that do you?"

"No good except the learning," said he.

So down I went, an inch further until my cheek met the floor-boards. A humming in my joint told me any second now. Would I give? My body would—soon. It filled me with relief to know there was a breaking point and my body would find it before my spirit.

I could relent. I could bow. I could say I was loyal—but it would just be another ploy between us. I wouldn't change my mind. I'd only learned it was better not to have a broken arm. He kept me trembling, knowing he could push, me knowing he was choosing not to.

Then he hauled me upright and the shock of the release stung my eyes with tears.

"You done learning then, Miss Lubchen?"

When I nodded, he let go of my arm.

"Do it again. Like I told you. Don't make me wait."

I turned to continue, fighting back tears, but my joint was in agony and it made me angry.

"You don't know what they want," I told him.

"What's that now?" He was cracking his knuckles, mean-faced, grinning.

But I was the Lady Pale-Throat so who was he to me?

"Poise and polish, aye, that you can teach, but where's the substance? Where's the lure? I want them more than cuntstruck out there. That'll dazzle them for a moment but I want more than that. When I tell them how the world is, I want them to know it for truth. I want to write it in their bones, hear me? So deep if you crack them open you'll find my name written inside."

He caught me in his vicious gaze. "You reckon you know how to do that, wonder-child? Show me then. Find a new spectacular, something that will charm them the way you're talking. But make it fast. No more delays."

"Oh, I will, Uncle. I will."

And I gritted my teeth, smiling like a killer. He smiled back, ready to meet me bruise for bruise, violence for violence.

✴ ✴ ✴

That night he came to my dressing room. I was alone as I always was when he found me. As if he had the place mapped out, as if he'd tracked my comings and goings. Which meant he knew me well. Knew my magician too, when he was occupied.

I expected another lesson, was ready for it. "What will you teach me now, Uncle?"

This time he didn't speak. There was a heavy scent on him, bitter and green like pinesap. He had throttling hands and when he moved, he moved quickly.

I was standing by the mirror and I saw him there first, the three of him coming toward me, feral as a wolf pack. I half-turned and he caught me round the waist. His fingers measured the jut of my hips. They spun me toward him.

There was a woolen rug covering the floor, a shapeless thing kept on past its prime. Nothing in this room was supposed to be beautiful but the woman in it. He lay me down. I let him. I welcomed him, even, thinking maybe his hotness was a victory. It seemed I'd left him cuntstruck after all.

"What you got—"

I didn't give him the sentence before I was at him with certain maneuvers, swift then slow, using what I'd learned from my magician until his voice grew hectic. Soon he was trembling.

Then so was I.

"Tight as a noose," he said, coming in first with his fingers, then with the rest.

Heat spread from my crook, rolling on through until my wrists seemed to burn. Then my own body was bucking. He pressed his palm against my mouth, his skin a saltlick. His left hand touched my throat, then came up under as we rolled, him capsized, me astride now. Then it was my hand on his throat, feeling the thick walnut-bulge of his Adam's apple. His face went the color of gunpowder. The thing moved between my fingers, rocketed up and down. A quick pulse beat against my mound of Venus.

"What you gonna do?" he gasped.

"I'm gonna show you what I am," I told him, matching his drawl, taking everything in his voice and flinging it back at him. "Here and out there too."

He pushed me off him, making his own noise—that hyena laugh. I looked into his eyes, which seemed a slick wet red in the light. But I had seen it truly. Something in him was afraid of something in me and I wondered if he had ever looked at Mistress Sostary like that.

35

onna show you, I'd said—but it was no easy thing. The preview crowds the Deep admitted were capricious as titmice and even the General's approval wasn't enough to bind them truly. Every night on the stage felt like a foray in a never-ending campaign to first claim new ground, then hold it. I wanted neither their pity nor their purchased support. What I wanted was to ravish them.

Yes, I wanted their love.

And sometimes I swear I had it. I could see their expressions seize with wonder. The fear they all carried—every last one of them—would vanish behind their eyes. But when I missed a cue or failed to find my light then the moment would rupture and the blankness I knew so well from Stary would creep in. *Look but see nothing, hear but forget.*

It was difficult work and each misstep left me exhausted and exposed. All this was made worse by the lingering suspicion I'd had when I'd first seen my magician: that it wasn't his story, that the fit was awry. The show was Vesna Sostary's through and through and though I could put some of her damn-bitch in my expression, I couldn't hold it the way she could.

If I was to master the rabble then I'd need to find a way to tell my own story.

Uncle and I met often in the weeks after, him hunting me or maybe me hunting him, throwing him to the floor, stripping him bare and moving my body until I felt him breaking up, going under. He never left a mark—he knew he couldn't—but I had no such restrictions. I scratched and I used my teeth. Some nights I slept with fingers dipped in gore.

As time went on I grew colder with Erastus. He was my moonchild but now I had something else: a monster. A monster on a leash, so I thought. Still the magician kept trying to win me back. Shyly he read to me from the book of poems he kept with him:

> *You think it strange that I could love the darkness.*
> *But I have moved beyond these things—light, love.*
> *I have no need of you.*

He was trying to get me to fall in love with him. Just as I wanted their love so it seemed he wanted mine: my heart, my soul, that spirit of song that lived inside of me. But whenever he turned to the book all I could think of were my mother's poems, how I'd let them burn when I released her spirit.

She had left me and now I was alone. I had only these two: the magician and the monster, and in neither was there any care nor comfort. So I would feign interest as best I could, rubbing my big toes together for distraction. My new shoes had made blisters the size of chamomile blossoms on my joints.

On and on Erastus would read, his sad eyes begging me to listen. If at first I'd privately scorned him then as his voice took on a surprising richness, I began to pay attention. Some of what he said had power.

> *Then your face brilliant with sunlight*
> *as you speak my name.*
> *I had forgotten.*

"Tell me about that one," I said one night as he ran the filigreed hairbrush he bought for my birthday through my tresses. My hair was growing quickly, losing the blunt shape Mistress Sostary had given it. The Deep had told me to let it grow, that it made me look younger than I was.

"It's the story of the Sun-King and the princess of the north. You never heard it?"

It reminded me so much of you on the morning we first met. Trivia, trivia, trivia, you'd snapped. But I buried my sentiment. I couldn't allow myself any weakness.

"I know all the battles General Cvetko ever fought. I know who died at Cheyory Bridge, and why. I know the fourteen shades of blue that wool can hold. I can run a mile faster than most. I can hold my breath for over a minute."

I'd said as much to you, hadn't I?

"But you don't know poetry."

"No." A hot flush of shame at this, as if I were a traitor. I knew only the snatches my mother had read aloud. But those were seldom by the poets of Strana whom I'd once heard her call too compromised in their sentiments.

"Not even when it holds your own name?"

"What do you mean?"

"Lady Pale-Throat," he told me. "It's one of the old stories. Here. Let me tell it to you."

Well. Men like him were always quick to remedy ignorance.

"This is Oblonsky's reworking. There are variations, of course but—never mind. You know how it begins—with a girl, a princess of the north named Lady Pale-Throat. The Sun-King fell in love with her and watched her through her window. He slid into her dreams. He wanted her love but he was hot as Heaven and that made her afraid. So she fled as far as she could on this earth but it still wasn't enough."

It was a story I knew, of course—one of those stories of men loving women too much and not taking the hint—but the words he had been saying seemed different to me. She'd spoken of forgetting, of being without need. It reminded me of my mother's poem...

> *I shall not see the shadows,*
> *I shall not feel the rain...*

"What did she do?" I asked.

"This part you must know. She hid herself in the house of an old woman, a witch, who promised her if she served for a year she would find remedy for her distress. But while Lady Pale-Throat served, the hag had her own plans. At the end of the year she took out her carving knife. 'Only in death will you find an escape,' that one said as she hacked the young princess into pieces. And so she sojourned to the kingdom of the dead."

A faint chill ran down my spine. An idea was coming to me. Kindling and sparks. "Did he find her?"

"Of course he did. And see—" his face was excited "—this is where Oblonsky is best. No one else has such subtlety. He describes how the Sun-King worshipped her. And you know—love is like that, it can drive a man mad."

"Mad?"

"With *desire*."

"Is that how it works then? For a man in love?" I was toying with him now. I knew what Erastus Fortunato was like in love.

His fingers were warm and feverish as he stroked my arm. "The

233

Sun-King traveled to the underworld and won back his princess. I'd like to think she was grateful."

But what he was saying didn't make sense. "Why is she so melancholy then? In the poem?"

"Oh." His eyebrows screwed up. "Well. *I* think she was happy. She had forgotten who she was but his touch helped her remember. Besides, what woman would want to live among the dead?"

"There's no pain in the kingdom of the dead."

"But there could be love," he said hopefully.

No, I had meant to tell him—not love, but freedom. But by then it was clear the poetry lesson was over. He was putting the book aside and moving toward me, nostrils flaring as he started in. Pleasing him was just another kind of trick, watching his pupils shrink in concentration, delaying and delaying and delaying. When I pushed my weight down upon him and felt the give of his body, the sound he made was like a string plucked, a timpani.

"Like this?" I asked him, thinking of Victor pressing his ring to my lips, thinking of what I might press to Erastus's instead.

"Oh, Lady," he moaned. "Lady, lady, lady…"

I bucked against him until he took my nipples between his teeth. He could only last so long before he craved release but if I touched him just right I had learned how to find a pathway to surprise, pushing want toward need until need became something else: immolation.

The girl who dreamed of fire…

Maybe all stories were one story in the end. The princess in the cage, sharpening her claws. The princess on the stairs to the Kingdom of Death. I didn't resist, though it wasn't love the poem made me think of at all.

36

"This will be our spectacular," I told my magician soon after, "the story of Lady Pale-Throat and her pursuit through the underworld."

We were in the theatre workshop, which over the weeks had been populated with small-scale painted backdrops, faux-marble cathedrals, a forest of trees made of nothing but tissue paper as I sought to find a new direction for the show. One wall had been covered with posters featuring my own silhouette, kneeling before the General. ALL HONOUR TO YOU THIS DAY! proclaimed its florid, hand-scripted writing.

"It's a fairy tale, princess," Erastus told me nervously. His pet name. He'd taken to calling me that since our little school lesson. "A story that mothers tell their children. Shouldn't we select something more modern?"

Of course he had his own ideas and had been pressing them on me for days. They went like this:

"Borrow a gentleman's firearm in good working order and discharge it into his mistress's breast; when the powder smoke dissipates, she must give him the most passionate kiss."

"Take a person of quality's daughter, well-dressed with fine shoes, and all suitable accompaniments; slice her head from her body with one swift stroke. From her neck should pour forth all sorts of dainties."

"Select a lady from amongst the gallery seats and, by means of a rope tightened fiercely about her neck, raise her heavenward. Once aloft, invite her to sing the General's praises."

Such illusions were performed by our rival companies, Madam Nikolayevna and her lot, many of which they'd pilfered from our own repertoire. I had seen several of her productions by this point and found the switches and swindles elegantly executed but nothing that truly moved me. They were lies, not stories, and at the end of the performance they made me feel foolish for the belief I'd ever placed in them.

"It needs to be a tragedy. Like your poet Oblonsky."

When Erastus had read to me I had felt something within his words, a pattern I could make my own.

"Why a tragedy?" he asked. "A man likes to laugh."

His sketches were intended as drolleries. A man likes to laugh, a man likes to fuck. What I wanted had to go deeper than that. I had seen it was possible in the way my mirabilist had sparked the secret combustible matter of dreams.

A story had to be like a treasonist. It had to be something you already trusted. But how to explain that to my magician? He was as far from a turncoat as I could imagine. I saw the way he was with the Deep: cringing and deferential, eager for praise. When he went to Madam Nikolayevna's performances he chattered like a magpie, crying out for more. I didn't understand him.

"How did you come to the theatre, Albin?"

He had been pacing until now, tinkering with the little models I'd had Otto create for me. But now he went still and pale. "Those were bad days, princess. Why worry about yesterday's rain?"

Love grows tired, history vanishes, and nothing needs to linger past its day. So I'd always been taught. But a story needed to start somewhere, to come from something if it were to have any power at all...

"Please. I want to know. Will you tell me?"

Confusion passed like a cloud across his features. "I was an accountant."

"Here in the city?" I coaxed him.

"Yes," he said softly, staring at a miniature castle with hinging parts and a cantilevered balcony. It was as if he was discovering the words anew. "The city. It was different when I first started, just after the armistice was declared. There were many new firms then. Money was flowing into Strana and it passed through my hand... it seemed to melt without a trace."

I drew in close, watching how his eyes went slack when he took in my perfume: cypress and salt, the same scent my mistress had worn.

"Some days it seems like I dreamt it," he told me. "There were government raids but we all knew the drill. Shred the books and show them the props. Keep a kit full of cash and a clean shirt in case you had to run. I had a friend named Tisha who joined at the same time as me. 'This peace is just a lie, brother,' he used to tell me as we shammed up receipts and balanced the slantways ledgers. 'The fighting never stopped. All the hoodniks have done is rebranded.'"

In Stary they had talked about the armistice, of course, but no one had believed it. The factories kept spitting out munitions and the old war songs still sounded in the city square. Perhaps we'd never wanted peace. In war you always know who you are, the old-timers used to say.

"What happened?" I asked.

"You wouldn't understand, princess—even I barely understand

237

it myself. There was something frightening about the firm. The scale of the excess, the sheer level of frenzy. Even after the armistice came crashing down and everything started changing. Especially then. Everyone was into something. Tisha wore samite and sang opera on the weekends. My supervisor, a beady little man named Vojislav Pap—he slipped on crinolines so he could pose at the Academy of Fine Arts. There were week-long bacchanals. And me…" He waggled his long, delicate fingers theatrically. "I played for pennies mostly, trying out my tricks at the summer cafes and rooftop terraces. All that play-acting kept us sane. It meant we never took the world we lived in for real." He drew in a ragged breath. "But I was *good* at my job. I did what I was told. But then Tisha—well, he taught me how to skim a little from the top. 'It's nothing, brother,' he kept telling me. 'The money's not even real. It never was.' And he was right. But then—he wasn't thinking about the men who owned that money…"

The rest of the story I could imagine well enough. *Someone marked you for a reason*, Mistress Sostary had said to him and she had been right. He'd gone silent now and his look was desperate. I knew that gnawing feeling. He was wondering if perhaps he had said too much. I didn't have to ask what happened to Tisha.

He was an innocent, an elf-child. *Whisper something in his ear and he'll spout it like gospel.* But how different was he really than any of the others in Hraná City? How different from me? I'd written my compositions and dreamed of a glorious death, I had knelt at the General's feet when I could have chosen otherwise.

I felt a sudden surge of tenderness for him, turning his face so I might kiss him. A taming kiss, a gentling kiss, perhaps, but in that moment I swear I would have spun a cocoon of silk around him, coddled him as he desired to be coddled—safe as a songbird.

It wasn't love. It would never be love.

Once there had been a dream inside him, a kindling spirit, if only I could find a way to light it. Here was a man who quoted poetry while the noose hung around his neck. Mistress Sostary had been a cynic—but he was a believer. There was something noble in that.

He turned to kiss me back but by then I was moving past him. I plucked from a stand of arranged props a golden crown adorned with a shock of blue-green peacock feathers. "Those days are behind you, Master Fortunato. Whatever you were, we can make something of this together. You and I, the Sun-King and the princess from the north."

"Something they know already," he murmured.

"But bigger than they've ever dreamed it. Like nothing they've seen before."

"A love story."

"A tragedy," I whispered, gaze caught on the miniature sets Otto designed for me. One was an underground grotto, with green-gray stalactites that hung like dripping wax. An underworld. The shape of the thing was becoming clearer in my mind.

"Sometimes good can come from tragedy," he said hopefully, the skewed paste gems sparkling above his brow.

"That is what we must show them," I answered.

37

There are passages of time that feel more like a story. What has no hands, no feet, but passes by?

Love. A shadow in springtime. A song your lover sings.

As the sun blanched the city and died, the early frost starbursted upon the windowpane. The summertide campaigns had been successful though we had been warned to settle in for a difficult autumn. Supply shortages, incursions along the border in retaliation. The Minister for Public Works resigned in disgrace and was discovered to have hanged himself in his dacha. In the far east a former economics professor declared himself a messiah only to have his congregation tear him to pieces in a frenzy. A touch of that same madness could be felt on the streets of Hraná City where a celebratory mood had swept aside the memory of seizures and suicides, the heavy fall of military boots in the streets.

"Needs must," Victor would tell me, with that shark grin of his. "It will be soon. Before the snows come."

"But *when*?" I asked him.

He never gave me a straight answer, only cupped my chin until I felt the marbling of bruises beneath his fingertips. "Your problem, Miss Lubchen, is you worry for the future," he'd tell me. "But this is a country whose future is scrawled in the past. You think you're hurtling into the unknown but really you're hurtling into history. Superstition and paganism, isn't that what you're after? Let me worry about when and you worry about your own readiness."

And so I did. Day by day, the shape of my spectacular was growing clearer in my mind. Pieces came to life in my dreams, kaleidoscopic, all confetti and cut glass. It would be a carnival of searching, the princess seeking an escape, taking shelter with the witch woman who promises her the only way out is through death. Then her body hatcheted apart to feed the crone's hunger. What then? What next? A journey through the underworld, with sprites and spirits, monsters and demons.

As the vision swelled in my head from seedling to thicket, I tried my best to give it substance. A horde of workers were made available to me. Carpenters, joiners, hoisters, fitters, framers, hangers, cabinetmakers, and all those legions of the workshop, laboring under the direction of Leon himself. I was given into Renata's care, her bloodless leather fingers pinning me into bright fabrics, flashing with sequins and faux-pearls, testing the swish of this and that drape of that.

Our spectacular took on the proportions and logistical necessities of an army. The Deep found me knife-throwers, dancers, and musicians. There were women who could hurl themselves through the air like birds of paradise, somersaulting fifty feet above the bare boards. A parade of strongmen: hulking, square-jawed fellows. Sword-swallowers and fire-eaters. A child who contorted her limbs into a sailor's knot. Some came from the streets, some he stole away from Madam Nikolayevna and her menagerie.

I wondered if I might see my mirabilist but neither he nor any other escapist or maybe-magus appeared. I never dared ask Uncle about him. It would be a sign of wanting he could use against me. In truth I loved my ignorance. It was easier, I was learning, if you didn't know for certain who the dead were.

"But we never stop owing the dead, do we?" Sara Sidorova asks.

"No," answers her granddaughter, "we don't. Some things take time to understand."

I focused upon what was before me: the procession of silver-lit figures. Sheer excess, Master Fortunato had said, and here all my excesses were accommodated. Thus my spectacular became a psycho-drama, encompassing every snare and stratagem I could devise. Men with the faces of animals. Women melting into angels and sirens. We would have song and pageantry, the heavens plastered on the circus's curving dome like wallpaper.

Amid the hustle of rehearsals, there were hushes and hiatuses. I slid from the heights of performing to troughs of reflection and worry. Of course there were moments when I thought of you, Baba. How could I not? I wondered if you felt the same scissoring of self. If you too had been galvanized by the spotlight. And then after—did your certainty vanish?

"You never came to me to ask?" says Sara Sidorova.

I was angry. What kind of grandmother gives her only blood away? To me you were Baba Yaga, the witch in her castle, sending Lady Pale-Throat to her death. You were a treasonist, you'd betrayed your own blood. I had seen the glint in your eye but I hadn't known what it meant, not truly.

Instead I remembered the corset and what it had said to me about

242

the self: how one could delight in excess, in beauty, a certain wildness. I wanted my patrons to know beauty. To understand how beauty was the life of the soul. But my heroine would be beyond it, a frozen thing, an iceberg queen, unmoved, uninvolved, incapable of pain, incapable of love. That was what made her free.

"What your cold-fish princess needs," Uncle told me, "is a little heat. A little sexing up." He had come to me in my dressing room as he often did in those days, to discuss the particulars of my plans. The door was locked. Had I locked it or had he? I couldn't remember. There was no bed here but that hardly mattered.

"Give me the spectacular," I told him, knowing he took his pleasure in my resistance as much as my pliancy, "and I'll give you their hearts."

He laughed his hyena laugh.

"She's a stuck-up bitch, she is—Lady Pale-Throat. Maybe you call yourself that but you're still just the beast girl at heart, aren't you? And stuck-up as you are, I know how to unstick you." I squirmed away but by then he had me laid flat against the floor. One hand clamping my shoulder and the other working at me. "Don't tell me you don't enjoy this. I know your swelter. Like an ever-loving combustion engine."

Light sparked in my vision, good and bad, but he held me and he held me through it all until my throat was hoarse.

"The spectacular." I was struggling not to breathe in his canker scent. "Let me have it. I'll whisper a word in their ear…"

"And what word is that?" He leaned in close.

"Whatever word you want, Uncle."

It was all that mattered to me now.

"Good," he told me. "Soon I'll whisper it in your own ear, Miss Lubchen."

After he was gone, my body pulsed like a drum. I felt slow and sluggish. The mirror gawked at me: skin pinked with fever and a single thought burning in my mind. Who am I? Who am I? Had I really chosen this? So what if there was another voice inside me who said, "Hold fast now. Enough." It was me who had shut the door. Now I remembered turning the lock, hearing the tumblers fall.

But then the question blanched and the frost set in. Whoever I was, I didn't want to be the girl from Stary anymore. In the mirror I watched my limbs compose themselves. I studied their resting angles. How would I hold my head when the Sun-King kissed me? Would it be like this? Or like *this*?

I measured myself against the specter in my mind. Her—the dead princess, cut down by the witch's knife, fled into the underworld to escape his steaming touch. But I knew he would be after me, always after me, always dogging my step, hunting my shadow until even that last moment of release.

Mistress Sostary had told me as much, hadn't she?

I moved my head and saw the plane of my cheekbone now, the bolt of my shivering lips. When he came, he would find me on my death bed, inert as all fable maidens are. Encased or entombed. Tangled in constriction. Beyond his reach at last, just as the crone had promised.

I saw myself rising into the air. Imagined wires holding me, invisible to the crowd. Glimpsed a staircase from the underworld and me upon it.

I lost myself in the tableau. My spirit at its highest point, gazing outward with hawk's sharpness, stripped down, soul-clothed in the regalia of the dead. It would be a pantomime of sorts, with body doubles. I held onto the image. Played it again and again until I could hold it perfectly inside myself. The finale I needed—the princess was frozen, yes, but soon enough she would burn. After all, she was the girl who dreamed of fire. Every night she dreamed of fire…

She would choose differently than I had. It was a story, wasn't it? And in a story a girl could do the impossible. A woman could turn into a tiger, she could escape the trammel that held her.

But when I opened my eyes, I saw my own reflection thrown back at me, my hair tangled, a dirty thumbprint on the shoulder he'd pressed to the floor. And beyond that a third Irenda, a fourth, a fifth: the printed silhouettes of that other girl who had promised to make a torch of her body but had kneeled when the moment came at last.

✦ ✦ ✦

He chose Teresa to play the role of my double even though her hair was lighter than mine, threaded with gold. I was quick to point this out.

"We can darken it." Victor's voice had a new quality: self-satisfaction mingled with a measure of control. I understood then that he believed what I had told him. Though he might call me the beast girl in private, he knew on the stage I had power.

I would win over the people, just as I had won over the General.

"Isn't she too old?" From our vantage in the balcony, we watched her descending. She had an aristocratic delicacy, not more beautiful than me, striking, perhaps—but I wouldn't have said more beautiful. Over-honed, I thought. She had ghost-wrinkles.

"We'll have her as the crone first. But don't you worry, Miss Lubchen. In a few years you'll catch up and—well. At your age you shouldn't bother with professional jealousies."

His eyes fixed on my simulacrum but I could tell it was my

response he was measuring. Would I fight him? He wanted me to. It would be an excuse for retaliation.

"She'll pass with distance but a veil would help."

"Too priggish. You don't want a prioress up there."

"Her eyes are blue." I could see their pelagic sheen from the gallery.

Victor cracked his knuckles and laughed. "Dress her right and no one will be looking at her eyes."

They worked through the tableau's choreography and the effect was uncanny. I'd spent weeks practicing those gestures and she had learned them in an hour. The line of Teresa's shoulders, the cant of her jaw. There was a danger in making a double of yourself. Was this how Mistress Sostary had felt when she laced me into the corset?

To settle myself I took my leisure with Amba.

My tiger demanded nothing of me. His hunger was easy to sate. No fretting or strumming or wondering what life was. When quiet he was gentle, when happy he showed his affections. I never got a whiff of wildness from him. Not as I had in the beginning, looking at the beast and seeing only death. But by now Death seemed like a pussycat himself. Death crept along beside me, halfway tame.

What was life anyway? Just a song in your throat. A pulse, a gurgle in the gut. Sever any part and life—whatever it was—just bled out. Try to clutch at it and still it slipped away. Only in the world of dreams was it more than that: desire and fury, all commingled, all interknit.

That was what I wished to breathe into my spectacular. Showing Death's smallness through my performance. And I could feel we were nearing readiness.

38

Then it was showtime.

September had fled and the autumn winds carried ice and sleet, twisting the withered stems of the leaves and letting them go. By seven o'clock the circus had become a madhouse. Leon was fretting above the proscenium like a blackbird, territorializing the younger crew with his blue cusses and slaps. "Fall in line, fall in line, you speckled mickeys," he cried out. "Hell to pay for the first one to slip up."

"What about the second?" some cutup rejoindered.

"The second's dead meat on a platter. And the third—well, you don't want to be the third, d'you? That third little pissant goes belly-up to His Nibs."

Opening night and the crew were raucous and full of themselves. Those that were left, anyway. Many of the old crew had vanished, and the new lot, with their flinty grins, had been hard to keep in line. But today their high spirits were welcome. Today would be the test.

I was taking my leisure in the balcony, checking the sight lines. It was too late for adjustments but it kept me busy. "Do you think they'll understand about what happens when the Sun-King touches her?" my magician was asking. "We could still add a line, princess, to make it clearer."

"No time," I told him. "It'll have to hold for tonight."

He nodded uncertainly and left me to myself.

My body ached with all that had been done to it: all those pinches and prods and loving administrations. Earlier when I'd looked in the mirror it was some other girl I saw, some woman—not the girl from Stary. I was the Lady Pale-Throat now. And it made me glad, seeing her smiling back at me, not fully knowing where that queenly look came from.

Leon appeared beside me. We seldom spoke these days. Sometimes I caught sight of him crossing the street to the Strelka or, if I were restless, stumbling home before dawn. But today his presence was welcome: he knew what he was doing and I needed him. "Those bastards'll keep at it if I watch close enough. I reckon we're ready as we'll ever be."

"Show-ready?" I asked. My bowels were contorted and my stomach all in knots. That morning I'd chuntered with nerves and now the bile was back in my throat. I felt the Lady stutter, felt her slip away from me. Leon must have seen it for his next words were kinder.

"Listen. Never know 'til the show, that's what the old mistress always said."

We watched as his boys scuttled about the overhangs. They had an easy way of moving.

"Would she like it, do you think?" I asked carefully.

He shrugged and chewed on his thumb, unwilling to answer.

"Where is she, Leon?" This was invasive but I needed to know: was he my man or hers? Could I trust him?

First he looked careful, then he grimaced, running his hand over the baldness that must have once been a proper head of hair. "I reckon she's where she wanted to be. She won't be returning to claim all this if that's what you're asking. You're safe from her."

Safe from her. Is that why I had asked after her? Was it fear?

He continued softly: "We'll speak after. The mistress used to have me in for a rundown, see, so we could tally up the good and the bad then steer ourselves a course."

"That won't be necessary."

"Ah," he said, "you have others to consult with."

I let the Lady in.

"That's enough, Leon," I said haughtily, preparing to withdraw to the dressing room.

That made his face turn stony. "I saw you, y'know," he said softly. "Saw that time you showed yourself to her." He ran a bitten nail over his bottom lip, remembering. "You said you'd take away her pain. Aye, that was it. So what'd you do with her pain after all that?" He sidled a step closer to me.

I said nothing.

"You wouldn't be the first to choose a bad life over a bad death. But don't let yourself be shammed, girlio. Men like that one can't abide competition. Arkady was the same sort, too. But he was just a baby goblin and here's the master miscreant himself. This isn't a good life, despite the silks and the fineries."

"She bent," I murmured in reply. "You both did. So why not me? Maybe I just learned that to live with wolves, it's best to howl like a wolf."

But by then he was putting the old distance between us again as if I was bad news and he didn't want to hear it. "Never know 'til the show," he said, giving me that old half salute of his. "Is she ready or not? No way to tell past testing."

✶ ✶ ✶

Eight o'clock and the familiar hush was falling, a silence like the end of the world. Then the musicians set bow to string, breath to reed, and their efforts conjured the show into being.

Was I ready? Was I ready? We had practiced and practiced and practiced but never before a true crowd. And these ones were true—not Victor's comped-in punters. He'd been drumming up publicity for the opening for weeks now. When I walked down Stradaniye Street I saw a line of Ladies, miraged onto banners that hung from every street post I passed from here to the Capitol Buildings.

My hands were shaking like a rattle, the wrists loose and fragile. Renata had teased my tresses, fit my forehead with paste gems. I glittered like a chandelier but I couldn't remember how to walk. I tottered, fought for balance, fought to find my light. Would it be enough? How could it ever be enough?

But then time slipped and it didn't seem to matter anymore. My spirit slunk out of me and the Lady swept in. Her hands were poised. She knew how to hold herself. A second hush scudded over the crowd. They were watching me closely now, watching for the sort of lie Madam Nikolayevna might tell them: a man likes to laugh, a man likes to fuck—and what more to life is there, really?

But the Lady never lied.

"Once upon a time there lived a princess in the kingdom of the north. Every day she slept while the Sun-King made a circuit over his lands. When she dreamed she dreamed of him. But she didn't love him," Master Fortunato crooned.

The words were right. His voice was that of a poet, starry-eyed and chimerical. Music to match skirled up from the orchestral pit and my audience watched it unfold with a hunger I'd only seen on one face in my life: Cvetko as my tiger bore down on him.

As I bore down on him.

The Lady Pale-Throat with the ice-touch of death.

And oh, she was beautiful.

And oh, she was deadly.

And oh, for a moment—for a moment!—she was me.

"The princess wouldn't have him," the magician was declaiming. "When he came for her, she fled his burning presence. She traveled through a dark forest until she came to the house of a witch."

Then there went someone whooping in the dark air above me, a flash of satin and silk. Baba Yaga descending in her cloak of indigo and mauve and deepest black. She wore a mask with a long-hooked nose, a wig of silver hair. Braids, I had demanded—she looked like you, of course. Ill-omen, outcast. But still I could see Teresa's blue eyes gleaming in the darkness.

"Stay with me a while, Granddaughter," she cackled, "and the two of us shall strike a bargain. Everything you desire I can grant you."

The overheads dazzled and my cheeks glowed like a hot pan. I felt green and full of life, full of lies—but they were beautiful lies and the Lady would loose them on the world. My soul was splitting into two.

Beside me pranced a trick-man in a demon mask: varnished red paint and two curved bull horns almost kissing above the crown of his head. He slipped a cavalry sword down his throat. That close and I could see how his neck muscles worked, how he turned himself half-python for it. Then the blade was out again, silver edge flashing and him all in one piece. We would use that blade again. Baba Yaga would plunge it into me…

I glided to the next spectacle. A child with a yellow, star-petaled flower. Now it floated. Now it was tall as she was, then taller, towering like a ladder. She scampered up thorns as thick as railway spikes and disappeared into the upper reaches of Heaven.

"You've served me well, Lady Pale-Throat," the witch declaimed, "and a bargain is a bargain. The only escape is death. But I am hungry, oh so hungry…"

Then she was putting me in the oven: a metal contraption specially designed to hold me. Her demons were dancing, passing her flashing blades to plunge into me, severing my arms, my legs, my poor head at last. But of course I felt no pain. I was too elated. The show was a beast and we were riding it together. Teresa in her mask, Leon and his crew by the fly rails, Erastus in the wings, even Uncle from his purchase in the upper balcony.

And down I went, down and down and down, until I entered the underworld. Dream logic held me and the Lady moved. *I* moved. This was a phantom land of twisted, hellish limestone, shadows at all angles. The audience could hear the ceaseless drip of water, they could smell the sulfurous fumes.

"So Lady Pale-Throat descended into the kingdom of death. But the Sun-King was filled with passion and he kept up the chase." My magician stood on a platform, announcing his conquest. He wore a titian-tinged cloak that shimmered under the ring-lights. The crown of peacock feathers was perched upon his brow. Whatever work Leon did with the lanterns cast stilliform swatches of pomegranate and blue-violet behind him.

Those same lights beat down on me. The curtains fell. The noise beyond them was ecstatically silent—worse than thunder. We were coming to the finale.

"Here now, move. Move!"

Renata stripped me down, fingers snicking through taut laces.

Her daughter powdered my face, draped a white robe across my shoulders. The backstage light dyed it pewter. They set me on a wheeling pedestal and it was as if I had died after all. I remembered the dream of my mother's death, thought I could smell the scent of apple blossoms. I went away, then came back into my body with a jolt.

A brutish pain was working into my stomach, exploding into my ribs. Suddenly I felt dreamy and disconnected. I couldn't think straight. Was it Mistress Sostary's blast caps? Of course not. I'd buried them, hadn't I? I'd laid them in the darkness in the secret hatch she had showed me.

Something cramped inside me and there was a terrible slickness gathering between my legs. Red stained the whiteness, red so dark it was nearly black. Renata clutched my arm.

"What you been doing, girl? And who have you been doing it with?" she hissed, working quickly, stripping me down again and cleaning me. It felt as if a second body were lodged inside of me: a twin, a ghost, trapped by the cage of my flesh. Something fibrous was strapped against the offending region, a second shift hauled over me.

Somewhere backstage I could hear Amba calling for me, a questing howl both mournful and full of rage.

"Try not to move." Renata's lips were close to my ear. "It'll hold, princess. It'll hold long enough." They smeared gel over my arms and legs where otherwise my flesh might burn in the grand conclusion. The pain had enlarged but the Lady didn't feel pain. The Lady was an iceberg drifting through a trackless sea. How could such a woman dream of fire?

I lay upon the pedestal and the magician grew close. His moves were fluid and practiced. We'd practiced all of this.

"You think it so strange that I could love the darkness." I tried to hurl my voice out to the crowd but all I could smell was the tang of gore, blood between my legs. Where was Amba? Was he ready? He had to be ready, or else… or else…

I saw Teresa on the staircase, playing out the tableau just as we had prepared it. She was my soul-twin. The Sun-King called to her but she turned away. She didn't want to be alive.

"I have moved beyond these things—light, love, life. I have no need of you."

Then I began to float. The magician's fingers fluttered above my breast, sparkling with tendrils of fire. Real flames, they had to be. What a spectacle it would make! He was the Sun-King and I was his pyre. His love was too dangerous for a woman such as me.

"I fear the way your mouth burns when you kiss me. How could I live with such knowledge?"

I couldn't, of course. I was being consumed by it.

The crowd watched closely. Their eyes were gleaming, famished.

Flames licked against my skin but I couldn't feel them. I was shining so brightly, half-fire myself. A roaring in my ears. As loud as a mortar, as harsh as death. It was my tiger coming, wasn't it? It was teeth and jaws and pain…

Was I Lady Pale-Throat or the Tiger Lover? For a moment I couldn't remember. My lines vanished from my head. Silence where there should have been a finale. The moment stretched and stretched and stretched.

The magician laid his finger upon my cheek and on the tableau staircase the boy too reached for his lover. But Teresa turned away and raced downward. She didn't want love. It was too late for her.

Then the magician's double began to glow with heartache. He was the Sun-King after all, and he burned with a passion so real that flames sprouted from his fingers. He reached for the girl and where his fingers touched, the fire crept up her dress. In an instant it was licking every inch of her body.

Now came the difficult part. She leapt into the air, held aloft by a web of wires. Slowly she began to spin, then faster and faster.

She soared like a comet, moving closer and closer to me, to her true self. The flames leapt from her to me as our bodies touched, conjoined in the midst of an inferno.

The magician stumbled away, shielding his face from the torching gusher.

Still the audience was silent.

Wider and wider whirled the flames, a supernova, a sun exploding in the heavens while a drumbeat thundered from the orchestra pit.

"I'll never be yours," I called out to my magician.

It was different than we'd planned it but sometimes a story moves through you, sometimes you think you know it but it *changes*.

"Death means nothing to me. I'll live again. But not for you. If you love me, let me give my people your light in dark times. Let me live and I'll shine for them! Let me take away their pain!"

The Lady set something loose in them. Now the crowd was wailing. Someone rushed the stage. It was more than a performance. Even the magician knew that. What they were doing was…

I couldn't describe it. We were crossing a threshold together.

"Lady Pale-Throat!" they cried.

I hovered above them, timeless and unreachable. Brighter and brighter the fire burned. I took their rage, their pain and I dissolved it in the boil of my blood. But all the while through the murderous glare I could see Victor in the wings watching. Now his hands were clasped together, now he was grinning like a hyena.

I had done it, that grin seemed to say to me. I should have felt triumph—hadn't I accomplished what I had set out to do? Hadn't I got what I wanted?—but instead all I felt was a rising sense of horror.

✶ ✶ ✶

Then it was over. The lights fell away, the cooling shadows gathered against my skin. The scent of char like a halo. The stagehands threw a damp blanket over me to smother the last of the flames. My shift was ash and what was left flaked away.

I checked my body for damage. Nothing but frazzled smoothness, just as we'd planned it. The ache in my abdomen abated.

Renata's girl slipped a new shift over me and cinched it about my waist. Then the curtain was pulling back again and I could see the mob howling for me—for *us*. For what our company had done together.

I stepped forward as we'd decided. I bowed to the portrait of Cvetko, and then to the crowd beyond. The noise of their approval stitched me together, masking my tiger's howl of concern. I wanted it to make me whole but something was wrong.

Something had happened. Something new had come into the story.

39

"Y ou're a damn fool," hissed Teresa, "a nestling, a doll. Don't you know what happened out there?"

She was waiting me in my dressing room, still clad in her performance gear. Off the stage some of her natural aspect had returned. She had a masculine way of standing, solid, straight-backed. Her jaw was sharper than mine and her stride was longer.

"What are you doing here? You know this place is private. You shouldn't have come," I said. The show had left me exhausted. While I was on the stage it was as if a current ran through me but now it was over that energy was gone. I gritted my teeth and sought out the Lady to answer her. My stomach was molten and a damp sheen swamped my forehead.

"I saw the blood. And the tiger. He was going wild as if—"

"It's just my monthlies," I told her, flushing with shame but prepared to brazen it out.

"Not likely." She had a cloth wrapped around a chunk of ice. She gave it to me and I held it against my belly. The feel of it was welcome and I relaxed a little. "It's not your time, is it?"

"They come at odd times now."

"When was the last?"

I didn't know. In Stary, we girls had followed a regular pattern but in the months since then I'd been careless keeping track.

"Who else knows about this?" she asked.

"Renata," I said quietly. "Her girl."

"Do you trust them?"

Renata had a coarse sense of humor. She laughed often and she cursed often. Her daughter was cut from the same cloth, if a touch quieter. Both were easy with me in conversation but I remembered what Leon had told me. Fingers and Ears, he had called them. But whose fingers and whose ears?

"No," I said.

"Good. You've got some sense. If Renata knows, then assume that everyone knows. Or more likely just one—*that* one." Meaning Victor, I understood. "I needn't ask if he's got your trust."

"What makes you think *you* have my trust?"

Her laughter was deep and fulsome. "Trust me neither, Lady Pale-Throat, and you'll be wiser for it. But I know what's happening to you. Didn't your mama teach you where babies come from?"

Her words hit me like a bolt of blue light.

"You thought, what?" she continued. "That you were too young? That it couldn't happen?"

The truth was I'd thought nothing at all about it. What I had done with my magician seemed so distant from the act of making a child I had never thought through where it might lead. And with the Deep? It hadn't seemed possible. It hadn't seemed like a thing in this world at all.

"I've been stupid."

"You and half the girls in history. How many of our mothers were just as stupid as you were? Most, I'd reckon. But the question is what next?"

"Is—is the babe gone, do you think?"

"Was there blood only? Or any mass?"

"Just blood."

"Then mayhap it'll live. Don't look at me like that. I had some training with the medics—not that this was their area. The question is, do you want it to live?" Her frosty eyes challenged me to answer.

"I don't know," I said.

"Babies are fragile. You want something around with a soft skull in a place like this? Tiny hands, tiny feet, something puny and growing?"

I thought of my mother then, the way she'd sometimes rub her belly. How she dreamed of vanilla and vernix. How my coming along must have been a muzzle on her protests.

But Teresa was flicking her dark-dyed hair impatiently. "Guess I better knock myself up too or I'll be out of a job."

Or you'll wait, I thought. *Let me get big on my own.*

"You go on," I told her. "I can do this." I was having trouble thinking.

"Want me to give you some breathing room? I can simper for them if you like."

Leon had said he would come for me. Victor would as well. I didn't have the will to resist either of them. But now Teresa was twinning me again. Her spine took on my silky way of moving. When I glanced in the mirror I saw myself thinned out and spread, too much of me for comfort, too little of me for strength.

* * *

And so it seemed that time was a spinning top. You, then Mama, then me—now her, this little one hanging onto life. I touched my stomach and wondered if I'd feel her squirm. Of course not, it was far too early. Whatever it was would have barely had a chance to take hold.

Tiny hands, tiny feet.

How tiny? I remembered Estes' grain of rice, a whole landscape carved upon it. Did I truly want to love anything so much? It would be helpless but hungry. I knew women in Stary who'd broken teeth when they were pregnant, the little imps stripping the hardness from their bones. I needed all my hardness for myself.

But when I ran my fingers along the black grain of the doorway, I wondered how many fingers had touched it before mine. The Swallow of the Night? The Goddess of Love? Now Lady Pale-Throat. Such a simple thing, this door—yet I felt neither free to open nor close it myself.

I'd asked you for riches, Baba, but what I'd wanted was love. That had been foolish, I realized. There was nothing of love in a place like this. Whatever bargain we had made had been a mistake. I knew that now. I had wanted freedom but all I had found was a cage—and if I wanted out I reckoned you were the only one who could help me.

40

I t was dark when I left the circus, wearing a simple gray jacket over a black dress that reminded me of my mourning clothes. Cheapnik, Mistress Sostary had called them, but they had made me invisible. No one saw me now, but everywhere I went I saw myself. The patchwork brick of the tenement buildings had been painted with over-sized murals, me kneeling before Cvetko. A thousand times I must have seen them until when I closed my eyes there she was: the Lady with her head bent low, neck exposed.

The subway didn't frighten me. I crossed my knees, let my face slacken so it no longer showed an expression of lively intelligence. This is what I'd learned at school: no one minds an idiot.

Much had changed in your neighborhood since my months with the circus. I crossed streets bearing the names of those killed in combat, their regiments, their place of dying. I touched each one like a charm. The back alleys were empty, the cafes shuttered up. Signs of old violence, broken windows, smashed doors. At old Fedkin's shop, I found a bullet casing lodged in the gutter, which shone like treasure. Then I saw your tenement block: concrete balanced on twisted steel. Fearing you gone like Mistress Sostary, Estes, all the others I had come to care for, I pounded on the door and waited. Pounded again. Had they taken you in the night?

But no—there you were, immovable, it seemed. Still dressed in your widow's weeds, eyes dark as a secret, some furious word twisting your mouth. But whatever that curse was it dissolved when you saw me.

"So the Lady's come home."

I searched for the words, not knowing what was in you then, joy or sorrow. But you were quicker, urging me inside.

"Come then. You look well fed. Has someone been stuffing you with figs? Give me your finger, let me see—aye, there's meat on your bones. Will you have tea? Or something stronger?"

"Stronger," I managed.

I made it over the threshold before my bones seemed to melt. Then I was down on my knees, down as I had been before Cvetko. Except it was you, Baba. And you cradled me to your body and rocked me as you never had when I first came to you.

"Oh, child," you said. "Don't you cry now. Your mama's here for you. Oh, Else."

My glance was all horror. Where was the witch woman who had raised her voice in the circus that day? Where was your cunning and your anguish and your hate? What I needed now was the marquessa who had tamed Death. But here you were—just an old woman, lost in time, thinking your dead daughter had come home.

As you held me your heart thumped in your chest like a caged bird and your arms were thin as kindling. I wanted to rail against you, curse you for leaving me, but instead I let myself be held. The feeling of rocking was good and I couldn't bear to tell you the truth of who I was. You needed a daughter and I needed a mother. Soon enough there were tears on my face. I let them come. We sat like that for a while until you stirred back to wakefulness. Saw me, knew me, and smoothed back my hair.

"I'll get the bottle," you said. "Then you'll tell me all."

I helped you stand. My knees were better than yours. Since you kept the bottle on a high shelf, I helped with that as well.

"Arrivals should be met with feasting but I'm afraid my cupboard is bare these days. This will have to do." You poured out a measure of samogon and set it on the table. "Is it known you've come to me?"

I shook my head.

"Ah."

We sat. The liquor tasted faintly of onions but I drank it down anyway. Behind you I could see the little teacup we'd used to grow dill together. The seedling was withered now, without my hands to care for them. The little apartment was silent.

"Where are your neighbors? I don't hear them."

"Gone."

"Were they taken?"

"Them?" you snorted. "No, not those ones. Some go up and some go down, isn't that the way of it? And they were obedient to a fault."

You refilled my glass but instead of drinking, I stood, went through to the sitting room, took up the picture upon the mantle above the fireplace. You as a young woman, my age, your expression fierce and joyful. I recognized something I had not seen before: the straightness of your back, how striking your body was, its careful positioning. "You were pretty," I said.

"Too pretty to be safe."

Beneath the picture was the ancient wooden chest with its three broken brass lever locks. You hadn't moved it since I had lived with you. But when I pulled the corset free it was not the watery shine of the silk that caught my eye but a darkened stain, nearly black, and in its center a tear as big as a thimble. A bullet hole.

"I don't understand what happened that day in the circus. What you said to those two to make them take me in. Was the tiger yours once? Really?"

Are you a witch? I was asking you. Is there a way out of this? Can you help me? But your eyes were crafty and then it was exactly as it had always been between us, me ever asking and you refusing to tell me straight.

"Does he still make that sweet sound when he approaches?" you murmured. "Is he as jealous as he ever was? Does he put on airs for the crowds?"

"Please, Baba."

"A big animal makes you think of death. Did I tell you that? These days I keep forgetting myself. There are times it's good to think on death. No one should meet death as a stranger. Fetch me some olives from the kitchen, will you? Set them there."

I could see you were stubborn still but I did as you asked and returned with a porcelain bowl and a fist-sized jar. Then afterward you wanted me to make you a fire but there was no fuel. How small your apartment seemed to me then, with its crooked hallways and jigsaw rooms. Your things were shabby compared to Master Fortunato's palatial quarters: his silk sheets, his fine wines, his oysters.

You narrowed your eyes as if you had pulled the thought from my head. "What do you want then, child? Didn't I keep my promise? You have your magician, you have your crowds. Haven't I seen your likeness on every poster and pamphlet from here to the Capitol Buildings?"

"And all it cost me was a cage," I spat back, the old anger flushing my cheeks.

Suddenly a cough shook your whole body. "The cost is everything, little mouse," you told me when you had your breath again.

"Life lives in the costing. But you chose, didn't you? Just as I did once." You unstopped the jar and plucked four olives for the bowl. "Only your mother had the wit to walk away. A fool, I called her when she left, and a traitor too. But she wanted a different life than the one I could give her. In those days they encouraged you to get married early, settle down. You know why? So you had something to lose. She had you—in love, she said, not in fear—perhaps she was right. Perhaps I held onto my hate too long."

"Baba…"

You took up the corset then and spread it on the table beside the olives like an offering. A thousand tiny mirrors winked at me. "And yet I lived, didn't I? In some places it's expected that a wife will follow her husband into death. She'll pass away from grief, or perhaps throw herself upon his pyre. But in my village—in Garsk where I grew up, the Village of the Brides—we had a different tradition. The women were supposed to wear black even when their husbands were alive. They took up mourning from the day they wed and when their husbands were gone, the women married each other. Mother married daughter, sister married sister, so they wouldn't be alone. How do you like that, my darling granddaughter-wife?

"And so I always knew you would come. There is something in you that demands an answer from the world. I was the same." Another cough rattled your lungs and you pulled at the knot of your midnight-black scarf to loosen it. "You must burn my things when I'm gone."

"So, this is it then?" says Sara Sidorova. "This is what becomes of me?"

"Everything ends eventually, Grandmother," the other says.

"You aren't going to die," I insisted. I wanted to believe it was true. Omen of ill luck, teller of tales, outcast, thief—but also blood of my blood. The only kin I had in the world except for that little one who nestled inside of me, and what was it? Just a cramp in my stomach, a jelly, hardly anything at all.

"What, never?" you snorted. "What a soothsayer you've become. Will you point to a lump of tea leaves and say, 'Aye, Granny, that one's a cloud and that one's a bird and therefore an angel has whispered in my ear you're destined to live forever'?"

"You know I didn't mean it like that!" I wondered if there was a book I might set alight, to help the flame catch. You were shivering. "Let me fetch some meat. You could use a good meal, Baba."

"I'd just peck at it like a bird."

"You're just a lousy cook is all."

The truth was you were fading. The skin of your arms showed fey blue veins beneath. But I didn't want to believe it. The deaths I knew were violent deaths and disappearances: extravagant, staged, deliberately comprehensible. I had never seen death like this before, when it slipped in quietly.

"The girl I knew wasn't any better at domestics." A half-whisper, your eyelids already drooping.

"The girl you knew is gone. I'm someone else now. Isn't that what you wanted?"

41

Outside the apartment I watched night take hold. I passed through the back alleys, saw a dog with a tumor hanging from his belly. Strangers rolling backgammon dice watched me from their stoops. A murmur rose up behind but for once I didn't let it be my guide.

Stradaniye Street was monstrously grandiose but here the laneways felt intimate as those in Stary had. For a moment the years seemed to melt. I remembered walking between my parents, their hands holding mine on either side. How I'd swing myself between them.

"One, two, three and up!" Papa would holler.

"Again, again!" I'd demand.

How old had I been the last time I had done that? Five or six, perhaps. I tried to imagine the child I had been, not yet willing to do the things that would bring my own child into the world. Then sickness boiled inside me and I stumbled toward the gutter to rid myself of it all.

So. That was a sign at least, wasn't it?

I touched my still-taut stomach and tried to sense the baby moving beneath, thinking of a fresco I had seen in Stary's old quarter of a black-clad holy woman with a child in her womb, long-limbed, fully formed already. Her eyes had been scraped out by vandals but her smile was beatific. What had you said? Mothers marrying their children, sisters marrying sisters. My own little one would have no father. It could be yours if I wished, it could still be born from love.

Suddenly a fierce reflex of joy whispered through me. *Boom*, went my heart.

Now I was ravenous.

✦ ✦ ✦

"Baba?" I called when I returned from the late-night kiosk clutching what little I could find—two tins of sprats and some packaged crackers. In desperation, I'd snatched a handful of dill from an untended garden.

No one answered.

At first I thought you must have managed to light the fire, for the sitting room glowed like a little oven. But beyond the doorway to the kitchen there were only shadows and the bitter aroma of coffee brewing.

"There's something I must tell you." I peered into the darkness, alive with a new feeling of wonder. You would be happy, I thought. Whatever black spirit had entered you would be banished by my news. It would be as I'd sworn when I left: all you needed was a good meal to set you right. Didn't I know how you liked to eat?

Still no answer. The broadcast radio was blaring so loudly I half-expected Madam Trout to pound on the walls in protest.

"Look what I've found for us," I tried again as I headed through, expertly juggling the tins. They clattered to the floor when I saw Victor waiting for me at the kitchen table, smiling flatly.

"No kiss for your uncle?" His voice was placid and he nodded to the cheap-suited men beside him. Then someone turned off the radio and took the bread loaf from me and someone pushed me into one of your rickety chairs. There were heavy hands on my shoulders, the scent of gunpowder and sweat. I felt young and dumb, immobilized—a little mouse, indeed. The change sent Victor's lips curling above his eye teeth.

"This is civilized, isn't it?" he said as someone else poured coffee from your long-handled pot. "You were looked for last night. You ought to keep yourself available, you should know by now. I had thought we had an understanding." His gaze fell on me as weighted and inescapable as those leviathan hands.

"What understanding, Uncle?"

I was playing for time. Where were you, Baba? Just in the other room?

And suddenly Sara Sidorova hears a noise, like a freight train bearing down. "What is that?" Her whole body is shaking.

"It's coming now. That's the roar of the All-Dark."

"You were good last night. They were more than cuntstruck. Well. You did what you wanted. You made them good and ready."

"Ready for what?" I asked.

"What's coming? That sound... it's rattling my bones! Make it stop!"

"I'm sorry, Grandmother," says the other, turning away.

The muscles in his shoulders moved like a rockslide. "The General is slipping. Three visits to the hospital in the last month

269

alone. He's an old man and old men don't live forever. The Party has called for a day of prayer."

"What has that got to do with me?"

His eyes widened so I could see the colors of his iris: brown like a sweat stain edging to rose madder. He scrutinized me carefully. I could feel his eyes like fingerprints all over my body.

"Those punters trusted you more than they trusted their own understanding of the laws of nature. You told them you were a princess and they believed you. You told them you could raise the dead and they believed that just as easily. So, you tell them to, they'll love the man who replaces Cvetko. Better yet—tell them you've brought Cvetko back. Relax their eyes, make them look where you want. Tell them I'm Cvetko. Tell them the General's spirit lives inside of me."

I tried to turn away but then he was quick, pincering my jaw between his fingers. "Or maybe you're unhappy with our arrangement. Maybe you've gone feral same as your mistress did. Sometimes it happens. A woman can be gentle for a while before she bolts. So what I want to know is, are you breaking cover? Is that what this is?"

"Where is my grandmother?" I needed to know.

A sound from the bedroom: the rustling of cloth, maybe. Victor pricked his ears and glanced to the hatchet-man behind me.

"Tell her, Dimitry."

I heard the Deep's guttural voice close to my ear. "That old piece of gristle? She was dead when we found her. Her spook was long gone."

"He's lying, isn't he?" demands Sara Sidorova. "Those are the kind of men who lie about such things. I know, don't I? I remember... Oh, mercy. I can't stand it!"

270

"See now," Victor said softly, now taking an olive from the bowl you had left out. "It's just as Dimitry says: dead when we found her. We aren't animals. I remember that one. She howled, didn't she? Like a she-cat caught in a trap. Well, I reckon she'd suffered enough. If you like we can find a way to honor her—a memorial perhaps. Only whisper her name to me and it'll be so." He crushed the dark flesh between his teeth. "It's as easy as that, Miss Lubchen. We're not so different, you and me. You tell them what to believe. You tell them what they know of the world is wrong, that you know better—that your way is better. I do just the same."

"I meant it to be palliative," I whispered, a taste in my mouth as bitter as if he had filled it with quicklime. "The world hurts them too much. *You* hurt them."

"Have you seen pain? Seen it up close?" He leaned toward me. "Leave a man with no light for twenty-one days. If you set a candle by his window, he'll believe it's the sun. Blow it out and he'll believe it's night."

I heard the noise again from the bedroom. What was it? Was I only dreaming?

"Better yet," Victor continued, "you can sit in that cell beside him. Night and day, day and night. Feed him stories about what they've done to you and tell him the place you go to escape." His body seemed to grow larger then, the shadows stitched to his elbows, his shoulders, multiplying and gathering like his own private army. "See, every man has such a place. If he trusts you, he'll tell you how to reach it—where he goes when he goes away."

He stood and his helpmate made me stand with him.

Now he was leading me toward your bedroom but I didn't want to see inside. I didn't want him to open the door.

"You're my candle, Irenda. You create that place for them. You burn away their thinking and you make it easier for us to hurt them when we want to hurt them."

"I don't want to look."
"Of course not. No one should see themselves like that."

The door swayed and fell open. A bright slant of sun had fallen over the bed. You were there but your face was waxy and still. The windowpane had been lifted. I saw a flash of white and gray and glimmering green—a pigeon. It fluttered around the room, throwing itself from wall to wall until the Deep stepped in beside me and snatched it from the air.

"I'm taking you home, little niece," he said and that purr had come back into his voice. That civilizing softness. He took the bird to the window, nudged aside the dirty linen curtain and released it gently. "Renata told me you were poorly. You'll be given time to rest, of course. Time to recover yourself. But not much. Be ready."

I thought of the fluttering I had felt inside me. Tiny fists knocking at my ribs. "What if I won't perform?"

Then he was close beside me again, those same fingers gripping my upper arm. I could smell the buttery fug of his scent. "We had an agreement, little niece. You said you'd whisper a word in their ear," he told me, "and that's what I need. That word is my name, you hear? I want them singing it on the streets tomorrow. I want you showing them how to kneel for me, just like you did for the old man."

"I won't do it." I couldn't bear the bleakness of your body.

"Won't you?"

He moved quicker than I would have believed possible. Now his hands were at my throat and he was forcing my spine into the carpet. His fingers crushed my windpipe, hard enough to bruise. He didn't care. The bloodlust was in him.

"Why, tell yourself to let go then. Do it if you can."

My heart was hammering against my ribcage. The light speckled at the edges of my vision. I gagged and threw myself against him. I could see your hand hanging past the coverlet, veins purple as a sea urchin.

But the air in my lungs was all used up. I tried to speak, couldn't, then I tried to go blank. To slip away from him. *One day*, I thought, *I'll die in the name of...*

"No one *wants* to die. There's always some part of them thrashing away, trying to find a way out. You know why? Because here's the truth. I'll follow you wherever you go, Sara Irenda Lubchen. Even into the kingdom of death."

"What's he doing?" says Sara Sidorova. "I can't see properly!"

"He's killing her, Grandmother," the other says calmly. "Killing me."

He wasn't going to stop. The lights were going off, mine and the little one's too. The air began to shimmer above me. Lights, lights and more lights. A rent in the world, a staircase, a figure climbing and climbing past the gray tower blocks into a sky the color of cement. I recognized your gait, your black scarf, the swing of your hips, the silver braid of your hair.

You were turning on the staircase. You were calling to me, trying to tell me something.

"What? What?" Her pulse is slowing in her throat, her wrists. Something shining whispers out of her.

"What would you tell her? What would you tell *me*?"

I couldn't hear it. Not then.

The Deep's face leered above me. A vein throbbed near his temple, twisting like a guy wire. I jerked beneath him, slapped uselessly at his face. That only made him laugh. Ha-*hah*, ha-*hah*. He laughed and I hated him.

"Fight, Granddaughter. Come on now, you must fight!"

"Why should I fight? You sent me into that place. You knew what would happen. Now you want me to fight? For what?"

"I don't know!"

Then his hands slipped away and air ached into my lungs.

"Breathe," he said. It hurt but I did it anyway and he laughed at me doing it. "When the time comes tomorrow you'll choose the same. So make yourself ready."

"How will I know what to do?" I gasped.

"All you have to do is kneel, child. Kneel and they'll kneel right along with you."

✶ ✶ ✶

Afterwards Victor's corporals handled me brusquely. I was hurried down the stairs where a black sedan was waiting for me. The windows were tinted. As we drove I could hear the throb of heavy engines—passing trucks? Military jeeps?

They returned me to the circus where I was locked inside my dressing room. When I pounded at the door there was a hiss I thought I almost recognized—one of the new troupers with their dark, deep-set eyes and hacksaw noses. "Behave now. We'll come for you in the morning."

So.

I was to be primed and prettified, sent out to glamorize the shabby violence the Deep had prepared. And they would be prepared already, wouldn't they? Didn't the newspapers spit out their incendiary headlines faster than history could feed them? Hadn't it been the same with the blast that killed my mama and papa? Whatever was to come would have all the stage cunning and preparedness of one of Madam Nikolayevna's counterfeit productions. I knew nothing would be left to chance—not if Cvetko was falling.

My own reflection showed a necklace of bruises.

Foundation, concealer, powder. I'd need them if I were to do as he'd said.

Had you worn the same necklace, Baba? I didn't know. Your face had looked calm, that much I had seen—and you had called Death an old friend. Perhaps you had gone to meet him on your own. Perhaps the Deep hadn't lied.

"What now? The noise is gone," Sara Sidorova whispers. "Why did it stop?" In truth, she knows the answer.

"That's the end."

"The end of what?"

"The end of your story, Grandmother."

My mother first, and then you. Who next? Who else remained? Only the little one, my daughter, and my terror. You had told me once when the dead leave us they can make a path for the living. But that, it seemed, was a lie. One more among so many.

And thinking that my old grief returned, doubled then trebled. Not just grief for Mama, but grief for you—and with it I felt your own grief for those who had been lost crashing against me like a wave, my child's grief for the grandmother she would never know.

Now my grief hung upon me like a heavy veil.

Now it shone like polished metal.

There were no blankets, no bedding—nothing but Mistress Sostary's abandoned mirror. I curled up beneath it and wept.

42

I was bruised and hungry but still I slept like a stone at the bottom of a lake. When I awoke in darkness sometime before dawn I still half-expected to hear you singing, "Juniper, juniper, juniper"—still very much alive. But of course it was a dream only. Whatever spirit of song roosted inside you was gone and I would be allowed no forty days of mourning.

And yet I wasn't alone. I heard harsh breathing like a rasp drawn over difficult wood—too close. Footsteps on unfamiliar floorboards.

My pulse leapt in my throat and my hands squeezed into fists. If it came to that I would not go kindly. I had been the beast girl once: I knew how to bite, claw and scratch.

But then an electric torch flared and neither a ghost nor goblin stood before me, not even one of the Deep's hatchet-men. No, it was Leon I saw, eyes red-rimmed and sparking with a jeopardous light. "Looks like you were show-ready after all," whispered the old circus master. He had a long-necked bottle in one hand and a stenchy cloud of liquor hung on his words.

"What are you doing here?" I hissed, pulling myself up.

He had not slipped in through the door, of that much I was certain. He kept his voice low so the syllables wouldn't carry. "I told you I'd come. There are words that need to be spoken, girlio."

"You're drunk."

He searched out a chair and slumped in it. "Aye, drunk is good sometimes. Drunk is good for what I've come to do." He took a swig.

"And what's that?"

"My mistress left you in my care."

"Your mistress would've seen me dead," I shot back.

"Only because you said so." His hands went wide and the samogon dribbled onto the floor like an offering. "You never saw yourself then."

"I'm flesh and blood."

"Oh, I see what you are. Just a little thing caught up in a bigger thing. You lay with the beast and you thought you could do it forever because he was gentle for a while. But I reckon by these ill-appointed quarters of yours that you've found out it ain't so."

I was silent for a while. "Where is she, Leon? Your mistress?"

How many hours had I spent staring at the shape of her arms? Hungry for whatever it was she had that no one had ever offered me in Stary. I had been drawn to her shine, not to love it as it was but to steal it for myself.

"Seized, I expect. Or fled over the border. Same as Estes, same as all the others." He looked away.

"What threat could he have posed? He wasn't a traitor or a—a—"

Leon stood abruptly. His eyes were china-white as he dared me to keep on with my assessments. "Your lad was a threat all right. He wasn't settled, he wasn't safe. He had a brother and his brother died in debt. But in this country a man's debts don't die with him. They follow after."

"I didn't know. I *swear*—"

"You knew well enough, I reckon," came his tired reply. "Even back then. You saw things, didn't you? Barely more than a ghost yourself. You snaked in the shadows and at night you lay soft with that ever-loving tiger. What girl would do that? Myself, I thought you were some creeping child like my nan warned me about. A changeling." He sighed. "'Twas the only reason I went along with the mistress in the first bleeding place. I'm a watcher myself. You see enough and you know the bad ones. The ones who get men killed for nobody's glory but their own. See enough and you know sometimes it's worth a good one just to take the bad one out. Nobody likes it but that's how a soldier thinks if he wants to live."

It was the longest speech I had heard him give and when it was over he seemed to lean in exhaustion against the mirror stand. Now he pulled up the edge of his shirt-tail so I could see the terrible work some ancient hunk of shrapnel had done him. "See, I knew Cvetko in the old days. He was a glory-hungry old snake and he didn't care what happened to the men beneath him. Four hundred of us there were at Cheyory Bridge and only twelve survived. So maybe I wanted it for him too, thinking he was doing the same bastard thing to the country. But I didn't take those munitions, I let the mistress pass them onto you."

"And I knelt."

"That time you did." Now he leaned harder against the mirror. There was a gentle click. Suddenly I understood. It wasn't that his legs were weak or his vision wobbly. Gently the mirror slid as if on rails.

The next step Leon took was a secret one. The wall opened up and swallowed him.

✳ ✳ ✳

I followed him into the passage because I couldn't think of a reason not to. Otherwise the night would die slowly while I waited to do what I had been told to do.

279

Drunk as he was he moved with a quickness that left me struggling to keep up. The corridor was narrow, one of those leftover spaces: dusty, ancient, and damp. Details of its original life remained intact. A golden border, topped by a scratched frieze of chubby cherubs. I thought I knew the circus but now I was beginning to realize how deep it must truly go. Mistress Sostary would have known. But then she had understood so much more than I had.

We passed a branch in the path and now Leon was pressing me to the wall. He made the stage gesture for 'silence' and 'be ready'. The breath went into me and hovered in my throat. I saw them: two men with unleavened shoulders and bulges beneath the breasts of their backstage trouper gear. They passed by an arm's length away, never the wiser. When their footfalls had receded down the other corridor Leon at last released my arm.

"Where does that lead?" I wanted to know but the old man pulled me along.

"Let's hope you never find out."

"Why not?"

"Because, girlio, down there is the place that people vanish to."

Victor's lair, he meant.

Now I understood why the Deep came and went as easily as he did. He had made his own hideaway in the recesses of the circus.

At the top of the rise I signaled to hold. I had lost the hard muscle of my days in Stary. A year ago I could have run ten miles but nobody needed my running here. They wanted me dainty and well-formed. "Where are you taking me? What *is* this, Leon?"

"They were wild last night. In all my days not even the mistress could touch them like that."

"The show is over," I told him. "There won't be another."

"It is and it isn't. All that hotness of theirs is its own kind of munition. Maybe you lit the fuse but it's that one down there who knows where to place it. I reckon now he's seen what you can do all that matters is the timing." He was staring at me, inscrutable. "So hurry up, girlio. They'll be coming for you soon enough and we want you ready."

"Who does, Leon? Who wants me ready."

But he turned without speaking and continued on his way.

✦ ✦ ✦

Fresh air. A cool breeze on my face that smelled of smoke. Whether Hraná City was mourning or delighting, I couldn't tell. Perhaps they were two sides of the same thing.

A moment later Leon was hauling away a heavy metal grate and leading me up into the training yard. Even in the crepuscular darkness I knew it, by scent if not by sight. The ivy that covered that southern wall had begun to blaze scarlet though the gloom had leached it of color. It would die before November's snow arrived.

"Grandfather Death," I murmured, as Amba came to meet me at the fence. More grandfather than death. His eyes were rheumy and I rubbed his dove-white beard. Had I truly seen a shadow tiger walking beside him?

When I first came to the circus I had believed in marvels, the secret world that lived beneath the world we acknowledged. I wasn't a fool, you see. I'd known you had lied when you claimed the tiger was yours—had been, when you were young. He was old, yes, but even the oldest tigers live barely more than two decades and it would have been many more than that since you were a girl. But I had recognized that sound you made: a phantom memory of my own body howling the night I had learned of my parents' deaths. A sound like that couldn't be faked. It was a rivet popping, which signaled the collapse of some great edifice.

So I had believed you, even though I knew tigers are made of the same bone and blood as men and of course they don't live forever. I had let you bind me to your design, never knowing what that design truly was.

Somewhere above me the planets hurtled along. The moon, the sun, the stars—the same stars I had seen as a girl, casting a light that would take years to touch my skin. It seemed I hovered in a dreamless sleep and when I blinked the sun was rising. Its colors dissolved the pale grays with a flourish of gold and orange.

Teresa coughed behind me. She was standing next to Leon. A cigarette rested between her fingers, a slash of red lipstick smeared across it. "Listen," she said softly. "Do you hear that?"

It came to me slowly, a rush of noise that advanced and receded like a wave. I had thought it was just the wind but now I understood it was something else. A growing mesmeric howl from beyond the walls of the courtyard.

"What is it?"

"The talk in certain circles is Cvetko has been poisoned. Headaches and nausea, diarrhea. Maybe a stroke. Can you imagine? Our glorious general shitting his bed." A slow, spreading smile as her eyes flicked again to Leon. "Do you think they'll gather round like soothsayers? Speak now, faithful, speak with grace. Who will come to take his place?"

"I'm not political," I tried to tell them, shivering though there was enough sun now to warm my wrists, the back of my neck.

"Even animals are political," said Teresa. "And I reckon you're more than that, Lady Pale-Throat—or you have been made to be."

"What am I then?" I pushed myself toward her. Close, too close. A feeling in me that this was a schoolyard scrap to be settled with fists or teeth and nails before the wardens found us.

But she didn't flinch. An uncanny stillness about her, the signs of a person rigged for violence. "A good question, that one. How long has it taken you to ask it then?"

Amba must have sensed the tension between us because now his tail was scything back and forth. His lips curled over his teeth. Good. I'd had enough as well. I flipped the latch and he flashed between us, a bolt of lightning with thunder in his belly.

Teresa stumbled away, real terror writ on her face. I was glad for it. Let her be afraid, let both of them be afraid. Leon darted for the whip but my tiger was faster. Up he leapt, snatching the circus master's wrist lightly in his jaw.

"Be gentle, my love," I called and as easily as that Amba turned about face, releasing the old circus master and coming to my side.

"Tell me what this is," I commanded the two of them.

"Call him off, princess," said Teresa. The tiger licked his chops and I could see her eyes on him still, watching with ugly fascination the curl of his pink tongue. Then he sniffed the air and snarled. The noise was a ripsaw starting low in his throat. She didn't like being prey. Well. Who did?

"He's a beast," I told her with a grin. "He has his own ways. But I reckon he'll behave if you will. So. Go on then. Speak."

Leon nodded slowly to Teresa. "Better do as she says. We always knew it would be a risk coming here but this is the only place those boyos of Victor's never venture."

"You're sure?" she demanded. Then Leon made a gesture and she seemed to relax, pulling her cigarette shakily to her lips. "All right then. Let me tell you a story."

"Haven't we had enough of stories?" I spat back.

But it was Leon who answered. "Stories is what we trade in, girlio. People like us folk? Stories is all we have. I thought you knew that by now."

I made my own gesture for her to continue and she sighed. "I told you where I came from, yes? Well. There was an old tradition in my village. No one practices it anymore, of course, but they used to. I remember my mother telling me about it. How it would start with a girl, any girl, not the loveliest or the richest or the wisest. Just a girl. And that girl would begin to dream of fire."

I had heard of such stories, of course, but it had not been that way in Stary. We were too new, too modernized. Yet even Stary had been surrounded by its own savage weald where there were rumors of villages that lived as they had always lived: hunters and trappers and charcoal burners, shamans, shape-shifters, demons.

"This was how it was then. That fire-thought was like a sickness. First the one girl, and then others, they wouldn't sleep, they wouldn't eat, they would begin to starve themselves, thinking about the fire. See, my grandmother was one of these women. She had the fire-thought. When she spoke, whatever she said was the truth. And maybe they would have found a way to keep her quiet but then the other women started whispering, and then crying, saying all the same things, saying, 'Why are we having babies? Why are we putting seeds into the ground at all when war is coming?'"

A crimson light was bleeding across the sky and I thought of the ivy red as a flame on the southern wall. My tiger seemed calm enough but there was still rancor in his eyes. "How did it end for her?"

"How do you think?" Her mouth twisted. "The men came and built a big bonfire. They burned her things, all her beautiful clothes, whatever it was she loved best—hers and those of the other women who thought like she did. They thought the shock would make the women sane but they kept wailing anyhow. See, they had seen what was coming and which of the boys was going to live."

The light was behind her, just as she must have known it would be. Not an accident, that positioning.

"And did the men die?"

"Of course the men died. A regiment came to the village and took them away. Some of them tried to hide in the woods but these were the ones who had burned the women's things. My grandmother said the smoke followed them wherever they went. That was how the regiment knew where to find them. Then they were given boots and jackets, they were given rifles, but no one taught them how to fight. All they learned was how to march, then how to die."

"So what?" I asked her bitterly. My throat was aching with the damage Victor had done. How many grandmothers had howled the same way you had then? *All of them*, I thought. *Every one of them knows how it will end because it always ends the same way.*

My mirabilist had been fair-haired as Teresa was. He'd had blue eyes: poppy blue, not her bleak, military gleam but still. Did I imagine they shared that dimple in the chin? He could have been her brother. But what did it matter now? Her brother had disappeared and once you disappeared that was the end of you. A knife to the gut, a cord around the neck. What did we really owe the dead? Would it have helped to have my knowledge of Estes officialized?

"We saw what you did last night," said Teresa. "You're the girl who dreams of fire. I know because now I'm dreaming of fire too. We all are."

The noise from the streets beyond the courtyard was getting louder. I swore I could hear singing and I wondered what they were singing for. Not for me, I thought, whatever it was that others believed. I imagined them waving small, desperate flags while men in kilim jackets watched from their balconies.

"It doesn't matter," I told her.

"We think it does," said Teresa, her carrion-dark lips curving into a smile. "The folk out there are like kindling, I reckon, so dried up and parched all it will take is a spark."

I turned to Leon and he was primed like a wire trap. "That's why I brought you here, girlio," he said. "So together we can turn the whole ever-loving cunt circus against its master."

43

They spoke their piece and I listened carefully, asked my questions, and received what answers they were able to provide. Then they made their offer and I accepted. "Meet at the Strelka when it is over," Leon told me once Teresa had left. She had her own preparations to make, it seemed.

Together Leon and I watched the slick of the cobblestones reflecting the pale hues of dawn. The chamomile blossoms I had seeded were past their prime, the white petals attenuated and crinkled as old paper. Mama would have pinched the flowers from their heads by now and set them to dry but she had never taught me that final act of preservation.

"Is a thing like this ever over?" I asked him.

He shrugged. "Keep your own records, girlie. Remember your debts and pay when you've the coin for it. That's all we have in this world."

I knelt then beside Amba and he curled toward me, seeking out my hand. I touched the secret spot that always pleased him and felt him purr in response. But I knew I couldn't keep him by me. Once I had done what I had promised I wouldn't be returning. "Go on," I said to him. "Let one of us be free, at least. Mayhap I'll join you."

Then he was up in a flash, staring at me. His eyes glistened yellow, then acid green. I turned away. Where would he go now? What life for him was there beyond these walls? I loved him but sometimes, I was learning, love isn't enough. Sometimes you abandoned those you loved.

But perhaps these were only the thoughts of a little girl. Perhaps he had never truly loved, not as I loved him. What need had a tiger for a one such as me? Silent as a specter he left me. I had expected him to turn. Wanted him to. But no, without a second glance, a moment later he was gone.

＊ ＊ ＊

Afterward they returned me to the dressing room and it wasn't long after that the seamstress and her daughter—Fingers and Ears—appeared beside the Deep's man. They had instructions about which I had not been consulted.

Of course I had known someone would come for me eventually. Someone would dress me in scarlet and someone would place a hand on my shoulder to be sure I remembered how to kneel. But when I saw Renata's smirk my first thought was to plunge her scissors into her bastard tattletale heart. What can I say? At least she had the grace to recoil from the heat of my wrath.

Then she leaned in close as she pinned up my dark tresses: "Peace now, m'lady," she said. "Maybe I watch you but my girl watches me and her cousin watches her. It is what it is."

Another of Strana's maxims.

As I looked closer I saw how suffering had accumulated in the sag of her jowls. Her daughter was stamped with the same look. They whispered to one another and worked away with blood-pricked thumbpads, lacing me up in my performance regalia. What was there left to say? I had made my bargain. All that remained was to see it out.

✳ ✳ ✳

When they were finished I was brought to the theatre forecourt where Master Fortunato was waiting for me. The peacock feathers of his crown shuffled in the breeze. Their blue-rimmed eyes seemed to blink as they moved.

"I was worried for you." His face was pale as soap but the appearance of the Deep's jackals—and me with them—did not seem to surprise him.

"Were you?"

He exchanged a look with my handlers. I wasn't part of it, merely something to be traded from person to person. My arm was gripped with clammy fingers. No tenderness there, not anymore—but perhaps I didn't deserve it. "You shouldn't have left," my magician hissed into my ear.

I turned on him. "Why? Why shouldn't I do exactly as I please, Master Fortunato?"

He stared and his headdress wobbled in the wind. No one had thought to pin it properly. His mouth wasn't able to make an answer to me, even now. There were things we had never spoken of. For all he loved his Oblonsky, his Egorov, he still didn't know how to say two things at once: the thing that was allowed and that second unthinkable thing.

Whatever he might have been, there was no resistance left. He would become what was needed: a banker, a magician, a poet—but not a treasonist, never that again. The Deep had placed a seed of fear inside him that had grown long, choking vines.

"Just follow my cues," he told me. "Everything has been made ready for you."

I could see it for myself, of course, the banners on the street proclaiming the same story Victor had told me. That I had knelt once, that I must kneel again. Time was a vast spinning wheel, shooting off flecks of light. A demon whose stare creates frenzy, neither cruel nor kind, only unstoppable motion.

I could feel the wheel turning, that gaze on me. Your gaze maybe, from the staircase. I don't know. Only now they were pushing me out into the streets.

By then the thin layer of cirrus had dispersed leaving a sun-brightened sky that seemed to reverberate with crowd sounds. Side by side we walked, my magician and I—like lovers, like royalty.

We passed scores of people, grizzled men with sly features, children hid behind their mothers' knees, women in black clutching ikons with the General's imprimatur. The boulevards were filled with stragglers and lags in groups of three or four and everywhere we went they strewed flowers in our path or waved homemade banners.

"Lady Pale-Throat," they cried. They were weeping and roaring, asking me for an answer I didn't know how to give them.

The red poplar leaves skirled around us, kicking up against the state houses, the impressive oaks, the guarded railings. It seemed the air had been shaken and filled with blood. Faces peered from smoky windows, waiting for the masses to tip one way or the other as they always did, whenever there were such crowds. Someone handed us a flask of wine and a loaf of bread flavored with cherry stones. We didn't need it but we drank anyway. Master Fortunato clutched at the hands of strangers and wished them well. He kissed their cheeks and they kissed his.

We spilled out into the main square, which was lined by the old civic buildings. The painted banners soared above me and we were met by a multitude who welcomed us with cheers. From somewhere I heard an old war song:

> *It seems to me at times that the soldiers*
> *who never returned from the bloody fields*
> *did not sink into the earth at all*
> *but instead flew off—pure white cranes.*

Even more amazed was I to hear Master Fortunato's voice blending with theirs. He had a low, husky way of singing. I started weeping then as Estes had wept in my arms. I couldn't understand why, only that the image of the birds was so powerful. How many times had I sung that song in Stary? Suddenly I wanted to be the child who believed without question and never asked who gave the orders and why. I wanted to remember how it was to be a joint, or a ligament, or a hand, or a finger, some part of a moving whole.

The crowd swarmed around me—mobbing, dancing, and praying—and I let them do it. My hand twisted free from Master Fortunato's and I sank into muscles, meat, and sinew. They surrounded me. Fingers clutching after me, tearing sequins from my gown to be kept as private treasures.

Red hips, red waist, red breasts.

Aye, and there was Teresa among them. I saw her hawkish features, those wintry blue eyes, and then the rest of her. She was wearing a ragged wool jacket which she cast off and swung around me while the pressing flesh formed a curtain.

Then we moved together and I couldn't tell where she ended and I began. She stood while I sunk, her body clad in a twin of my own corset. It fit her beautifully. Indeed, her body knew it better than mine.

Let it be her, I thought. *She is stronger than I am. She knows how to do this.*

Now it seemed it was Teresa who was kneeling in each of the banners, Teresa dressed in red, Teresa promising glory and honor and wearing the mark of the General's approval. When she moved away from me it was like a weight was lifting.

"You must pray for the General," an old man said to her. His eyes were wild as yours were the day you handed me over, Baba. He was missing an arm, had only the smoothly pearled joint of an elbow. Was he an innocent or one of Victor's? No longer could I tell the difference. Perhaps they were all innocent, perhaps they were all in disguise.

"Please, pray for him," said another who was blind but seemed to know her anyhow.

"Take away his pain!" cried a third with a mutilated mouth.

"In the kingdom of the dead there is no pain," she assured them with a flourish. They receded, rapturous with her news. Her gestures were perfect for the newsreels.

✳ ✳ ✳

Above the dome of the Capitol Building a rocket threw up a shock of white sparks. A thunderous roar—petards bursting and firecrackers skittering, wheezing, whistling, and hurling flames into the sky.

"Is he dying?" asked a child of ten with glorious yellow locks. "Is the General's spook going out of him now?"

I thought of my mistress and the trick she had performed, a hand squeezing his ribs and forcing out the sounds it wanted. But then the boy was looking at me and I could see wonder written on his face. Here was a boy who believed without threat or cudgel.

Teresa was mounting the stairs to the Capitol Building and I wished it was me and I was thankful it was not. She had a terrible, ravishing beauty about her. *Touch me and do not ever dare to touch me. If you touch me I'll curse your line and poison your blood forever. But if you don't I swear you'll die of a heartbreak no other can cure.*

Women curled her hair in their fingers as she passed, grasping after her. "Is it you?" they murmured. "Is it her? Lady Pale-Throat?" And: "Will he come back from the dead? Will you give the General life?"

"Is that what you want?" She was using my voice. It rebounded across the square and scythed through the congregation.

"Such things we have seen!"

The spirit of the crowd was changing too. One by one they were swept up in a storm of knowledge: *it is her, it is her*. They were howling now as you had howled in the theatre, Baba—a cry of irreversible loss. It wasn't for the General. It was for Lady Pale-Throat swathed in red like an avenging angel who had hidden herself in the underworld to escape the eyes of the watching emperor. The fire I had lit was beginning to blaze and it seemed Teresa knew better than I how to breathe it into an inferno.

Teresa was standing beneath two banners now: twenty feet tall, each bearing the stylized portrait of the General. The wind seized them in its teeth and shook them. The General's mouth seemed to grin horribly, the eyes opening and closing as if he could step down from the cloth, a new man.

Then it was Victor's face staring down at me—the bull neck and narrow, purplish lips. There was a light flashing in my eyes. When I looked out into the crowds it seemed I could see the faces of the dead multiplying among the living. My mother and my father, gaunt skeletons bending before him. A handsome soldier with the horns of a ram sprouting behind his ears. A giant clutching the moon between his fingers.

And you, Grandmother, you as well—on the staircase beside her. You were whispering a promise in Teresa's ear.

* * *

The moment was almost upon us now. I could sense it in that clangorous energy field, the people's *passionarnost*: resonating, amplifying, blistering. All it needed was direction, a voice that would remind them what the world was and who they must be to live in it.

There was Victor himself coming among them. He wore the General's beige kilim jacket and a legion armed with Kalashnikovs ensured his safe passage. "What is a country that has no bones?" he called out. "What is a family without its father? Who will protect you if not I? Who will care for you if not I?"

And he looked down at the lady clad in crimson who stood before him. He looked down and he waited for her to kneel.

44

Teresa smiled at him and in that smile was defiance.

She raised her hands to the sky. Now flames danced from her fingertips—a blue-white glare which leapt to the banners, blazing like tar paper—and for all I had studied the swindles of our circus even I couldn't tell how she had done it.

"Let me be your light in dark times," she called out in the Lady's seizing voice. "Let me show you the way forward."

She was the hammer ready to strike the cap. The flame that burned down the house while the household slept.

The cluster were wailing and gnashing their teeth. More than a performance. The moment was burning away their thinking. It was lovely and terrible and it frightened me and I wanted to be consumed. Her voice unfurled over the crowd, unearthly, inhuman as if she were no longer an actress, but an oracle.

Prorok, elf-queen.

They were giving themselves over, utterly and completely.

All except one.

✳ ✳ ✳

How had I forgotten him?

Now I saw the sway of blue feathers, dyed red by the light of the blaze. The emperor's crown sat crookedly on my poor magician's head. His face was ecstatic but empty, a strange shadow show of a man—no substance at all.

He looked to the Deep and Victor nodded. Then Master Fortunato raised his own hand, a mirror likeness to his princess. And nobody saw, nobody minded him, why would they? It was her they had come to see. Lady Pale-Throat, not the Sun-King.

But I recognized those fearful lunatic eyes as he moved to embrace her.

I wanted to call a warning, but I was too far away now, hidden beneath her cast-off rags. Invisible as I had wished to be, as Leon had promised me I would be if only I stepped aside. If only I let her take up my mantle. Escape, they had promised me, just as I had promised it to Mistress Sostary.

But there was my magician and the rabble parted before him like waves before the prow of a ship. "All glory to the General," he cried in the voice my mistress had taught him how to use. "Look! The General has come again!"

Where had those words come from? Who had taught him what to say and what to do?

Too late now I saw the gleam of his knife, its progress, and at last its fall. His hand had faltered when he held a rifle. Now it was steady. Down he stabbed, the blade moving in and out. Red was the flame and red was the blood and red was the corset that came apart beneath it.

A trumpet blast sounded overhead and the sky exploded into light, and more light.

✳ ✳ ✳

When it was over I stared in horror at Teresa's ruined body. Her throat had been punctured with an oyster knife. Why an oyster knife? Was it a joke?

I couldn't move. Air sirens wailed in the distance and the cloy of blood haunted me like perfume, splatters of it speckling my clothing as I reached her. Elbows and shoulders jostled me. The golden-haired boy ran between my legs to gawk. "I seen her before. She's that faery woman." He sucked placidly on two of his fingers. "She comes back from the dead. Come on now, come on and do it."

Nearby was my magician. Blood shoestringed his face. He stared at Teresa's body as if he half-expected it to rise and take a bow. Then he was down on his knees before it, his face irradiated by the burning banners. Smoke wreathed his shoulders like a mantle. The crowd rushed forward: joyous and desperate.

"She's dead, she's dead again," they cried. "She isn't dead, here she comes, watch for it."

Almost, I thought, their belief might carry us through the day. But of course in Strana the dead did not rise again. Only in stories, no matter what I had promised them. And now it seemed they were remembering that: remembering who they were and what world they lived in.

The magician raised his bloody hands and the red sun dipped behind him.

A breath later, they were sinking their nails, their teeth into him, pulling the crown from his head and shredding the titian robe he had worn like armor. I couldn't move. Their silhouettes flashed through the flames of the burning banners: dark against the light, shuttling limbs, the brightness behind.

Then the Deep's escort raised their rifles and the bullets began to rain down.

45

What happened next was inevitable. The Deeps had been ready for those whitecaps of panic and they were quick to close. Riot shields hemmed in the crowds while truncheons cracked bone and skull alike. There were arrests: those few who turned to flee or reacted, unthinkingly, with protests. It wasn't real resistance. The older women—the grandmothers and aunties, the women in black who had seen such gatherings before—began to peel off from the crowds like carrion birds when the carcass has been stripped clean. They wiped the blood on their skirts.

And hadn't I seen such things before? I knew enough to move quickly.

But where to go?

A slow and settling gloom fell over the city while I wandered the back streets, avoiding the magistrales with their military barricades and traffic-calming barriers. The subways had been converted into makeshift bunkers and the train stations were closed. All passenger carriers were to be delayed for military transport. Didn't I know what was happening?

"What?" I asked.

"Invasion," said some.

"Coup," said others.

The rest merely shrugged. They would be told what it was in time. No point worrying until then.

As evening descended the noise from the streets had quieted to the hush of the wind, spiraling leaves from corner to corner. A few flakes of snow swirled among them—or ash perhaps. Soon the faceless men would be out to return the streets to a tender cleanness. It was an intermission only. Victor had known all, had been as prepared for my disobedience as he had been for my surrender. Both served his purposes equally well.

✳ ✳ ✳

I went to the Strelka because I couldn't think of a reason not to. Otherwise the day would die slowly while I waited to be rooted out. Red stained my wrists, my neck like splashes of scent.

Inside, the canteen was little more than a cramped root cellar with a touch of old-world charm. Yeasty wooden floors, handbills from the armistice years now papered over with my own stylized image. Or Teresa's, I supposed. I shook my head, still seeing the horrible pageantry behind my eyelids. My magician's face had been a ruin, his body a mass of sloughing naked flesh and twisted muscle. I had known him only from the rags of his titian robe—the Sun-King, fallen to earth. Who would wear his crown now?

"Here now, drink this. It'll help."

Despite everything, there was Leon easing onto the bench beside me. He was wearing a thick greatcoat with fraying seams and a tell-tale military bulge beneath the breast pocket. A swig from his flask made my head reel but at least it calmed my palsying hands. My teeth had been clattering so hard my skull ached. He settled down beside me with a cracked ceramic bowl and a washcloth, not speaking, only waiting until whatever was left of the frenzy had shaken itself free and I could clean away the gore.

"I didn't think you'd come," I said to him at last. He had no answer for me, not right away. I dipped my finger in the water in the bowl, which was tinged with pink now. A deeper vein of crimson swirled round like a galaxy.

"I spent the last twenty years of my life in this place. Even animals have their graveyards," said Leon after a long stretch. He smelled of cordite.

Tired words. Not enough, not ever enough.

"She deserved better."

"Aye, well." He seemed restless, gray eyes flicking to the door, the boarded-up windows. A couple of old-timers with their heads down occupied a stall on the far side but otherwise the Strelka was empty. "Who in this world gets what they deserve then? Heroes buried in unmarked graves and murderers given their glory. We are the bone that will choke you. Well. Seems we'll be choking on nothing but our own bones now." He drank down what remained of the flask and shuddered.

Estes had once told me at the point of annihilation the soul recalls its origins. I had never put stock in priestly gabble, but that single aspect had a whiff of truth about it. There was a moment in that hollow in the cage, with death riding close, the scent of it thick around me, when my mind would go wandering. I had that same feeling now, slow breaths in and out, drifting in memories. There was Mama filling her chapbooks with tiny mementos: pressed flowers or the mottled cream-brown of a skylark's feather. Estes' head cradled in my lap as he told me about his dead brother. You too, Baba, kneading dumplings sprinkled with our filched dill.

"What do we do when the show is over?" I said to Leon at last.

An echo of history, the world repeating itself. "Flee," he said harshly. "Run as far as you can. That's what you wanted, isn't it? That's what I promised you—you and the little one."

Deserter, I thought, *treasonist*. So Teresa had told him what she knew.

I shook my head. "Victor will follow me to the ends of the earth. But you know that, don't you? You know what happened to our mistress."

"Sometimes we never learn what happens. Maybe she lived."

But she hadn't, of course she hadn't.

A new thought was coming into me then. Maybe it was my own or maybe it was Teresa's fire-thought: the spark passing from me to her and back again.

Had it been the same with you, Baba? Surely there must be a place where all such thinking begins. Surely there must be a story for that: a story about what fire was before it discovered how to burn.

"It's coming now, isn't it?" whispers Sara Sidorova. It is as if she knows this moment: not from a vision but from a story of her own, a story she lived or a story she has told herself.

"Aye, Grandmother. Another ending. Will you watch it with me? Will you see what it is you set in motion?"

My hand whispered to my belly, searching out that pulse of life, knowing the baby would have never been permitted to live. A round-thighed, smooth-skinned little bundle. She was a dream only, as delicious as escape. Admitting that to myself brought a strange breathless feeling, closer to terror than sorrow. I had wanted to be born... and now... and now...

Now the fire-thought was sparking hot and cold at the same time: the sun on your neck as you prepare to descend into shadow. I understood then why it was I had come to the Strelka even after everything had gone so horribly wrong. It wasn't for escape.

Through a gap in the boarded-up window I could see the circus.

The marble columns were rotting from within, their facades crackling like ancient eggshells. Even the bronze figures on the balcony had begun to green and weep, their acrobatic poses now looking more like contortions of pain. I knew every creaking floorboard, every loose panel, every hidden path where the old caravans used to roll in their beasts. The basement still had its tunnel system from when they'd housed the elephants. Security never watched it—they thought it had been sealed decades ago.

I knew the workings of that place, its weaknesses and tender belly, didn't I? Tonight it would be thick with Victor's bootlickers but such monuments as those are always built skew-whiff. They are weak enough if you know the place to strike them. No matter how many Deeps were stationed at the doors, they couldn't guard against a place's memory of what it used to be.

I took the coin that Cvetko had given me and laid it on the table. Then I told the old circus master what I was thinking. "I have a debt to pay, Leon. But will it be enough?" I asked. "If I were close to him?"

The old stagehand listened intently and when I was finished he rubbed his jaw. "Maybe. If you were close. But those blast caps will be chancy and if it worked at all, it would be death to you both." A pause then. "I shouldn't have listened to her the first time round. Shouldn't have let you go out there."

"Will you help me?"

This time it wasn't the Lady's voice I used. I was speaking with my own, asking his blessing for my own death.

"I'm done fighting, girlio. I seen enough. Sometimes you lose. Sometimes you have to live with your losses."

"Not tonight," I told him.

46

I went alone. The fire-thought was stronger now, impossible to resist. I knew the way, didn't I? Leon had shown me the route to take to keep myself hidden. As I crept through the secret corridors of the theatre, I searched out my old spyholes. The offices and storerooms, the old bear prisons were empty or else populated by the Deep's ghouls. The old-guard partisans had scattered. Otto had vanished and in his place was another: ashy skin and a face like a claw hammer. The seamstering room had been deserted, the mess hall, the training yard.

Good, I thought. *Good*.

No one saw me as I went to the private cache Estes had revealed. It took a moment as I pried at the boards with my fingernails but eventually they came loose. There, behind Arkady's bottle of first-class brandy, I found an abandoned corset and performance gear of a very special sort. Its pockets were loaded with munitions, canisters crammed with powder, a nest of wires running akimbo. I was ready to don it again.

✶ ✶ ✶

Then down I was stumbling, through the hidden warrens, the passageways and stairs, charting a hopelessly twisting path. Down into the earth, into the underworld.

Newly clothed and laden with my burden, I crept quietly. The passage was narrow, one of those leftover spaces: dusty, ancient, and damp. Then I climbed a ladder to another cramped service hallway, then another, moving instinctively as much as by Leon's directions. Here electric bulbs studded rough concrete bricks. I had known there was a basement to the circus and a sub-basement and a sub-sub-basement, places I hadn't explored. But this one—I recognized the smell of rot. I had been here before: the place where people disappear to.

And I knew the Deep, didn't I? His proclivities, his predilections. Perhaps some would be celebrating their victory with champagne and cigars, but not that one. He was a watcher, even now. He would want to fully understand what it was he had wrought upon the city.

The hallway emptied into a chamber and somehow I was up high on a catwalk and below was a second circus I'd never seen. A platform of wooden boards surrounded by a ring of chairs. Pieces of worn-out circus machinery cast angular shadows. Broken staircases, cracked tanks large enough to house a body, faded backdrops. Here the ramparts of a military fortress, there the shattered mast of a ship.

I had been here before.

My breathing was hoarse with the effort. Sweat streamed down my face but even that didn't matter. I was smiling as I imagined the fire and the spoilage that would follow me: the gunpowder crackling, the walls buckling and caving, the tissue sets blazing, the staircase alight and all our pageantry with it. Was that smoke I could smell? I welcomed it like a gift from the future.

Soonest started, soonest done and over. I could have imagined my mistress saying such lines to me. Now I was wearing her corset again, making good on the promise I had made her. Making myself ready to walk into the Kingdom of Death.

The grounds were empty now but a single bulb of light was still burning. A wooden platform had been erected, a little stage, private, for a performance that was only ever supposed to be secret.

I remembered how my footsteps had thudded against the boards, how the General—or a man with the General's face—had loomed above me. Was that man dead? Had he ever truly been alive?

There was blood everywhere, wet fans of rust and vermillion. A heavy leaden bar, one end tipped in gore. I knew what it was for. What it was that Victor had been doing in this place. He *had* been here though and could still be close.

My hands shook with something like fright but I stepped forward, summoned my voice like a ball of energy and hurled it in the darkness. "A bargain is a bargain, Victor, and I'm ready to make good!"

I never doubted he would come. Leon had often said that a man's strategies seldom play out as he expects, so perhaps that was foolish of me. For a moment there was only silence. I stood in that place, dressed in the corset I had longed for, loaded up with death, speaking only to myself: the empty walls, an audience of ghosts.

Then his footsteps sounded from the shadows and his rasping, secret voice hissed after. "Miss Lubchen," he said in such a way I could not tell if I were expected or not. His eyes grazed my performance gear. "I'm glad you've come. It makes things easier. There were reports of riots on the streets. A girl was killed, they say, stabbed by a fanatic and he in turn… well, let's call it a piece of bad luck."

The breath jerked into my body. I tried to hold it and calm myself. I had to wait, I knew. He was moving toward me, his hoodnik gait still lithe and relaxed.

"Are you ready to be friendly. Let us mourn them among the others then. Let us write their names in our register of martyrs."

His eyes glittered. "It is, after all a time of mourning, isn't it? The General is dead. He died in his sleep. They say it was a hemorrhage. An artery burst in the old man's brain."

He was dressed still in the General's counterfeit jacket. It was a military look he had never worn in all the time I had known him. But then he hadn't been a soldier, had he? His violence was never the violence of the front line, with its summer campaigns and winter holds, its uniformed battalions, its conscripts and commandos. His was the violence of the street where any man, woman or child could be drafted into service. Where any district or ghetto might become a theatre of war.

"You're thinking it's a tragedy, aren't you?" he continued. There were no tears in his eyes, no pretense of sadness at all. "But then you're a child of tragedy, aren't you, Miss Lubchen? You understand what a tragedy can do." He paused, waited for me to catch up with him. "See, there are two worlds at play here: the world of law and the world of belief. The world of law is made up of rules and regulations but the system of belief is more —shall we say—nebulous than that. Possibilities appear. They must be seized instantly."

He paused.

Patience now, and caution.

Still I let Victor get close to me even though his presence sent a shudder of terror running through my body. I felt a squirming sensation, a fluttering beneath my ribcage. I did not want to think of what it was. *Why are we having babies? Why are we putting seeds into the ground at all when such a thing is coming?*

"You were here before once, weren't you? I remember it: a little girl grieving for her dead mother and father. But then how many other spirits did you oblige to keep them company? I think you know better

307

now. They were our enemies once but we called them our heroes." His grin was wide and flat. "We could do the same for you, of course. If you were willing. Think what we could do with ten such circuses as we have made together. A hundred. So tell me, little niece—can you be loyal? Who do you want to be in this world?"

Nearer he came, then at last near enough. The ring glinted on his fist as he pushed it toward me. It seemed engorged like a tick.

"Oh yes," I told him. "My name is Baba Yaga and I have come for your skull, you bastard. I am as loyal as you have taught me to be!"

I closed my eyes, breathed in one last time as Teresa had taught me, breathed out.

Goodbye, little one, I thought. *Find a world better than this one.*

Else, I had named her in my heart. For her mother's mother.

Then I flicked the trigger.

47

Nothing happened.

His eyes screwed up in expectation of... something as his thoughts worked their way to his brain. I tried the trigger again, then a third time, before the truth of the situation came to me. Somewhere was a chink, a misplaced wire, a signal that wasn't transmitting.

Victor let out a shivering laugh. Ha-*hah*. There was death in that laugh—my own death coming at last—and with it a kind of joy.

"Oh, Miss Lubchen," he said, his hot breath touching my neck. "You aren't the first she-bitch I've had to tame. Nor will you be the last. Shall I show you how it's done then?"

He yanked my hand away from the munitions, then leaned his weight, pushing me backward, crabwalking me across the blood-stained stage. His fist closed over mine and language deserted me in the pain of the moment.

"Carefully, carefully now. Those are amateur charges, I think, so best to treat them kindly. But I can be kind..."

One hand kept me pinned while the other clamped down over my elbow. I screamed as he forced the joint backward and the bone snapped like wet wood. He was fastidious as a ship surgeon. I thought I might pass out then—wanted it, in fact, wanted the darkness, a quick end to what he had started. He was going to kill me. That much was obvious from the moment the trigger had failed.

"Normally I have questions," he said. "I like to search a man's soul. Hardly a need this time as I know your soul very well already, don't I? I've put my fingerprints upon it. You're mine still, it's just you seem to have forgotten it. So let me remind you."

He pulled himself close to me, as if he were going to whisper a secret in my ear. But already I knew what that secret was. We are weak and other men make of our weakness what they will. He would come for Leon, the company, any I knew and loved. I'd proven turncoat once before and I would again if he wanted it.

Then it wasn't even the pain that made me tremble though that was very bad. It was his leering face, his teeth tiny, sharpened by the shadows and the light. And with his grin the now certain knowledge that he *could* break me. If the pain were bad enough… and of course it would be.

"Shall we begin?" he asked.

Then I heard a thunderous roar from the darkness.

Victor glanced away and his grip slackened. It wasn't enough for me to move, only enough for the ebbing pain to leave me my wits.

Something hurtled toward us like a comet, a flash of flame-colored fur. My vision darkened and there were stars and sparks as a heavy blow sent me reeling.

I landed badly. My ruined arm gave out under my weight while my good hand clenched the trigger. There wasn't time: not to think, not to act. The rank smell of animal filled my nostrils.

It was my tiger.

The beast's ears were laid flat against his head, his barrel chest puffed out with fury. He was baring his teeth, nearly the length of my finger, and then those same teeth were sinking into Victor's shoulder. The Deep struggled under the surprise weight, trying to find purchase. Amba held him up in his jaws and shook him violently.

Where had he come from? How did he find me?

The tiger's forepaws anchored themselves in Victor's chest. A shock of brilliant red blood sprayed out from a rent in the Deep's body. It seemed it should be over then. The human body was weak. Didn't I know how little it took for bones to fracture and sinews to fray? For all else he was, Victor was only a man. It shouldn't have been possible for him to resist a beast like that.

It shouldn't have been possible—

"No," whispers Sara Sidorova, "no, no, no…"

—but hadn't I longed for the impossible moment? Hadn't I been drawn to those times when reality seemed to fissure? When someone with the right instincts could transcend the laws of nature?

A fist shot up from the hurley-hurley mass clenching a fat orange agate. Once, twice, the tiger swiped it aside. His claws hatcheted through muscle and meat but the Deep was strong, fast-moving.

"He can't survive it!"

"Come on, you," the Deep muttered. His voice was ecstatic. Again the hand went up and this time my tiger clamped his magnificent jaw around the wrist and crushed it down.

But Victor, it seemed, had been waiting for this. He'd been prepared to lose the wrist if it meant saving the rest of him. With a wrestler's agile maneuvering he flipped my tiger over. Now Amba began to yowl piteously, unused to being on his back.

Unused, it seemed, to hunting at all.

"What's happening?" says Sara Sidorova. "Is he—?"

"Don't you want it?" the Deep was saying. "Thought you had me. But you're old, you're well past your prime."

Now the Deep moved on top of my tiger and wedged his knee against the other's windpipe.

Ha-*hah*, ha-*hah*. Despite his crippled arm, despite the blood that sheeted from his shoulder, the Deep was laughing. He threw the whole terrible weight of himself down.

"Is this how it ends then? After everything?"

Impossible moments, Grandmother. I had spent my life searching for them and now I had found one. Time slowed. The world seemed to vanish and all I could see were millions of stars, stars beyond counting.

Only one star was brighter than the others.

One star burning like a premonition.

My spirit flew out of my body. I saw a staircase reaching out of that terrible place, felt myself traveling upward. Below me the world grew smaller, even as Amba thrashed and choked and his life guttered in his beautiful yellow eyes.

There was a body below me, a girl's body, dressed in red and primed for death.

"It's coming now," whispers the Evening Star, her granddaughter. "It is upon us."

I had promised my mistress it would end in fire.
And then—and then—

EVENING

48

Past gloaming now, past dusk. The rich hues of sunset—lavender, porphyry, vermillion—spill into cumulus grays then the deepest black Sara Sidorova has ever seen.

"A door opens, the snare is loosed," whispers the Devourer, "first one, then another, the dead vanish like smoke. Is it ending enough for you, my love? Do you understand now?"

Smoke. Aye, it seems she can still smell it even here: a smothering, ashy musk that hangs like a blue gloom in the air, stinging her eyes. The sisters too are gone, their thrones abandoned. Only the Devourer remains, the standing bulk of him grown massive now, his shoulders as wide as three wagons set side to side, his banded tail as thick as an alder. The scent of ash follows him like perfume.

Grandfather Death. The fire-beast.

"Where is she, Amba? Where did my granddaughter go?" she demands.

"What is a body after its spirit has gone out of it? An empty eggshell, a husk, nothing but bones and char and cinders and dust."

When he inclines his head to meet her gaze, his black-rimmed eyes are banded as well, shades of amber, flax and venomous green-gold. He is ancient, she realizes, far older than the world she knows. Ancient and implacable.

"Then what am I? I saw my own death, too." Her words are halting, as if she is only remembering the gift of speech. "Teller of tales, she called me. Outcast, Baba Yaga in her palisade of human bones—why would my granddaughter tell me such a story?"

Something had flown out of Sara Sidorova when she watched her death. Now when she stares at her wrists it is like staring at a stranger. She has forgotten the landscape of her own body. It could be anyone's, it could be her granddaughter's. She cannot remember where the smear of blood came from. Hers or the elf-boy's? The elf-boy? What elf-boy?

Still the Tiger's gaze holds her. It burns.

Her voice is desperate. "There must be something more than this. What else remains?"

Is there nothing else? her granddaughter had asked. And in the end, what had there been? Only the devouring fire. Only its hunger.

She knows she cannot stand the force of that gaze, alone, as she is, in this place. He brought her for one reason and already her life is slipping away from her. Blood, a necklace round her throat as the bullet parts her flesh.

"You know what remains, Sara."

Of course, she does. As she looks closer she can see, even from here, the collar that circles the expansive width of the Tiger's neck. Iron, cold iron—binding him still. Dwarfed as she is, her hands tiny against the gargantuan scale of him, she could still open it. Would it really be so awful to forget? She is forgetting already, isn't she? Forgetting everything but her rage, her need to see them dead—every last one of them.

"My granddaughter..."

"You've heard her story," thunders the Devourer. Growl like a rockfall, an avalanche barring her way.

"Not all of it," she cries. "Show me Victor's death."

"I cannot."

His eyes are plummetless and unblinking. *There are stars in their depths*, she thinks, *new constellations of light unseen by any mortal. How is a woman supposed to look into such vastness and resist?*

"But every man dies," she pleads with him. "Show me his day. Show it to me!"

"The spirits are gathering closer, my love. You can see them twinkling in the night sky. But his is not among them. Some things... persist. But you know this, don't you? You've only forgotten."

A sudden flash of remembrance then: the guttering campfire stove and the captain of regiment speaking to her. *Come on now, Victor. This lady is our guest and I won't have her disappointed.* Then a face with a murderous grin and that dry, hyena laugh. *Ha-hah.*

"Oh, my love, you're losing yourself, aren't you?" the Devourer asks softly, so softly now.

And despite all her practice, her years of training, Sara Sidorova finds she cannot lie to him. "Yes."

"It happens. Even here. Not all tales survive their teller. Sometimes one story inhabits another, comes to replace it."

There are other memories behind that first one, but they are distant: circling like a flock of mourning birds. "If I'm to die, then let me go. I don't want to remember," she rages. There are no stars in the sky. Had he been lying when he told her there were? It is pure black, not a gleam, not a glimmer of light.

"But you must now," says the Devourer relentlessly. "Remember your own hunger, my love. Remember why it was I brought you to this place. A final gift then: your own story returned to you."

"Please, I don't want it—"

"But you need it, I think. If you are to do what must be done."

And the Tiger lifts his paw into the air, the claws gleaming, as curved and as sharp as a scythe blade. The movement is delicate and precise.

The point of one talon rests against her brow. Then it begins to dig, parting the flesh, opening her up.

"Grandfather," she whispers, "devil."

"Perhaps."

Then there is a noise, sizzling in her ears. A starburst of flame.

THE MIRABILIST

49

"It's a day of deep grief for all of us," crackles the radio. My hand floats above it and the announcer's voice waves, reappears. "There has never been another man like him, so astute a performer, one so attuned to the crowd…"

When the voice vanishes again, a sharp sadness wells up in my stomach. Goosebumps on my skin. I think I might be close to tears.

"I'm eight years old." Sara Sidorova makes a strange noise. "What is this? How are we…" Still the voice comes out of her, whispering her story.

Of late I've come to feel these sudden squalls of emotion more acutely: a happiness that bowls me over, a languor that saps my strength. I don't fight them. Instead my mind fills with a dark cloud which I slowly release into the world. A dramatic sigh. I wish I could return to bed now. My limbs are heavy as stone. My head lolls.

"Enough of that!" says my mother, dressed in black as all the women of Garsk are. We are the Village of Widows, aren't we? "Don't let your papa catch you moping."

"But Valentin…"

"Yes, we know. Of course we know."

I won't look at my mother. Instead I stare at the black-eyed crows.

They could be mourning with me. Will my mother let me charcoal my eyelids now? Better to wait until Valentin is dead.

I wish I had been born prepared for a world of sorrow, like the crows. I'm too joyful. I sing for no reason. The words just appear in my head. *Juniper, juniper, juniper…* Now I'll have to make do as best I can. Poor Valentin. My papa promised to take me to see him at the circus but like so many promises, this one has been deferred. Soon it'll be too late.

She takes a breath, tries to master herself. "It hurts. Seeing it like this."

"I know," says the Devourer. "It must. That is the way."

Now my mama's hand waves in front of me. The nails are well presented but her skin is speckled in the heat. My own hands are lovely. I've tiny fingers compared to my papa's, the nails of which are often bitten down, with a line of red dirt lodged beneath the ragged ends. He has miraculous hands. They do miraculous work. He smells of chestnuts, vinegar, the metallic dust that coats everything. He has a voice that makes things go quiet inside and his presence is almost invisible. He's good with horses.

I wait and listen for him.

50

How beautiful is Garsk at the end of autumn? Star-shaped flowers drift in the air. Spirals of dust trail the breezes and I walk through the cemetery, thinking a little on death. The gravestones are askew, old teeth-wise, and little curls of ivy have shot up between them. I know the names. Estes. Kanter. Moebus. Minow. Their professions too. Strongman. Acrobat. Clown and clown.

"I'm ten already. It's all running by so quickly..."

I practice poses for my act. There are nine basic passions: joy, sorrow, fear, scorn, anger, amazement, jealousy, revenge, and pity. I promised Papa I'd master them while he was away. It's been a good task for me. Once I know these I'll have felt everything there is to feel in the world.

There's Papa coming down the road at last. Amazement! I helped to paint the wagons last spring and their colors are still very new and fashionable. The red's particularly good. You can see it from far off and it makes you wonder what's coming toward you. Only I know. Papa is coming. Joy! There he is, waving to me. I don't like waiting but today the waiting feels good.

One hour. Two hours. Was he really so far? Sorrow.

"Come here, little mouse!"

There he is. He scoops me up in his arms and waits for my kiss. Love.

"Very good."

"I've been practicing."

His beard has gotten quite overgrown. Mama won't be pleased. So. I comb it with my fingers and he laughs.

"I promise to shave right away."

"Is there news of Valentin?" I ask him.

Now his face is sorrowful. I wonder if I can do my face like that.

There's a fairy tale Papa tells me sometimes, which he says is famous. I love to hear it.

"This isn't a story, is it?" Her voice is full of wonder.

"It's your life, Sara, your memory."

"I remember a time when the world had three suns in the heavens. Back then it was so hot the world bubbled like asphalt and the people were skeletons walking, begging for respite. They knelt in the dust and their tears boiled to vapor."

I can almost glimpse it: the earth like a dying ember. I can smell the char on the wind, woodsmoke, ash, even the ancient oaks of the wildwood alighting like candles, and all the small things running in terror.

I know the lines. I whisper them with him.

"Two warriors were sent to them, both crack-shot twins. Together they turned the sky into a shooting gallery. By the end, they had struck two of the suns clean through with their arrows."

I wait for the ending.

"They fell to the earth, which cooled and hardened and bore life once more. Afterward many children were born, which the people thought of as gifts from the trees."

I can't resist any longer. "I know what happens, Papa."

"What happens then?"

"Even now the remaining sun travels to the underworld each night to search for his kin."

Papa pulls me so close his beard tickles my ear. "Good girl. You understand then?"

I nod.

"Sometimes even the sun must die so the world may live. Only mourn for a short while, my little mouse. Forty days, then let him go."

I nod my head solemnly and make myself watch the crows circling the horses. When they land they run their beaks through the manes, preparing to thicken their nests. The horses love the birds who tend to them. My papa loves the horses. I love my papa. The world's a dancing circle.

"Now," he says, "I have a present for you."

He takes me by the hand and I greet the performers as I see them. The show has been a success. I can tell because they all look well-fed, which isn't always the case at the end of the season.

Together we come to the animal train. An unpainted wagon I don't recognize—a bit small and a bit funny-looking. There are bars on the side and a window looking in. "You must go slowly now," says Papa. He points to a ball of pumpkin-colored fur in the farthest corner. It moves and there is a face. A little pink tongue. His back is all lined as if someone has painted on it. What a little darling. He blinks his yellow eyes.

"This one is for me?"

"Your responsibility, Sara. The two of you will grow together.

For now he's little but he won't be for so long."

"I'm growing too, Papa."

"Yes, I know."

"May I hold him?"

Papa takes a key from his chain and hands it to me. It's old and heavy. "He's yours now."

I haven't felt like this before. The sensation is close to pity but not pity. Why are there so few good passions? I try pity and love and they are close. Perhaps I'll need to invent the rest myself.

"He sleeps like a grandfather so I call him Grandfather Death. But in the east they call these ones *amba*," says Papa.

"Is that where you got him?"

"There was another caravan on the road. They had only just split up. Most had fled."

I've heard stories about this: caravans attacked by thieves or mercenaries. Sometimes the bosses take the money at the end of the season and cut the performers loose without pay. If there are other circuses on the road, they might pick them over for good acts. But no one new came home with Papa. Only this one.

"His mother was injured. Someone put a bullet in her shoulder."

Sorrow and anger. Revenge!

"She wouldn't have survived the trip back, little mouse."

"She might have." I won't cry. "May I call him Amba?"

"Call him whatever you wish."

I reach out and the little one comes to me. He's squirmy and affectionate. His tongue touches my chin and I laugh out of my expression. Now the sum of my joys is greater than the sum of my sorrows.

"Will you wear black tomorrow?" Papa asks lightly.

Judiciously I answer: "Tomorrow I'll wear the red."

51

Years pass.

I tend to the beastie and the two of us grow. I stroke and feed him egg mixed with milk mixed with brandy. Sometimes I wear the corset Mama made me with bright red stockings. It's getting chilly but I need practice the wearing. I am sixteen. I've learned how to take dainty sips of air. For a while it made the poses harder but my body is smaller in some places and larger in others. Now it's all right.

"Show me what you've learned then," says Papa.

I let Amba outside his cage. He has trebled in size in the last two months and that's made him proud. The aspect of pride is very close to anger. Eyes open, the mouth pouting, mostly shut. He struts around for a few minutes like a soldier. Then he flattens his body against the ground.

I match the roll of his joints, head down and spine supple. He sees the chicken and stalks toward it. Its tail feathers are a glorious, white fan. Then Amba races forward. The bird is spooked and takes to the air, juking and diving when its feet touch the ground. The tiger cub is too slow but not me! I pounce and my pounce is proper. I can almost imagine the bird's gamy neck between my teeth.

"Let her go, child. Don't be greedy."

I turn to Papa and toss him the chicken. The old girl squawks and buffets until he coaxes her to silence. Amba is embarrassed. He slinks back to the cage and crawls in himself.

"You wounded his pride."

Why is there no pose for contrition? Well, I know what it should be. Big fearful eyes and a downcast mouth. Papa laughs.

"Oh my girl, you're wonderful. But how will we use it, do you think?"

I shrug. I can see one of the farm boys has stopped his carrying to watch. I give him a little curtsy and he quickly gets back to his business. "When Amba is older he'll make them think he's fierce. The two of us will learn all sorts of tricks."

"It would be better with a second big cat."

"You have me," I say, pouncing. The chicken startles out of Papa's arms. Suddenly Amba is alert again. Papa swings me around. His feet make beautiful patterns in the dirt.

"You're a girl." Staring at me more carefully: "Almost a woman."

"A tiger!" I make a face like Amba's.

"Only sometimes. Sometimes you must be my daughter."

"Always."

He ruffles my hair gently and sets me down.

52

I practice love, but it isn't right. I know it should be natural, not imitative, if it is to convince an audience. To be a great performer I must understand love from the inside. But how? I decide now is the time to fall in love.

"Sixteen and already a widow," jokes Papa but Mama only looks on with a strange sad smile. I don't talk about Valentin anymore. I was a child then. Now I'm a woman and a woman must be more careful with her love.

I take stock of the men around me. Oral and Alek and Lev are all too old. They would if I asked but I won't ask them. I spent my first summer traveling with the caravan, so I know too much about them, the sounds they make at night, the smell of their wind. The younger Estes is too big. He's quick to smile and slow to anger but I'm afraid how much it would cost to feed him if we ever got married.

I've timed this badly. There were boys in the towns I visited that I might have tried. The caravan had worked its way up the coast so it was mostly fishermen and sailors. If I'd gone with one of them, the rest of the crew would have had no respect for me. Once Vana took up with a townie and they teased her mercilessly for the rest of the season. But there aren't enough of the right age in Garsk. I was conceived in the festival that marked the end of the last bad years of the famine. Not many babies were born during that time so now there are only a few young men and most of them are idiots. I'll have to keep an eye out and choose the best of them.

There is one with a nice look about him.

"You're talking about Feliks Lenko," says Vana. I frequently practice with the acrobat. Her trim body can do amazing things.

"Who is he?"

"His family is from across the border." Vana is smiling at me in the way older women always seem to. I hate it.

"I think he's in love with me," I say, just to shut her up. "But it isn't anything to me if he is."

So. Feliks.

His teeth are straight and they give him a good smile. He could do the trick. But he doesn't truck with the circus folk much. His farm is farther away, over the hill, closer to the border than any of the others—almost in the killing zone. He likes to work so I seldom see him. At least all the work has given him nice broad shoulders. Not too broad. No, he's the right size.

I go to Feliks's farm. The state issues maps with false edges to confuse those tempted to cross outside the checkpoints. The locals know better and so do I. I take Amba for a stroll down the road to see if I can catch his eye. Amba isn't impressed by these antics. Now he's reached his adult weight he pretends nothing impresses him. He spends more time cleaning himself than I do. Papa says it's because tigers are careful of their scent but I know better. He's vain. I hum a little song of admiration for him.

"Hey now, you!" calls the farmhand—Feliks—waving from the field.

Good. I've got his attention.

I pretend not to notice and I do my best walk. I know how good I am at it. He waves his hands some more and I smile to myself. This has been easier than I expected.

"That beastie is spooking the cows! Get on, get out of here!"

"You're an insolent fellow," I shout out of spite. Spite is easy. Everyone in Strana can do spite.

"And my heifer has better manners than you."

I spin on my heels with dignity so he won't see the heat dying in my cheeks. Amba's eyes follow the slow-moving creatures as they form a defensive circle.

My tiger is pleased with himself. He leaves a spray of urine on the fence.

✳ ✳ ✳

It takes me a week to pluck up the courage to try again, if only because I think Amba is laughing at me. If there is one thing I've learned about tigers it's that you must always appear to have the upper hand. So. I must show Amba I can own that stupid boy.

When the sun is high and hot, I go alone, with a loaf of bread I've baked myself and a little bottle of brandy. "Ho there," I say from the road.

"What?"

"You must be hungry."

He shrugs.

"I think we should make up."

"If you like."

He comes over. The sweat makes him glisten and that glistening makes me light-headed. Perhaps I'm coming down with something. He does have nice teeth though. And nice eyes too. The people in

333

Garsk don't have eyes like his, which are the color of moss. His hair is blue-black and darling.

"Where's the beast then?"

"Sleeping."

"Lazy," he snorts. "What have you got for me?"

Suddenly I don't want him to have the brandy. Papa bought it for Amba. "Nothing," I snarl.

"Hey now. You wanted to be friends, I thought."

Damn those green eyes of his.

"I suppose I could share."

"That's a good girl then. I've got the right place for us."

My face goes red again, but he's turned away and started off down the road so he doesn't see. I follow, a little afraid, but I like the way his body moves. This liking is part of love so perhaps I've had enough now, perhaps I've got it. But he keeps walking and I keep following. We crest the hill together. From here the field is yellow. The sunflowers are huge and flaming. They must be taller than me!

"What do you think then?" says Feliks and now his voice is a bit shyer.

"The ones in the back look terrible. Are they dying?"

"Just for the season. They'll be back next year. You've never seen them before?"

"It's too close to the killing zone. Papa told me not to come this far."

He's standing close to me. "I thought you might like them."

I love the flowers with their gently nodding heads. Their colors remind me of Amba: the gold and the orange and the brown. "Aye, I do." I take the bottle from the basket.

53

So this is love then.

I'm lying with Feliks in the cozy warmth of the shippon where the straw is softish and the cold air doesn't get in. I've asked him to describe my face so I know what I look like but the farmhand is useless. "Your skin is pale," he says, "and your mouth is a little bit open."

"What about my eyes? Are they shining?"

"I can't tell. It's too dark."

Probably my eyes are shining. They feel as if they are shining and they often do when we're together. But how can I make them do that if he isn't with me? Tricky.

I don't bother describing his face. His body is good, very nice. I love the cindery little trail of hair that leads to his navel, gold and copper and brown and a few stray blacks. His skin has a dark coloring because he's from the other side of the border. He won't tell me about that.

"But you know my family," I plead. "So surely it's only fair?"

"My father doesn't speak the language. He wouldn't understand you. I don't want to talk about it."

"But then how did you learn?"

"Because I'm very clever. The cows taught me. Why are you so full of questions?"

The look I give him is like jealousy but softer and with a smile. "I don't like you keeping things from me."

"I won't hold back," he says and then he uses his fingers to make me make a different face.

Well. He's very good at what he's doing. When I think on it my eyes shine and my face and breasts go all hot and at least none of the others will tease me about this. I take him in but when he goes too quickly I move him out again.

"I can't have a child."

His breath is hot beside me. "You can if you let me keep going."

"No. I don't want to."

He rubs himself against me and that's enough for him. Afterward he's careful to make sure I'm satisfied. He does a thing. I don't want anyone to know about it but it makes me feel very good. I'm glad he can't see my face while it's happening though. The one time I schooled my features. I wanted my look to be something like joy. Actually what my mouth does is like anger and what my eyes do is like astonishment and the rest doesn't have a passion attached to it.

"That's good," I say.

"I know."

"You're so full of yourself!"

"You could be full of me too." He is joking but I don't like it.

"Aye, then I'd be full of a big, fat, farmhand baby. And what would I do?"

"Clearly you'd have to hang yourself," he says.

I'm silent for a long time, enjoying the pulse between my legs, which makes me lazy and unwilling to argue. But as the warmness recedes the worry is still there. Eventually I say: "I couldn't perform anymore. Papa wouldn't take me with him."

"Do you need it so badly?"

"Yes."

Now it's his turn to be silent. I wish I had a light so I could see his face. Is it jealousy? Is it sorrow? I reach out but my fingers don't look as well as my eyes do.

"Then I promise you, no babies until you're old and your joints are stiff and your breasts are sagging and no one wants to see you anymore anyway."

"You don't like my breasts?"

"I adore your breasts."

"What if you don't love me when I'm as old and as ugly as all that?"

"Don't be a dolt," he says. "I want to marry you. Then we can both grow old and ugly together."

"What does my face look like now?"

"Quite astonished."

"I suppose that's how you'll look if I ever say yes," I tell him.

54

The thought of marriage is gray. What would it mean?

I love Feliks, that much is easy to know. But there can be love and all manner of good things without marriage too. It's dangerous. I could grow fat and pregnant like some of the other girls and that would be it for my performing. I could get rid of the baby, if it came to that—an option, anyway. Vana has done it. I held her hand after and brought her boiled water to settle her stomach. There was crying, lots of it, and a mess of redness. I've never been afraid of blood but I hate the thought of some raw and unformed thing coming out of me. Me but not me. Me and Feliks but without all its working parts.

Which limits my choices.

Who do I know who has done well out of marriage? Mama? She seems happy enough, and she has my own charming company for now. But then Papa is away so often and now I'm going with him. What's left for Mama then? The cousins, maybe, and their own little ones. So, little ones and little ones and little ones. They have such small squalling faces. Are they enough to fill up a whole life?

There's nothing inside of me that wants rest.

I like the idea of my stomach ballooning outward with the child but only because of the change it will cause. It'll push me into something else. I like the push but not the something else. I feel as if I've reached the border in my life between childhood and—the next thing. The next age. Thus far I've been powerless but power is flowing into me now, my breasts, my graceful neck. This is why I must know the signs for love and joy and terror and sorrow and jealousy and all the others. To put on their mask is to be free. It means choosing for myself. Once I'm the master no one else can put the mask on me.

I have a strong, flexible build but the end of my growth spurt left me small enough to look petite, which is a good thing. Extra height would make me unstable. Tall girls are not welcome in the circus unless they are very tall, in which case the circumstances for them are different.

I'm healthy. I broke my arm once when I was five and now it seems stronger for the weeks it took to heal. I'm less careful with it than I should be but it has proven itself to be exceptional.

Where is the self anyway? Pain lives in the body and so does the mind. Vana's first husband was kicked by one of her horses. Afterward there was a spot on his skull that was soft and he changed completely if you touched it. He had been a bastard, always swearing and drinking, but if you touched the soft spot he would turn gentle as a child. He wandered off six months after the accident, got lost in one of the small towns the caravan visited; maybe he fell in love and stayed; maybe someone strung him up. No one knew, least of all Vana who now has the fear that fate is terrible and the only way to beat it is joy and joy and more joy snatched from wherever you found it—which means, for her, far too many men, sometimes women too.

The women are often kinder because they know they are dealing with someone broken.

I'm good with animals. Animals of any sort are my friends. They are born thespians. The signs they give are very clear, even if they are lying.

The masks are good. They're a defensive mechanism. With a

mask a small beast can seem very large; a large beast almost invisible. The world is full of things that hide themselves by pretending. I do it myself. There are things I refuse to allow myself to see.

The Nay-Saying Tree, for example. Someone has stabbed a railway spike through a human shoulder and put it up there. There is a mass of bones at its base and everyone knows they are human bones. They call it the Garsk Girl because the border guards want them to believe it was one of their own found in the killing zone.

I know if I were to see the Nay-Saying Tree it would break my heart.

But I don't see it. I walk past with my eyes shut. Amba never sniffs the bones. He isn't interested. There are live things, deer in the forest, the rancid stench of bears, which intrigue him but don't seem to cause much alarm. The cows on the other side of the fence. Feliks, whose smell is on me always.

But perhaps the mask means something as well—a sameness to be put on? A singular notion. I'm not singular. I am everywhere, everything: watching, listening, contradicting.

I surprise myself when I say yes to Feliks. "I'll marry you," I begin and this makes the bastard farmhand smile as if he's caught me in a trap. But that's only the outward smile. Inward is another smile that speaks more truly. It says he's the one to be trapped; he'll give me anything I want, he'll serve me however I wish. He'll bind himself to me and follow me to the ends of the world.

Or at least the country.

Which is what I ask of him. One summer of traveling together. I wouldn't use an animal on its first tour if I could help it. It needs breaking in. Familiarization. That's what I want from him. One summer first.

55

We spend the winter together in a kind of hibernation.

Both of us get a little fat but I don't mind because it's warmer that way and we're both practical people. I meet Feliks's father, who never seems interested in talking much. He gives me lumps of sugar after dinner and this always makes Feliks embarrassed but I don't mind. After eating when we're alone I whinny like a horse and prance around, until Feliks grabs hold of me and puts a stop to it all with kisses.

The bad months blow in, lay down the freeze, and no one moves more than necessary. My hair smells of burnt tallow but it's too cold to wash. I learn things about Feliks: the way he likes his coffee, the way he shaves, doing the hardest bits first. His accent seems to vanish overnight. Mama is unhappy about the arrangement but she makes lace in the evenings and presses it against my forehead, asking my opinion. Is it too fancy? Is it too light?

"It's beautiful," I tell her.

✳ ✳ ✳

Then spring comes and Feliks helps with the calving. He seems to tug the little pups right out of their mothers' wombs. Even the backward ones find their way when they're guided by his knowing hands. This impresses Papa more than anything else but Papa loves anyone who treats animals with respect.

It's difficult for Feliks to leave but he begins the preparations, hires laborers to help his father, and watches them carefully in the early months to be sure they can be trusted. Two of them he lets go for stealing and a third for keeping quiet about it. It's hard. The folks in these parts are suspicious by nature and never say more than they have to but he needs to know who is loyal. The other three are good and he gives them as much as they want for the job so they'll stay through the summer. They don't rob him blind. Their terms are fair.

Then the caravan sets out.

The air is still brisk. There are patches of snow in the ridges of the mountain but late started, late returned, so Papa says. At first the other performers see Feliks as an appendage and suggest various forms of surgery. They laugh but I keep silent. Vana warned this might happen and I listened to her advice carefully.

After the first show I find the knife-thrower Oksana, an aging starlet prone to terrible bouts of jealousy. I beat her with a pole wrapped in fleece. I'm careful not to leave bruises that might show, careful not to touch her hands, her wrists or her fingers. But they all hear Oksana shouting when it happens—canvas walls are thin—and that's enough to be sure no one bothers Feliks again.

The rest of them fall in line when they see how hard Feliks can work: like a bull, but smarter. He learns how to set up the big center pole that props up the tent. He watches the acrobats—Lis and Lil—and shows them how he can help, flinging them up into the air just as the younger Estes does. Sometimes he's a stooge when Oral and Alek and Lev require a stooge. He's handsome but foreign enough with that blue-black hair that the crowds like it when the barbs are vicious and he never seems to mind.

342

I hear stories on the road about what is happening in other places. Papa tells Feliks to keep his head down. After that the clowns leave him alone too and he makes do with tending to the horses, which is still good honest work.

After all that is settled mostly my days are happy. The nature of the acts changes from village to village. It's Papa, the ringmaster, who decides how it'll go. He sends spies ahead of him, often Vana, because she's good at making friends. She creeps into their camp in the morning then comes back to reveal how poor the people are, what their likes and tolerances are, what might offend them. And then the show is altered. Sometimes the shows of strength performed by the younger Estes—bending bars, catching a cannon-ball in his bare hand—are symbols of military might and what might be accomplished by the state army. But if they hate the army then he performs without a uniform, dazzling the crowds with the possibility of what an ordinary man might accomplish. The clowns are the most astute of the lot. They have jokes for any occasion, and their best friend one night will be their most bitter rival and hated enemy the next. Thus the circus reinvents itself endlessly. Sometimes they praise our people's warlike ferocity, sometimes they announce they live in the best, most peace-loving place in the world.

We travel to desolate port towns and bustling markets, always avoiding the bigger cities, the army, when we can help it, which isn't always. If we're stopped then Papa pays a bribe and we go hungry for a few days, which isn't so bad. What's worse is when the soldiers ask for a show. I keep close to Amba during those performances, and after. When the men approach me then Amba snarls and snaps and that's often enough to send them on their way. "He's so bad-tempered!"

I fuss apologetically and even if they want to linger, those unblinking gilded eyes sour their spirits.

Otherwise, Amba has a sweet temperament on the stage, a willingness to show off. The two of us move in sync. I can do a shout that's a little like his roar and he always pretends to jump like I've goosed him. The crowds love that.

"You have to work with the inclinations of the animal," says Papa but I know all this already so I just smile at him demurely until he laughs. "All right, little mouse, I'm an old man now and I'm only saying things you've heard before. Do it how you want. I know he's yours." He means in my heart. The tiger, he has always told me, belongs to no one but himself. It's up to Amba how long he wants our friendship to go on.

Me and my tiger are popular, of course. Sometimes when I get to a town already a crowd is waiting. I wave from the wagon, which is painted orange and black so everyone knows where to look. Feliks hoists me up onto his shoulders so I can blow kisses to the ones who are furthest, the wives and the little children standing in the back. When he does that I feel myself going up higher than even he expects, as if I'm weightless, floating, looking down on all the tiny people. I see myself too, the corset which I've molded to my body, the thousand tiny mirrors Mama sewed to the bust to ward off the evil eye. But not just myself in the present, a line of selves radiating outward in many directions, each waving and blowing kisses and smiling. They wear red, not black.

Then he sets me down and it's all work, work, work, getting the tent ready, and the stage, the animals calm and fed. I starve Amba on travel days because I've found food gives him indigestion. Six days of meat and play, one day of fasting and travel.

Then we're off again, the dust cloud blowing out behind their wheels and the clowns happily soused and Vana mourning another lost love.

A good life.

The days get longer and longer, their shadows stretch out, then everything tips into autumn and too soon the summer is over.

56

The sunlight slips away. The sun itself is a burning ball grown faint enough I can look at it directly, fat, orange as a pumpkin.

"Have I done my penance, Baba Yaga?" Feliks asks, and he's smiling that straight-toothed smile that captured my heart.

But the question is real. Has he done well? Has he worked hard? Will I give him my heart now that he's done as we bargained?

I take his hand in mine, kiss it, kiss his mouth, let him take me. My hair will look lovely under the lace Mama has made, the trees dipped in the fires of the sun's death glow. Red, red all around me, beautiful, beautiful red.

So it seems I'll get married.

I want to wear the red but Mama is traditional and so the linen is dyed midnight black and shaped against me. My corset has no steel in it, only animal bone. I stand up properly. I don't even remember what it feels like to slouch. When I sleep it is with a straight spine. Sometimes Feliks complains he's marrying an iron rod and I give him a look that says, "I beat a woman with an iron rod for you so keep your mouth shut." And he gives me a look that says, "I love you and I'll say whatever I want."

I laugh. We don't really need words, that's how far we've come.

But not far enough. Fear flutters through me when I see my love. I'm snappish in the mornings, queasy after breakfast. Mama turns to the old rituals for help. I meet an old woman in a room filled with ikons. She accepts from me a bullet used to kill a wild animal, which she places under my pillow. When I return the next morning the woman is waiting with a pot of water with herbs, a small fire burner, and a wide metal spoon.

"Do you know what frightens you?" the old woman asks.

I shake my head while the woman retrieves the melted bullet from the bottom of the pot and shows it off.

"This is your bullet heart," she says but it doesn't look like a heart. It's smooth and tear-shaped. While she melts the bullet again she whispers prayers over my head, my breasts, my arms, my pubis. The next shape is nettled, threads of copper like lightning in all directions. "It's bad luck," she says.

"My wedding?"

"Your dreams have been bad of late?"

I nod and the old woman brings the spoon to the fire again. Metal has a particular smell when it dissolves in flame, sweet like garlic.

"I'm remaking your bullet heart."

The threads go soft, pool together, into two smaller tears.

"The left is larger than the right," says the old woman. "You should marry your husband. He loves you very much."

I don't ask what it means that my own heart is smaller. Perhaps that's how it is for all women. "What about the bad luck?"

The woman shrugs. "There's always bad luck. But love is a rare beast. Few truly snare it. If you've got it in your trap, take what you can get and be happy. Besides, there's good luck on the way too." She points to a third nipple of lead, practically invisible, nestled between the other two.

That settles it. I stand beneath the Nay-Saying Tree because Mama insists. We'll all get very drunk tonight but for now my mind is clear. Feliks is holding steady in a wedding suit that makes him look dashing and strange. A stranger. How am I expected to come to him? But I do. I close my eyes and follow his smell. Good things. The horses. Resin. A musky sweetness all his own.

Papa lets me go. That moment is strangest of all. When was the last time I thought of Valentin and his fading heart? I promised to love Valentin forever but I never saw his tomb. This early in life and I'm already unfaithful. I reach for Papa but he has taken a step back. I must go forward, away, away. Toward.

"Come to me, my love," says Feliks. There are other words. All the old oaths, some in the language I know and others that sound strange in my ears. Feliks's native language. No one seems to mind if he speaks it here. I have to repeat the words and trust I haven't promised away some vital part of myself. Or if I have that the trade was fair and I'll want what I've bargained for.

The bridal hooks sink into my spirit. I think of what love is to me and what I'd be willing to promise. Today I am a wife, a widow. I love Feliks. The women around me wear black as I do but when I whisper the words, they are green. There's no lie in them, nor could there be. He's already a part of me now and I could no more kick him loose than I could my own shadow. So I whisper it again and again and then I say it louder because I want to make this promise fully. I want to bind myself to this man so his fate is my fate, his life mine.

Somewhere inside me is an answering flutter. Somewhere, deep, a kick. A breath. A spirit quickening. Can joy make one fat and full as the moon? I hope it's joy in my belly, nothing but joy.

"Bitter, bitter, bitter!" shout the men as they take a drag of the samogon in the cups, so Feliks and I kiss, to take the edge off, to chase the bitterness from the world for all of them.

57

I look around the house in winter and take each thing in, examining it for cracks or disturbances, for soundness and longevity.

It is my house now, my house to share with Feliks. What a remarkable thing! I'm used to the dust of the road, sleeping where I can, ignominious assignations in whatever hidey-hole can be managed. In barns and under the wide-stretched alder.

But here's a bed whose purpose is to give me comfort. I've a chest to keep the insects out of my clothes. Blankets so I won't be cold, a stove for food, cupboards, plates, bowls, and other things. Everything around me has a soul. It was made for me, a luxury.

Now life slows to a crawl. I've no duties beyond the preparation of food, the cleaning of the house, caring for Amba, training him with the waggoneer's whip.

I'm not so much cut off from my old life as it has become arrested. Banished. My things are now a married woman's things. When I drink coffee early in the morning and tend to Amba's needs, I'm conscious that I'm doing it as a married woman. How would a married woman walk? What are the faces of a married woman? Are they the same? No, I think. Love, envy, sadness, jealousy—I still have access to the same range of emotions but there's a new inflection in my performance, like a flourish at the end of a written letter. Feliks doesn't insist I wear my hair up but I begin to do it anyway, thinking it is more practical, and besides, my ears get cold in winter. I tie a black scarf under my chin, but when Feliks sees it, he laughs, tugs the knot free, and kisses me.

"You look like my grandmother," he says. "Shall I get you a cane? Do you want ointment for your feet now?"

I snarl at him.

"Ho there, Mistress Tiger!" He holds out his hands to placate me. "I've never seen a more beautiful grandmother in my life. Only wait a bit, will you? I want us to grow old together."

I adore this about him, the way he imagines the future as a land we'll explore together. I undo the tresses in my hair and down it flows like water. "It's very soft," he murmurs as he takes it in his hands.

"And you're very stupid," I say but I kiss him anyway. No point in fighting. He takes me to the bed and we lie down together. The mattress envelops us in the scent of straw. This is good, I think, this is better than good. Because we can take as long as we want now, which seems to be forever. We're inching along into that future Feliks imagines, getting closer, day by day.

I feel like a pilgrim approaching some holy relic in a temple. I'm not anxious to arrive but I know that ahead lies the keys of Paradise and tomorrow is good enough to try them out, tomorrow, tomorrow.

58

Then bad fortune comes down the road.

Papa tells me the news. I'm exercising Amba in the yard. The last of the winter snows don't vex him much but he's still dainty about the mud. I'm dainty too. My belly has swollen with the baby, and so have my feet and ankles. My back aches now and I know I'll be too big to travel this year.

If only the little thing had waited to take hold… a few months, no more. I could have sat out the winter getting fat in my beautiful straw bed, but no, I'm too far along now. I'll have to wait until next year when the baby is older. There are other women who have nursed their children in the caravan though Feliks isn't happy about the idea of it.

"Decide in a little while," he said to me and I know he hopes that once I hold the thing in my arms I'll want to stay home. But I also know that mustn't happen. It's bad enough I have to sit out this season. Amba won't travel without me, but it's clear he's getting anxious too. The winter left him bored. He misses the crowds.

The black birds are back, circling overhead. Amba watches them. If they land in the pen he hunts them like the chickens. A week ago he was very still. Birds see too many colors, all that plumage. It blinds them to ordinary dangers. They didn't see him waiting. He snatched one right out of the air.

But there's Papa and Papa is telling me the bad news. "Look, the soldiers are coming…"

My eyes snap to the birds. The birds follow the soldiers. The soldiers are always leaving bodies behind and the birds are clever. They're happy little scavengers.

It isn't unusual to find soldiers on the roads, not with spring approaching. No one tries to cross the border in winter. The snow makes them easy to find. They'd have to carry more provisions, scarves and thick boots and heavy jackets and food. If they laid down to sleep the snow would cover them and they would freeze. So the soldiers relax in winter. They come to the village to play cards or gamble or drink or try their luck with the women. But in spring the soldiers don't trust the villagers. The border isn't real for the villagers. Some used to live on the other side, many still have family there. Over there. Beyond. Where Feliks came from.

The children are trained to watch for strangers in the village and report them in exchange for sweets. When they get older they're shown the Garsk Girl and they all take turns touching the bones and shivering. Some of them will become soldiers. Not my child, though. No, already the little one is doing flips. She'll be an acrobat. Lis and Lil will train her to fly through the air so if she ever escapes it won't be on foot.

"What do they want?" I ask.

Papa shrugs. "Keep that husband of yours out of sight."

"He has papers."

Papa shrugs again and then touches me gently.

My eyes drift to Amba. Snowflakes settle on his face. He wrinkles his nose in distraction and his tail stands up high—curiosity, not threat. He has already eaten his fill today.

59

Captain Olender is surprisingly handsome. He has a distinguished mustache that makes the younger Estes jealous. "If I had a mustache like that..." he begins sometimes. It's hard to take a strongman seriously when he's jealous.

Captain Olender speaks with a cultured accent. I've few opportunities to see him up close but at one point I find myself with him in the tavern. Mostly the soldiers drink in their camp but the captain is different and this is because, as he says, he must establish links with the locals. "You're the tiger girl, aren't you?" he asks and I tell him quietly, yes, I am. "He's a good-looking brute. Have you seen him kill?"

"Only birds. Only the crows."

"A beast like that wants to hunt."

"He's a sweetheart."

"Oh, the girl thinks her tiger is a sweetheart! Bring him to our camp then. There's one among us who knows a thing about tigers."

Feliks tells me not to go to the camp but I can't refuse. When Captain Olender sees me again on the streets, he calls out, "Tiger girl, tiger girl, are you coming now?"

So. I go with him because I have to.

In the garrison they live like men away from home. Mostly they sleep in canvas tents, though none so big or well-appointed as our own big top. The smell of the cook fires is everywhere. They breathe on their hands to keep them warm, stamp their feet. Their beards are thick and heavy, combed through with crumbs no one has bothered to tell them about. Only Captain Olender seems to care for himself. This is part of his charm. He's like Papa: he has a big voice, a big personality.

"This way, this way." He ushers me into the mess hall. I know at once that this is a dangerous place. My belly presses against the soft fabric under my woolen shift, under my coat, and though the men can't see it, I know they've stripped me naked with their gaze. They all want something: sweetness, softness, a touch, a kind word, even just my smell. There are men who are standing close, trying to sniff me. "You just smell so much like home," says one. "My mama smells exactly like you."

"Never mind them," says the captain. "You! Victor! A moment of your time."

Victor is a large man, not so large as the younger Estes, but still pretty big. His head is bald with an angry purplish shine. He has barely any neck at all.

"This one wanted to hear your tiger story," says Captain Olender and the soldier grunts. Slowly he undoes the buttons on his gymnasterka. The flesh beneath, like his skullcap, is the color of root vegetables. But whereas his pate is perfectly smooth, there I see a hideous puckering of flesh. It is matched by a mess of deep, scarified lacerations on the meat of his right arm.

"My story," says Victor.

I study the expression on his face but I can't read it. I wonder if that's how it is with men, if they are taught not to have expressions.

Captain Olender claps his hands. "Come on now, Victor. This lady is our guest and I won't have her disappointed."

"My story…" he says again and the captain urges him onward.

"All right. Here it is. We were sent to the steppes. Bastard lands, those, too ever-loving cold and no good soil. But they said it would make good farmland. That's what Captain Olender told me." A slow, bad look. "Only there were tigers—man-eaters, they reckoned. The croppers were fearing 'cause they butchered the livestock, sometimes the dogs. Worries about the womenfolk and their youngsters. Sometimes hunters went missing, mostly only the foolish ones, or the drunks—the old hunters weren't scared of the tigers. They got on well enough but the shavelings were churlish and didn't show respect. So the croppers went to the landlords and the landlords went to the governor and the governor went to the army so we went to the steppes and made ready to hunt. They paid us for each skin. You know how we did it?"

I shake my head, feeling sick. It's the baby, I think. The baby doesn't like this story.

"We were riflemen, see, and we took pack horses with us. We had snares and shot but we barely needed them. Some of the villagers—the old hunters—had their own strategies. When they came across a tigress and her cubs, they'd let slip the dogs. The beasties would startle in all directions so it was easy as jacks to nab a cub that way. And the mama never knew where it had gone. You'd see tracks after, that mama tigress looking for her young'un. Then the hunters would sell us the skin and keep the rest for themselves."

"Tell the lady why they kept them," says Captain Olender.

"Oh, those croppers were an ever-loving superstitious lot. They ground up those tiger bones and they pickled the cubs in wine. Their claws were a cure-all for sleeplessness. Sometimes they needled a whisker into a rotten tooth, saying it would stop all the soreness in an instant."

The baby kicks again and I wonder about asking for a chair. I don't want to show myself weak. I clench hard as the pain passes.

"So that's what I'm thinking when I see you and His Nibs parading round the village. If the beastie were mine, why I'd strip him down for my salvation. Never another toothache. Those croppers said a tiger could make you live forever. Just swallow him whole, tongue to tail."

And then he spurts laughter. Ha-*hah*. Ha-*hah*.

"Aye, so what happened to you then?" I stare pointedly at the scar.

"What indeed, madam. Maybe the beasties told the same tall tales to each other. Gobble up a man and you'll live for bloody ever. That one came at me like a thunderclap. We were tailing her but she doubled back, the old damn-bitch."

"She didn't kill you?"

"The captain here was quick with the rifle. Shot clean through the two of us, he did. Look." And Victor points to a little pucker beneath his collar bone. "No one thought I'd live, least of all me. I said, 'Go on, boys, who wants to drag a dead man through the snow?' But Captain Olender cut out the girl's heart and he fried it up right there."

Now he wipes his mouth with his sleeve while the other men howl. Afterward Captain Olender escorts me from the mess tent with a look halfway penitent.

"It isn't a good place for women," he says. "It comes from coarse living. You know how it is. A man has to survive how he can in this world."

"I need to return to my husband."

"A man would be lucky with a pretty girl like you on his arm."

Suddenly I say, "I'm nobody, please!"

"It would be a pleasure," Captain Olender continues, stroking his mustache, "for the men, you understand? If your troupe would give us a performance. It's easy for morale to slip out here, so far from our own families. You'd do that for us, wouldn't you?"

When I nod at last, he lets go of my arm and gives a genteel, little half bow.

60

I return to my little cottage but now I'm afraid.

"All this worriment and bile must mean the baby's coming soon," teases Feliks. He has seen the soldiers but they don't bother him. Sometimes he drinks with Captain Olender at the tavern. "They aren't so bad," he tells me, "just lonely, just far from home."

But I find a footprint I don't recognize near Amba's pen. Sometimes he seems agitated. Then the weather grows warmer and the nights throw off their chill, embracing the light for longer. Bees and insects visit the budding ginseng plants which grow bright red berries the size of peas. The workers seed the sunflowers as the last of the spring frosts vanish.

"The flowers will be up before long," Feliks promises.

During this season it's all graft and preparation. The wagons must be painted again. The younger Estes works off the winter's fat by lifting stones in the field or pulling the plough. Lis and Lil stitch silk scarves to their costumes.

But I catch Captain Olender following me. He has a way of standing that's demure, somehow ladylike. "Ho there," he says. "The wagons are almost ready. You must perform for us soon or it'll be only your sweet self!"

Papa is against it. "These things bring trouble with them. Don't give an inch, my wonder-girl. When you get a little rounder he'll leave off and find another to bother."

Vana tries to distract the captain but he only smiles politely and says, "Good day, madam," when she approaches.

Mostly things hold. Then a bad spring storm blows in. In my cottage I can hear the hail punching the walls, then rain again, then more hail.

"The river could flood," Feliks murmurs.

"So soon?"

"It's a bad sign," he says then spits to ward off the spirits.

After, the banks are palisaded with branches swept down from the mountains, hagberry and hawthorn. A body is fished out a week later but no one knows the fellow, probably a shepherd from across the border. He has a rifle slung across his shoulder which jammed between two rocks as he floated past. Without that he would have drifted downstream, been pummeled by the rapids and thrown into the gorge.

But the rifle worries Captain Olender.

Feliks isn't the only man brought in for questioning. His father too, and some of the farmers, as well as a chapman who set out early that year, lulled by the fast-melting snows. Most are released within a day and they spend the evening grousing at the tavern, not too loudly. They offer salutes and toasts with their beer whenever the captain's men are within earshot. But Feliks isn't with them.

"Don't vex yourself," says Papa though he's stroking his beard. "I'll bring his papers to Captain Olender tomorrow and all will be well. But stay with us tonight."

So that night I sleep in my old bed.

The tang of the woodsmoke and Mama's singing are a kindness. I remember how it was when I was younger and Papa would tell me such stories. He has the best sounding voice of any man I've ever met. No one can spin out words the way he can.

It's good to be here again, with family. But a cramp in my stomach keeps me up and gasping. The baby playing tricks, bigger now, pressing her face against the skin of my belly.

"You were the same way," says Mama with a smile in the morning but I find little comfort in it. Papa comes back from the camp alone.

"They say he's being held for questioning. Sara, I think you should go to Captain Olender. What they said is quite serious. They don't believe the papers are true. They say Feliks had a different name when he lived on the other side of the border."

So now the baby is kicking but I'm holding my wrist to it, singing, "Juniper, juniper, juniper, don't be afraid while I'm here."

61

I'm eighteen today.

The garrison is a vat of mud with little canals between the tents covered over with wooden boards. I have to be careful to keep my balance. I'm wearing a simple green shift cinched above my waist, which shows off my belly. Green, because I want them to know I'm telling the truth. A young man with a trembly voice, his army shirt clearly too big for him, and unwashed, takes me to Captain Olender's tent.

"Ah, the tiger girl!" He curls the tip of his mustache around his finger. "You're here about Feliks Lenko. I know him and I'm sorry if I've caused distress. It's only a little thing. I'm sure the matter will be cleared up soon. These situations often resolve themselves but I've a duty, understand, and it's for your safety as well. That's topmost in my mind, if I'm honest. You're such a fine woman but you don't understand what sort of men there are in this world. So it falls to people like me to protect you."

"He has papers. You've seen them now."

"Aye, but your husband is how old, twenty-five? It's a long time and when he was born—well, let's just say the officials in those days were not as scrupulous as we are now. There are reports of unrest across the border. My men reported seeing your husband near the killing zone."

"Are you sure it was him?"

"That's the very problem! The soldier who gave the report is away on a training exercise. So. You understand my position. I can't release your husband until I'm certain, yay or nay."

Blood quakes in my ears. "I want to see him."

"Impossible, I'm afraid. It isn't me, but the men. I can't be seen to give you special treatment or else when we release your husband they won't trust him. That would be a bad situation for you both."

Soon the young soldier returns to escort me from the camp. His boots are mud-splattered, his trousers too, almost to his knees. Only Captain Olender has fresh clothes. He clasps my hand as he says farewell. "Don't abandon hope, Madam Lenko. This parting between lovers is only for a little while. But perhaps if you found it in your heart, you might speak to your father about a performance."

"The caravan will be gone soon."

"Best to be quick then."

✵ ✵ ✵

After that, a terrible feeling of waiting comes over me. Sitting in my mother's kitchen, drinking fitful sips of water, I remember what it was to be ten years old watching for Valentin's death. How the world seemed to stretch out his final hours. I never saw the mausoleum. It's been too political in the cities. But politics, Papa says, never comes as far as the countryside. In Garsk the dead aren't given so much fanfare. Just a little stone. Estes. Kanter. Moebus. Minow.

I don't want to think about death.

I cry whenever I see the Garsk Girl until Mama tells me a secret: "It isn't what they say. They found those bones in the cemetery after the last bad flood and they put them up there to frighten people."

"But why?"

"Because the idea is enough to scare you."

Still Papa won't let the circus perform for the soldiers, even when I beg. "It would be better if we left today. Sara, we could take you with us. And your mother too. All of us could go with the caravan this year and when we return Feliks will be waiting for you."

"What would he think if I left now?"

And Papa takes my face in his hands, which are rough with years of working the tent ropes. There's a warmth in them that flows out of him and into me.

"Your husband loves you. Your child is coming and that's what matters. Every father knows. He gave away his life the moment he stood with you under the Nay-Saying Tree. The part he has left is just a little thing."

"Papa, he's my world."

"You only think so. But your world is much bigger than him. I've spent my life trying to make it so."

Then a week passes. Not much time, but enough for the first of the sleep-grass blooms to burst and the white-capped rhododendrons to open their red, fragrant throats. Though I visit Captain Olender every day there's no news. I don't see Feliks. The soldier on his training exercise doesn't return. Then Papa and the caravan are ready to depart.

"Please. It would be so little to you. And it might make a difference." I try sorrow with him, I try love.

But Papa only kisses the top of my head. "Come with us, Sara. Your mother is coming and if you don't you'll be here alone."

"I won't leave him."

"If we don't go now the performers will starve. There's never enough for the winter as it is."

"Why won't they do this for me, Papa?"

And now he won't look at me. "Because they know, Sara. It's you the captain wants. The men would, the younger Estes, Oral, Alek, and even Lev who has as much to fear as Feliks, given his history with the army. But Lis and Lil won't. Oksana won't. Not even Vana. They're afraid of the captain. But don't worry, soon you'll be past his wanting."

"So what then? What's left for me?"

"Come with us."

"No."

"I'd make the younger Estes put you in a barrel and carry you away with us if I thought it would help."

"I'd come back for him."

"I know. Your mother warned me."

So. It seems as if that will be all between us.

I watch as the horses champ at their bits and start to pull. The wagons look so pretty, freshly painted, like the toys of a young child. So small they seem to me. I let my hatred go with them. I don't want to keep it close where it might curdle my growing child. I want nothing but love in her life.

But now the village is quiet. Spring should be happy but there's too much ice and it'll be many months before they return.

I go back to my cottage. It still smells of Feliks, smoke and resin and his own sweat, our musk on the sheets. My back aches and my feet are sore and my gums hurt but I find the old trunk with its three brass latches locking down the lid.

I take out the corset. How will I even lace it? My stomach is too big now. No one is left to help. Red silk shot through with purple. Beautiful colors. I tuck the silver comb of the headdress into my pinned-up hair.

62

Now there's a light blinding me.

I know what I'm doing is dangerous, for me and the child I carry. It's bad luck for a pregnant woman to even clasp her hands above her head lest the cord tangle. But I'm in a cage of my own wants. What's happening must happen. I look ahead to the future where it has already happened—where Feliks is safe beside me, teasing me about the strange fancies that can take hold when the blood is high. "Were you really so anxious for me?" he'll say. "What a worrywart you are!"

"I love you," I whisper to myself, to my husband's ghost. Love. What is my face doing? Are my lips parted? Are my eyes shining?

The caravan has taken the performing tents and so the soldiers have cleared the mess hall for me, set up benches at the back where they can watch. They've hung lanterns as I instructed. I glance at Captain Olender but his expression is hard to read in the glare. I must judge his mood by the sound of his applause, the sound of his breathing, which is heavy now, excited.

But then Amba is beside me and it is easier.

My body is so closely attuned to his moods, and it must be: because no matter what's between us he's still wild at heart. There are scratches on my arms from the times I've been careless or he showed his love in the language of beasts. But today Amba is gentle and performs with good humor. The smell of his body is calming. He rises onto his hind legs. He places his paws gently on my shoulders. I lean forward to kiss him—my mouth close to his, a trick that Feliks would never watch. It frightened him so much, how vulnerable I made myself.

The Tiger's Wife, they called me, for this. For so little.

My act is barely more than a quarter of an hour. I know of other acts which are longer but those circuses have more animals: bears, lions, leopards. Papa told me never to outstay my welcome or trespass on the good will of a crowd. "They can turn quickly," he warned me. "If they're bored, if the harvest has been bad or there's no work or they're drunk."

I've seen that side of them and always forgiven their misbehavior. But in the past I was protected. Papa was the ringmaster and he always gave me the best slot. There were others to help. The clowns who are used to deflecting—Oral, Alek, and Lev. But now there's no one to judge the mood for me, no one to coax the jackals to kindness.

I bow as gracefully as I can, given the constraints of the corset. No longer does it fit the contours of my body. The baby squirms and I feel a wetness between my legs. Blood. I imagine I smell it. I bow again, quickly, and then call for Amba. Normally someone else would lead the tiger to his pen while I enjoyed the applause. The transition is awkward. It steals the suspense but I can't let Amba roam free in this place.

I clip the leash to his collar and bury my hand in the ruff of his fur, reassuring him. He lets me lead him out the back of the tent. Despite the lengthening days the night has settled the sky into indigo, the last burst of sun leaving a sulfurous stain on the hills. The first stars have appeared. Soon the Thresher will be visible and the Swan.

"You're a natural performer," says Captain Olender, who has

stolen beside me. On another night maybe he would look gallant, with his pressed gymnasterka, his polished boots. "Tell me, you're never afraid?"

"Never."

Captain Olender matches my pace, careful to help me across the uneven boards. The two soldiers at the gates of the camp salute us smartly. They are a little in awe of the tiger though neither wants to show it. "Don't worry," the captain says with a consoling smile. "He's as gentle as any house cat, isn't he? The girl has tamed him. It's magnificent."

For a minute I think it's been enough. But he turns from the men who are grinning at one another. "May I escort you home, Madam Lenko?"

63

I never feed the tiger after a performance.

Amba isn't good-tempered about it. Better for him to eat in the morning when he can spend the afternoon drowsing. But tonight he's slow to leave my side when I come to the pen. He makes the noise which means he is hungry. I don't have any meat. Tomorrow I'll need to ask one of the farmhands to slaughter a sheep—or else catch a deer in the woods—if Feliks doesn't return soon. A tiger's meal is measured in pounds and the weight of it can be astonishing.

"I wonder if we could speak for a little," says Captain Olender. "Do you have wine, perhaps?"

"Of course."

I won't take him to the house.

There's a shed near the enclosure where I keep my tools. Inside I have a small bottle of brandy I use to treat scratches. It's foul stuff, mustard-colored, like urine.

There's no place to sit so Captain Olender stands. "To your health," he says as he downs it. I've poured myself a half measure and even this I only sip.

"Did you like the performance?" I ask. I know I can't show love, not even a little. The nine passions are no use here. Maybe only the young are so pure in their displays. As a woman my emotions only come in parts now: scorn, fear, sorrow, pity.

"I enjoyed it, very much," says Captain Olender. "Please. Drink. I don't like drinking alone."

"You lead a company of men. Surely they're your best companions."

He smiles. "How old are you?"

"Eighteen."

"Why are you looking at me like that?"

I glance downward quickly. He's sharp, the captain is. Frighteningly sharp. "I don't like drinking in the evening. It muddles my head."

"Come now." He fills my glass to the brim. I don't want to offend him so I drink. It's like air, this brandy. It goes into me but I barely notice at first. "Good girl," he says.

"When can I see my husband?"

"Please," he says, "let's talk a little first."

Now the brandy is burning my stomach. I feel light-headed but he pours another measure and he watches me drink it down. The bottle is almost finished.

"I didn't always want to be a soldier, you know," he says. "I wanted to be an artist. Oh, my sketches weren't very good. Trifles, really. I loved the classical style. What they do now is too modern for me."

The night is softening like velvet around us but a cold wind whips through the trees. Somewhere a dog is barking. On the far side of the training pen Amba lifts his head.

"Art helps the soul to recognize itself."

Captain Olender is delighted. "That's just what I was thinking. I felt a moment of recognition when you were on the stage. I can't easily express it."

"Many men say that when they see the tiger."

He cocks his head. "Why is that, do you think?"

"The tiger makes them think of their own death."

I don't tell him that's the secret of my show. The tiger's wife is Lady Death. Their pulses quicken because they're thinking of death.

"Where is my husband?" I ask again.

Captain Olender turns formal but his voice carries a mocking edge. One performer to another. "I'm afraid to inform you, Madam Lenko, that last night your husband escaped from our garrison. We think he's fled across the border to join his compatriots."

"I don't believe you."

His eyebrows lift. "It isn't for you to believe or disbelieve, Madam Lenko. I am telling you it happened."

"I want to see his body."

"There is no body."

Captain Olender is standing very close. Traces of beeswax glisten in his polished mustache. His gymnasterka is freshly laundered. Someone in the village must do it for him. A collaborator. *Who is it? I'll kill that woman*, I think. *I'll strangle her with my bare hands*.

"This is why I wanted to speak to you privately. We have his papers but it's clear they were falsified. Your husband is a traitor. It is my personal belief that you didn't know. How could you? What husband tells his wife all his secrets?"

"Please. Will you give me his body to bury?"

I'm thinking of the Garsk Girl. Where would they have done it? Did they take him to a cliff and push him over? Lis and Lil once tried me on the trapeze. The hardest part, they said, was simply stepping off the edge. Trusting your strength. But I hadn't minded. It had seemed like a game to me, like Papa swinging me over his shoulders.

Would they have blindfolded Feliks first? I imagine him stumbling in the darkness, a hand at his elbow to guide him. Would he have guessed? Would they have lied to him? And then the ground gone beneath his feet. Did he think of me at the end? Was it too fast?

"I said there is no body." Captain Olender looks annoyed but he schools his features. Only another performer would recognize it. "You must listen to me very carefully now, Madam Lenko. In situations such as this it is normal for us to take the family into custody. The state has a responsibility to its citizens. We can't know what is in your heart."

There is nothing in my heart. That's the curious thing. It's as if all the true passions have frozen solid like a river in winter. I could feign anything I like now. "What do you want from me?"

"I want you to be a good citizen."

He touches my cheek. In truth, I barely feel it. What shall I give him then? What does he want? Sorrow? Anger? Is he the type of man who enjoys those?

Captain Olender continues. "You're young, barely older than a child. I'm sure you were deceived by him. If you wish I can annul the marriage."

"We made vows."

He shrugs. "Such things can be undone. Else you have vowed to give our enemy shelter. Vowed to comfort him with your body and to raise his child. We can't allow that, you understand. Instead let me place you under my protection."

"My father will come home again."

"It is a long time until autumn, Madam Lenko."

Still he is touching me. Why doesn't he feel the cold coming off me? I've seen elks frozen in a winter river, their weight enough

371

to crack the surface and send them plunging in, one after another because the herd is bound to follow wherever the leader goes. Maybe this is how it is with the soldiers. They follow their captain even when the ground gives way. He follows his commanding officer. On and on, everyone following, marching blindly. One false step and the river takes every bastard one of them.

"I can't come with you tonight." My voice is perfect, my gestures are perfect.

"You need to grieve," he says.

"No." My smile is perfect and he looks no deeper. "I can't grieve for a traitor. But he might come back for the child. I need to prepare myself."

"You're a good woman, Madam Lenko. We will need to take the beast, of course. Tomorrow then. I'll send Victor for him."

"You must call me Sara. I am Madam Lenko no longer."

He is content we understand each other. I watch him going away along the path until the night merges with his spirit and he's only a little shadow, then nothing at all. When he's gone I don't allow myself to weep. Only children weep. My mind is sharp as a carving knife.

Estes. Kanter. Moebus. Minow.

I wonder what it's like past the killing zone. I've never once thought about crossing. But if that's where Feliks is—it must be a city of the dead. There must be great edifices of marble and porphyry and ash. That's how the dead live.

The bridal hooks tug at my spirit. But I can't go yet, not so soon as this. There's work to be done. I think of Victor startling the cubs from their mothers. I think about their bones cooked down for soup. He's a cannibal, from a long line of cannibals. They devour what's good in the world so they might live forever.

But I know better.

Amba stirs drowsily when I call him. "I give them to you. Take them tonight. They're yours."

Then I let the beast slip through the gate.

"Do you see then?" the Devourer asks her.

"Don't speak just now. This is my story."

64

In the morning comes a storm of crows. It could be autumn already, the sky is so full of movement. I wake in the tiger pen and pluck straw from my shift. My back is stiff but for once the baby is still. For whom would the child perform now? The watchers are gone.

Not gone, not entirely. I find traces of them on the road as I walk toward the garrison, slowly now, for my knees are aching. Blood in the flowers. Sleep-grass and white-capped rhododendrons in the dappled shade. The crows have pulled the bodies apart, searching for hair to thicken their nests. I wish them warm beds tonight.

When I reach the garrison I stall at the threshold. There are no fine young men to salute me here. I see a paw print in the mud. It's enough to know. Beyond is a thunderscape of such crimson I need not see it myself.

"Goodbye, my love," I whisper.

Then I let the road take me away from Garsk, past the fields with their hidden sunflower seeds, waiting for the light to come again. I take the right fork because I know this path. I went this way with Papa and the caravan. I don't carry food because I won't need it. I've moved beyond such things now. I should be wearing black but all I have is the corset.

I drift, a straggler on roads of dust that stretch between one place and the other. When I see the shadow of others approaching I hide in the forest, between trees as bleak as old houses. Once I discover a body in the woods. It startles me. There's a hole in the man's gymnasterka, no bigger than a thimble. I could place my finger in his body, plug him up. But his eyes have the quality of glass. I stare but I can't see inside. Perhaps he vanished into smoke.

I take his boots, which are too large. I cut strips from his uniform and stuff the rags in my toes. I steal his knife, which is misshapen from over-sharpening.

"Juniper, juniper, juniper, my juniper," I sing, "under the green pine, lay me down to sleep."

"Hush now, my child. It's enough. You remember and it is enough."

"I want you to come to me, Amba. I want to be Lady Death."

"Come away then. We're finished."

Time loses its meaning. I can't tell the borderlines, the bright concentric rings that dance and surround me. I make no effort to be lucid. What concerns me are these questions of light and time.

"This way now."

The road is a staircase and I step lightly upward. This, I imagine is how the constellations are born. How easy it is to live forever! All I need do is reach out and touch the vault of heaven.

I see the arc of the earth, the trembling of small creatures, storm, sun, the parched dust, the wide, trembling eyes that burn with the fire of love and the fire of hate equally. And in the distance I see—what?

Another staircase, and a girl upon it. And another, and another.

"Welcome, princess. How long have I awaited your arrival?"

TWILIGHT

65

"ello, husband," whispers Sara Sidorova. Her legs are tired from the effort of climbing. She has never felt such a weariness in her life.

"Devil, you called me. Grandfather Death."

"I know you better now, don't I?" she asks.

She wishes suddenly for small, familiar things to look to. A quilted blanket or her mother's hairbrush, her chest with its three brass latches. Everything in this place is grossly gargantuan, a scale of being too far beyond her. It smells fierce and fresh as live coals.

"Who am I then?"

She forces herself to look into the deathless depths of her Tiger's chimerical eyes. Takes up the postures of widowhood: pride, defiance, enduring grief. "You are the beast who eats the world. My angel of mercy."

"Aye, Lady, you're right. And I loved you in my way—but my love is no easy thing. It cannot be, given what I am and what I was put in this place to do." The black triangle of his mouth relaxes into a smile. White whiskers, black stripes. *Like cinders*, she thinks. *The devouring flame.*

Bitter, bitter, bitter, the men cheered at her wedding. The world was bitter so why not then let him take it? What is there left for her? Only the work of a widow—

"Are you ready then?" he asks gently.

—and after that, then what? What could ever follow? Grief like salt in her mouth, bitter indeed. Her fingers shift to her belly but even then the movement is so faint it could be nothing more than a dream, a memory of life.

Perhaps the child is already dead. After all, she herself is dying. The blood leaking from her wound as the bullet continues its inexorable course. She has her memories but it isn't enough. Even the sun must die, thinks Sara Sidorova. Sara Lenko. Every night it dies and leaves the earth in darkness. It travels to the underworld in search of—what?

She looks out now to the night sky: charcoal-dark with a spray of stars, beautiful in its own way but desolate too. A wasteland. And yet she saw someone traveling through it: a burning man, a figure in the heavens vanished now, too, into the shadows.

And with that thought a sudden sweetness floods her mouth. Circles and repetitions. She *had* known him, hadn't she? Like an echo, a spirit. Only she couldn't bring herself to believe. Even for the circus master's daughter, some things still seemed beyond the ken of mortals.

But how many impossible things has she witnessed today?

"Amba," she says at last, reaching out to touch the flaming gold of the Tiger's crown. "You have brought me to this place and named me your guest. But there is one thing my heart still desires."

And the Tiger inclines his leviathan head, the inky scrimshaw on his brow like a tale of bad fortune. "I can be generous in victory. But the time is short—" she knows he is right, she can feel the cold stealing into her limbs, a deadening of sensation "—so what would you ask, my love?"

"Where are your sisters?" she says softly.

The question is a snare in its own right. Once asked, she can see the shock of it ripple through him, a slow cloud of anger passing over him. Only now does the Tiger blink, the bronze of his eyes guttering into mistrustful midnight black. Rage, she sees there, and something else: a surprising tenderness. An acknowledgement he has been bested—at least for a little while. For it seems, at the end, that some things might still be allowed to her.

A farewell, she hopes.

66

S ara Sidorova climbs until her legs begin to buckle, until great blisters as red as carbuncles form between the calluses on her feet. This time the Tiger is with her, his fetters extending as far as they need to, iron links gleaming like a whipsnake's scales.

For a second time she passes through the gates of ivory and bone with its chattering skulls. She does not—will not—linger. Not even to marvel at exquisite craftsmanship: the filigreed details of a ceaseless, still-form psychomachia. Devils and angels, miracles and murder. But she has seen things already, hasn't she? Lived them, in fact, possibly found her death in the mad hurley-burley of it all.

She looks out and sees the world below, shrouded in the darkness. Weaving upward through the air she sees a staircase of twisted gold and ebony. The same staircase she walked upon herself? Perhaps. There is a girl upon it, a girl who looks very much like her.

Never mind. Into the foundations, then.

She can hear a distant susurration, growing closer, deeper, richer, more complex and resonant as she travels. It is sweeter than the skulls. Birdsong, a chorus of waxwings and bluethroats. And as she thinks this, the shadows begin to coalesce around her. Hundreds of them, thousands, their plumage silk-gray tilting to pallid jade-white. Touches of morning glory and red, like a thousand watching eyes—

Sweet Sara, little Sara, I know a place the birds go in the winter and our souls go after death...

—and black too, feathers like night, feathers like charcoal. The mourning birds gathering close to begin their terrible labor. He had told her there was little time left and as the dream-fowl flock to her and she lets out a cry of concern, she can only hope there is time enough.

But then—oh, mercy!—their throats open...

"—it was only a little while and then I—"
"—but at dawn he came for me—"

"—green as glass and I knew I loved her but her father—"

"—it was a wreck, I was drowning, the storm—"

"—he followed and followed—"

"—the taste of raspberries I'll never—"

"—my sister was a—"

"—went west but by that point—"

"—we never see, don't understand but how could—"

"—for me and it hurt—"

"—dreamed of fire—"

Stories, she thinks, *endless stories, a thousand, thousand stories ushered forth from the mouths of the dead.* So much raw and glittering sensation: the shadow of love and the brilliance of pain, growing until its pitch is as thunderous and stultifying as the All-Dark.

Sara Sidorova knows she could stay and listen. For her this is a temptation in its own right. Hasn't she learned as much about herself in this most sacred of precincts? A story can be both a shackle and a tether, a thread in the darkness that helps you find your way, a hook that lodges in the tenderest part of you.

She covers her ears. She *must* because what living ears were meant to hear so many stories? Who could hold all these stories inside of them? Yet there is one voice which she doesn't hear among them. His. And so hope flickers inside Sara Sidorova, its own warm pulsing light.

Through the hallways of birds she travels, stepping softly, her skin brushing dark gossamer feathers—"Not yet, not yet," she whispers to the mourning birds—and the tracery of their reply rising up before her, behind her until at last the passage opens and she finds herself in a vast, wide throated cavern.

The gloom is thicker here, the shadows become leaches of color. *But of course,* she thinks, *it must be this way.* The sun has died and nothing remains now except the grief work of the sisters: the Morning Star and the Evening Star. It is their light alone which keeps the darkness from owning every inch of this space. A silvery glister emanates from their faces, their hands, their unshod feet.

"It is you," she whispers—and it is and it isn't. A veil has been drawn across the Evening Star's face, a dark curtain which hides her features. She doesn't speak. The story is finished, Sara Sidorova understands.

Between them lies a body.

The sisters are gentle with their ministrations. Carefully now they peel back the blood-stained robes to reveal the tender human flesh beneath. An ugly sight. A livid, raw wound stretching beneath the collarbone. His fingers have been broken, his skin slashed open in half a dozen different places.

Feliks.

He suffered before he died then. Aye, she thought he would have. Only his face has been left unmarked, that beautiful, familiar face.

"What have they done to you, my love?" whispers Sara Sidorova as she kneels before her husband.

Except, of course, the dead man is not her husband, not wholly—or rather, not only. And Sara Sidorova knows this, understands it immediately for she has always been precocious. Didn't her own father teach her how to watch, how to learn, how to ward off sadness and discover a crowd's hidden character so she might better play to it?

No, this one's hair is golden where her husband's was blue-black and wiry. And his body is too *large* to belong to Feliks. After all, he was—despite all she may have felt for him—only a man. And this is the Sun-King. He has ridden into the darkness and burned there, loving the world until it devoured him, until he too had to fall.

Sometimes stories are wrong, she thinks. Hasn't it been *her* seeking *him*? Past the ends of the earth and into the kingdom of death itself. Cycles and repetitions. She imagined a body left out on the steppes, pulled apart by wild animals. Flesh scattered like starlight—*but sometimes,* she thinks, *our dreams are wrong.*

Still, Sara Sidorova kisses his bruised knuckles. She touches his moon-glow cheek, some portion of reflected light still held there, fading fast. This final kindness is allowed to her before the sisters kneel beside her, long-limbed, undying.

They are not, she realizes, of the same substance as the man before her. They are watchers, eternal and he is something less than that.

Something less and something more.

Together they lift the body and wrap it in silk, red as heart's blood, shot through with purple. And suddenly the birdsong is tremendous, the trilled notes resounding and triumphant. Light breathes across the sky, banishing the nebulous grays, and the spirit of color arises.

"It's time now," says the Tiger. "Long past time."

But Sara Sidorova is listening to the birdsong now. She lets it fill her up, wanting to chase the moment, to linger in it. It isn't fair that she should travel so far and still, at the end, there should be this: a broken body, wrapped in silk. Magnificent—perhaps, but still beyond her, so far beyond her that the pain of it seems somehow worse.

To remember what she has lost and why.

"Will it happen again?" she asks.

And now the other turns to her—Zorya Utrennyaya, whom some call the Morning Star. It is her time, Sara remembers. This child, this young one—except, of course, she is hardly young at all. Centuries have flowed beyond the gates of the palace and she has seen it all.

"Every night," she murmurs.

And her voice is familiar.

"Why?" Sara Sidorova asks.

"Because this is the world as it is, little mouse. A man may be a beast and a beast may be a man. Nothing follows unless it chooses to follow, not even the sun. There was a time when the sun had two brothers but no one speaks of it anymore. The earth bubbled and the people were walking skeletons. Even the sun has known loss."

"What do you want from me?

The other smiles. "The universe wants nothing," she says, folding her graceful hands, "but that you go your own way. Look, now. The light is spreading. A flock of birds has come to greet the morning..."

There they are: brilliant points of light in the wash of lemon yellow, peach, and palest blue. One among them shines brighter than the others.

"What are they?" breathes Sara Sidorova in wonder. Her own fingers are dipped in blood but as she watches, the red sheen begins to glow like a ruby. Brighter and bright it burns, offering no pain, only warmth.

It is the Tiger who answers her, a surprising tenderness in his voice. "They are souls coming home. Soon they'll vanish into the All-Dark. Would you go with them?"

As a child her father taught her to feel the pulse of a story. Each story, he said, has a line of energy, a heart, a soul. And if you find it—if it is in you to pluck it, to make it sing—then you will own the listener entirely.

All her life Sara Sidorova has believed it. This is the work she lived for—because she loved them, didn't she? Truly she loved them: the watchers and the witnesses, the bevy of punters, patrons, accomplices, and rivals.

But it isn't enough, she realizes. Bitter, bitter, bitter. It was good work but it mended nothing. A story is only so good as its ending and in life who knows where that end may fall and what significance it brings when it does?

Staring at the body of her husband, seeing the awful damage he has suffered, she knows how little a story is. Hadn't Captain Olender told her a story? And the captain's lieutenant, Victor? And her granddaughter, blood of her blood, if she lives. And she herself—Sara Sidorova, the Tiger's Wife. She had cast a net around the child and sent her into that palace of misfortune with only a wild beast as her helpmeet.

"No," whispers Sara Sidorova at last, looking out into the vanishing darkness. Even now new light is claiming the world, making a stranger of even its most well-known features: the amethyst spine of the mountains, the rivers like old tin, the coastline ragged as torn paper. "I won't be forced. I told you that once, my angel of mercy, and I say it again. Let me speak to my granddaughter. I think I have wronged her. I'll give her my death, if she wants it, but let it be her who chooses. That much I owe her."

"She has asked us, brother," calls the Morning Star, "let it be so."

And now that other pulls aside the veil.

"Ah," whispers Sara Sidorova. She knows who this is, of course she does. How many times has she seen that face? Sorrow, pity, love. She knows those expressions because she practiced them. They both did. It is like looking into a mirror: an echo, a perfect repetition.

"Oh, Baba. This was never what I wanted for you," says her granddaughter. Here is the smoothness and polish of the wonder-child, here the glowing luster of her skin. The line of her jaw seems sharper now, more angular. Her eyes somehow more expressive with the glister of youth. Her feet are bare. There are blisters upon them. Sara Sidorova has those same blisters upon her own feet.

"It is good to see you, Sara Irenda Lubchen," says her grandmother.

"Who is that one? She has a name that sounds like nothing," the Morning Star muses. "A name that sounds like a mistake."

And Sara Sidorova discovers a new inflection to her grief. Longing— she heard it in the voices of every spirit who came before her. "Your mother loved you," she says. "She gave you that name."

"She gave me your name as well."

"Princess."

"Aye."

Carefully, Sara Sidorova takes the other's hand in her own, feels the hard calluses that mar her smooth skin. "Perhaps it was a bad name. I'm afraid I might have cursed you."

At this her granddaughter laughs and the sound is surprisingly rich. "Blessings and curses, dear Baba. What else is life for? You warned me, didn't you? You warned me but my heart was set and I made my bargain."

"What did I tell you that night?" she asks.

"You told me many things. You told me of a staircase that rises into the heavens. You told me there was a beast at the center of the universe. You told me the spell to tame him."

"And what was the spell?" she wants to know, *must* know.

"What has no feet, no hands, but passes?"

"A story," whispers Sara Sidorova.

"Aye. You told me to tell a story. And I did, didn't I?"

"Not fire then."

The ghost woman smiles again but this time there is a sharpness to it. A trace of mockery, its edge directed inward. "No, that was always my own. You didn't give me my hunger, Sara. You only helped me give it a shape."

Sara Sidorova looks into the dark, expressive eyes of her granddaughter. Else's daughter—and thinking that, she feels the baby kick. Unbidden tears come to her eyes. She had been afraid... so afraid...

And now she moves the other's hand with hers, presses both gently against the mass of life beneath. Again, the baby kicks. Else. Around them whispers the scent of lemon and apple blossoms. The child will grow, thinks Sara Sidorova. She will dry chamomile blossoms in the autumn and sing songs throughout the winter.

"In all my travels in this place," whispers her granddaughter, "I never found her here. I thought—I wondered, did I do wrong by her? Letting her go the way I did?" There are tears in the other's eyes as well now, but a look of wonderment on her face. And hasn't Sara Sidorova seen that same look before, on the faces of the crowds when she took to the stage?

"A story," murmurs the circus master's daughter. "Will you tell me your ending, Irenda?"

At last, the other smiles. "No, Baba. My death is dull. Don't you see? Everything ends the same as everything else." Now her gaze turns to the

Tiger who has drawn himself up, made himself as elegant and solicitous as a suitor. "It shouldn't be the end that we look to, should it, my love?"

As Sara Sidorova looks on, her granddaughter lifts her fingers to the other's collar, digs them into the white-tinged underside of his mane. And where once there was anger, now his eyes close in satisfaction as the beast lets out a contented purr, followed by the sweetest of chuffing sounds.

"Let us choose together," says Sara Sidorova. "Will you do it with me?"

"I will," says the other. "Of course I will." Now her smile is widening.

The Tiger pricks up his ears, white-spotted, like a daub of snow. "I could take the world, if you wished," he rumbles.

"But we do not give you the world," says Sara Irenda Lubchen. "Not now, not yet. What would come after if we let you go?"

"An end."

"Yes," she says softly. "But even now I'm not ready for that. But there is one who has offended me... I give you that one, husband. And I hope he will fill you up. Let it be enough."

And with that her granddaughter, blood of her blood, undoes the catch.

There is a moment then—a long one, a very long one—when the Devourer rouses himself, his hips low to the ground, his bull neck swelling up, his ears laid flat. The ruff round his neck is ashy white, tinged with soot.

When he turns his implacable, ravenous gaze on her, for a moment Sara Sidorova feels afraid—deeply, truly afraid. Well, only a fool denies her fear. And she learned long ago how to master it, let it fuel her art. For fear, it seems, can be a tool as much as pain is, a way of shaping something beautiful.

"For a little while," growls her granddaughter's Tiger. He turns away from them both, his body lithe and liquid, the gorgeous stripes beginning to blur and double and triple: darkness, then brilliance then dark again. She can feel the heat of him, gathering in intensity, burning hotter and hotter until he is a creature of flame—a supernova—and she has to shield his eyes from the blaze.

It is almost too much to bear.

Almost.

Then the fire-beast is gone.

"I let mine go as well," says Sara Sidorova at last. "I loved him."

"I loved mine too. Just as I loved you in my own way, Baba." Then more gently: "Just as I think you loved me. And you were promised a story, were you not? It is not yet over. Shall we watch what comes together?"

THE MORNING STAR

67

Deeper we go, back and down, through the hallways and the tunnels where an inferno devours everything. Dull reds and salamander oranges, cadmium yellows and torching blues.

"It's burning, all of it. How did it happen?" whispers Sara Sidorova.

"The one we sent is fire, isn't he?" says the other with a smile.

"It's beautiful."

"Oh yes. Let us watch together now."

And here, of course, we find him: the faithless soldier, the layer of snares, the perverter and persuader, the hatchet-man. In the chamber beneath all other chambers—the charnel house. Still the soldier, barely disconcerted, is pressing his advantage against the beast.

"Come on now," he mutters, "gonna go, any time."

He can feel the life flowing out of that one and though his own flesh has been mutilated, the wounds slicing meat and gristle, still the value is all in the costing and he cannot escape the joy of the moment.

This moment, when the lights in the eyes of his enemies vanish to pinpricks, then gutter.

And what is pain for him in any case? What's the body? It is only one more instrument, no more precious than any other. It is not his own life he values. In the end, he believes, there will be darkness. His own spirit will gutter, his own light will go out. Because of this he has never felt fear in his life, only seen it in others, that gnawing of the soul, like maggots working through a man.

But the hatchet-man knows the truth. One day it will be over, all the pains of the body, the indignities of flesh. Nothing lasts forever, not pain, not hunger, and so each of them can be borne in their turn. After all, it's only a little while…

Once he had thought it might be otherwise. He had seen something in the girl, something that seemed to rise above all the vicious hurley-burley. But in the end even that had proven false. It was nothing, just another lie.

He can feel the beast giving way now. Just meat after all that. Well. He plans to take his time with this one after, butchering the carcass. Sometimes the old ways are the best ways. This will not be the first tiger he's eaten.

A moment longer and it will be over.

He can smell smoke now, yes. Is it the girl? He glances to where he left her crumpled on the floor but she is nowhere to be seen. Her vest lies on the floor, discarded. His gaze searches the darkness. Then he feels the prickle of heat.

Suddenly, a bitter, scalding wind lashes into the chamber. He chokes on searing ash, masters himself, cocks his head. What is it charging down on him? An ugly carnival fug, the acrid perfume of charcoal and sulfur. Then a halo of orange and gold that glimmers like a firebrand.

Even then he does not fear his own death coming.

It is a distraction, nothing more. And there is still the work, before him. Beneath him. "Not finished," he whispers as he pushes his full weight down and waits for the spark of life to vanish from the beast.

But instead it burns brighter.

Impossible, he thinks. He is a master of death. He knows all its signs and manners, he has made death his own righthand man.

Turned traitor at last, it seems.

For the tiger isn't dying, isn't *obeying* as he should be.

"Hello, brother," comes a voice from the darkness.

And that voice is rage. That voice is flame.

"It's you then," Victor whispers in a tone of fury and bewilderment and—for the first time—terror. He can smell charred meat, and then he knows it is his own hands, his own flesh, seared by the heat of the beast beneath him, erupting into fire.

Impossible, he thinks again, before the conflagration swallows him. And he is right.

"It's not enough," whispers Sara Sidorova. "It's no more an ending than anything else. Show me more, show me..."

68

There is a light blinding Sara Irenda Lubchen.

Her own body feels heavy as if her bones hold a hidden landscape within them. She is on a staircase, traveling toward...

"What?"

"You know, Grandmother. Of course you know. You traveled this same path yourself. It was you who taught me the way. When the dead leave us, they can make a path for those brave enough to follow. Isn't that what you said?"

Around her the circus is burning like a third sun come to earth, so bright the girl can't bear to look at it. Even now flames are whirling through the passages, hot like a tiger's breath, thick with the clot of carnage. Or perhaps it is only she who is burning as the fusillades rip her apart. But no, she doesn't care. For once she will not question it. Instead, she closes her eyes. She climbs and she climbs and she climbs.

The scent of lemon and apple blossoms surrounds her, cradling her, lifting her. She dreams she can feel her mother close beside her, singing: "There's the missing moon, no harm done I know..."

"A last gift, I think."

When she emerges into starlight and darkness, the coolness of the wind is a blessing against her cheek. She stares at the streets around her, the elegant balconies of Stradaniye, the line of snowcloud trees with their pendulous purple berries. All around her the people are staring, marveling at a vast cavernous pit that has opened up where the circus used to stand. A peacock screeches and skitters above the cracked flagstones that surround it. The foundations have sunk in on themselves and she can still see the lick of orange flames in the depths. A child sucks her thumb while her mother dandles her, breathing in the dust of collapse.

Sara Irenda Lubchen moves through the crowd easily. She has taken off her shine, let it burn with the Lady. No one recognizes her now and with a sudden jolt, she finds there is a pearl of peace in that.

"I think I must have learned that in time."

"Of course, Sara. The true art of the mirabilist lies in knowing the unseen: the freedom of invisibility."

Ashes crown her hair. Her eyes are gleaming with that murderous light reflected. In the distance there is noise and chaos, screaming and shouting, dancing and singing.

She wants to know how this has happened, how she lived. But she knows now that a story is not the same as an answer.

A bitter wind whips through the shuttered buildings, promising snow. It will be a bad time to travel.

Even so.

There is nothing to weight her down. And she reckons she won't be the only one on the road. She will find her own folk in time.

And the girl is imagining a landscape of green—forests and rushing rivers, the mountains opening up like a seam in the earth, green, green, green with no lie in it. A good country, over the border. A home for the life growing within her.

She slips like a ghost through the old streets.

IN THE END

69

"Are you content now?" says the Morning Star, her face aglow with the gleam of the cresting sun.

Beyond the gate, the heavens are alive with the glory of dawn, given substance and new form. One world taken and another world reborn. But still Sara Sidorova is not satisfied.

"Oh, what a greedy thing you are..."

AND IN THE BEGINNING

70

They find her at her husband's feet. He is dead, of course, and the flesh has been stripped from his body. Sara Sidorova knows him only by the scraps of cloth, the scarlet shirt he was wearing when the soldiers came for him.

They stuffed him in the trunk of a hollow tree, its flesh smoothed with the wasted years. Already the mourning birds have had their fill. They still linger among the grandfather roots, hopping from one foot to the other, curious at the stranger among them. The bleeding thing.

She had expected anger when she found him, a rage that would consume her. But instead there was only the sense of some great wheel coming to rest. It is done, it is over.

Now Sara Sidorova braces herself against the trunk of the dead wood and the blood goes out of her, little by little. It stains the white pith, mingling with that of her husband.

And so the soldiers stare in wonder at the girl before them: rail-thin and bleeding, wearing the dead man's gymnasterka over a scarlet corset. They take the knife from her carefully.

The boy is among them, the soothsayer, the one whose bullet is lodged in her shoulder. He cradles her gently in his arms. He is young but his hands are sure.

Later, he cleans the wound and removes the bullet fragments with his surgeon's tools. He tells her his name is Mirko, whispering it over and over again as if the word is a charm against bad luck.

He has a local accent so she allows herself to be lulled. When the soldiers break camp he insists that she sit on the wagon with him. He brings her a blanket and cabbage soup, which she eats as cautiously as a grandmother. But when she has finished the baby gives a sharp kick and her eyes grow heavy with tears. She is so thin she hadn't believed that the child would survive. Sara Sidorova doesn't know how it sat inside her all this time, waiting, like an animal in spring, scared by its own new shadow.

"The war will be over soon," Mirko tells her as they near the town. "It won't be very long now. We're winning, sister, you must understand that. But everyone on the roads is being taken in. It's impossible to know who might be a spy, and there was a garrison, not far from here… but they're all gone now. No one knows how it happened." He shivers as if someone has stepped on his grave.

Sara Sidorova asks him what she'll need in the refugee camp and he tells her, "Nothing, they'll provide whatever you want."

But what she wants is dancing shoes. How can she dance in these dead man's boots? It won't be so bad if they let her dance.

The rain is falling when she does. It licks her clean. She strips off her boots and walks barefoot so she can feel the cobblestones beneath her, the cracks and joins. She smiles.

✳ ✳ ✳

A week later a train takes her to the refugee camp. It isn't overfull yet but she must sit in one of the baggage cars. The other women fuss over her belly. Sara Sidorova has forgotten what it's like to be among the living and so at first she is sharp with them, but then her temper settles and she listens to their stories. So many stories. She tells them her own story and it's no worse or no better than any of theirs but they listen attentively and one of them says, "We must write all this down"—but the soldiers won't give them anything to write with.

When the baby is born she is glad for their company. They help her with the birth. They show her how to swaddle her daughter in a black cloth so she feels safe. Softly Sara Sidorova sings for her:

> *In the sky the weary flock is flying,*
> *their wings crash against the roof of storms...*

In the camp the wheel of time begins to circle backward. For a while she seems to grow younger. Her skin tightens, her breasts begin to shrink. She is prepubescent. Sometimes the women ask her to perform but she finds it's impossible, even with her dancing shoes. She doesn't know where Amba is.

Or perhaps she does know. Perhaps even now she remembers.

✳ ✳ ✳

Sara Sidorova lives peaceably enough, as much as she's able. She learns there are other camps, a whole network of camps with their own laws and regulations, teachers for the little ones, seamstresses, carpenters, an economy of barter and cooperation.

The camp is bigger than she thought it was. Big enough for her village, for the neighboring village, too. When the men are let into the camp she is greeted by all the people she once knew. Her papa is among them. He's older than she remembers him ever looking, with little strands of white hair and a mouth that crinkles. He has cracked lips, but that same smell: she didn't know what it was before, but now she does. It's the smell of blood. There are other things too, but the sweetest, richest scent is blood and it takes all things into it and turns them over gently, kindly, violently. She thinks if she had her knife she could cut a hole in him and cut a hole in herself and the blood would move from one of them to the other. She could make him young again. Her papa could make her old.

Sara Sidorova embraces him tenderly and feels the thinness of his bones. He whispers: "All the animals are gone…"

But then she shows him the little one, Else, his granddaughter, and she watches the explosion of joy on his face. And there are Lil and Lis and Vana and Oleg and the younger Estes. Her mother too. Not everyone is there, but enough. They're older. The younger Estes walks with a limp and someone tells her that he doesn't catch cannonballs anymore because of the pain in his hip.

✳ ✳ ✳

They watch little Else, four years old now.

They marvel at the well-turned shape of her limbs and the laughing smile she has, her slightly mocking brown eyes. She isn't beautiful the way her mother was once, but as to that Sara Sidorova only feels a kind of gratitude. She thought that everything had been poured out of her by the tiger, that the tiger had made a little puncture in her soul and all her feelings had come out through it.

But then there's her daughter who is tiny, yet so large. The child cries when she discovers an injured bird in the camp that one of the soldiers has been nursing back to health. It hobbles around, its black wing broken and dragging but the soldier is so tender with it. Then Sara Sidorova hears the soldier whispering a secret to her daughter.

"No one else will tell you this," he says, "but the true substance of the world is song. When we are born someone places a song inside of us and our song is our spirit. Then when we die the song shoots out of our mouths and it goes up and up and up toward the stars, which is where Paradise is."

"Even the animals?"

"All the beasts of the land."

"Even the birds?"

"The birds are different. The birds are confused souls already. They got lost on the way so they come back to earth to watch for a little while. But they're made of song too, and so they sing for us, to remind the ones they left behind that they're still watching. But when they get old and tired and when the winter is coming then they'll find a soul who is traveling to Paradise. Then they'll follow it as high as they can until their body turns to a stone and falls away from them. Only their pure spirit makes the rest of the journey."

"And the tiger?" asks the child, having heard what they say about her mother.

"The tiger alone lives forever."

Afterward Else's eyes are wide and hungry for knowledge. She pulls out the grass from the ground and throws it up into the air, watching for the direction of the wind, trying to tell the future. "Was the man lying?"

And Sara Sidorova wants to explain to her daughter what it had been like to sit among the stars with the Tiger. The things she learned, the spells and secrets.

"No," she says, but her daughter doesn't hear because the sun is setting. The child's watching the redness of it, and then the stars coming out after. The Thresher, the Trammel. Her grandpapa has promised to teach her the names. But for now he's too busy tickling her and she's laughing so much, laughing because her spirit is fresh and new, because she has already found so many good things in the world to be thankful for, what does she need one more miracle for at her age?

ACKNOWLEDGMENTS

I've always been one of those readers who lingers over the acknowledgments pages of other writers. Each one tells a story of community, of the invisible web of support and inspiration that brings a book into being. I know firsthand how a novel grows not just from solitary hours at a desk, but from conversations, critiques, and encouragement, from the generosity of other writers and the patience of loved ones. This book is no exception.

This novel emerged from several profound influences. Victoria Lomasko's striking graphic reportage *Other Russias* (translated by Thomas Campbell, Penguin Books) provided vital imagery and language that shaped my narrative. The haunting poetry of Anna Akhmatova resonates throughout, particularly her piece 'To the Memory of M. B.' from *The Complete Poems of Anna Akhmatova* (translated by Judith Hemschemeyer, Zephyr Press).

The soldiers who inhabit these pages owe much to Svetlana Alexievich's masterful *The Unwomanly Face of War* (translated by Richard Pevear and Larissa Volokhonsky, Penguin Classics). The landscape of the novel found its foundation in Kapka Kassabova's remarkable works of non-fiction: *Border: A Journey to the Edge of Europe* (Granta, 2017) and *To the Lake: A Balkan Journey of War and Peace* (Granta, 2020).

Excerpts from Christina Rossetti's beautiful 'When I am Dead, My Dearest' are quoted as a refrain as are lines from the Russian folk song 'Cranes' about the soldiers who did not return from battle.

Readers familiar with my collection *The Gold Leaf Executions* (Unsung Stories, 2022) may recognize elements of this world, including the tale of Erastus Fortunato in 'The Katalog'.

My research into stage magic became an unexpected obsession that deeply influenced this work. Christopher Priest's novel *The Prestige* (Touchstone, 1995) exploring the world of Victorian magicians opened my eyes to the rich possibilities of this territory. I am also indebted to several illuminating texts: Derren Brown's *Confessions of a Conjuror* (Channel 4 Books, 2010), Jim Steinmeyer's *Hiding the Elephant: How Magicians Invented the Impossible and Learned to Disappear* (Da Capo Press, 2003), Alex Stone's *Fooling Houdini: Magicians, Mentalists, Math Geeks, & the Hidden Powers of the Mind* (Harper, 2012), and Henning Nelms's *Magic and Showmanship: A Handbook for Conjurers* (Dover Publications, 1969).

This book would not exist without the unwavering support of my husband, Vince Haig, who patiently read countless drafts. I am deeply grateful to my early readers—Nina Allan, Anne Charnock, Nathan Ballingrud, Huw Evans, and Tashan Mehta, especially—whose insights proved invaluable. Anne Perry's editorial wisdom helped shape the manuscript, while Meg Davis from the Ki Agency skillfully guided its journey to Titan. I'm grateful to my current agent Max Edwards and his assistant Alex Osmond for their continued support and enthusiasm.

The entire team at Titan deserves my heartfelt thanks, particularly my brilliant editor Cath Trechman and my long-time friend George Sandison. Paul Simpson's meticulous copy-edits, the marketing expertise of Katharine Carroll, Kabriya Coghlan, and Isabelle Sinnott, and Julia Lloyd's stunning cover art all contributed to bringing this book to life.

Parts of this novel were written at a workshop in the south of France, led by the indomitable and wise Una McCormack. The Clarion West Writing Workshop has gifted me with some of my dearest friends and strongest supporters over the years. I'm also thankful for my colleagues and students at Anglia Ruskin University and the University of Queensland, who have created such stimulating environments for creative work.

On a personal note, I am profoundly thankful for my family, especially my sister Laura, whose steadfast support of my writing career has meant everything. To the Haigs and Hoptons, who have embraced me as one of their own—thank you for creating a second home.

This work was made possible through the generous support of a Canada Council Creative Writing Grant.

ABOUT THE AUTHOR

HELEN MARSHALL is Associate Professor of Creative Writing at the University of Queensland. She has won the World Fantasy Award, the British Fantasy Award and the Shirley Jackson Award and received endorsements from authors such as Nathan Ballingrud, Kelly Link and Paul Tremblay. Her debut novel *The Migration* was one of *The Guardian's* top science fiction and fantasy books of the year. She lives in Australia. Find her on Twitter/X *@manuscriptgal* and on Instagram *@hairside*

For more fantastic fiction, author events,
exclusive excerpts, competitions, limited editions and more

VISIT OUR WEBSITE
titanbooks.com

LIKE US ON FACEBOOK
facebook.com/titanbooks

FOLLOW US ON TWITTER AND INSTAGRAM
@TitanBooks

EMAIL US
readerfeedback@titanemail.com